PRAISE FOR THE HUMAN ORIGINS SERIES

An enticing and recommended tale, not to be missed.

Midwest Book Review
from a review of *Relic of the Ancient Ones*

Shiel uses her extensive knowledge of archaeology, anthropology, and Bigfoot to write a very rich story....I would highly recommend this book.

Paige Lovitt, *Reader Views*
from a review of *Lord of the Dead*

Incredible high adventure...The pace is frenetic and the story lends plausibility to an number of evolution theories. We rated this book a solid four hearts.

Bob Spear, *Heartland Reviews*
from a review of *Lord of the Dead*

The characters were well done and I found myself wanting to learn more about them. The action is well thought out and written with real dialogue...So, did I enjoy this book? Do I recommend it? Yes to both.

Dan Fabian, Bard's Ink
from a review of *The Hunt for Bigfoot*

A lively, exciting and gripping piece of fiction...If you are even remotely interested in cryptozoology, ancient cosmic visitors, the legends of Atlantis, human evolution and more, then grab a copy of [this book] as soon as possible.

Nick Redfern, *Phenomena Magazine*
from a review of *The Hunt for Bigfoot*

A good read for an evening-campfire setting gathered around in front of pitched tents near a lake.

Independent Publishing Review
from a review of *The Hunt for Bigfoot*

REVENGE
OF THE
ANCIENT
ONES

Other Books by Lisa A. Shiel

Fiction

From Jacobsville Books

Faces of Bigfoot
Faces of Bigfoot 2
The Faces of Bigfoot Collection

The Human Origins Series

The Hunt for Bigfoot (Book One)
Lord of the Dead (Book Two)
Relic of the Ancient Ones (Book Three)
Bigfoot Beginnings (Backstories, Vol. 1)
The Bigfoot Effect (Backstories, Vol. 2)
Traces of Bigfoot (Backstories, Vol. 1 & 2)

Nonfiction

From Jacobsville Books

Creature of Controversy (Forbidden Bigfoot, Part One)
Top Secret Sasquatch (Forbidden Bigfoot, Part Two)
The Evolution Conspiracy
Backyard Bigfoot

From The History Press

Forgotten Tales of Michigan's Upper Peninsula

From Trails Books

Strange Michigan (with Linda S. Godfrey)

REVENGE
OF THE
ANCIENT
ONES

Book Four in the Human Origins Series

LISA A. SHIEL

Jacobsville Books
Lake Linden, Michigan
Toll-Free: 1-866-341-3705

ISBN: 978-1-934631-61-4 (pbk.)
ISBN: 978-1-934631-62-1 (e-book: EPUB)
LCCN: 2012916154

Manufactured in the United States.

Jacobsville Books
www.JacobsvilleBooks.com
1-866-341-3705

Publisher's Cataloging-in-Publication Data

Shiel, Lisa A.
   Revenge of the ancient ones / Lisa A. Shiel.
     p. cm.
   ISBN-13: 978-1-934631-61-4 (pbk.)
   ISBN-10: 978-1-934631-62-1 (e-book: EPUB)
    1. Alternative histories (Fiction). 2. Michigan—Fiction. 3. Unidentified flying
objects—Fiction. 4. Egypt—History—To 332 B.C.—Fiction.   I. Shiel,
Kerrie, ill. II. Title. III. Series: Human origins series.
PS3619.H53 R48 2012
813'.6—dc23
                        2012916154

PROLOGUE

THE SURF ROARED. HARRY GLANCED OVER HIS SHOULDER. THE LIGHT FROM his lantern petered out at the cave's entrance. Beyond that lay darkness—and a fifty-foot drop to the lake below. The deep, cold waters of the lake. After a storm like this one, the waters would be even colder.

The air, damp and warm, clung to his skin. He swiped the back of his hand across his brow. The sweat transferred to his hand and dribbled down his wrist under the sleeve of his shirt. He looked at the ground in front of his feet. A bone, a complete femur, rested atop a pile of sundry fragments of skeletal remains. He felt like a heathen, invading this sacred space. He had no choice, or rather, no time left to find other options. The bones, though ancient already, mattered not one whit. The cave itself, as it existed now, mattered not one whit either. Only the significance of this place in the future mattered.

Only the item in his hand mattered.

Whoomp.

His heart thudded. Just a breaker, he told himself, a wave shattering against the cliffs.

He hopped over the pile of bones and approached the rear wall of the cave. At waist height above the floor, a niche was cut into the rock wall. The niche stood three feet wide by six feet tall, and a foot deep. A driftwood log as tall and wide as the niche itself leaned against the niche's back wall. He ran his hand around the niche's rim. Smooth, hewn with expertise.

He yanked his hand away. No time for admiration.

Grasping either side of the driftwood, he lifted. Nothing happened. Mud had congealed around the bottom of the driftwood, where it met the niche's floor. He tugged harder.

The wood popped out. The weight fell into his hands and he stumbled backward. His left heel stamped down. Crack.

Oh lord, the bones. He glanced over his shoulder at his heel. A piece of sandstone had split in two under his boot, but the bones lay unharmed a few feet away. Relief rushed through him. The bones may not matter to his current mission, but he was still loathe to desecrate this cave any more than necessary.

Harry hefted the driftwood aside, dropping it on an empty section of floor. The driftwood hit the dirt with a dull thump. Inside the niche, a rectangular slab of rock formed the back wall of the cavity. The slab protruded from the wall a few inches.

A scratching issued from behind him.

Harry half turned toward the entrance. Percy was clambering over the cliff's edge into the cave.

"Finally you're here," Harry said. "I know those handholds are murder, but did you take a coffee break on the way up?"

Percy said nothing as he tried to straighten to his full height. The cave was six feet tall, though, nearly two feet shorter than Percy. Bumping his head on the ceiling, Percy grunted.

Harry shook his head, then gestured at the stone slab in the niche. "Could use your help here."

He'd brought Percy along for this very reason. No one but Harry's odd companion could lift the slab, and no one else knew what lay behind it.

The gargantuan Percy grunted two syllables that sounded like "un-boo." Then he lumbered past Harry into the niche, grasped the right-hand edge of the slab with both of his stubby hands, and pulled.

Rock grated against rock as the slab inched outward like a great door. Harry winced at the sound. The slab door, its front edge now extending past the stone jamb, etched a curved line across the earthen floor. No one had opened this door in a very, very long time.

The door froze halfway open. Percy moved his hands back and forth as if trying to wiggle the door free. It didn't budge. With a grunt, Percy dropped his hands to his sides.

Harry sighed. "I guess that's it then."

He strode into the open doorway.

Percy grunted an almost-word. Suddenly Harry wished he'd made time for that lesson on the language of Percy's tribe, when a lovely young woman had offered to teach him. Later, he'd said. Now it was too late.

Harry patted his companion's shoulder. "I know you're afraid, but we have to do this. Someone has to save the world, right?"

The back of his neck tingled.

Lightning flashed. Harry winced. Percy jerked.

No, not yet. Harry's pulse pounded in his ears. More time, please, just a little more time. He looked down at the item clasped in his hand. She must find this, but she couldn't find it unless he placed it in the right location. Without it, she might reach the wrong conclusion—and every living thing on the planet would suffer because of one mistake. It wasn't her fault. It was his.

He held the power to fix it.

Lightning blinded him. Boom!

The earth shuddered at the detonation of thunder. Harry struggled to stay on his feet. He flung a hand out to brace himself against the slab door. Within a few seconds, the tremor faded.

"Step away from the door, Harry."

The voice was not Percy's. The timbre was female, and besides, Percy never spoke words that Harry understood. Harry squinted at the cave entrance. There she stood, painted with golden light, hands resting on either side of the entrance at shoulder height, head tilted to one side.

She smiled. "I've missed you, Harry. Now be a good boy and put that back where you found it."

This time her accent sounded Irish, with a tinge of French. Had he at last met the real her?

His hands felt cold. He looked down at the item in his hands. He was wrong. Neither he nor Percy would save the world. The item he transported held the power to save the world, once it reached the right hands. He had no idea what to do with it. He rather doubted Percy did either. And the right hands certainly did not belong to the woman standing at the cave entrance. No, the right hands belonged to another woman altogether.

Harry clasped the item to his chest.

The woman said, "Put—it—down."

Percy growled. The sound was more human than animal, though not entirely human.

She said, "Uh-uh-uh. Call off your dog, Harry."

"Easy, Percy," Harry said, patting his companion's arm. Percy quieted, though he kept his gaze fixed on the woman.

She cocked her head at Harry. "Why do you call him by a man's name when he is not a man?"

"I have to call him something."

Harry scuffled backward two steps. He stood just inside the doorway now, inside a dark and dank tunnel. Moving only his eyes, he glanced left and right down the tunnel. Couldn't see a blessed thing.

The woman marched halfway across the cave. When Percy growled, she halted. Her gaze flitted from Harry to Percy and back again.

"You know he can stop you," Harry warned.

She shook her head. "It didn't have to be this way. We were such good friends...for awhile."

With her right hand, she reached behind her back and pulled out a dark object slightly larger than her palm. She aimed the gun at his chest.

Percy slammed the door shut just as the gunshot exploded.

The darkness swallowed him. An inhuman shriek resounded on the other side of the slab door. A second gunshot popped, muffled by the door.

In the silence that followed, Harry knew what he must do. Place the item in the correct spot. Somehow, in the darkness, he must do it. There was no escape for him now, for he knew no other doorways lead into or out of the tunnel. Sometimes saving the world required great sacrifice.

Thunder rumbled. The tunnel shook so violently that he stumbled sideways. If they had their way, he might die before he ran out of air.

Yes, he knew it would end this way. Like a sixth sense, some part of him had felt it creeping up on him. His own death. But his death could still mean something.

Harry whispered a prayer, and then he marched into the darkness.

He marched into the arms of Death.

1

Revenant Point, Michigan
June 7

A SINGLE CLOUD, PALE AND FLUFFY AND BLURRED AT THE EDGES, SCUDDED across the sky. Erin Turner watched the solitary puff until it disappeared behind the treetops. Sometimes she wanted to be whisked away like a cloud swept on an upper-level wind, bound for glorious lands that awaited beyond the horizon.

Of course, back in the flat-earth days, mariners thought monsters waited beyond the horizon.

The handle of the retractable leash in Erin's hands jerked. She tore her gaze away from the now-cloudless sky to look at Freya, the black mutt straining at the end of her leash. The dog glanced at Erin and wagged her tail. The universal sign for hurry up, human.

"Okay," Erin said. "I'm coming."

Erin started toward the dog, who burst into a trot as soon as the leash got some slack. Freya stretched the leash to its full length and strained against it once more, dragging Erin toward the woods thirty feet away. Over her left shoulder, Erin spied the house. The Victorian-style manor hunkered at one end of the clearing, while the other end dropped off into a cliff. The precipice sat at the end of Revenant Point, the tiny peninsula owned by her employer, Samuel Wessick. More than anyone she had met or heard of, Samuel Wessick deserved the title reclusive billionaire. Then again, she didn't know exactly how much money filled his bank account. He might be only a millionaire, or he might've reached the exalted status of trillionaire.

Okay, she would call him a reclusive gazillionaire, because that term seemed to cover all possibilities. The man had money, period.

Wessick owned the entire fifty-acre peninsula, which itself attached to the Keweenaw Peninsula, which in turn jutted out from the Upper Peninsula of Michigan. So essentially, Erin now lived on a peninsula on a peninsula on a peninsula. At the moment, however, she was being dragged across that peninsula by an excitable mutt. As the dog hauled her into the trees, Erin glanced over her shoulder at Revenant House. The manor looked foreboding even in the brilliant sunlight, and she half expected to see a spectral figure watching her from an upstairs window. The house's name, revenant, did mean ghost after all.

The dog dragged her down the only human-made path leading into the woods. Then Freya veered left down a deer trail barely wider than the dog herself. The weeds already grew waist high here. Erin would have to check herself for ticks when she got back in the house. Ah, the joys of living in an untamed wilderness.

Through the woods they hurtled, canine and human bound by a nylon leash, swerving left and right around trees and bushes, trampling weeds and wildflowers. Erin yanked at the leash to stop, or at least slow, the dog's progress but Freya was stronger. Thorns snagged on Erin's clothes and skin as they ran through a thicket of wild blackberry bushes. She thought about letting go of the leash, but then where would Freya wind up? The dog must've caught the scent of something, maybe a porcupine. Freya's last encounter with a porky resulted in a massively expensive trip to the vet, thanks to the proliferation of quills on the dog's head, chest, and front legs. Yet if Freya ran into a porky today, Erin could no more stop the dog than she could halt a stampeding elephant.

They broke through a wall of weeds into a small clearing. Freya slowed, then stopped altogether in front of a thick tree. Pillowy moss blanketed the clearing. In the vicinity of the tree, however, the moss had been disturbed in patches. A divot of moss lay overturned a few yards from Erin.

A chill shimmied up her spine. The hairs at the nape of her neck prickled.

This was where Rassul died. Where she had killed him.

The evil bastard deserved it. She felt no remorse. Oded Rassul assaulted her, brutally, and later threatened to kill everyone she knew, starting with Alex MacKay. A memory unreeled in her mind, images of Alex tied to the tree she faced now, of Rassul holding a knife to Alex's throat.

The gun in her hand. Her finger pulling the trigger.

Rassul dead on the ground, eyes open but unseeing. His body had lain...

The body of Oded Rassul had lain in the spot where she stood right now.

Erin scuttled backward. Christ, why had the dog brought her here? The incident happened two weeks earlier, to the day. Maybe Freya could still smell the blood. Or sense the trauma.

Both Erin and Alex survived the encounter with Rassul. Thoughts of Alex banished the chill, though not the sharp need to get away from this clearing as soon as possible.

Tugging the dog's leash, she led Freya across the clearing and down the trail she knew led back to the house. It was the same trail she and Alex followed on that night, after Rassul died. Sometimes, in those moments when she really thought about it, an odd feeling of unreality flickered through her. It seemed downright bizarre that she, a lowly librarian, wound up fighting bad guys alongside Alex MacKay, an archaeologist who left behind a career in mainstream science to join an organization that, as far as she could tell, spent vast amounts of money and time searching for proof that human beings did not evolve on Earth. The Human Origins Project investigated many other topics as well, areas Alex referred to as ancillary phenomena. Those phenomena ran the gamut from UFOs and Bigfoot to out-of-place artifacts, meaning artifacts found outside of the normal context, either in place or time or both.

Alex had, supposedly, brought Erin into the Human Origins Project. Yet so far, she'd met only one of the group's members aside from Alex—Errando Warner, a German gazillionaire and Alex's mentor. Over the last two weeks, Warner had visited Erin at Revenant House numerous times. She hadn't seen Alex since the morning after their final encounter with Rassul. Erin convinced Alex to stay away, for his own protection. The threat from Rassul may have died with the man, but the threat from Rassul's masters lingered. Although the evidence suggested Rassul had worked for Wessick, the owner of Revenant House, the evidence also pointed to much more reclusive, and much more dangerous, beings who controlled Wessick.

Beings was the best word for the puppet masters. They were not of this earth, she felt certain, and neither were they human. From whence they came and what they were, she didn't know. At least not yet.

Freya halted.

Erin stopped alongside the dog. Freya was staring into the trees ahead of them, her ears up.

Though she stared into the trees, tracing the line of Freya's gaze, Erin saw nothing.

The dog growled softly.

Erin squinted at the shadows between the trees. For a few seconds she saw nothing, but then a shape moved, a shadow distinct from the darkness between the trees.

The hell with this. Tucking the leash handle over her thumb, Erin cupped both hands around her mouth like a megaphone. She shouted, "Who's there? Come out where I can see you."

The silhouette shifted again. This time she heard the rustling of branches and leaves.

"I have a gun," she called, knowing full well she didn't have her Smith & Wesson 9mm semiautomatic pistol with her. The person hiding in the woods up ahead didn't need to know that. When no response came, she said, "Come out or I'll shoot."

A twig snapped. Vegetation rustled against fabric as the figure separated from the shadows. The man walked at a brisk pace, shoulders slumped, head down, face hidden by the angle of his posture. He wore a gray T-shirt and faded blue jeans, plus dirty sneakers. When he got within a dozen yards of her, he lifted his head just enough to reveal his features.

"Greg?" she said.

The man, Greg Virtanen, shuffled closer. At arm's length from her, he stopped. He met her gaze for a second, then averted it to the forest floor. He picked out a rock with the toe of his sneaker.

Greg was the live-in boyfriend of Chloe Pelletier, one of Erin's closest friends. Since her circle of friends couldn't fill a broom closet, calling Chloe one of her closest friends seemed less of an honor than a default status. Chloe, Alex, and Warner were her only friends.

And a weird bunch they were.

She asked Greg, "What are you doing here?"

He shrugged and muttered syllables Erin couldn't make out.

What the blazes was he doing out here? Chloe might've told Greg that Erin lived and worked at Revenant House. But his reasons for trespassing in these woods remained a mystery. She had every right to call the cops on him.

As if sensing her thoughts, Greg cast an uneasy look at her. He said, "I gotta find Chloe. Find out why she's doing it, what I did wrong. Is she in the house?"

"No. I haven't seen her in days." She felt an unease burgeoning inside her too. "What has Chloe done? What on earth are you talking about?"

"She comes here, I see her. Tells me she's going to the shooting range, but I follow her and always she comes here." He hooked a thumb over his shoulder. "Parks in the woods back there."

"Chloe shoots? A gun?"

"Yeah, she got it for self-defense. Practices a lot—or that's what I thought. Now I know different." He leaned forward to whisper, "After she parks her car, she just…vanishes. Like zap, and she's gone."

Erin knew all too well that animals and people could seem to vanish in the woods, when in reality they ducked behind a tree or other obstacle. Yet she also knew that once in awhile a person really did vanish into thin air, and in her experience they did so accompanied by a flash of light.

Which possibility did Greg witness?

"She's with him," Greg said. "I know she is, I've seen it, his hands all over her, in the house, through the window—"

"Wait." Erin eyed him, feeling the unease swell. "You've been spying on the house?"

"Just her. I had to know. She meets him, and I don't know what he does to her, but when she comes home after, she's different."

Greg thought Chloe was cheating on him, that much Erin gleaned from his breathless monologues. She asked, "You've seen Chloe inside Revenant House, with a man?"

Greg nodded so vigorously a lock of hair flopped over his eyes.

"What did he look like?"

"He was older—" Greg jerked. He stared past her shoulder, eyes wide, mouth falling open. In a near whisper, he said, "Oh no. Oh God no."

"What's wrong?"

His face blanched. "She's here."

Greg took off into the trees. Freya whimpered and barked, but her attention was not focused on the man fleeing through the woods. Rather, the dog stared in the opposite direction. She tucked her tail between her legs and whimpered again. Freya acted like she saw someone or something.

Erin tracked the dog's line of sight into the trees. There, in a shaft of pale sunlight, stood a woman with long, dark hair. The woman wore an ankle-length dress, tan in color. The sun glinted off the jewels on her necklace. A slice of shadow obscured her face.

The woman bolted after Greg.

Freya took off after the woman, dragging Erin behind her. Erin tripped over a tree root and lost her hold on the leash. It bounced out of her grasp. Freya rocketed through the woods after Greg and the woman with the leash handle thwacking out an arrhythmic beat in the dog's wake. Erin raced after Freya. They were headed toward the cliff.

Soon Erin lost sight of the woman and Greg. She tracked the bouncing black blob that was Freya until she lost sight of the dog too. She veered around the tree behind which the dog had ducked. Seconds later she ran out of the woods into the clearing behind the house. Freya was nowhere in sight. Greg stood at the cliff 's edge, near the opposite side of the clearing. He was talking to the woman. Greg waved his arms as if emphasizing a point, while the woman stood straight and calm, her face turned at such an angle that Erin couldn't see it. Greg reached for the woman.

She shook off his grasp.

He grabbed for her again.

She shook off his hand and then, laying both palms flat on his chest, she shoved him over the cliff.

Erin skidded to a halt. Gasping, pulse thundering behind her eardrums, she gaped at the spot where the woman stood and where Greg had been a split second earlier.

The woman brought something out of a pocket in her dress. She held the object close to her side, where Erin couldn't see it. The woman's long hair shielded her face as she twisted sideways to fiddle with the object.

Erin sprinted toward the woman.

With a casual turn of her hand, the woman dumped the object over the cliff. She gazed down after it for half a second.

Then, with a slow and deliberate motion, she stepped off the cliff.

2

A GUST OF WIND LASHED HER HAIR INTO HER FACE AS ERIN STARED OVER the cliff's edge and down at the water below. Seventy feet of sheer sandstone plummeted to the surface of Lake Superior. Breakers crashed against the cliff. There, on a boulder that bulged out of the water, lay the crumpled body of Greg Virtanen.

A wave broke over the boulder, submerging the body for several seconds.

As the surf receded, Erin backed away from the cliff. She felt nauseous and cold, though the sun bathed the spring day with its warmth. She wanted to vomit but couldn't. She wanted to forget she'd ever seen the woman hurl Greg over the cliff.

The woman.

Erin tiptoed to the cliff's edge. Bending forward just enough to peer over the precipice, she scanned the area below for another body. Nothing. The woman's body might've been carried away by the surf.

Yet the woman had stepped off the cliff with such casual assurance, not desperation. When Erin watched the woman step over the edge, she got the impression the woman was stepping onto or into something solid, rather than plunging to her death. A second before she jumped, the woman dropped an object off the cliff. A flash of light followed.

Erin had recognized the flash. She saw one like it before, back when she chased Rassul into the woods, determined to catch and question him. A burst of light nearly blinded her, then a bubble-like portal split open, suspended in empty air inches above the ground. Still in pursuit of Rassul, her brain on autopilot, she raced after him through the portal—and straight into another place and another time. She might've been lost there, if Alex hadn't pulled her back.

The woman who killed Greg might've escaped through a similar portal. Until now, Erin had no clue how Rassul opened the portal. Maybe the object the woman cast over the cliff somehow ruptured the fabric of the world.

As the surf retreated, Erin caught sight of Greg's body. Nausea swelled inside her. Everything seemed to twirl around her. She stumbled backward, tripped, collapsed onto her butt. In a moment, the spinning subsided and she pushed onto her knees. She had witnessed a murder. What did a person do in this situation?

A noise echoed from the woods, drawing closer. Erin froze.

Thwack. Thwack-thwack. Thwack. Thwack.

She turned her head toward the sound. A black shape darted out of the trees, headed straight for her.

Freya ran a circle around her, then stopped to slather wet doggie kisses all over her face. Erin jumped up before the dog could plant one on her lips. She patted Freya's head, murmuring words meant to calm the dog. It didn't work. Freya flung her paws onto Erin's abdomen. Erin stumbled backward as she pushed the dog away.

A powerful wave broke against the cliff with a boom.

A picture of Greg's battered form flashed in her mind.

Erin nabbed the handle of Freya's leash, spun around, and sprinted for the house. This time, she dragged the dog.

Erin jogged down the main passageway, past the staircase, to the library door at the end of the hall on the right side. The door hung open, ready for her to return after her lunch break. She hurried to the desk and reached for the phone. As her fingertips touched the handset, she froze.

Who would she call? The police, naturally.

They might view her as a suspect. Although she saw the woman push Greg over the cliff, she could offer no evidence to back up her claim.

Alex. The last time they saw each other, he instructed her to send an encrypted text message if she needed him. Erin bit her lip. She needed him now.

The phone rang.

Erin yelped. Snatching up the handset, she muttered a weak hello.

A woman's voice, colored by an English accent, responded, "Have you called the authorities yet?"

The caller was Anna T. Newman, the go-to girl for Samuel Wessick, the man Erin worked for but had never spoken to or met. Erin supposed Newman, as the woman preferred to be called, was Wessick's executive assistant or whatever bigwigs called their secretaries these days. Still, Newman seemed like more than just a secretary. Erin didn't really know what to call her, other than Newman.

"Erin?" Newman said.

"Huh?"

A note of irritation crept into Newman's voice. "Have you called the authorities yet?"

Erin thought for a second, then asked, "You know what happened?"

"Yes. Have you reported it?"

"No."

"Good, don't. We will handle the matter internally."

"Someone died. He was murdered."

"As you are well aware, Revenant House is a special place. The rules that govern the rest of the world cannot be applied at the manor." Newman paused, but before Erin could respond, she said, "Trust that the matter will be dealt with appropriately. You have no choice."

Yes, Erin was well aware that Revenant House, aka the manor, existed inside a bubble where the rules of society—and indeed, of the universe itself—seemed to lose their power. Little made sense here, a fact she'd learned to live with over the past two weeks. But covering up a murder...

A line must be drawn somewhere. Problem was, Erin didn't hold the pen. Samuel N. Wessick did.

As Newman said, Erin had no choice.

"Do you understand?" Newman asked.

"I understand."

"Try to forget the incident and get on with your work."

Erin recognized that when Newman referred to work, she didn't mean the cover story of Wessick hiring Erin to catalog his private library. Newman meant to the real work. Finding the relic, an unidentified object sought by Wessick and his shadowy puppet masters.

When it came to covering up Greg's death, Erin may have no choice. But when it came to the job at hand, finding the relic, maybe she did have a choice.

"I need to consult a specialist," Erin said, "about the library collection. A lot of the books deal with Egyptian archaeology, and I could use an expert's advice about how best to organize them."

"Whom did you have in mind?"

Erin took a deep breath and said, "Alex MacKay. He's an archaeologist specializing in Egyptology."

Wessick knew about Alex. Erin knew this because Wessick's henchmen Rassul had known about Alex and how he'd helped her uncover evidence concerning the relic and Revenant House. Rassul had ordered her not to see Alex anymore and to find the relic on her own, or else Alex would die. For that reason, Alex had stayed away for two weeks. Erin hoped that by claiming she needed a specialist's help, she might earn permission from Wessick to see Alex without risking his life. Both she and Newman knew full well Wessick did not bring Erin here to catalog his library. She prayed Newman understood the subtext of her request.

Let me see Alex and please don't kill him.

Newman said, "That would be acceptable."

Relief surged through her. She could see Alex. Soon.

"However," Newman said, "if at any time we deem it to be no longer acceptable, you must terminate the relationship immediately."

Erin decided to ignore the statement. If she said nothing, then Newman couldn't claim she'd agreed to the condition. Before the woman could say anything else, Erin said, "Handle this incident your way and I'll get back to work. Goodbye."

She hung up the phone.

Letting a murder go unreported, and therefore uninvestigated, left a bad taste in her mouth, and not just metaphorically speaking. The unease that sprouted inside her when she encountered Greg in the woods had matured into a host of symptoms, from the acid in her stomach to the headache stabbing at the backs of her eyes. Her jaw ached. Realizing she was clenching it, she loosened the muscles. Her neck ached too. Seating herself in the desk chair, she massaged the nape of her neck with one hand. Partaking in a conspiracy to conceal a murder sure could make a person tense.

If she wanted to see Alex, she needed to send him a text message. Rather than using modern technology to encrypt the message, she would use a centuries-old technique known as a Vigenère cipher. The method involved substituting each letter in the text with a different letter, based on an alphabetic table and a keyword. Before leaving her, Alex gave her the key— the word power.

She brought out a copy of the Vigenère table, which she kept in the desk drawer. Within a few minutes, she encrypted her concise message and sent it to Alex via her cell phone. Barring any malfunctions in the cell phone network, and assuming his phone was on and in range, he should receive the message soon. Immediately, she hoped.

With nothing else to do, other than wait, she got back to work.

3

The Turner Home
Shadow Bay, Michigan

Alex MacKay sat in the backyard swing, rocking it slightly. The wooden frame of the standalone swing creaked a little with each forward motion. The swing itself, also wooden, seated two. Alex sat in the middle, alone.

Julie Turner, Erin's mother, had offered to sit with him. But he preferred solitude this afternoon. If Freya were still here, he might've let the dog curl up next to him. Mrs. Turner had sent the dog to Revenant House, ostensibly to guard Erin but realistically to keep her company. Freya loved people, even most strangers, and so made a hopeless guard dog. For the first three nights after Alex moved in with the Turners, Freya slept on his bed. Although he felt like a sissy for thinking it, he really did miss the dog.

But he missed Erin more.

Two weeks ago, at Erin's request, he moved in with her parents—because, Erin said, they needed his protection. So he took up residence in the guest bedroom next door to Erin's room, or what had been Erin's room until she moved into Revenant House. After living with Julie and Patrick Turner for two weeks, Alex knew the couple needed no protection, especially from a disgraced archaeologist with no training as a bodyguard. Errando Warner offered the correct skill set to guard the Turners, however the German billionaire/mercenary preferred to watch over Erin day and night and evening and morning.

Alex kicked at the grass. His boot toe lodged in the turf, halting the swing. Warner had spent more time with Erin than Alex had. Warner probably know her better by now than Alex did, and she knew Warner better than she knew Alex. The two of them were probably on the verge of getting engaged.

He leaned forward, elbows on his thighs, and cradled his forehead on the heels of his hands. Christ, he hated this. Because the villains ordered him to stay away from Erin, he was banished to her parents' house. Meanwhile, Erin lived in Revenant House—the epicenter of both the mystery they sought to solve and the danger brought on by the quest. There she sat, and here he sat. Useless. Superfluous.

During his banishment, he'd tried to uncover evidence on his own, or at least to unlock the secrets of the evidence already in his possession. Five days before they parted ways, he and Erin found a catacomb inside Cheops Pyramid, a mountain adjacent to the Grand Canyon. The network of unfinished passageways and chambers seemed to have been intended as a tomb, possibly for an Egyptian pharaoh, as suggested by a partial inscription composed in hieroglyphs. A powerful and distinctly unnatural thunderstorm collapsed the passageways one by one, forcing Alex and Erin to flee through a hidden escape tunnel. In that tunnel, they found the mummified remains of an individual clad in Celtic-style garb. Alex had taken a tooth from the mummy, for testing purposes.

Strontium isotope testing showed the individual was born in southern England. Radiocarbon dating suggested the individual lived sometime between 4000 BC and 5000 BC. However, the style of the brooch Erin found alongside the skeleton should've dated it to several thousand years later. The brooch was an out-of-place artifact, an object found in a time and/or a place where it didn't belong. Oded Rassul had stolen a dozen other out-of-place artifacts from both museums and private collections. Museums invented stories to explain away out-of-place artifacts, for instance by saying a flood must've washed an artifact into an older stratum, or they might simply redate the artifact without explanation.

Most archaeologists tried to erase out-of-place artifacts because their careers depended on maintaining the status quo. But on examining photos of the stolen artifacts, Erin realized the enemies she and Alex battled against had another, far more sinister reason for covering up the anomalous artifacts. They needed to cover their own tracks.

Their tracks through time.

The Aten, the unseen enemy behind everything that had happened lately, possessed the technology to travel not only through space but also through time. Once in awhile, it seemed, one of them inadvertently dropped a clue in the form of an out-of-place artifact. Over the course of six months, the artifacts were gathered up by Rassul, the Aten's minion, and taken to Revenant House. There, Samuel Wessick assumed responsibility for the artifacts. The day after Rassul's death, however, the artifacts vanished. Alex knew this only because

Warner shared the information with him—after Erin told her new best friend, the German mercenary.

Alex straightened in the swing. He sighed. Warner was his friend too, as well as his mentor in all things covert. He liked and respected Warner. Yet when it came to Erin Turner, he lost sight of their friendship and saw nothing except an attractive, virile man who clearly liked Erin. A man with money and charm and masculine wiles. And every time he thought about Warner's evening visits to Revenant House, he wanted to shoot something.

His cell phone vibrated. He slipped it out of his pocket and looked at the screen. A text message had been received. Opening the message, he saw it was from Erin. The text looked like a nonsensical series of letters. The message was encrypted, of course, per his instructions.

Alex rushed into the house, to his room, and dragged his attaché out from under the bed. He unzipped a side pocket and dug out the sheet of paper on which was printed the Vigenère table he found on the Internet. Using the word power as the key, he decrypted the message. It consisted of three words.

I NEED YOU.

He strapped on the shoulder holster with his Glock 9mm pistol snug inside it, grabbed his jacket and the attaché, and ran out of the house.

Revenant House

Two men tromped across the expansive lawn toward the rim of the cliff. The men wore gray jumpsuits and clunky boots, and each carried a duffel bag. Erin watched from her position just outside the back door as the men stopped at the precipice, peering over the edge, presumably at Greg's crumpled and lifeless body. Her gut twisted as if a large fist had clamped around it. She was watching the cover-up in action, from a front-row seat.

During the past hour, she tried to call Chloe five times. Each call went to voice-mail, and she left a series of messages that must've sounded vague and desperate simultaneously. Where was Chloe? Erin had neither seen nor heard from her in over a week, since the last evening she visited Erin at Revenant House, when Warner tried to convince Chloe to accept his protection. Everyone in Erin's life was in danger. Chloe refused the offer, rather angrily. Her reaction stupefied Erin. With a few exceptions, Chloe generally behaved in a polite, cheerful manner. Her response to Warner's offer of protection replayed in Erin's mind.

"I can *protect* myself just fine," Chloe snapped. "I don't need you to do it for me. You guys think you're hot stuff, brainiacs or something. You're all so—so—"

Chloe's face had flared red then, her cheeks as fiery as her hair. The rest of her face looked paler than usual in comparison. She fisted her hands so tightly they trembled.

"Are you all right?" Erin had asked.

Chloe snorted. Fixing her ice-cold glare on Erin, she said, "This is all your fault."

With that, Chloe had stormed out of the house. In the intervening days, Erin had neither seen nor heard from Chloe. Both Warner and Alex tried to find her, to no avail. The girl seemed to have vanished.

Two days after Chloe's departure, Warner found Greg. Chloe's boyfriend was holed up in the apartment they shared, alone, with the curtains drawn and the contents of a six pack in his belly. When Warner asked about Chloe, Greg told him to "shove it all the way to China." Apparently, even her boyfriend wasn't privy to Chloe's current whereabouts. He must've come to Revenant Point as a last-ditch attempt to locate her.

And died for his devotion.

Out on the lawn, the men in jumpsuits marched along the cliff's edge into the woods.

Where were they going?

Inside the house, on the other side of the back door, Freya barked. Ignoring the dog, Erin jogged across the lawn to the place where the men entered the woods. A trail partly overgrown with weeds led into the trees, skirting the cliff's edge. Erin had seen the trail before but never followed it, because walking that close to a sheer drop-off sent wormlike fear wriggling through her gut. The sandstone cliffs of the Keweenaw occasionally collapsed under the gradual but constant nibbling of the elements. Until today, she'd stayed out of the woods altogether. Her sole foray into the woodlands around Revenant House ended with a man dead by her hand.

She felt no remorse over shooting Rassul, considering he assaulted her brutally and terrorized her thereafter, not to mention his threats against her friends and family. Yet since the day she shot Rassul, the woods of Revenant Point seemed darker and infused with evil, the insidious kind that often masqueraded as normalcy. Her walk with Freya this afternoon marked her return to the woods. A feeling she could neither name nor describe had urged her to explore the land around the manor. Though the men had a head start, she caught up with them quickly. When she spotted the men up ahead, she slowed her pace and tried to move with more stealth than usual. She grimaced. Any stealth would be more than usual. In library school, they neglected to teach covert tactics.

Warner taught her a few things. She thought back to his lessons, conducted at a roadside park ten minutes from the manor to avoid the watchful cameras and listening devices hidden throughout Revenant House. She pictured Warner as he demonstrated certain postures and techniques for minimizing the odds of being spotted by the enemy. The sunlight, filtered through the trees, had glistened on his clean-shaven head. Though a few wrinkles fanned out from his eyes when he squinted, the overall smoothness of his features made him look younger than his fifty-one years. His favorite attire—dark jeans, long-sleeved black cotton T-shirt, and black combat boots—lent him the aura of a villain, especially when coupled with the black knit cap he often donned. His full lips rarely parted in a smile or even curved in a smirk, which made it hard for her to tell if he was joking. Sometimes when his dark eyes zeroed in on her gaze, she felt a slight tickle in her stomach. He was good-looking and charismatic, after all, and she was a woman.

Focus, she admonished herself. In her mind's eye, she saw Warner demonstrating one of his techniques. Mimicking it now, she stepped forward by settling her toe down first, then rolling backward to her heel. She repeated the motion with each step. It felt awkward at first, but within a minute she got used to it. Her footsteps made almost no sound when she walked this way. The men she was tracking seemed unconcerned with stealth. They clomped through weeds and cracked twigs under their boots. One man smacked his duffel bag against a tree, inadvertently. Both chattered and voices loud enough to carry some distance, although their words were muffled.

The man turned toward the cliff. They marched downward as if descending a staircase.

When the second man's head dipped out of sight, Erin scurried forward in a half crouch, careful to maintain the toe-down-first stride. At the point where the men had descended, she tiptoed to the edge. A series of steps carved out of the sandstone cliff led down to the water, perhaps fifteen feet from the boulder on which Greg's body slumped. Erin hadn't noticed the steps before. From her vantage point in the yard, the angle must've hidden them. The steps blended into the cliff rather well. Even from her current viewpoint, positioned at the top of the steps, she could barely make out where they ended.

The men had reached the bottom of the steps. They gestured as if discussing the best method for retrieving the body. One man squatted at the water's edge, while the other dug out of his duffel bag a coiled rope. The first man shook his head. He rose from his squat and dipped one foot into the water. Finding his footing, he waded out into the surf toward the body.

Erin turned away, closing her eyes for several minutes. She couldn't watch them wrestle with the corpse that had once been Greg Virtanen. It just felt…wrong. When she looked back at the scene below, the men were crouched at the base of the steps wrapping Greg's body in a brown tarp.

She'd seen enough.

Erin crept back down the trail.

4

A S SHE NEARED THE EDGE OF THE WOODS, ERIN STRAIGHTENED AND BROKE into a trot. The men would dispose of Greg's body, she assumed, though she had no desire to learn the details of that disposal. How could she let them do it? Covering up the crime, allowing a murderer to walk free.

She had no choice.

Maybe Wessick knew the murderess. Maybe he intended to deal with her himself. In this instance, Erin hoped for Samuel Wessick to mete out punishment.

Halfway across the lawn, Erin skidded to a halt. Freya was galloping toward her, ears flapping, tail wagging. Just outside the back door of the house stood a familiar figure.

Anna Newman did not wave. Instead, she spun on her high heels and marched back into the house.

A lump congealed in Erin's throat. As she fended off the dog's attempts to tackle her, she hurried to the back door, which hung open. She shut it after herself and Freya.

Newman stood in the passageway a half dozen feet from Erin. The woman wore a gray suit with a skirt that stopped halfway down her thighs. Her stiletto heels raised her an additional four inches, so that she towered a good six inches over Erin. Newman wore her black hair tucked back in a bun, with a perfect wave of bangs curving across her forehead. Her eye makeup, though heavily applied, was in earth tones that blended into her tanned skin. Matte lipstick tinted her mouth a shade pinker than her skin.

Dressed in jeans and a flannel shirt with white tennies, Erin figured she must look positively drab next to the fashion queen. The first time she met Newman, she let the woman's superior wardrobe and superior attitude push her into a sinkhole of self-doubt. Today, as she tilted her head back to meet Newman's gaze, she felt no inferiority. This woman worked for the same man who had employed Rassul. She allied herself with villains, and Erin refused to feel inferior to any of Wessick's minions.

Even the ones who looked like supermodels.

"What were you doing out there?" Newman asked without a hint of emotion.

Erin shrugged. "Going for a walk."

"The cliffs are dangerous. You should take more care."

"I'll keep that in mind."

Newman turned sideways to Erin. With a swish of her hand, she gestured down the hallway. "Your guest has arrived."

Her guest? Trying to look and sound like she knew exactly what Newman meant, she said, "Thank you."

"He's in the sitting room."

Erin thought for a second before she realized Newman meant the living room. Then she realized the most important word Newman had said—he. Her guest was a man.

Her heart thumped faster. A little over an hour ago, she'd sent the message to Alex. It took about that long to drive to Revenant House from her parents home outside Shadow Bay.

"I'll be leaving," Newman said. "I stopped in to see how you were doing."

And yet the woman had not once asked how Erin was doing. By "how you were doing," Newman meant that she came to make sure Erin didn't get in the way of Wessick's cleanup crew.

Freya and Erin followed Newman down the north passage and around the corner into the west passage. The door to the living room was shut. Erin halted in front of it to watch Newman proceed down the hallway. The woman executed a sharp right turn into the vestibule, disappearing around the corner. Erin heard the front door open and then shut behind Newman. She opened the living room door and walked inside.

Alex stood in front of the windows, facing away from her. Even from the back, she recognized him by the upright posture that made him seem taller than his six feet, the squareness of his shoulders, the suggestion of muscles visible under his shirtsleeves. The sunlight brought out the golden hues in his light brown hair, which he kept trimmed short. His physique was beefy yet not overweight, his muscles natural rather than the product of obsessive exercise. Today he wore khaki pants, a green plaid shirt with long sleeves, and dark brown leather hiking boots. His leather jacket, the same shade of brown as his boots, hung draped over the arm of the sofa.

Erin shut the door, locking out the dog. At the click of the latch engaging, Alex turned toward her. Face to face, separated by fifteen feet, they gazed at each other. After a few seconds he strode closer, narrowing the gap to a few feet. She hadn't seen him in so long that she almost forgot the effect his eyes had on her. The longer she stared up into his dark blue eyes, the more entranced she became by the lighter shades of blue and gold that swirled through his irises.

"Hi," he said.

A warm shiver coursed through her. Warner may on occasion inspire a tickle in her gut, but Alex gave her a feeling no one else could. She wondered if he knew that.

"Hi," she said.

His lips curved into a slight smile. "I got your message."

Erin wanted to fling her arms around his neck and hug him so tight he'd pass out from lack of oxygen. But she sensed a tension in him that acted like a wall between them. It was nothing palpable, just an underlying discomfort. Where it came from, or what it meant, she couldn't say.

He touched her arm with a pressure so light she barely felt it. In a soft voice, he said, "Maybe we should talk in your bedroom."

Uttered by another man, the words might sound like a come-on. When spoken by Alex, however, they referred to nothing of the sort. Her bedroom, along with the connected bathroom and walk-in closet, offered one of the few surveillance-free zones in the manor, along with the second upstairs bathroom and the downstairs bathroom. Every other room, including Samuel Wessick's study, hosted at least one camera-microphone pair. Most of the rooms hosted multiple pairs of such devices. Apparently, though, Wessick didn't want to intrude on Erin's most private moments. As a consequence, if she wanted to talk to someone in true privacy, she took her guest to her bedroom.

"Shall we?" Alex asked.

Her voice refused to work, and her mind had gone blank. As his eyes captured her gaze once again, she could do nothing but stare at him.

With the suddenness of a head-on collision, the reason for his question hit her. He wanted to go upstairs so they could talk, and all she did was gape at him. He must think she'd completely lost her mind.

With a nod, she swung the door open. Freya surged through the doorway like a furry tsunami. The dog licked Erin's hand with a flying pass on her way to Alex. Hurling her paws up and onto his belly, Freya whimpered and craned her entire body in an effort to reach his face with her tongue. Alex and Freya must've bonded during the few days they spent together at the home Erin once shared with her parents.

Erin tried not to notice the similarity between Freya's reaction to seeing Alex and her own urge to fling herself at him. She consoled herself with the knowledge that she drew the line at licking his face.

"Come on," Erin said.

She led Alex out of the living room and upstairs to her bedroom. Freya tagged along until they reached the top of the stairs, then the canine whirled around and galloped back downstairs. A tinkling sound had caught the dog's attention. The noise emanated from a tiny bell affixed to the collar of the manor's feline resident, Bastet. It seemed odd to Erin that Samuel Wessick, an agent for evil aliens, kept a pet cat. Villains could be inscrutable, she supposed.

Once inside the bedroom, with the door shut, she said to Alex, "Thank you for coming."

"You summoned me." He leaned against one of the bed posts. "I said if you needed me, I'd be here."

"I know, but you and your buddies have a lot to do, what with fighting evil aliens and all."

She meant the Aten, the unseen enemy in whose name Wessick labored. The Aten were beings not of this world, though exactly what that meant remained a mystery. Since they seemed pretty evil to her, and pretty alien, she figured evil aliens was as good a term as any for them.

Alex understood her terminology. He said, "Evil aliens notwithstanding, whenever you need me I will always come for you."

Erin knew he meant it. Despite his casual posture and offhand tone, she got the feeling he was anything but relaxed. Her latest news would add to his stress level. She needed to tell him anyway.

Sighing, she slumped down onto the bed beside Alex.

"What?" he said.

She bit her lip. "Greg's dead. I witnessed his murder."

ALEX HELD MOTIONLESS AS HE TURNED HIS EYES TO LOOK DOWN AT ERIN. SHE sat on the edge of the bed at arm's length from him, her shoulders sagging, head drooping. Her fingers curled over the edge of the mattress, though they hung slack rather than gripping the bed. Despite her obvious distress, he couldn't help admiring her form, the feminine curves that fleshed out her bones so that she looked like a real woman, rather than the stick-figure shape Hollywood convinced women they should strive to achieve. He wanted to hold her, to comfort her, but she undoubtedly preferred to receive comfort from Warner.

A ridge in the bedpost dug into his spine. He pushed away from the post and knelt in front of Erin. She lifted her head to meet his gaze. Both her light brown hair and her gray eyes looked darker in the false twilight of the room. Direct light, especially sunlight, would bring out the pale blue streaks in her eyes and the reddish highlights in her hair. He reached over to click on the bedside lamp. Its light, though muted, revealed the hidden colors in her hair and eyes—along with the half-moon shadows under her eyes and the pallor in her cheeks.

"What happened?" he asked.

She told him the story, her voice a near monotone. Her gaze stayed linked to his throughout her recitation. When she finished, she clasped her hands on her lap.

Frowning, he settled one hand over hers. "You didn't recognize the woman at all?"

"There was something familiar about her." Erin bit her lower lip. "But I can't place it."

"You sure it wasn't Newman?"

Erin shrugged. "I don't think so. The woman looked shorter than Newman."

Alex squeezed her hand briefly. "I hope my visit won't get you in trouble. Having guests during work hours is a violation of your employer's rules."

"I got permission. Said I needed an expert's advice on cataloging the Egyptology books." She yanked her hand free from his. A bitter tone infected her voice as she said, "Besides, I helped cover up a murder. An unapproved guest is no big deal in comparison."

Her expression had morphed from sad to angry. She was angry with herself, he realized, not with him and not even with her employer. He wanted to tell her she wasn't to blame, but he understood such words offered little comfort. Self-recrimination overrode reason, a fact he knew all too well based on deeply personal experience. Erin had helped him move past his guilt over the death of his colleagues, six innocent lives sacrificed by the Aten, to conceal their existence. For eight months, Alex blamed himself for those six deaths, because they died while he was away from their base camp. He left them at the height of the expedition—because another member of the team took ill and needed assistance to get to a hospital. The necessity of his departure offered no comfort, though, and no relief for his guilt. Erin showed him it hadn't been his fault. He owed her for that.

Now he could repay the debt. If he only knew how. Erin made it look easy.

He took a deep breath, grasped her hand, and said, "You had no choice. If you defied Wessick's orders, he could've hurt you." He sat on the bed alongside her and tucked his arm around her shoulders. "Greg's dead and nothing can change that. Under the circumstances, you did the right thing."

She let out a harsh laugh. "The right thing? I should've—"

"Stop it. You didn't kill him. The time will come when you need to stand up to Wessick, but this is not it."

"I'm supposed to have the power, remember? They need me, which means they ought to bend to my will, not the other way around."

Samuel Wessick and his masters, the Aten, believed Erin was the only one capable of finding a mysterious object they called the relic. As far as Alex and Erin knew, neither Wessick nor the Aten had any clue what the relic was. The text of an ancient Egyptian papyrus, which Erin found hidden in a secret compartment inside Revenant House, referred to the relic as "the object from another time" and spoke of a pharaoh having taken it against the Aten's wishes. The same papyrus mentioned a woman who could find the relic. The text called her the *amun renet*—literally, she whose identity is hidden—and labeled her the daughter of Seshat and Thoth, two Egyptian gods associated with knowledge and history. Seshat was the Mistress of the House of Books, a term Erin interpreted to mean librarian. Erin was a librarian, so it made an odd kind of sense that the Aten believed she was the *amun renet*.

The text also applied to the *amun renet* the epithet "incarnation of another time." Though both he and Erin agreed the Aten saw her as the *amun renet*, neither of them understood how she qualified as the incarnation of another time. Yes, the Aten possessed the technology to travel through time as well as through space. The out-of-place artifacts Rassul and Wessick collected for the Aten demonstrated the reality of time travel. Yet Erin was not a time traveler. She assured Alex she had never visited another time, except for the second or two when she stepped through a portal while chasing Rassul. Erin wouldn't lie to him. He trusted her more than anyone in his life. He would trust her with his life.

Maybe the epithet meant nothing. The ancient Egyptians referred to their pharaoh as His Incarnation or Your Incarnation. The epithet applied to the *amun renet* might be nothing more than an honorary title.

The salient point was that the Aten viewed Erin as their *amun renet*, the savior who would locate the relic for them, and in so doing, protect them from whatever they thought the relic might do to them. Their belief gave Erin power. They must keep her alive and, if not happy, at least not feeling threatened. He wouldn't call the situation a détente, but it was slightly better than a stalemate. Erin wielded a discreet amount of power against Samuel Wessick, and by extension, the Aten.

"I guess we were wrong," Erin said. "If I really had power over them, I wouldn't have let them cover up a murder."

"Then why did you?"

In slow motion she rotated her head to look straight at him. "I don't know."

Erin leaped up and ran across the bedroom. As she yanked open the door to the hallway, she paused to glance over her shoulder at him.

"Wait here," she said. "I have to make a phone call."

Then she left. Her footsteps clapped down the passage, fading as she rushed down the stairs. Within a matter of seconds, Alex sat alone in the silence of the bedroom.

A phone squatted on the bedside table.

She must've wanted privacy. From him.

Freya padded into the bedroom, her tail swishing, and approached Alex. The dog nuzzled his hand. He patted her head, a sign she took as an invitation to plant her feet on his lap, one paw on each thigh. While he struggled to shove her off him, Freya licked at his face.

He sighed. At least the dog enjoyed his company.

HER PALM HOVERING OVER THE PHONE HANDSET, ERIN HESITATED. HER INSTINCT was to call Newman, because the woman had so far served as a conduit between

Erin and Samuel Wessick. But Newman acted according to Wessick's orders. Erin needed to talk to the man in charge. She needed to talk to Samuel Wessick.

To do that, first she needed to get through Newman. Or get around her.

Start with option one. Erin picked up the phone and dialed Newman's number.

Ever since Alex asked her whether the mystery woman might have been Newman, the idea niggled at her subconscious. Erin tried to picture Newman with her hair down, the dark locks tumbling over her shoulders. Newman might've rushed into the house to change clothes, to prevent Erin from recognizing the outfit Newman wore when she murdered Greg. The theory sounded reasonable, but her instincts disagreed.

Newman answered after the second ring, uttering her last name in lieu of a greeting.

Erin identified herself then said, "It's about the incident this morning. What will happen to Greg's body?"

Her throat tightened on the word body. Her stomach did a quick flip-flop. In spite of the involuntary reaction, she managed to keep her tone even.

Newman's tone sharpened into a blade of ice. "It will be disposed of."

"That's not good enough. You have to notify the authorities. Greg must have family somewhere who'll be worried about him. They deserve to know he's not coming back."

"The package will be disposed of. That is all you need to know."

Erin gripped the phone tighter, feeling every muscle in her body tense. "He was a man, not a package. And I need to know a hell of a lot more than what you're telling me."

"I'm not authorized to divulge the details."

"Then get authorized." When no response came for several seconds, Erin said, "I need information and you're going to give it to me. Remember, if I'm not happy then I won't be in a good frame of mind to...catalog the library."

They both knew that "catalog the library" meant "find the blasted relic for your ET bosses."At least she hoped Newman knew that. Erin might not be as talented as her foes at speaking between the lines.

"I cannot help you," Newman said.

Click. The dial tone buzzed in Erin's ear.

Okay. Option two it was.

Now she just had to figure out how to implement option two. Going around Newman meant finding a way to contact Wessick directly. She doubted he was listed in the phonebook, and she knew from previous attempts to find information about him online that he was a virtual ghost. Even Alex's friends, with all their technology and resources, failed to gather much information about Samuel Wessick.

She lived in his house, dammit. His private study lay across the Hall from the library. Although the door remained locked at all times, she had a key. A skeleton key, to be precise, that opened every door in the manor. She found the key in the hand of a mummy, the mortal remains of a Victorian explorer named

Ridley Covington. Ridley was connected to Revenant House. She knew it but couldn't explain the connection yet. The skeleton key also opened the secret compartment above the library door where Ridley hid two items, an ancient Egyptian papyrus and a page from his unfinished book about otherworldly influences on ancient civilizations.

Two weeks ago, she and Alex had unlocked the door to Wessick's study. They found nothing of any relevance to their quest for the relic, nothing of much interest at all. The drawers of Wessick's desk were locked, and the skeleton key didn't work on them. She might force open the drawers with a screwdriver. But she had a feeling the answers she sought didn't await her in Wessick's study. She needed to talk to the man himself.

Without a phone number, she couldn't call him.

Then again, maybe she could.

Erin rummaged through her desk until she found a black felt tip marker. From the laser printer she stole a sheet of clean white paper, on which she scrawled a message with the marker. The sheet flapping in her hand, she ran out of the library into the passage.

The manor was riddled with surveillance devices, cameras and microphones camouflaged so well even the most observant person wouldn't notice them. Erin knew the exact location of each surveillance device, and yet she had trouble spotting them. When she first met Warner two weeks ago, he held in his hand a strange little contraption that turned out to be a super-high-tech device for ferreting out electronic bugs. In fact, the device was so high tech it outstripped anything available anywhere in the world. Not even the most clandestine military project laid claim to technology this advanced.

At first, she thought the device merely disabled, and re-enabled, electronic bugs. Later she learned the device could also pinpoint their locations. Warner and Alex had both wanted to permanently disable the bugs planted throughout Revenant House. Erin convinced them to leave the bugs in place. They could shut off the surveillance devices if necessary, and it would most likely look like a glitch in the system. Turning them off for good would leave no doubt that Erin and her friends knew about the bugs. For the time being, she preferred to leave Samuel Wessick and his minions guessing.

Erin faced the wall where the passage dead-ended. She stood between the doors to the library and Wessick's study. The wall in front of her looked like plain wood, with ornate moldings at the top and bottom. Thanks to Warner's device, she knew precisely where a camera was hidden in this wall. Three-fourths of the way up the wall, and Erin's eye level, she spied a faint whorl in the grain of the wood. This was no mere defect in the wood, she knew. The slightly darker core of the whorl concealed a tiny camera.

Someone watched, and she hoped it was Wessick. Otherwise her message might not reach him. His minions seemed intent on keeping her from speaking to or seeing him.

She had to try.

Positioning herself squarely in front of the camera, about ten feet from it, she raised the sheet of paper so that the message scrawled on it faced the camera. If Wessick received the message, if he understood it, if he felt like reacting to it, then she might have a chance.

After a good twenty or thirty seconds, she lowered the sheet and returned to the library. Alex was waiting for her upstairs. They needed to talk about the papyrus.

She slapped the sheet down on the desktop. The words she'd emblazoned across it stared up at her.

WE NEED TO TALK.

If her message didn't work, she'd try something more drastic. One way or another, Samuel Wessick would give her what she wanted. Answers.

Erin spun on her heels and marched upstairs.

5

WHEN ERIN REENTERED THE BEDROOM, ALEX WAS SQUATTING ON THE floor rubbing Freya's belly. The dog made little whimpery noises as she wriggled on her back.

"I hope you two will be happy together," Erin said.

Alex whipped his head around to look at her. He stared at her with wide eyes and cheeks that suddenly glowed pink. Not bright pink, the way her cheeks used to flush every time he so much as looked at her. His cheeks blushed in a muted shade that seemed more dignified, and certainly adorable. She fought back a grin.

The dog sprang up, darting to Erin. Alex leaped to his feet, shoved a hand through his hair, and struggled to regain his composure.

On her way upstairs, Erin had decided not to tell Alex about her message to Wessick. If it worked, she could tell him about it later. Hearing about it now would only raise his stress level and most likely lead to an argument. Well, a disagreement anyway. Alex had never yelled at her. In the short time they'd known each other, they experienced some of the most stressful situations imaginable, yet he rarely even raised his voice.

Except for that one time when he announced they were going to die. To be fair, though, at the time a thunderstorm of the Aten's making had been firing lightning bolts that, section by section, collapsed the tunnel in which she and Alex stood. They escaped that attempt on their lives. The Aten sent Rassul to attack her, but later dispatched a glowing orb to heal her injuries while she slept.

The memory of the orb hovering over her bed replayed in her mind, bringing back the fear and confusion that flooded through her when she awoke to the sight.

She remembered the heat from the orb's glow, and the redness in her cheeks that lingered after the orb left. These thoughts reminded her of a question she had yet to answer.

Alex walked up to her, halting a couple feet away. "Let's hear it."

She scrunched her eyebrows. "What?"

"You've thought of something. I can tell by the look on your face."

"I was just wondering," she said, "why sometimes the Aten try to kill us and other times they seem to protect us."

"Protect you. I'm expendable, remember?"

"Not to me."

He studied her, his expression blank. He didn't even blink.

She waved a hand in front of his face. "Did you have a stroke?"

Letting out a sigh, he said, "I don't why the Aten tried to kill you a few times and other times helped you. It makes no sense. Nothing I've learned in the past eighteen months makes any sense whatsoever."

Eighteen months ago he joined the Human Origins Project. She was a newbie compared to him.

His expression was no longer blank. He pursed his lips, compressing them firmly. His eyes were narrowed, with faint lines webbing out from the corners. Every muscle in his body seemed to have tensed.

She laid a hand flat on his chest. "We will figure this out, you know."

He said nothing, his gaze locked on the wall behind her.

"Things are better now," she said. "We're not alone. We have people like Warner helping us."

He hissed a breath out his nose, flaring his nostrils. As he flattened his lips into a line, the darkening of his expression seemed to both darken and chill the blue of his eyes. She wanted to ask him what his problem was, but asking a man a direct question about his feelings worked about as well as asking a grizzly bear to pretty please stop eating hikers. Instead, she changed the subject.

"I think the papyrus map is the key," she said. "We should look at it together."

Finally, he spoke. "Fine."

She turned to leave the room.

He seized her arm. She stopped, rotating to face him. His grip was firm but gentle.

"Where are you going?" he asked.

"Downstairs. The photos of the papyrus are on my laptop, which I left downstairs."

"I've got the photos right here."

As quickly as his expression had hardened, it softened again. The lines around his eyes smoothed out, his body relaxed, and he almost smiled. Striding to the foot of the bed, he picked up his briefcase, which he referred to as an attaché. She hadn't noticed he carried the bag upstairs with him. Flopping the bag onto the bed, he opened it and slid out a silver object the size of a hardcover book. It was a tablet computer, she realized. The back was silver matte, the front glassy. He turned on the device, then tapped the touch screen several times.

With a satisfied smirk, he handed her the computer. The screen displayed a close-up image of one portion of the papyrus map. The entire papyrus measured three feet wide by two feet high, with the map taking up three fourths of the width. The left-hand quarter of the sheet contained registers of hieroglyphs that talked about the relic and the pharaoh who stole it from the Aten. The text also talked about how the Aten believed only one person, an unknown woman, could find the relic for them. The papyrus text called her the *amun renet*— she whose identity is hidden—though the Aten preferred the term *satseshat*, meaning daughter of the goddess Seshat.

The map that took up the bulk of the papyrus had proved difficult to decipher. A squiggly blue line painted across the center of the map clearly represented a river. Green strips on either side of the river must indicate fertile land, either grass or crops. Farther out from the green strips, brown blobs edged with faint black lines seemed to indicate mountains. Other shapes sprinkled throughout the two-dimensional landscape must represent something too, but Erin had yet to figure out what.

On the tablet, Erin could easily pan across the image and zoom in and out on certain features. The map was most certainly Egyptian, as evidenced by the hieroglyphs and the decorative images that formed a border around the entire sheet. Egypt laid claim to but one river, the Nile. The obvious conclusion was that the river in the map was the Nile.

She looked at Alex. He was watching her with rapt, if slightly amused, attention.

"What's so funny?" she asked.

"When you concentrate, your tongue sticks out a little bit."

A blush fired upon her cheeks. After making certain her tongue was firmly in her mouth, she said, "Have you found any location in Egypt that matches this map?"

"Without knowing what those other symbols mean, it's difficult to tell for certain. Based solely on the positions of the mountains relative to the bends in the river, I have to say no."

Erin stared at the section of map displayed on the screen. Where on earth was this place?

Maybe it wasn't on Earth after all. The text accompanying the map described the Aten as beings not of this world. Alex's translation of the text echoed in her mind.

They are not Egyptians. They are more than gods. Their will commands the sky to open up and rain fire upon us. Their anger causes the earth to tremble. Only the dead are safe from them. Beware the Aten, the ancient ones who seem to give light but bring only darkness and death.

Ridley Covington wrote similar words, in the note he composed while he lay dying inside the Grand Canyon labyrinth she and Alex found. The note—dated August 15, 1858— warned "nothing but evil can come from allying oneself with those who serve the darkness that masquerades as the light." Since he hid the map and the missing pages from his unfinished book inside Revenant House, Ridley must've either lived here or visited the manor at some point. Both he and the Aten shared some kind of connection with Revenant House. In his last note, Ridley also mentioned his brother Broderick. That reference spurred Erin to scour the Internet for any information related to the Covington family.

Despite searching everything from genealogy databases to online collections of historical books, and everything else she could find, her efforts netted her zilch. The Covingtons seem to have left no footprints in the digital world. Oh sure, she found plenty of people with the last name Covington. None of them, so far as she could determine, shared any lineage with Ridley. Katy and Rick Bergren, the people who ran the Human Origins Project, had gotten some of their computer geek buddies to search databases not available to Erin, or to anyone other than hackers, but they turned up nothing either. Like the current owner of Revenant House, Ridley Covington was a ghost. She used the word ghost figuratively, of course, though she couldn't rule out literal ghosts. These days, she ruled out nothing categorically.

As she twirled her finger on the touch screen, the map image slid and zoomed on the display. One shape caught her eye, and she zeroed in on it. The shape was roughly rectangular, brown, and apparently hollow. If it represented an object then she would guess it was a canoe, like the ones ancient peoples in North America had fashioned from trees. But why would an Egyptian map feature a canoe? From everything she and Alex had learned in the past few weeks, she knew Egyptians must've traveled to the Americas long ago, though precisely how long ago remained a mystery. If the shape on the map represented an American canoe, then the map must not show any location in Egypt. It must show a location in North America.

Unless the Egyptians took some of their new American friends back to Egypt with them. Then a canoe might've floated down the Nile.

Alex said the map looked like no place in Egypt that he knew. The canoe suggested an American connection. The artifacts Rassul had stolen for Wessick also suggested a connection between Egypt and the Americas, as well as other cultures around the world. So the canoe shape helped her not one bit.

Blasted cryptic map. Why couldn't the person or persons who drew the map have written the name of the place on the papyrus? Oh, that would make her life too easy, that's why.

The Egyptians had clearly feared the Aten. Feared their power. Maybe that explained why the mapmaker omitted the name of the place depicted, and any details that might illuminate the mystery.

No, fear alone could not explain it. Despite fearing the Aten, the mapmaker included text that described the Aten, albeit in terms that fell short of crystal clear. Maybe the mapmaker simply didn't know where the place was. If he traveled there via one of those weird portals, then he might not know where in the world the location sat. Drawing a map of a particular locality was very different from recognizing the locality's position on the globe.

She had no idea where she ended up when she followed Rassul through a portal. Somewhere in the past. Somewhere not here.

Tapping her finger on the screen, she said, "This looks like a canoe."

Alex squinted at the screen. He leaned close to her, head ducked. His hair brushed against her cheek, triggering a tickle. She scratched her cheek lightly, and the heel of her hand bumped Alex's head. He twisted his head around to peek up at her through his eyelashes.

"Sorry," she said.

"That's my line." He straightened. "I apologize for everything, remember? You're the bossy one."

In the beginning, he had apologized for every little transgression, even the imagined ones. She only got bossy when they were in imminent danger of dying, which was about the time he would turn into Mr. We're Gonna Die. After their Grand Canyon expedition, he became progressively less apologetic and more…manly. Not that he'd been wimpy before. But his demeanor had transformed from overburdened with guilt to self-assured.

Over the past two weeks, she'd felt herself seesawing between confidence in her own power and abject fear that everyone she loved would die because she lacked the information necessary to find the relic. She might've gotten stuck in the latter position, if not for Alex.

She glanced sideways at him. "Thanks for reminding me I'm not a spineless little slug with lint for brains."

Trying not to grin, he looked at her. "Excuse me?"

A chuckle, half suppressed, chopped up the words.

Erin laid a hand on his thigh. "You reminded me I have the power here. Before you showed up, I was frolicking in Wimpville."

He let out a tiny chuckle. "I thought Warner inspired confidence."

"I didn't tell him about Wimpville. He wouldn't get it."

The humor on his face faded. He turned himself so that he faced her, with his left leg bent beside her and his right leg draped off the bed's edge. Propped up on one arm, he took hold of her hand. In a soft voice, he said, "I guess you still need me."

"Of course I do."

He averted his gaze to the quilt. "I thought you might prefer Warner's help."

"No." She hooked her finger under his chin and forced him to look up at her. "I like him, but he's not you." She planted a quick kiss on his lips. "Besides, he's way too old for me."

Alex smirked. Just as he opened his mouth to speak, his cell phone bleeped. He plucked it from its holder on his belt and punched buttons. His brow furrowed, then smoothed out. Returning the phone to its clip, he said, "We found your man."

"Huh?"

"T.R. Young, the architect who wrote about Revenant House."

On her first day of work at Revenant House, she'd searched the Internet for information about the manor and its owner. Her search for Samuel Wessick came up empty. Her search for Revenant House turned up a brief mention of the place on a blog written by an architect named T.R. Young, who included the manor on his list of unusual historic houses in Michigan. Young had also mentioned that he heard about Revenant House from the manor's former groundskeeper, a man called Ignatius Underwood.

"I e-mailed Young two weeks ago," she said. "He never replied."

"Warner assigned his most trusted investigator to the case and, apparently, Young has been located." Alex rose, reaching for his bag. "I'm flying down to Texas to meet him."

He took the tablet from her, tucking it inside his bag.

Texas? She wanted him close by, in case something happened, not two thousand miles away. He didn't have a magic portal, like Rassul.

For pity's sake, she was hardly helpless. She both owned a gun and knew how to shoot it. The Aten wouldn't harm her until she found their relic anyway. Of course, Rassul had worked for the Aten and that fact didn't stop him from assaulting her.

Alex bent down to look directly into her face. He grasped her shoulder in one hand. "In case of emergency, you can always call Warner."

She nodded.

"You've been alone here for two weeks," he said. "You can handle one more day."

"I know." She forced a tight smile. Then a thought occurred to her, and she asked, "What about Chloe?"

"Warner's investigator can't find a trace of her. She seems to have dropped off the edge of the world."

A chill raced through her. The woman who murdered Greg seemed to have stepped off the edge of the world, right in front of Erin. If the mystery woman killed one person, she could easily have hurt Chloe too.

"We'll keep looking," Alex said. "She must be out there somewhere."

"Yeah."

He kissed her forehead. Releasing her shoulder with a quick squeeze, he turned and marched toward the doorway. There, he paused to glance back at her.

He gestured at the window. "Remember, our friends in the woods are looking out for you too."

With that, he left the room. When she heard his footsteps creaking stairs, she leaped up and ran after him. She caught up with him halfway down the stairs. They walked the rest of the way side by side, until they reached the front door. As Alex opened the door, they turned to face each other. His blue eyes captured her gaze.

"Find out what Young knows," she said. "And be careful."

In lieu of an answer, he kissed her cheek.

Then he strode out the door.

6

E RIN WATCHED ALEX GET INTO HIS CAR AND HEAD OFF DOWN THE DRIVEWAY. When his car disappeared into the woods that surrounded the driveway, she shut the door. For a moment, she stood there with her hand resting on the knob. Finally, she traipsed down the hallway to the library door. The wood carving above the door depicted two Egyptians worshiping the sun. Lines representing sunrays stretched down toward the figures, with each ray terminating in a tiny hand. A few of the hands proffered small crosses, the tops of which formed loops. Known as an *ankh*, the looped cross symbolized life.

The wood carving concealed a cavity, Ridley's secret hiding place, where she'd found the papyrus map and the missing page from Ridley's book.

If Ridley kept one secret compartment, why not another? He might've hidden other clues elsewhere in the manor. For two weeks she'd wondered about this, and for two weeks she explored every nook and cranny in the house for anything resembling a hidden doorway or panel that might pop open. So far, she'd found nothing.

The existence of Ridley's secret compartment suggested he lived here at some point. She supposed he could've installed the secret compartment at any point after the house was built, or even during construction. During Erin's job interview at Revenant House, Newman gave her a tour of the manor, complete with a brief history of its origins. Newman said a lord somebody-or-other built the house, and though Erin couldn't remember the name now, she felt certain it hadn't been Covington.

But it had started with a C. She dug through her memory, hunting for the name. Colgate. No, that wasn't it. Cumin. Duh, that was a spice. Colban.

Yes, that was it. Lord Colban.

She trotted to the library desk, plunked herself down in the chair, and grabbed the computer's mouse. Once she'd navigated to a web search engine, she typed in the name Lord Colban. Mentally crossing her fingers, she hit enter. The search results displayed a couple seconds later. Her effort yielded a handful of links to fantasy websites that featured games and stories about ancient Scotland. A number of other links led to pages about various ancient Scots who went by the name Colban. None of the links related to Revenant House.

Another dead end. She slumped in her chair. This maze of clues often drew her down the wrong path. The answers she needed could not be found online or in any books publicly available.

Gradually, she became aware of a grumbling sound outside. How long ago the sound started, she couldn't say. Her own thoughts often drowned out the world around her. She got so engrossed in whatever task occupied her that she forgot to eat and missed the phone ringing. The grumbling sound might've begun ten minutes ago, or two hours past. Before she moved into Revenant House, her total immersion in intellectual activities seemed innocuous. Now, as she realized anyone might've entered the house without her noticing, the idea of her total immersion in her own thoughts sent a chill skittering down her spine.

She sprang out of her chair, leaning across the window ledge to check the driveway. A black Cadillac Escalade, the huge SUV her employer provided for her, hunkered in the drive. No other cars were in sight. The grumbling sound seemed to originate behind the house.

She recognized the sound. It was a riding lawnmower.

On the first day she worked at Revenant House, the second day she lived in the house, she saw the groundskeeper ride his lawnmower into the woods. A mosquito net had shielded his head, obscuring his features. She couldn't even be certain the groundskeeper was a man. A baggy canvas jacket and jeans concealed the groundskeeper's body. Such clothing might mask the figure of a not-too-voluptuous woman. On that day two weeks ago, Erin decided against following the groundskeeper. Concerns about making a good impression on her first day of work overrode her curiosity. Today, she felt no such compunctions.

Trotting down the passageways to the back door, she flung it open and raced outside, past the ends of the east and west wings into the open lawn. She stopped there to survey the area. Halfway between the house and the cliffs, the lawnmower zipped back and forth at top speed. The groundskeeper, clad in the baggy canvas jacket and jeans she saw before, sat ramrod straight in the seat of the riding lawnmower, with his gloved hands tightly gripping the steering wheel. The mosquito net covered his brimmed hat and head, draping down to his collarbone. The section of lawn between the house and the mower was neatly trimmed. She breathed in the scent of fresh-cut grass.

The grass had grown to ankle height, which explained why the groundskeeper fired up the lawnmower. If he really was a groundskeeper.

Someone cared for the property. Someone cared for Bastet too. The cat looked healthy and was well fed, as evidenced by her lack of interest in the scraps Erin offered her. Newman had told her the groundskeeper fed Bastet. At what times he fed the cat, and whether he had a key to the house, Newman didn't mention.

Erin waved at the groundskeeper. As on the first day she spotted him, he either ignored her or didn't see her. She moved to stand in the shadow cast by the east wing of the house. If he hadn't seen her, then she could watch him from the sanctuary of the shadows. Watch him do what? Mow the lawn? Fascinating.

Leaning against the house, she observed the groundskeeper's progress. It took another ten minutes for the lawnmower to traverse the remainder of the grassy area. The groundskeeper steered the lawnmower back toward the house along the edge of the woods on the west side of the lawn. He passed the trail taken by the men who retrieved Greg's body, the one that that led along the cliff's edge to the steps carved out of the rock face. A little further on, he turned the mower into the woods and pushed through the boughs of a pine tree. The limbs billowed in his wake, settling back into place.

Erin sprinted across the lawn toward the pine tree. From five feet away, the area looked like woods with no trail evident, aside from the faint parallel tracks where the mower's tires depressed the grass. Erin sidled around the boughs of the pine tree. The mower's tracks continued in a straight line for a dozen feet, then veered left down a track way too wide for a deer trail. Although grass had overgrown trail, it looked like an old two-track slightly wider than the mower, the tracks of which traced a double line into the depths of the woods. Erin trotted down the two-track, careful not to step on anything that might snap or crackle underfoot. The mower's engine grumbled up ahead, the vehicle itself veiled by the foliage and shadows. Within a minute, Erin got close enough to glimpse the mower and its rider through the screen of foliage.

Remembering what Warner taught her, she tried to look through the foliage rather than at it. She let her vision slide out of focus and back in again. Suddenly, behind the branches of the evergreens and hardwoods, she spied a shape. A structure of some kind. The groundskeeper was putting toward the structure. When she got within fifty feet of the lawnmower, she slowed to a brisk tiptoeing gate. The structure looked like a gazebo, round and perhaps twenty feet in diameter.

The groundskeeper parked his lawnmower at the foot of the gazebo steps. Shutting off the engine, he hopped off the mower.

Previously, Erin assumed the groundskeeper was Rassul. She had been wrong. The groundskeeper's identity, even the person's gender, eluded her. A frozen ball congealed in her stomach. She didn't like not knowing.

Erin crouched behind a fir tree. Its branches, she hoped, hid her from view.

The groundskeeper stood motionless, facing the gazebo. After a moment, he trudged up the steps to the platform. The gazebo was constructed from wood that had grayed over the years. The remnants of paint, mostly white and blue, flecked the roof and posts. The glass that once closed in the gazebo was cracked, and large chunks were missing. Wooden benches sat in a semicircle in the middle of the gazebo.

Halfway to the benches, the groundskeeper froze. He turned sideways to gaze back the way he'd come, past the lawnmower, into the woods.

A shiver rattled through her. The hairs on the back of her neck stiffened. The mosquito net concealed the groundskeeper's face, yet she felt his gaze zeroing in on her.

While she kept her gaze on the groundskeeper, still in a crouch she backed away step-by-step. Her footsteps produced only the slightest noise, nothing the groundskeeper could hear from this distance. He stood as motionless as the trees.

A deer bounded out of the woods to her right, flying past the lawnmower and gazebo.

Erin stopped. Her heart was pounding so loud she thought for sure the groundskeeper heard it too.

He turned to watch the deer until it bounded out of sight. Then he faced her once again.

Though she couldn't see his face, she felt certain he was smirking at her. Just like Rassul.

The groundskeeper reached a hand behind his back.

A memory flashed through her mind. Rassul with a knife, its blade glistening in the sunlight. Rassul brandishing it at her. Threatening her. The sound of his raspy voice as he commanded her to find the relic or else.

Erin swallowed hard.

And then she fled.

SAMUEL WESSICK PULLED THE HANDKERCHIEF OUT OF HIS BACK POCKET. AS he wiped sweat from the back of his neck, he watched Erin disappear into the distant woods. The mosquito netting blocked much of the airflow, which caused him to sweat beneath the net. So now Erin knew about the summerhouse. Two weeks ago when she witnessed his journey into the woods, she hadn't followed. At the time, she had lived in Revenant House for less than a day. After two weeks in the manor, she seemed thoroughly comfortable exploring the property. Good.

Though once he visited this spot often, to enjoy the tranquility of the garden that surrounded the summerhouse in years past, these days he rarely made the journey. The garden was gone, but more than that, the summerhouse had lost its power to incite joy within him. Joy was a foreign concept to him, something he recalled through hazy memories. Until two weeks ago, he had stayed away from the summerhouse for twenty years. Or longer, depending on which calendar he counted the days by.

Why did he come here?

Sentimentality, an outsider might say, lured him to this place. No one who knew him would attribute sentimentality to Samuel Wessick. Even he himself found it hard to blame his actions on nostalgia. Something else drove him to visit the summerhouse, a feeling he couldn't identify. For the first time in his life, an existence that spanned more decades than he admitted, he failed to understand his own psyche.

The feeling would pass.

When he received Erin's message informing him that they needed to talk, he knew she meant in person. The time had come, he realized. Bringing her into the fold would require a delicate touch, for if he overwhelmed her with the truth of her destiny she might well balk. He must gain her trust, no matter the cost. She must aid him. Without her help, all was lost. Not for the first time, he realized that the fate of all history, of every living thing that ever lived or would ever live, rested on the shoulders of one woman. Erin Turner had begun to recognize her own importance, but she remained largely ignorant of the details. He must enlighten her.

He reached under his loose-fitting sweatshirt to withdraw his cell phone from its holster. On the touch screen, he tapped icons until he'd opened the app that accessed the manor's security system. The vestibule camera caught Erin as she entered the house. From there, via other surveillance cameras, he followed her through the house and into the library. He observed as she settled into the chair behind the desk and commenced clicking away at the keys on the computer keyboard.

Closing the app, he tucked the phone back into its holster. The sweatshirt drooped over his hips, concealing the phone. As he took in his own appearance, his lip curled involuntarily. He despised wearing such ill-fitting, unattractive clothing. Yet anytime he ventured outside the manor, he felt the need for camouflage. At first, he masked his appearance to keep Erin from identifying him. Perhaps the time had come to strip away the facade. She must know the truth.

But not all at once. He would mete out the facts bit by bit, ensuring she could digest each morsel before feeding her another.

He strode to the lawnmower. A sack was strapped to a metal rack behind the seat. He unbuckled the sack's closure, slid a hand inside, and grasped the smooth, round object nestled in a bed of soft cloths within the sack. With a swift flourish, he withdrew the object from the sack. The *akhet* ball felt warm in his hand, its temperature a few degrees warmer than his skin. Its interior writhed, though not with a snakelike motion, but rather with the fluidity of oil and water. Within the ball, blue and white substituted for the blackness of oil and the transparency of water. The colors swirled, coalesced, separated. The skin of the sphere was firm, yet it puckered slightly under the pressure of his fingers. He knew nothing of the science behind the *akhet* balls. He knew only how to use them, and that they worked. Their construction, their exact mechanism, of those things he was ignorant.

The *akhet* would ferry him into the manor, directly to his study. Erin, working in the library across the hall from his study, wouldn't realize he had entered the house.

He turned away from the lawnmower. Visually surveying the area, he selected an open spot just in front of the summerhouse. He closed his eyes for a moment, initializing the ball. A breeze pressed mosquito netting to his face. The material tickled his skin but he ignored it, focused on the task at hand.

As he opened his eyes, he loosened his grip on the *akhet* ball. With a quick thrust of his arm, he tossed the ball toward the selected spot. A burst of pure white light blinded him. Wincing, he shielded his eyes with his hand until the brilliance diminished to a tolerable glow. The light, though still white, iridesced with a blue tinge. The glow ringed the bubble-like portal, which floated a foot above the ground. The bubble's interior revealed another place—his study inside Revenant House—seeming to float in midair, surrounded on all sides by the forest.

Wessick stepped into the portal.

His foot lifted off the forest floor and set down on the wood floor of the study. Once his other foot settled onto the wood floor, the portal behind him telescoped shut.

On the sofa in front of his desk, Desheret lounged. She sprawled lengthwise on the sofa, her torso nestled into the junction between the arm and the back, her legs stretched out across the sofa's length with her ankles crossed. The long tresses of a black wig cascaded over her shoulders. She wore a diaphanous tan gown, the hem of which grazed her ankles. The thin fabric revealed suggestions of the feminine form beneath it.

Without looking at him, she said, "Ah there you are, Samuel."

Desheret spoke the words with a casual tone, to match her body language. Since he had not seen her in over a week, however, he knew what her presence meant. The Aten sent her.

Before Rassul's death, the Aten preferred to communicate with him through their orbs, the glowing spheres that blinked in and out of sight. Unlike the *akhet* balls—which performed one action and one action alone, and only at the behest of the user—the orbs often behaved as if they possessed intelligence, though he suspected the impression was an illusion. He knew the orbs responded to commands from the Aten, like computers executing code. The orbs could also convey knowledge.

Wessick crossed in front of the sofa. He walked behind the desk and settled into the chair. Since Rassul's death, the Aten no longer communicated with him via the orbs. They no longer communicated with him at all. For the greater part of his life, he served the Aten and their cause, seeking the *satseshat* through every means available to him. Now his link to them was severed. Perhaps Rassul's behavior and his inability to control the brigand incensed them, or perhaps once he identified Erin Turner as the *satseshat* they felt they no longer needed him.

Desheret's presence suggested they might reestablish the link.

He resisted the urge to ask Desheret. To ask signified weakness. It implied he needed the Aten, rather than vice versa. Therefore, he would wait until Desheret felt like informing him of the Aten's decision. When one undertook a mission such as his, patience was not simply a virtue but a necessity. Death awaited those who rushed to please the Aten.

A memory rose in his mind, an image of one who rushed headlong into disaster, spurred onward by a desire for truth, and died for it. The face lingered in his mind's eye like a video on pause. His throat tightened. His hands ached. Glancing down, he discovered he was grasping the arms of the chair so tightly that the ligaments on the back of his hand arched beneath the skin.

He inhaled a slow, deep breath. As he released the breath, his muscles relaxed and he flexed his fingers.

When Rassul died, and the Aten pulled back from him, Wessick feared his plan might never reach fruition. Desheret's return signaled a change—in his favor, he felt certain.

"Will you speak?" Desheret asked. "Or have you not missed me at all?"

"You deign to return, and expect me to fall at your feet."

"No, love," she said, her original accent peeking through for a split second. "But you must be curious about why I've returned."

He shrugged one shoulder.

She blew a breath out her nose and flung her legs off the sofa, her heels clapping on the floor. A frown pursed her lips, knit her brow, and narrowed her eyes. "You care for no one and nothing. You're a machine, Samuel."

"Dear child," he said, fixing his gaze on hers, "let's dispense with the dramatics, shall we? Our masters sent you with a message for me. Deliver it."

Her eyes widened with feigned anger as she exhaled loudly through her nostrils once again. He knew better than to let himself get ensnared by one of her emotional traps. Admittedly, he contained his emotions inside a tightly sealed box within himself. She was the machine, however, capable of imitating but not experiencing the full range of human feelings, programmed to serve the Aten and fulfill her duties without mercy or conscience. It was not entirely her fault. For all the years he'd known the child, he fought the urge to empathize with her. For she did harbor one genuine emotion, a feeling made dangerous by her inability to control it.

Anger.

Desheret approached the desk, leaning a hip against it. The anger had vacated her features, and her voice took on a purring tone as she said, "Wouldn't you like to kiss me hello, Samuel?"

Clasping his hands over his belly, he steepled his index fingers as he regarded her. Though she often invoked his Christian name, he rarely spoke hers. Odd, he thought. But then again, perhaps not. In her young life, she had adopted many pseudonyms—so many, in fact, that on occasion he struggled to recall her birth name. That name came back to him now, but he refrained from speaking. The ancient Egyptians believed words held real power and that to know a person's name granted one power over the individual in question. In Desheret's case, perhaps knowing her true name did grant him a measure of power, for she had no idea he knew her name. He must hold the power in reserve until he needed it the most.

Desheret laid a hand flat on the desk and she leaned toward him. In her dark eyes, golden specks glittered in the lamplight. Her tone grew soft and throaty, with a hint of menace. "They are displeased with you, darling."

"Rassul was their choice, not mine. I warned—"

"You misunderstand. They approved of Rassul's tactics. He produced results." She leaned closer. "You have failed them too many times. And they know you held onto the artifacts, only destroying them after Erin Turner found them."

The artifacts. Rassul collected them over the course of a year, at Wessick's instruction but ultimately by the will of the Aten. The artifacts exposed one of their deepest secrets, that they possessed the technology of time travel.

"Erin already knew of the artifacts," he said. "Alex MacKay tracked Rassul's movements and documented the thefts. If I had destroyed the artifacts earlier, Erin still would've realized the truth."

"But she would not have known *you* commanded Rassul."

Since Rassul's death, he'd realized he never commanded the man. Rassul obeyed Wessick's orders only when it suited him, and when it helped him gain the Aten's favor. At some point, without his knowledge, Wessick lost control of his own plans. He must regain it, and to do so he needed assistance.

From Erin Turner.

Desheret recoiled from the desk. She stood straight, her body relaxed, her face without expression. "They give you one final chance, Samuel. Get rid of Alex MacKay and use Erin Turner to find the relic."

"It was your idea to allow Erin to form an attachment with MacKay. You assured me it would improve her odds of finding the relic."

"I have changed my mind." She lifted her chin to gaze down her nose at him. "Get rid of MacKay."

"I'm well aware of my duties."

"Then fulfill them." She bored into him with her diamond-hard gaze. "You know the consequences of failing once too often."

He returned her stare with equal hardness. Beings far more malicious than this child had failed to intimidate him.

Lips twitching, she whirled away from him. Her skirts flounced around her.

Temper, temper. So like a child, in years and in disposition.

Desheret marched to the doorway.

As her hand closed around the knob, he said, "Not that way. Erin is in the library."

She hissed out a breath, like a snake preparing to strike. Then, she spun and stomped back to his desk. He pulled open a drawer and brought out an *akhet* ball, which he offered to her. She snatched it from his hand.

He let a cold smile warp his lips.

She faced the open area between the sofa and the bay window. After a hesitation, presumably taken up with initiating the ball, she tossed device. Wessick shut his eyes until the brilliance faded.

Desheret walked toward the portal. At its periphery, she paused to glance back at him over her shoulder.

"Once you find the relic," she said, "kill Erin Turner."

She stepped into the portal. The bubble telescoped shut behind her.

He stared at the spot where the portal had hung suspended a second earlier. *Kill Erin Turner.* Her words echoed in his mind, eliciting an icy tightness in his chest. This was the first he'd heard of killing Erin. Once they possessed the relic, she was of no use to the Aten. Their order should not surprise him, yet it did.

Though death was inevitable, he disliked acting as the Grim Reaper's agent.

A sigh slipped from his lips unbidden. He would fulfill his duties, by whatever means the task required. After thirty years of searching, with his plan so close to its culmination, he could afford no doubts and no hesitation.

The relic would be found.

No matter the cost.

North-Central Texas

THE BRICK HOUSE LAY AT THE BOTTOM OF A LOW, SLOPING HILL. THE TREES that surrounded and camouflaged the house looked squat compared to their Michigan cousins, which would've towered high above the tallest trees in this area. A two-track dirt driveway, riddled with potholes and weeds, traced the contour of the hill as it wound toward the house. Alex didn't see the home until he steered his rental car around the last curve.

An old van, rusty and dented, sat parked in front of the house. The garage door was open, revealing the cardboard boxes and plastic bins that filled the space, save for one corner that housed a riding lawnmower. The house itself looked dark, the windows curtained.

Alex parked behind the van. After the long journey from Michigan, he really hoped T.R. Young was home. He really hoped the man still lived here. The current phonebook included no listing for a Young with the initials T.R., so he'd resorted to searching the public information databases available online—for a fee—to find an address for the man.

Swinging the door open, Alex jumped out and gazed at the house for a moment. If Young was inside, he didn't want anyone to know it. The house seemed lifeless, in spite of the van squatting out front. Alex shut the car door and strode up the overgrown path to the house's front door. He punched the button for the doorbell, which chimed faintly inside the house. A minute passed, then another, with no sign of movement inside the house. Pulling open the outer screen door, Alex knocked on the wooden door behind it. The door was solid wood, without so much as a peephole interrupting the grain.

Still no response.

He knocked three more times, suppressing the urge to pound on the wood, then shouted, "Mr. Young, I need to speak with you. Please, it's very important."

Another minute passed, maybe more. He did not travel all this way only to find an empty house. He would've preferred to call ahead, to make certain Young would be home, but even the public databases yielded no phone numbers for the man. Like many people these days, he might use only a cell phone, rather than a landline, as his home number. There was no phonebook for cell numbers. Given time, his contacts at the Human Origins Project could locate a number for him. But he did not want to wait that long.

Now it seemed he had to wait anyway. Find a motel, spend the night, and drive out here again in the morning. More time wasted. More time away from Erin. Dammit.

Letting go of the screen door, He spun on his heels and marched toward the car. The screen door banged shut.

Behind him, a lock clicked.

Alex froze. He glanced over his shoulder at the front door. It swung inward. A man in a wheelchair rolled into the doorway, halting at the screen door. The man said, "Well, you're persistent anyway. Might as well come in."

Relief washed over Alex like a cool rain on a hot day. He strode back to the door and asked, "Are you T.R. Young, the architect?"

"Once upon a time I was. Who are you and what do you want?"

"I'm Alex MacKay. And I want to talk with you about Revenant House."

Young looked to be in his mid forties, with a ring of salt-and-pepper hair around his bald spot. He spoke with only the slightest drawl. "You're the second person in the last two weeks wantin' to know about that place."

A knot tightened in Alex's gut. "Someone else asked about it?"

"A lady e-mailed me, said she worked there. Think her name was Karen something."

Alex sighed, relaxing. "That was my friend, Erin Turner." The word friend seemed inadequate to describe their relationship, but he didn't know if Erin wanted to be called his girlfriend, so he played it safe. He continued, "I'm here on her behalf, because we both need to know anything you can tell us about Revenant House and, specifically, the man who built it."

"Why?"

"Because lives are at stake."

Young wheeled his chair backward. "You better come inside."

Alex swung the door open and walked into the house. For a few seconds, he felt blind. Then his eyes adjusted enough that he saw he was in a living room, though not a single light burned in the space. To the right, the kitchen was also dark. But to the left, down a short hallway, light spilled out of a room.

His host ushered him down the hallway and into the lighted room at the end, on the left. It was an office, furnished with a rickety desk and file cabinets. A computer and its associated peripherals filled the desktop, overflowing onto the top of the short file cabinet adjacent to the desk. Young stopped in front of the desk. He angled his chair so that he could look at Alex.

"Grab yourself a chair," Young said, gesturing at the corner behind Alex.

Three metal chairs, folded flat, leaned against the wall in the corner. Alex grabbed one and, unfolding it, set it on the floor beside the desk, kitty-corner to Young. As he lowered himself onto the seat, it creaked once.

Alex rested his elbow on the desk's edge. "When I said lives were at stake, you didn't seem surprised."

"Nope."

"What can you tell me about Revenant House?"

Leaning back in his wheelchair, Young exhaled a long breath. "I know curiosity is a dangerous thing when it comes to that house. You seem relatively normal, so I'll give you some advice. Get your girlfriend out of Revenant House—today." He patted the arms of his wheelchair. "Before you both end up like me."

"I don't understand."

Young leaned forward. A dour smile darkened his features. "A week after I wrote about Revenant House on my blog, I was hit by a car while walking down my own driveway. I got hit so hard it broke my back. The cops found the car abandoned along the freeway, but they never could find the driver. Turns out the car was stolen. The old man who owned it was found dead in his apartment, murdered by whoever took his car."

Alex felt as if his flesh had frosted over, the chill seeping deeper and deeper into him. Erin's face popped into his mind, and a hot spike of anger sliced through the cold. Wessick sent Rassul to attack her. If she failed to locate the relic, or if he just got tired of waiting, Erin might suffer a fate similar to Young's.

He would *not* let that happen.

"I'm sorry," Alex said. "But I need your help to make certain the same thing doesn't happen to Erin. What do you know about Lord Colban?"

"Let me guess, Anna Newman told you about the mysterious Lord Colban." Young shook his head. "She fed me that story too. I stopped by to interview her about the manor, and she gave me the grand tour. She also fed me the fairy tale about Lord Colban, the occultist who built Revenant House."

"Fairy tale?"

"There is no Lord Colban."

Alex stared at Young. "What do you mean there is no Lord Colban?"

"It's a red herring," Young replied. "Anybody who tries to research Lord Colban will find about a million Colbans from old Scotland, plus some in Italy, but none who match what the lovely Miss Newman said about him."

The light snarl in his voice when he called Newman "lovely" belied his words. No one who met the woman would refer to her as lovely, despite her physical attractiveness. Anna T. Newman radiated the exact opposite of charm, which her polite demeanor failed to mask completely.

"By the look on your face," Young said, "I can tell you've met the lady of the house. Ain't she special?"

Alex fixed his gaze on Young's. He didn't have time for games, or reminiscences about Wessick's steely handmaiden. He said, "If Lord Colban didn't build Revenant House, who did?"

"Leave it be."

"That's no longer an option."

Young frowned. He pulled out a drawer on the desk, rifled through the contents, then brought out a sheet of paper. He said, "This is the only piece of evidence still in existence that says who built the manor. I found it in a musty old library at a musty old museum in one of those bump-in-the-road towns near Revenant Point. Good thing I xeroxed it, because when I went back the next day, the paper was gone." He snorted. "Misplaced, they said."

"You don't believe it."

"I believe the folks working there had no clue about what really happened to the paper. But I don't think it got misplaced." He proffered the sheet to Alex. "Somebody stole it."

Alex took the sheet. The words THE UNITED STATES OF AMERICA were emblazoned across the top of the page, above the words CERTIFICATE NO., which preceded three digits scrawled in a script he could barely read. The photocopy was splotchy and faded, or perhaps the original document looked this way. Whatever the case, he made out two of the digits—a seven and a one—but the third proved too faded to read. The main body of the document began with what sounded like the opening of a Christmas greeting card.

"To all to whom these Presents shall come, Greeting," it said, "WHEREAS Broderick Covington of Houghton County, Michigan, has deposited in the General Land Office of the United States, a Certificate of the REGISTER OF THE LAND OFFICE at Sault Ste. Marie whereby it appears that full payment has been made by the said Broderick Covington..." The text continued from there with more legalese that described a plot of land. The document was dated "the eighteenth of April in the Year of our Lord one thousand eight hundred and fifty-four."

Young tapped the back of the sheet. "It's a land patent. The government sold this parcel of land to a man called Broderick Covington."

Alex squinted at the text, frowning. "Where is this parcel?"

"Today they call it Revenant Point."

Alex ran his finger over the elegantly handwritten letters that spelled out the name Broderick Covington. In the note he'd scrawled while dying, Ridley Covington mentioned a brother. What was the brother's name? He needed to check on that later.

Without looking up from the document, Alex asked, "Do you know who owns the property now?"

"Nobody knows."

Looking up from the document, Alex arched an eyebrow at Young. "How is that possible?"

"I don't know. I searched every public records database on the Internet, contacted every government office that should have a record of it, even went to the National Archives in Washington. That document in your hand is the only evidence that anyone ever owned the parcel."

Young shrugged, giving a little shake of his head. "It's like Revenant Point doesn't exist."

Revenant House

FOR AN HOUR AND A HALF, ERIN HAD STARED AT THE IMAGES OF THE PAPYRUS map displayed on the screen of her laptop, which sat on the path Despite her efforts to make sense out of the shapes on the map, they still looked like nothing more than colorful splotches. Why in blazes did every clue have to be so cryptic?

Well, if the clues were simple and easy to resolve, then the Aten would've found the relic on their own a long time ago.

When did they start looking for the relic? They didn't want her to know, she supposed, since Rassul never mentioned when they started looking for it. For all she knew, they started looking for the relic on the day Rassul confronted her on the road near her parents home. The day he wielded a knife to scare her and ordered her to find the relic or else.

Two days after he attacked her.

The assault left her bruised and dazed, lying in the ditch where Rassul had thrown her. The bruises and scrapes made sense, given the violence of the struggle, but the marks on her arm still baffled her. After the attack, she discovered what looked like a puncture mark on her upper arm, with a two-inch scratch extending out from it. She knew Rassul had slammed his fist into her arm. A simple punch, however, failed to account for the marks.

That night, she woke to find an orb hovering above her bed. In the morning, all her injuries from the attack were gone. It seemed like the orb healed her, an act that baffled her as much as the puncture mark. The bulk of her experience with orbs suggested the Aten controlled them, and her experience with the Aten's henchman, Rassul, suggested they wanted her alive but cared nothing about how much she suffered. Why did one orb help her, when others helped Rassul?

The orbs must answer to more than one master.

She couldn't sort out the entire mystery today. For now, another enigma tickled at her brain. She closed the images on the computer screen, opening the web browser. When she typed the name Samuel N. Wessick into a search engine, it retrieved the zilch she expected. The first twenty searches she tried over the last two weeks netted the same results. He was a ghost, which made him an appropriate owner for Revenant House, the manor named after spirits.

The term revenant referred to more than ghosts. During medieval times, the folklore about revenants concerned deceased sinners who rose from their graves, condemned to walk the earth as penance. Revenants were akin to the modern concept of zombies, though in modern times the term had come to refer to spirits. The word revenant derived from a French term that meant to return, and the term literally meant one who returned. A revenant could also be someone who seemed to come from another age, a sort of living anachronism.

What any of this had to do with Samuel Wessick, she didn't know. He was a ghost in the sense that neither she nor Alex, nor Alex's buddies at the Human Origins Project, could find any information about Wessick. His company, SNW Inc., was a mystery too. She executed another search she'd done countless times before, typing in SNW Inc. The effort got her the same results as every other time—a handful of vague, congratulatory articles on business sites that mentioned Wessick's company and its expansion across the globe. Every article described the company in identical language, explaining that SNW Inc. specialized in "robotics for military and civilian applications." The company itself had no website, and none of the articles included a photo of Wessick.

No portraits.

When she'd interviewed at Revenant House, she noticed that not a single one of the paintings that hung on the walls depicted a human being. The only human figures found in any of the manor's artwork were the Egyptian figures in the wood carving above the library door. The ones worshiping the sun, or more precisely, worshiping the Aten.

Erin stared at the computer screen. The initials SNW appeared throughout the list of search results. Something about those letters bothered her. They stood for Samuel N. Wessick, she knew. It was his company after all. But in the back of her mind, something else about the letters niggled at her.

Pulling open the center desk drawer, which held pens and paper clips and similar items, she sifted through the contents until she found a business card. Newman gave her the card when they first met. Erin shut the drawer and laid the card on the desktop. The card read "Anna T. Newman, Recruitment Director, SNW Inc." In its upper left corner, the card featured an odd emblem—the company's logo, she assumed—that looked like a feather laid lengthwise across a downward-pointing arrowhead. The first letter of each word in Newman's name appeared in larger type than the rest of the letters, causing them to stand out from the rest of the text. She looked at the initials. ATN.

The niggling in her brain intensified. She grabbed a pen from the drawer and a scrap of paper from the desktop. In block letters, she wrote the initials ATN. Directly beneath that, she wrote the initials SNW. Then she stared at the letters. Let her mind go blank. Let her vision swim in and out of focus. ATN. SNW.

Wait a minute. She scratched out the letters she'd already written and wrote them again, reversing the order. SNW ATN.

Holy mackerel. She wasn't fluent in ancient Egyptian like Alex, but even she knew what those letters stood for in the language of the ancient people of Egypt. They spelled out *senu Aten*. Brothers of the Aten.

The text on the map scroll spoke of Egyptians who aided the Aten, doing their bidding so that the Aten need never taint themselves by consorting with humans. Those agents called themselves the Brothers of the Aten.

She knew Wessick worked for the Aten, so naturally he would belong to an ancient secret society that operated with the sole purpose of serving the Aten. His initials and Newman's together spelled out the name of that society. Why leave such a clue for her? Did he think she was too dense to figure it out? Or did he want her to know? If so, why? She really didn't need more questions. She needed answers.

The company logo caught her eye again, and she focused on it. The feather and the arrowhead reminded her of something. In the web browser, she pulled up a site that included a dictionary of Egyptian hieroglyphs. She browsed the pages, skimming over the symbols. After a few minutes, she found a feather symbol. The symbol could represent the concept of a feather, or it could represent the goddess Maat and the word *maat*, meaning truth.

Harry used the Latin version of the word truth, *veritas*, as the key to his Vigenère cipher. Ridley Covington also used the word *veritas* in his favorite saying, *vincit omnia veritas*, or truth conquers all. The word *maat* also appeared in the wood carving above the library door, where it marked the keyhole that opened Ridley's secret compartment. Variations of the word truth bore some sort of connection to the mystery of the relic.

Maybe the groundskeeper knew what it all meant. She hadn't heard the lawnmower again, so it seemed the groundskeeper never came back from the gazebo, or whatever the structure was. Maybe the structure hid answers, or at the very least more useful clues than the ones she currently struggled to decipher.

Erin leaped up from the chair. In the moment when she'd felt the groundskeeper saw her, she bolted like a frightened deer. This time her inner wuss would not convince her to flee. She ran upstairs to retrieve her gun, then headed out. Freya wanted to follow, but she made the dog stay inside. Getting from the library to the gazebo took five minutes of brisk walking. When she reached the spot where she'd hidden earlier to observe the groundskeeper, she stopped to reconnoiter. The lawnmower sat parked at the foot of the gazebo steps, as before. The gazebo was empty, however, and she saw no one in the vicinity.

Keeping an eye on the woods as she moved, she tiptoed past the lawnmower to the gazebo steps.

The hairs on the back of her neck stiffened. Goosebumps cropped up on her arms, spreading out to the rest of her body. As if in slow motion, she withdrew the gun from inside her waistband and turned to her right.

A figure stood before her, less than a dozen feet away. He was huge, close to eight feet tall, with shoulders twice as broad as an average man's. Muscles rippled beneath the coach of black hair that covered his entire body, save for his palms and a swath across his cheeks and nose. A heavy brow ridge protruded over his eyes, which glowed a deep amber in the muted sunlight. She knew he was male because of the bulge in his groin, though hair concealed his genitals.

Her heart thudded so hard and fast she couldn't breathe. This was a Bigfoot.

She knew they existed, because of the evidence she'd read about and because Alex told her they did. Tribes of Bigfoot lived in countless locations around the world, Alex said. At least one tribe lived here in the Keweenaw. She knew because Alex's friends at the Human Origins Project had asked the local tribe to help guard her while she stayed here at Revenant House. She remembered seeing red eyes glowing in the woods. Alex told her that was the Bigfoot. But knowing it and seeing it were vastly different experiences.

The creature canted his head, squinting at her. He grunted syllables that sounded like "oogah."

Alex told her the Bigfoot spoke a unique language that mostly sounded like grunting. They also understood ancient Egyptian. Unfortunately, she didn't speak Bigfoot and her Egyptian wasn't too good either.

The creature jerked his head upright. His nostrils flared as he sniffed the air. It reminded her of the way Freya would sniff the air when she caught a scent.

No longer sniffing, the creature stared past her. He grunted something, not "oogah" this time.

"Sorry," she said. "I don't understand."

"Perhaps I can be of assistance."

The words issued from behind her. And she recognized the voice.

The gun still grasped in both hands, she spun around.

Warner arched his eyebrows at her.

North-Central Texas

Alex returned his attention to the land patent. It granted the land "together with all the rights, privileges, immunities, and appurtenances of whatsoever nature, thereunto belonging, unto the said Broderick Covington and to his heirs and assigns forever." Alex's understanding of legal jargon, especially the nineteenth-century variety, was less than perfect. However, the document seemed to say that Broderick Covington's heirs owned the property forever, so long as they retained a copy of this document. The current owner must be a descendent of Covington.

"May I keep this document?" Alex asked.

"Sure. Damn thing's brought me nothin' but trouble."

Alex folded the document and tucked it in his shirt pocket, under his jacket.

The grumbling of a car engine approached from down the driveway. A moment later, the grumbling ceased and a car door slammed shut.

"My wife's home," Young said. He wheeled his chair toward the door, then paused to eye Alex sideways. "She doesn't know about this stuff. Thinks a drunk scumbag ran me down."

"I won't say anything to her."

Young flashed a tight, closed-mouth smile. He escorted Alex back through the house to the front door. Just as they reached the door, it swung inward. A brunette woman stepped through the entrance, halting when she saw Alex. Young's wife cast a questioning expression in her husband's direction.

"It's okay," Young said. "This gentleman's just leaving."

Mrs. Young glanced at Alex and back at her husband, then walked past them toward the kitchen. She flicked on a light. A yellowish glow blanketed the kitchen and living room, petering out before it reached the entryway.

Alex stepped into the open doorway. Glancing at Young, he asked, "What will you tell her?"

Young winked. "I'll spin her a tall tale, don't you worry."

Alex nodded. "Thank you for your time. The information you provided may be vital to me and Erin. I appreciate it."

Young nodded. "Just take care of yourself and your girl."

"I will."

Alex turned to walk out the door. Young grasped his coat sleeve, and Alex hesitated. The older man glanced back at his wife, then spoke to Alex in a hushed tone.

"When I say you don't want to end up like me, I don't just mean being crippled." Young gazed out the doorway as if the outside vista were a painting of a utopian kingdom, unreal and untouchable. "I don't go out into the world much anymore. They might've forgotten about me for now, but eventually they'll want to finish the job. I still know one of their secrets."

Alex opened his mouth, intending to reassure the man he wouldn't have to worry about Wessick and the Aten for much longer. But he closed his mouth without speaking, because he knew he shouldn't make promises. He and Erin strove to uncover the Aten's secrets and, he hoped, to sever their stranglehold on humanity. Yet how could they do that when they still didn't understand the Aten's motives? They didn't even know precisely what the Aten controlled, or how they had influenced human history. Until he and Erin learned the answers to those questions, their quest to defeat the Aten remained a wish rather than a feasible goal.

Now they knew who built Revenant House. It was a start.

As Young shut the front door, Alex hurried to his car and climbed inside. A minute later he was driving down the road, with Young's house no longer in sight in the rearview mirror.

The rear tires slipped. He regained control and checked the speedometer. It registered sixty miles per hour. Alex lifted his foot off the accelerator, letting the car slow to a more reasonable speed. He drove too fast, unconsciously, because he wanted to get back to Michigan. Back to Erin. He knew she was relatively safe at the moment, or as safe as she could be inside Revenant House. But he wanted to get home, to know for certain.

Home. When did he begin to think of the Keweenaw Peninsula as home?

He thought of it as home because Erin lived there. As long as she stayed there, so would he. If she moved, he would go too. Anywhere in the world. Anywhere in the universe.

A flash of movement drew his attention to the side mirror. Nothing there. A bird might've flown out of a tree behind the car.

Movement flashed again, this time in the rearview mirror. He glanced up at it.

A glowing orb hovered behind the car, keeping pace with the vehicle.

The engine died. With the power steering out, he couldn't turn the wheel enough to navigate the curve looming up ahead. He stepped on the brake. The car rolled to a halt.

The orb was gone.

He turned the key in the ignition, but nothing happened. He got out his cell phone, flipping it open to find it too was dead. He tossed the phone onto the passenger seat. A quick glance in the rearview and side mirrors revealed no orb. It could be hiding in a blind spot.

As he opened the door, he slid the Glock out of his shoulder holster. A gun might prove rather useless if an orb confronted him, but it was better than nothing. He jumped out of the car, leaving the door open, and turned in a circle to scan the area. On the opposite side of the car, the hill sloped upward. On his side, the hill dropped away into a precipice that formed one side of a small ravine.

Nothing. He holstered the Glock.

An orb swooped down from straight overhead. It stopped in an instant, without seeming to decelerate, to hover in front of his face an arm's length away. He stared into its mottled bluish white interior. A rim of pure white encircled the interior. The heat from its glow washed over his face.

The orb rushed at him.

He ducked sideways. The orb grazed his jacket sleeve. If he hadn't moved, it would've smacked him in the chest. He whirled around to see where the orb went.

It rushed at his head. He dropped to the ground, hearing the orb whiz past and feeling its heat scorch the top of his head. He rolled onto his back.

The orb had vanished.

Still flat on the ground, he turned his eyes to survey the area. No sign of the orb. Maybe it just wanted to frighten him, though to what purpose he couldn't say.

He sat up, pushed onto his knees, and glanced around again. No orbs.

Rising, he checked himself for burns. Where the orb grazed his jacket sleeve, the leather was singed but it had protected him from the heat. The top of his head felt fine too. The orb had aimed for his chest, more specifically his heart. He lifted up his jacket. The land patent, folded in half twice, stuck out the top of his shirt pocket. Right over his heart.

It aimed for the land patent.

The orb wanted to destroy the sole piece of evidence concerning the origins of Revenant House. They wanted the land patent, and him, incinerated before he told Erin what he'd found.

He took a step toward the car.

The orb swooped up from the other side of the car, hurtling toward him.

He scrambled backward, tripped, righted himself.

The orb rushed past his chest. It seared through his jacket and shirt, scorching his skin. Pain stabbed through his chest. He cried out, stumbled, grabbed for a tree branch. His fingers scraped the bark but the limb popped out of his grasp.

He tumbled off the precipice.

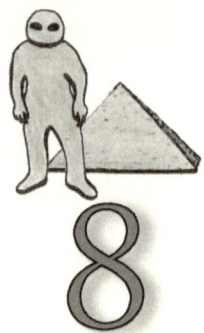

8

As the landscape whooshed past him, Alex flung his arms out and flailed for a handhold. He could see nothing except one big blur, hear nothing except the thundering of his pulse, feel nothing except the air scouring his face and the burning across his chest.

He smacked into the ground. On his left side. Hard. Pain lanced through his shoulder and across his chest. He gasped, tried to suck in a breath.

He flipped over and tumbled down the hill.

Spinning, bouncing over rocks, spinning, crashing through brush. Cuts and scrapes stung on his face and neck. Burrs stuck on his clothes and in his hair. He wanted to shout but couldn't catch his breath.

He rolled onto his back and stopped. Though he felt solid ground against his backside, and knew he was no longer moving, the world around him seemed to keep spinning. His gorge rose high in his throat. He did not want to vomit. If he just held it together for a few minutes, the nausea would pass. It had to.

Deep breaths. He forced himself to inhale slowly, filling his chest, and then released the breath an ounce at a time. His breaths, at first ragged, evened out little by little. The spinning slowed into a rocking sensation. He saw the blue sky above him, felt the sandy loam beneath him. In another minute or two, the sensation ceased altogether. The nausea subsided.

The pain, however, lingered.

The burn on his chest stung, as did the many cuts and scrapes scattered across his exposed skin. His left shoulder ached. He pushed up onto his elbows. Hot pains stabbed through his shoulder. He winced and groaned, but pushed through the pain to rise onto his knees. What the hell had happened?

Raking a hand through his hair, he swept his gaze up the hill. The precipice off of which he'd fallen dropped for ten feet, then segued into a slope that gradually leveled out into the spot where he now lay. As he struggled to his feet, new pains pierced his muscles. He stretched each muscle group separately, gently, until he ironed out most of the kinks. His chest still burned. He looked down at it. His leather jacket now sported a circular hole with a neat but singed boundary. His shirt was singed too. He unbuttoned his shirt and peeled it up to check his skin. In a circular area the exact size of the burn on his shirt and the hole in his jacket, the flesh was red and slightly swollen. Since the wound looked like a first-degree burn, he shouldn't need medical attention. When he got back to the jet, he could apply a cold compress and bandage the wound.

He shoved a hand through his hair again. Burrs stuck to his skin. He plucked them off his hand, and turned his attention to the rest of his body. More burrs dotted his clothes and boots. He removed one, then another, then another. A few minutes later he'd cleared himself of the burrs.

The car awaited him at the top of the precipice. He glanced up the hill. The base of the precipice lay a good hundred feet up the slope. About fifty feet to the left of where he'd fallen over, what looked like a game trail led up a less vertical section of the hill.

He stretched, groaned. Christ. The slope seemed steeper now and the cliff taller, more imposing. Just looking at the grade sent spasms through his muscles. He could make it, dammit.

But it wouldn't be a pleasure hike.

Sucking in a deep breath, he started toward up the slope. He tried not to think about the orb that might be waiting for him at the car.

Revenant Point

SHAKING HER HEAD, ERIN TUCKED THE GUN INSIDE HER WAISTBAND. WARNER strode closer, until they stood an arm's length apart. Erin half frowned, half smiled at him. She was annoyed he had scared the crap out of her, but she was glad to see a friendly face, so she opted not to chastise him for sneaking up on her.

"Where did you come from?" she asked.

"The woods." She must've looked peeved at his answer, because he added, "Though I enlisted the creatures' help in watching over you, I decided to augment their protection with a daily reconnaissance trek of my own."

An odd feeling bubbled up inside her. Not only did she have Bigfoot keeping an eye on her, she also had a German commando roaming the woods in her name.

She felt a little like a medieval princess held captive by an evil lord. If she was the damsel in distress, who was her knight in shining armor? Warner? Or Alex?

Nothing said she couldn't have *two* knights in shining armor.

Not that either one of them had saved her from much so far. She dealt with Rassul herself. Still, she kind of liked the idea that two attractive, manly guys watched out for her.

As for the Bigfoot…the jury was still out.

Gesturing toward the hairy creature behind her, she said after Warner, "What makes you think you can help with this?"

"Over the past several years, I've gained a decent understanding of their language."

"Really." She settled her hands on her hips. "You speak Bigfoot?"

"Not fluently. But I believe I can bridge the gap."

She turned sideways and motioned for him to approach. "Take your best shot."

He stepped up alongside her. The creature stood perhaps ten feet away, eyeing them with an expression that in a human she would interpret as suspicion. Warner, dressed in camouflage with a knit cap shielding his head, gave off a less-than-congenial vibe. Though she doubted a Bigfoot felt threatened by Warner's height or his muscular build, since his stature dwarfed in comparison with the creature's, this one nonetheless seemed wary.

Warner issued a series of grunts and almost-word-like noises. His utterances sounded like the vocalizations in a hokey caveman movie. She cast a sidelong glance his way.

Catching her glance, he said, "Trust me."

Erin focused on the creature again. She did trust Warner, though not completely. She completely trusted only three people—her parents and Alex. Everyone else had a tendency to disappoint her. Not that she expected Warner to betray her. But she'd trusted Chloe and the girl flaked out, vanishing without a trace after throwing the weirdest tantrum. She'd known Chloe for over a year. She hardly knew Warner.

Then again, she hardly knew Alex. She met him a few days before Warner, yet in that time their relationship developed and deepened in a way she'd never experienced with anyone else. She certainly hadn't experienced anything similar with Warner, despite spending more time with him than with Alex.

A fist tightened around her gut. Where was Alex? In Texas, he'd told her. Though he left mere hours ago, his absence felt much longer and, ever since he left, she resisted the repeated urge to call him. He was following up a lead, for her. He would call after his meeting with Young. Unless something went wrong.

Inside her, the imaginary fist cinched tighter.

Nothing was wrong. Alex would call soon.

Warner grasped her shoulder. "Are you unwell?"

"Huh?" She met his gaze as the meaning of his words broke through her reverie. "No, I'm fine."

He nodded toward the creature. "This one says you remind him of Aset."

"You mean Isis? The Egyptian goddess?" She knew Isis was the Greek version of Aset, the original Egyptian name for the goddess. The Aten viewed her as some kind of quasi-mystical woman who could find their relic, whatever it was, for them. They called her the *satseshat*, meaning the daughter of Seshat, the ancient Egyptian goddess. Why in the name of Michigan anyone, much less Bigfoot or evil aliens, would mistake her for a goddess was beyond her comprehension.

"Actually," Warner said, "in this instance I believe he means you remind him of Katy Bergren. One of the hairy hominids she met mistook her for Aset—the goddess whose legend, as it turns out, was based on the real life of a human being from an ancient civilization with advanced technology."

"The people you call the Planners?"

"That is the name they gave themselves. The Planner known as Aset was born over twelve thousand years ago, before the ancient Egyptian civilization arose. The Egyptians derived their mythology, their language, and many of their customs from the Planners, whom they called the Spirits of the Dead."

"The original gods. The ones who supposedly created the world."

Warner nodded. "Katy is a direct descendent of Aset."

"Well, I'm not." She glanced at the creature. "Your new friend is mistaken."

A faint smile curved his lips, but he said nothing.

Two words he spoke a moment ago popped to mind. She crinkled her brow. "What in the world is a hairy hominid?"

Warner chuckled. "It's what Katy calls the creatures. She prefers it over the terms Bigfoot or Sasquatch. When DNA testing proved the creatures are the true descendents of the ancient hominids, the extinct creatures from whom science says we are descended, Katy's preference was vindicated. They are hominids—and they are undeniably hairy."

Alex had told her about the DNA testing. It proved more than that the Bigfoot were descended from the ancient hominids. It also proved that human beings were not. Later Katy and her husband, Rick, unearthed the Book of Thoth, a tome that archaeologists either dismissed as myth or assumed contained nothing more shocking than information on ancient medical techniques. The Bergrens discovered the Book contained far more than that. Although most of the text was indecipherable, one section explained how beings from Mars emigrated to Earth and created humans from their own DNA. Erin still didn't quite understand the story.

The hairy hominid standing before them uttered a long phrase, which he directed at Warner. The German responded in kind.

To Erin, Warner said, "He says that he has never met Aset, but he has seen her likeness. I believe he means he has seen a statue of her. He says the goddess is quite beautiful, and in that respect, you remind him of her."

Erin felt her jaw drop open a smidge. Clamping it shut, she stared at Warner. "Are you sure you translated that right? I'm no goddess."

"But you are beautiful."

Her cheeks flushed. She averted her gaze to the creature, who in turn averted his gaze. Out of deference to his goddess, no doubt.

For pete's sake. She was no goddess. She was a librarian, and a pawn for evil aliens, but she had neither the powers nor the wisdom of a divine being.

Erin cleared her throat. "What else does your friend say? Did he see the groundskeeper?"

Warner attempted to translate her question into Bigfoot-ese. The hairy hominid wrinkled his nose, letting out a noise that sounded for the life of her like "huh?" Warner tried again, and the creature shook his head as he launched into an extended response that involved grunts, guttural croaks, clucks, and growling sounds.

She almost laughed at the absurdity of it all, then she realized insulting a Bigfoot might not be the smartest move. They were reputed to have great strength.

If she had to deal with this creature at length, which seemed likely, then she ought to give him a name. Calling him the Bigfoot or the creature, or even the hairy hominid, would get old fast.

"Does he have a name?" she asked Warner.

"Yes, the creatures do give each other names. But the names are impossible to translate into English and incredibly difficult to pronounce in their original tongue."

She believed that. If the creature's name consisted of grunts and growls, she'd have a heck of a time remembering it, much less pronouncing it. She needed to give him a nickname, for her own use.

Nothing sprang to mind.

After another, briefer exchange with the hominid, Warner turned to her. He said, "The creature tells me he and his tribe have long been charged with guarding this place. A legend passed down through the generations speaks of a man who buried an object of great importance in this location. The creatures have been guarding this sacred place until a certain person arrives to retrieve it."

"Who?"

Warner grunted to the creature. The hominid knelt, brushing away twigs to clear a spot of bare earth. In the dirt, he drew symbols with the tip of his stubby finger. The symbols were Egyptian hieroglyphs.

"I'm afraid," Warner said, "my grasp of the hieroglyphic language is minimal at best."

Erin knelt across from the creature. She studied the symbols etched in the dirt. If Alex were here, he could translate the hieroglyphs in five seconds flat. Despite recognizing the symbols from having seen them on the map scroll, she needed significantly longer than five seconds to sort out the meaning.

Realization exploded in her mind like a firework.

"It says," she told Warner, "she whose identity is hidden, the daughter of Seshat, the daughter of Thoth, the incarnation of another time." Erin rose to her feet without looking away from the glyphs. "The Aten think I'm the daughter of Seshat. Is he saying the Aten buried something here?"

"No. The legend says a hairy man buried it."

She made a face at him. "Doesn't that mean a Bigfoot buried it?"

Warner shook his head. "He is quite clear in saying that it was a man, a human being. Strangely, he is using the English word hairy, rather than the analogous term in his own language."

She'd take his word for that. To her ears, nothing the creature said resembled any English words.

"Hairy?" She thought for a moment, then asked, "Are you sure he doesn't mean a man whose name was Harry?"

Warner stared at her for a couple seconds. "Your time-traveling friend, Mr. Harry Harriman."

"Exactly. We know from Ridley's book that Harry traveled back to the Victorian era, where he met Ridley. Who's to say he didn't also stop off here to bury something?"

"But why not simply give it to Ridley Covington?"

"Because Ridley may have been working for the Aten."

"Or perhaps the hairy man was not Mr. Harriman."

"One way to find out." She sighed. "Where exactly is this thing buried?"

Warner grunted to the creature. Instead of answering with his own grunts, the creature slowly raised an arm perpendicular to his body. He aimed his fisted hand straight at the gazebo.

Harry hid something under the spot now occupied by the gazebo, something intended for her. And he hid it so long ago that the story morphed into legend. How much stock could she put in a legend told to her by a hairy hominid? It wouldn't be the weirdest thing she ever did, but it would certainly rank in the top five.

What the heck.

Erin pulled the gun out of her waistband and unclipped the cell phone from it as well. She handed both to Warner. "Hold these for me."

"What is your plan?"

She shrugged. "Climb under the gazebo and see what I find. Maybe whoever buried the whatsit under there left some kind of clue that's survived the ages."

"A marker of some sort?"

"Maybe." She shrugged again. "Worth a shot."

She marched to the gazebo and walked around it looking for an opening where she could access the space underneath. The gazebo sat on posts that raised it two feet off the ground. Latticework closed in the gap. On the right side of the steps, the latticework had come loose from the structure. She grasped the end of the latticework and pulled. A three-foot section of it popped free. Tossing the latticework aside, she dropped onto all fours to peer into the dark space now revealed.

"Here," Warner called.

She sat back on her heels, turning to look back at him. He held a small flashlight, which he tossed to her. The slender, four-inch-long flashlight was a dull silver color. She saw no button or switch to turn on the light, so she tried twisting the end. The light came on, spraying a narrow cone of illumination into the darkness beneath the gazebo.

Erin grasped the flashlight's end between her teeth, dropped onto her belly, and slithered through the opening. The dank smell of damp earth and old wood filled her nostrils. The flashlight shined its cone straight ahead of her. With her toes sticking out from under the gazebo, and the rest of her body under it, she swung her head left to right and back again. The flashlight's glow struck an object, which gleamed pure white in the beam. Even when she turned her head, and the flashlight's beam retreated from the object, it still glowed in the ambient light, a tiny ghost hovering in the crawl space.

The object looked like a rock. She crawled toward it. The object was a rock, white in color, measuring approximately twelve by six inches with a height of three inches. She tried to lift the rock, but it refused to budge. When she ran her fingers around its base, the rock felt as if it were lodged in the ground with some portion of it buried. She took the flashlight in one hand and aimed the light at the rock's top. The surface was relatively flat, though marred by scratches.

She traced the scratches with her fingertip. No, these were more than scrapes. Someone had etched symbols onto the rock, symbols partly worn away by time—and exposure to the elements, before the gazebo was built. Getting the stone wet might bring out the carvings. She could turn around and crawl back to Warner to ask if he had any water with him, but she didn't want to wait. Besides, she hadn't noticed any canteen or water bottle attached to his belt and he carried no bag or backpack. The flashlight he'd produced from his jacket pocket.

Oh well. She'd make do with what she had on hand.

She spit on the rock. Repeatedly. As she rubbed the spit over the scratches, the surrounding rock darkened just enough to highlight the carvings. Luckily, the inscription was short. By the time she ran out of spit, her mouth dry as a mummy's, she had wetted the entire inscription.

The text was in Latin. It spelled out three words.

Vincit omnia veritas.

North- Central Texas

THE LAST TEN FEET OF THE TRAIL PROVED STEEPER. BY THE TIME ALEX REACHED the top of the precipice, he was panting so hard he had to stop to catch his breath. Leaning forward with his knees bent, hands braced on his thighs, he stood there until his chest no longer ached from the heaving breaths, but only from the burn wound.

Finally, he trudged to the car. No orbs so far. Destroying the document must've satisfied the orb, or the being who controlled it.

He climbed into the car and shut the door. His cell phone still lay on the passenger seat where he'd dropped it. Grabbing the phone, he dialed Erin's cell number. It rang three times. The fourth ring was cut off as a male voice on the other end grunted, "Alex?"

"Who is this?" Alex asked.

"Warner."

"Where's Erin?"

A pause. "She is…indisposed at the moment."

Alex's hand involuntarily tightened around the phone. Indisposed? The word triggered a vision in his mind, one involving a bed and lingerie. He shook his head, blinked. It was ludicrous. Erin and Warner would not—

Actually, Warner might. But Erin wouldn't.

Would she? He knew she liked Warner. She'd spent a great deal of time with the man lately. Alex silently cursed himself. This line of thought did nothing to help anyone.

He cleared his throat. "What is Erin doing? I need to speak to her."

"Currently, the lovely Miss Turner is crawling under a gazebo in search of an object that may have been buried there, possibly by your friend Harry, sometime in the distant past."

Though Alex tried to make sense of the statement, he was too exhausted and in pain to comprehend what in hades Warner meant. Gazebo? Harry? Warner might as well been speaking an alien language. Right now, Alex wanted nothing more than to talk to Erin, to tell her about what he learned today but mostly to hear her voice and know she was all right.

The lovely Miss Turner.

The memory of Warner's phrasing made Alex clench his teeth. Ridiculous, he knew, yet he couldn't quash the feeling. Anger. Jealousy.

Idiocy.

"Perhaps you should call back later," Warner said.

"No, I—"

A sharp noise in the background of the call made Alex's heart skip. The noise sounded like a cry of pain. From Erin?

"Achtung!" Warner shouted away from the phone. Then to Alex, he hissed, "I must go."

Warner disconnected the call.

Alex stared at the display on his phone. Call ended, it said. In German, *achtung* meant "watch out" or "warning." Since Warner never panicked, his exclamation must mean something terrible happened. An accident. An attack.

Erin.

Alex tossed the phone onto the passenger seat and jerked the key in the ignition. The engine turned over with a sputter and a grumble. He jammed his foot on the accelerator. The car rocketed down the road. Gravel sprayed up behind the vehicle. The airport was forty-five minutes away. By the time he got to Revenant House, hours would've elapsed.

He nabbed the phone off the seat and punched redial. The number rang six times, then went to voicemail. Dammit.

Erin's cry. Warner's shout. He must get there.

Now.

Revenant Point

E RIN COUGHED AT THE CLOUD OF DUST THAT HAD PLUMED UP AROUND HER. She shoved the rock off her hand, biting back another cry. A minute ago when she tried to lift the rock out of its longtime home, she lost her grip on it and the stone flipped over onto her hand. The pain had been acute, her cry reflexive. Her index finger, which got pinched under the rock's edge, still throbbed.

A great tearing sound erupted behind Erin. She rolled partly on her side, just enough that she could look back at the opening through which she'd entered the crawl space.

The latticework was being peeled back from the base of the gazebo. She could see nothing but a pair of hair-covered legs and the huge, flat-bottomed feet attached to them. A pair of hands, hairy on top but smooth on the bottom, reached down to grasp the bottom edge of the gazebo platform. The stubby toes dug into the earth as the creature lifted.

"*Nein!*"

The voice belonged to Warner, who shouted in German from somewhere behind the hairy hominid. The creature paid no heed. His muscles tautened and bulged as he lifted again. The gazebo creaked and cracked.

Erin opened her mouth to yell at the creature, then stopped. He wouldn't understand her any better than he understood Warner's exclamations. The creature spoke neither English nor German.

The gazebo shivered above her head.

She scrambled across the dirt toward the creature.

He let go of the gazebo and it whumped back into place.

A dust cloud enveloped her. Coughing, she dragged herself into the opening the creature had made when he tore off the latticework. His toes were inches from her face.

He grasped the underside of the gazebo.

She seized one of his ankles in each hand.

The creature froze. She held fast.

Through the gap between the creature's calves, she spotted Warner sprinting up behind the hairy hominid. Warner spoke to the creature, between gasps, in the hairy hominid language.

The creature released the gazebo. It settled back down with a lighter whump this time, and virtually no dust cloud. Thank goodness. Her eyes were still watering from the previous cloud.

She let go of the creature's ankles. He shuffled backward from the gazebo.

Warner took the hominid's place, dropping onto one knee in front of Erin. He squinted at her, his mouth set in a line. She must look like somebody tied her to the bumper of a pickup truck and drove it down a dirt road at sixty miles an hour.

"I'm okay," she said. "I found something and I'm going back under there to get a better look at it."

Warner shook his head. "The gazebo may be unstable. The creature nearly tore it apart."

"Why would Jerry do that?"

"Jerry?"

The nickname had just popped into her head that second. She explained, "Our hairy hominid friend. He needed a name, so I gave him one."

Warner's mouth twisted in a half-suppressed smile. "You named the creature. Katy Bergren also names them."

"For pete's sake, would you people stop comparing me to the exalted Katy Bergren?"

"It's meant as a compliment. But I will stop if it offends you."

"I'm not offended. I'm—" She sighed. "Never mind. Why did Jerry try to destroy the gazebo?"

"You cried out. He believed you were in danger."

"He tried to kill me in order to save me. Terrific." She crawled backward under the gazebo. "I'll be back in a few minutes."

She crawled back to the rock, which lay facedown in the dirt alongside the hole it had covered. The rectangular rock was, she now saw, six inches thick. No wonder it hurt like hell when it landed on her hand. She crawled to the hole the rock had plugged, positioning her face directly over it with her hands on either side. Warner's flashlight, which she grasped in her right hand, illuminated the hole's interior. Slabs of sandstone lined the two-foot-deep space. The rough, irregular edges of the slabs hinted they had been ripped from a layer of sandstone and placed in the hole with no effort to smooth the slabs. At the bottom of the hole, a tubular object rested on the sandstone amid a small puddle of muddy water.

She reached into the hole with her left hand, closed her fingers cautiously around the object, and lifted it out of the hole. The object was a tube, six inches long by two inches wide, fashioned out of metal. She couldn't tell what kind of metal, though it looked like it must've once been silver in color. Countless years stashed in a rock-lined hole had darkened the metal's color, and rust laced its exterior.

Setting the tube on the dirt, she dived her hand back into the hole to feel around for anything else that might lurk inside. The makeshift compartment held nothing else.

She tucked the tube inside her shirt, nestled under her bra for protection. Then she scuttled back toward Warner. To keep the tube from getting squashed, she moved in an awkward posture halfway between a belly-crawl and a full hands-and-knees position, with her buttocks low and her elbows bent. When she reached the opening, Warner held out his hands to her. She took them, and he helped her shimmy out from under the gazebo.

He glanced at her breasts. His brow furrowed.

Of course, he wasn't looking at her breasts. He was looking at the object inside her shirt that pushed the fabric up into a little tent. She reached in and brought out the rusty tube. Its shape seemed familiar somehow. She gently turned it in her hands.

It looked like a thermos.

She took hold of the cap, and with great care attempted to unscrew it. The rust held it tightly in place. Flipping the thermos upside-down, she scrutinized the other end. The rust was more entrenched here. Holes had formed in the metal, which looked brittle enough to break if she squeezed too hard.

Shattering it might damage whatever was hidden inside.

Back at the manor, she might find a tool that would allow her to breach the metal without damaging the precious whatsit inside. Assuming she could find where the groundskeeper kept his tools. Assuming they weren't in a locked shed.

Oh screw it.

She smacked the end of the thermos against a tree. The rusty metal crumbled.

She tipped the thermos so that its contents would slide out onto her hand. A scroll fell into her palm. Tossing the shattered thermos onto the ground, she examined the papyrus scroll. One end of it bore water stains, tinted red with rust. She unfurled the scroll. An outer sheet concealed a piece of fabric, rolled neatly but loosely. The outer sheet looked like papyrus, but the writing on it was not hieroglyphic. English words, written in a messy cursive, filled the one-foot-square sheet. Erin recognized the handwriting.

"Harry wrote this," she said.

The missing page from Ridley's book, which he hid in the secret compartment above the library door, mentioned that Ridley met a man named Mallory J.

Harriman while in Egypt. That was Harry's full name. Ridley died a century before Harry was even born. Somehow, Harry used the Aten's time travel technology to go back to the Victorian era. Why, Erin still didn't know.

The rolled fabric consisted of a material so thin and delicate that it probably turned transparent in the light. Egyptian artwork depicted clothing made of similarly translucent fabric, though most historians dismissed the artwork as fantasy, since Egyptians should not have had the technology to create fabric of such delicacy.

Erin turned her attention to the papyrus scroll. She read the opening lines aloud. "Dearest Erin, I know we have never met but I feel I know you already. The day I first read your blog, I knew you would be the one person in all of history who could find the relic—with Alex's help. Through circumstances that can best be described as fate, I found a clue that I believe to be vital to your search."

Fate? Harry must've cracked if he thought she believed in fate.

Yet she couldn't dismiss it out of hand. Bizarre things had happened to her lately, things that lacked rational explanations. Time travel was possible. Why not fate? But she needed a little more convincing before she plunged headlong into belief, where fate was concerned.

She continued reading. "The story of how I found this item is too long to fit on the single piece of papyrus I was able to get. You might not believe it if I told you anyway. I wish I could tell you what this item is, but I know only that it has some bearing on the item Ridley left for you, or rather, that he left for the *satseshat*. I'm sure by now you, like me, have realized you are the *satseshat*. Anyway, Ridley told me exactly where to hide this item, and with a bit of help from my other friends, I felt sure you would find it. If you're reading this, then I succeeded. Good luck. Sincerely, Harry."

Ridley told Harry where to hide the thermos. She knew Harry must've traveled back in time, where he met Ridley Covington, but the rest of what Harry said confused her. If Ridley helped Harry find the "item," then why did he tell Harry to bury it under the gazebo? Why not stash it in his secret compartment inside the manor, along with the map scroll?

She could figure that out later.

Warner gestured at the fabric bundle. "What is it?"

"I don't know." Erin looked at the fabric bundle in her hand. If she unrolled the delicate fabric out here, it might get damaged. "I'll look at it once I get back to the manor."

Warner withdrew her cell phone from his pocket and handed it to her. She returned his flashlight to him.

"I will finish my patrol," Warner said, "then return to my hotel."

A grunt reminded Erin of Jerry's presence, and she looked at the hairy hominid. He'd backed away to stand alongside the nearest tree, about fifteen feet away. Erin smiled at the creature.

He ducked his head, turned away, and loped off into the forest.

She looked at Warner. He nodded, and retreated into the woods too.

Erin lingered there for a moment. The lawnmower hunkered a few feet away where the groundskeeper had abandoned it. She wondered why the groundskeeper traveled here by lawnmower, but departed using one of the orbs that created a portal. Why not come and go by the same method? Well, for once the answer might be both simple and obvious. Somebody needed to mow the lawn, which explained the lawnmower part. As for the departure by orb, she'd felt the groundskeeper looking at her. Maybe he decided a quicker exit was required to prevent her from following him again.

Birdsongs echoed through the woods from far away, the sound faint and ghostly. As she listened, she imagined the birdsongs emanated not just from a distant location, but from a distant time.

A woodpecker hammered nearby. The clacking shattered her reverie, yanking her back to the present.

She trudged down the path that led back to the manor.

H ER FIRST IMPULSE HAD ENCOURAGED HER TO HEAD BACK TO THE LIBRARY. When she reached the library door, however, she suddenly remembered the bugs hidden throughout the house. She abandoned the library in favor of her bedroom. This task required privacy.

Erin seated herself cross-legged on the bed. The fabric bundle she laid on the quilt in front of her. Harry's papyrus note she set atop the bedside table.

Her cell phone buzzed. She looked at the screen to see a new text message had been received. Punching buttons, she opened the message. It was from Chloe Pelletier. The message contained four words: I'M FINE STOP CALLING.

Erin stared at the screen. That was it? The girl disappeared for two weeks, then responded to Erin's numerous phone messages with a couple terse sentences. No explanation. No apology. Just irritation that Erin cared enough to check on her.

As she clipped the phone onto her waistband, the truth struck her like a slap to the face. She really didn't know Chloe at all.

No time to worry about it.

The open edge of the fabric she flattened out on the bed. In a slow and careful motion, she rolled the bulk of the bundle in the opposite direction.

Her cell phone warbled.

She jumped. Snatching the phone from its holder, she saw that her mother was calling. A cold fist tightened around her gut. She answered the call.

"Are you all right?" Mom asked.

"Yes. Did something happen over there?"

"Sort of." Her mother exhaled. "A few hours ago, Alex took off like a bat out of hell and we haven't heard from him or seen him since."

"He's in Texas, following up on a lead."

"Good, I was starting to worry he got abducted. These Aten people are aliens after all, right?"

"Um, yes. But as far as we know, they don't abduct humans."

Her mother harrumphed. "Somebody does. I'm living proof of that. If the alien tracking implant hadn't gotten infected, they'd probably have kept on taking me."

Erin knew her mother's story well. But it didn't jive with what she knew about the Aten. She said, "The Aten see us as dirty, unfit to socialize with them. They recruit humans to act as their agents on the ground so they don't have to touch or even see us."

"Uh-huh." After a couple-second pause, her mother said, "So Alex isn't dead in a ditch somewhere or being experimented on in a flying saucer."

"No. He's probably on his way back as we speak."

Another pause. "You should marry him. He's a sweetheart."

Erin felt the familiar heat in her cheeks. She muttered an excuse about having work to do, then exchanged goodbyes with her mother. After returning the phone to its holder, she faced the fabric bundle again.

The fabric looked delicate enough to disintegrate in a breeze. She recommended unfurling the fabric, touching it only with her fingertips, rolling it in a slow and cautious motion. Within a few minutes, she had spread out the fabric across the bed. The piece measured three feet wide by two feet high. Splotches of color peppered the fabric—a dot here, a swirl there, a blob there. The thing looked like an exceptionally bad example of modern art. The right-hand side of the sheet was discolored by the rusty water stains, which had smeared some of the paint blobs.

She let her gaze wander over the abstract patterns. The splotches and blobs seem to be contained in two separate areas of the fabric. In a rectangular area on the left-hand side, the splotches almost seemed to line up in registers. A blank border rimmed the entire canvas.

The pattern tickled her memory. She took a deep breath, releasing it gradually as she let her vision swim out of focus. A rectangle. A border. Registers.

The map scroll.

She bent forward, laying her palms on the bed at either side of the fabric. The map scroll Ridley hid in his secret compartment featured the same general layout as the image before her now. It was too big a coincidence to accept. The fabric bore some relationship to the papyrus scroll. But what did the connection mean?

She slid the tip of her index finger under the fabric. The color of her skin showed through the gossamer fabric.

From the bedside table, she retrieved Harry's papyrus note. This would do for a test. She slid the papyrus sheet under the fabric, easing it into position under some of the dots and swirls painted on the fabric. The handwritten text showed through the fabric, clear enough to read the words. The hieroglyphs on the map scroll would certainly show through at least as clearly as the handwritten text.

What would happen once she aligned the splotches on the fabric with the text on the map scroll, she could only imagine.

Erin bit her lower lip. She needed the scroll. The computer in the library held images of the scroll, but the laser printer there only produced black-and-white images, which dulled the hieroglyphs. She needed the real scroll, or at least a high-quality facsimile of it.

Alex had the scroll.

Abducted.

The word her mother used echoed in her mind. She didn't think the Aten abducted humans, but then she never thought Chloe would vanish without an explanation either.

Grabbing her cell phone, she dialed Alex's number. He picked up on the fourth ring.

"What's wrong?" he asked, tension roughening his voice.

"With me? Nothing. What about you?"

He said nothing for a second. "Why did you call?"

"I need the map scroll. Preferably the real one, not the digital version—but a high-quality, full-color printout of it might do."

"I'll bring it to the manor this evening." A jet engine whined in the background. "We should be landing in about an hour. I'll come straight from the airport."

"Okay." She frowned. He still sounded tense, either agitated or annoyed. "Are you mad at me?"

He sighed heavily. "No. It's been a long day, that's all."

She wanted to question him more, but in addition to the agitation he sounded tired too. Instead, she told him, "I'll be waiting."

He said goodbye and hung up. She stared at the phone for a few seconds, then returned it to her waistband and focused on the painted fabric. Soon, she would discover its secrets.

ALEX ARRIVED TWO HOURS LATER. WHEN ERIN OPENED THE FRONT DOOR, HE gazed at her with an expression that seemed to mix fatigue and annoyance. She didn't mind that, but she let her jaw drop open as she took in the rest of his appearance.

A wide scratch drew a red line across his right cheek. A handful of smaller scratches and scrapes marred the rest of his face. A scab at his hairline extended backward over his scalp, mostly concealed by his hair. His clothes looked relatively clean and unscathed, though she noticed he wasn't wearing his leather jacket. His boots looked a bit dirty, with a few scratches. In his left hand he carried a two-foot-long plastic tube.

She reached up to touch the scratch on his cheek. Thinking better of it, she pulled back her hand. Meeting his gaze, she asked, "What on earth happened to you?"

"I found a piece of evidence that the Aten would prefer to keep hidden."

"What did they do to you?"

In lieu of a response, he sidled through the doorway past her. She grasped his elbow to stop him. He half turned toward her, his expression unreadable. She laid a hand on his chest.

He winced.

Under her hand, she felt a mass like a piece of thick fabric or…a bandage.

Her heart thudded. Taking hold of his shirt collar, she lifted it so that she could peek under the fabric. Although he tried to back away, she pulled him back. Beneath his shirt, a square bandage covered a six-inch-wide swath of his chest. Jesus.

She looked up at him. He averted his gaze.

"Tell me," she said.

He cleared his throat. As his gaze connected with hers, he said, "One of their glowing orbs attacked me. It wanted to destroy the document I had tucked in my shirt pocket."

Words tumbled through her brain, colliding and spinning like debris in a tornado. She wanted to ask questions, but she feared the answers he might give. Maybe it was better she not know the exact details of what happened to him.

Like hell. She refused to let the coward in her win. She needed to know.

She sucked in a breath and asked, "What exactly did it do to you?"

"It hit me in the chest and I took a little tumble."

"You make it sound like a game of flag football."

"It was no game."

Not a fun game, she thought, but definitely some kind of power play in a game she never signed up for and didn't understand. "Why didn't it kill you?"

He pursed his lips. "Thank you. I needed a reminder that I'm expendable."

"I didn't mean it that way." She hovered her fingers above one of the scrapes on his face. "But why did they let you live, if they want the information you found covered up?"

Alex shrugged.

Another question with no answer. He must be as tired of the conundrums as she was.

Erin dropped her hands to her sides. "You mentioned a document."

"Yes. A land patent showing that Broderick Covington bought Revenant Point in 1854."

"Broderick Covington. As in Ridley's brother?"

"It's a reasonable assumption."

This explained Ridley's connection to the house. His brother built it. He must've lived here at one time with his brother. She said, "If they don't want us to know about it, then it must be important. Beyond the connection to Ridley, I mean."

"We can figure it out later." He set the plastic tube on the floor and grasped her shoulders, ducking his head down close to hers. Both his voice and his expression softened. "What were you doing crawling around under a gazebo? I didn't even know there was one on the property."

Now it was her turn to act nonchalant. "I followed the groundskeeper and discovered an old gazebo hidden in the woods. One of Warner's Bigfoot buddies told me a man buried something underneath it, something for me. Or rather, something for the *satseshat*." She hesitated, then asked, "How did you know about the gazebo?"

"I called earlier." A muscle pulsed in his jaw. "Warner answered. He told me."

"Guess he forgot to tell me you called, what with Jerry making a ruckus and all."

Alex lifted his head, fixing his narrowed gaze on her. "Who's Jerry?"

She choked back a laugh. Of course he didn't know what she was talking about. She recounted the story for him, including every detail she remembered, because she knew he wanted to know everything. She certainly wanted to know everything about what happened to him, but she wouldn't force him to tell her. Not that she could, even if she tried.

When she finished her story, he let go of her shoulders and straightened. "May I see what you found?"

"Of course. Did you bring the map scroll?"

He picked up the plastic tube. "It's right here."

Taking hold of his left hand, she led him upstairs.

THE MAP SCROLL LAY SPREAD OUT ACROSS THE BED. ALEX SIDLED UP TO ERIN as she lowered the fabric onto the papyrus, positioning it so that each of the four corners lined up with the corners of the papyrus beneath it. The dots, swirls, and splotches on the fabric aligned with the hieroglyphs underneath. The marks on the fabric altered the appearance of the hieroglyphs on the papyrus.

They changed the symbols. They changed the meaning.

Alex was focused on the map scroll and its new overlay. He hovered his fingertips a hair's breadth above the fabric, moving his hand left to right as if tracing the path of the hieroglyphs.

"What does it say now?" she asked.

"The section about the *satseshat* is unaltered. The changes mainly concern the section that talks about the pharaoh and the relic."

Two weeks ago when Erin first discovered the papyrus, Alex had translated it for her. The text spoke of the *duat*, the Egyptian underworld that the sun god Ra descended into at dusk and emerged from at dawn. It also mentioned a pharaoh who ran off with the "object from another time," aka the relic, an act that profoundly ticked off the Aten.

Alex indicated a series of hieroglyphs. "The original text said the Aten sent his double, the god Ra, to escort the pharaoh through the *akhet* and beyond the *duat*, to a place of darkness where the pharaoh was reborn as a son of the Aten. The king returned, and ruled Egypt with cruelty and disregard for the old gods, forcing everyone to worship his father the Aten, whom he had come to resemble."

"And now?" she asked.

"It says the pharaoh journeyed through the *akhet* and beyond the *duat* to a place of darkness where he ascended to the Aten. When the king returned, he was no longer the pharaoh Amenhotep. He had been transformed into Akhenaten—the effective spirit of the Aten, the living image of the gods who dwell behind the light, an enemy of the people who ruled with cruelty and disregard for the old gods, et cetera." He bent forward over the scroll. "It says the pharaoh was gone. Akhenaten replaced him, but the people didn't know what had happened. Only the Brothers of the Aten and the priests at the temple knew."

The Brothers of the Aten served as the agents of the Aten on Earth. What they gained from their service, she didn't know but felt certain she wouldn't understand if she did know. She could not comprehend why anyone would abet the atrocities committed by the Aten. She knew they murdered people, by controlling the weather and through their human surrogates. How many people had they killed over the millennia? How much had they influenced human history, for the worse?

She recalled another portion of the text, one referring to a river that ran into and out of the *duat*, ending at the excellent lake. According to the text, the pharaoh was buried near the lake. The new version of the text said the Aten took Amenhotep IV, replacing him with one of their own. Might Amenhotep IV be the pharaoh buried near the excellent lake?

No, of course not. The Aten despised humans and preferred to hide in their sky-borne craft high above humanity, a race they deemed too impure to deal with, for fear of contaminating themselves. So they cowered in their spaceships, or whatever the craft were, sequestered from the human race and from Earth itself. They haunted the planet, yet never deigned to set foot on it.

At least as far as she knew.

The point was, they wouldn't make the effort to bury Amenhotep. They probably dumped his body in the desert for the jackals to munch on, or chucked him in the Nile for the crocodiles to consume.

She rested a hand on Alex's shoulder. "What about the section that talks about the river? Has that changed at all?"

"Unfortunately, no. It still says the river runs into and out of the *duat*, then back into it before emerging in the excellent lake. The pharaoh was buried in a tomb near the lake. First buried in the land between the river, in the pyramid mountain at the doorway to the *duat*, he now rests for eternity in the land at the river's end." He sighed. "Which makes no more sense today than it did two weeks ago."

Beware the Aten, the ancient ones who seem to give light but bring only darkness and death.

A shiver coursed down her spine. In the note he wrote as he lay dying, Ridley Covington spoke of the darkness that masquerades as the light. No good can come from allying oneself with it, he said. Had Ridley joined the Brothers of the Aten? If so, he clearly came to regret that decision.

"Hmm," Alex murmured. "Do you remember what the scroll said about the pharaoh disappearing with the object from another time?"

"Yep."

The scribe who wrote the text explained how the Egyptians desperately tried to appease the Aten with the usual kinds of offerings they made to gods—bread, wine, meat—but the Aten's displeasure with them only grew. The reason for their ire stemmed from a mystery no one could solve. The pharaoh had disappeared, along with his favorite wife Nefertiti, their children, most of their possessions, several servants, and a dozen soldiers. Most importantly, to the Aten anyway, the pharaoh took with him the one thing the Aten coveted more than anything else, the object known only as the relic.

The Egyptians knew nothing of the pharaoh's whereabouts and, in fact, the evidence suggested the king and his entourage never left the palace. It seemed as if they simply vanished into thin air. When the Aten found out, they were not happy.

She asked, "Has the text changed?"

"A little, after the part where the Aten threatened to destroy the entire city of Akhetaten and the vizier pressured the priests to intervene. The Aten relented, abandoning Egypt altogether. But they gave the high priest a message."

"I know this part," she said. "They told the high priest the relic must be found but only the *satseshat* can find it."

He glanced up at her over his shoulder. "Actually, it says the relic can only be found by she whose identity is hidden, the daughter of Seshat, the daughter of Thoth, the incarnation of another time."

"My version is easier to say."

His lips twitched in a ghost of a smile.

She leaned her hips against the tall bed, resting her hands on the mattress. "I get that the Aten think I'm the *satseshat*, though I have no earthly idea why. But what the hell do they mean by the incarnation of another time?"

"I don't know." Turning his attention to the scroll, he grazed his fingertips over the fabric just below a sequence of hieroglyphs. "Here's the part that's changed. Additional text has been inserted at the end."

"What does it say?"

"We, the priests of Amun-Ra, aided the pharaoh in his escape and we alone know where the relic is interred with the king. We provide this scroll so that the *satseshat*, the peaceful one, may find the relic and destroy the source of the Aten's power—"

"Peaceful one?" she interrupted. "What does that mean?"

"Maybe they think you're a pacifist." Smirking, he cast a sidelong glance at her. "They don't know you like I do."

She poked his shoulder. "Read the rest."

He ran a finger over the text until he located the right spot. "It goes on to say that once the *satseshat* destroys the source of the Aten's power, then the true light of Amun-Ra shall shine down upon all humanity. The *satseshat* shall find the relic and become the ruler of time."

"Ruler of time?" she said. "Why does everyone have to be so damn cryptic?"

He straightened. "You're the *satseshat*. They assumed you would understand."

She snorted. Thus far, her attention had zeroed in on the hieroglyphic registers with an intensity that blocked out everything else. She scanned the rest of the papyrus, which contained the map.

It looked completely different. The splotches and smears on the papyrus merged with the splotches and smears on the fabric to paint a vivid picture of a landscape. Most striking of all, however, a black squiggle now split the river into two sections.

She leaned closer to examine the squiggle. It was more than a wavy streak of paint. It was a hieroglyph— specifically, the hieroglyph for *akhet*, the horizon.

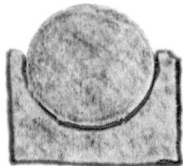

With her gaze, she traced the river rightward until it ended. There, a bizarre symbol towered above a hieroglyphic phrase. The phrase read, "the object from another time."

The relic. This map pointed the way to it.

The symbol above the phrase resembled nothing she'd seen before. It appeared to be a combination of two hieroglyphs—an *ankh*, the cross-like symbol for life, nestled inside a round sign known as a cartouche. Resembling a loop of rope, the cartouche represented the world as a whole, and in hieroglyphic inscriptions an elongated cartouche often surrounded the names of kings. The combination symbol on the map, however, did not include a name.

Indicating the combined hieroglyph, she asked Alex, "Have you ever seen this symbol before?"

Alex planted his left hand on the bed beside her, with his arm touching her. He ducked his head over her shoulder to squint at the symbol. After a few seconds, he shook his head and murmured a "no" in his husky whisper. His hair brushed against her cheek. A warm tingling raced through her body, and she fought the urge to turn her head and kiss him. Ridiculous. She needed to concentrate, not get lost in the pleasant but totally irrelevant thoughts ricocheting through her mind.

She switched her attention back to the map overlay. Unfortunately, the area around the strange symbol was obliterated by the water stains. She could tell the other hieroglyphs, as well as some kind of blue blob surrounded by black lines, once occupied the spot. The rust had worn holes in the thermos, however, allowing water to invade the interior. The damage to the overlay was localized but substantial.

A series of nasty curses flashed through her mind. Harry thought fate helped him find this item, but fate was apparently playing a practical joke on both of them.

The part of the map she most wanted to see, most *needed* to see, no longer existed.

10

E RIN FOCUSED ON THE *AKHET* SYMBOL THAT BISECTED THE RIVER. IN EGYPTIAN mythology, the *akhet* was more than the visible horizon. It was also the place where the sun, known to the Egyptians as the god Ra, descended into at dusk and arose from at dawn.

When they first found the map scroll, Alex had told her about the mythology surrounding the Aten. The name Aten signified the disk-like face of the sun, and it had served as a minor deity until the third year of the reign of Amenhotep IV, who at that point changed his name to Akhenaten. He banned the old gods, replacing them with a newly elevated and revamped Aten, the vehicle for the sun's light, the deity Akhenaten referred to as his father. As part of the Aten's reinvention as the premier god, Akhenaten bestowed upon it a new series of epithets. The Aten was the living one, the ruler of the *akhet*, he who awakens in the horizon and is known as the light of the sun-disk.

The ruler of the *akhet*. To Egyptologists, the Aten was an abstract god. She knew better. The Aten were a race of beings not of this Earth. For the Aten to rule the *akhet*, the "horizon" must exist as a physical location, either on this planet or elsewhere. In the mythology, the *akhet* was also the entrance to the *duat*, the underworld that souls traveled through during the night. If both the *akhet* and the *duat* represented physical locations, then perhaps the *akhet* served as a way station on the journey to the *duat*. The pharaoh's body might've been kept there while his tomb was being finished, similar to the way human bodies were kept at a morgue or funeral parlor prior to burial.

The pyramid mountain mentioned in the text referred to a mountain in the Grand Canyon known as Cheops Pyramid. She and Alex found an underground labyrinth there, perhaps intended as a tomb and littered with artifacts from the ancient Egyptian, Celtic, and Old Copper cultures. She recognized the artifacts belonging to the Old Copper culture because that civilization hailed from the Great Lakes region, and left a deep mark on the ancient history of the Keweenaw Peninsula.

She assumed the Grand Canyon labyrinth was intended to serve as a tomb mainly because rock art inscription that led them to the Canyon spoke of a king who died and was buried in the pyramid mountain. But the map scroll said the king was *first* buried there but later moved to the land at the river's end. Maybe the Grand Canyon labyrinth was the way station where the embalmers performed their tasks, which according to Egyptologists took about seventy days. Then after the body was prepared, the pharaoh's people moved his body to its final resting place in the vicinity of the excellent lake.

Alex turned sideways to sit partially on the desk, with one knee bent over the edge and the other foot planted firmly on the floor. She glanced at him sideways, and caught him eyeing her with the expression he gave her when he thought she'd experienced a vital insight. He once told her he thought she possessed some kind of special insight that he compared to extrasensory perception.

The comparison was baloney, of course. She did not have ESP, or even extraordinary insight. Sure, her thoughts tended to move in patterns different from those of other people's, but that hardly made her extraordinary. So far, she'd failed to convince Alex of that. And now he was giving her the look that told her he expected a monumental revelation. She had an idea, yes, though she couldn't tell yet whether it was monumentally important or just monumentally stupid.

"Tell me," he said.

She told him her idea about the *akhet*, the *duat*, and the land between the river and the lake. When she finished talking, he stared into space for a moment. She waited, drumming her fingers on the desktop.

He locked his gaze on her face as a smile spread across his. "I think you may be onto something. Any ideas about where the excellent lake is?"

"Nope." She swept her hand through the air above the right-hand side of the overlay. "That section of the map has been literally washed away."

"You'll figure it out."

"I'm not so sure."

"I am. You are brilliant, after all."

She rolled her eyes. "I don't feel very brilliant at the moment."

He pulled her close, and for a heartbeat she thought he was going to kiss her. But instead, he hesitated. Unable to move, she watched his face and waited. He stared into her eyes, their noses millimeters apart.

"I need to know," he said, "are you and Warner an item?"

"What?" She couldn't stifle the laugh that bubbled out of her. "No, of course not."
"You have spent quite a bit of time with him. And I've been told he has charisma."
"Oh yes, he does."

Alex scowled, leaning backward.

She took his face in her hands. "I'm not interested in Warner."

He pulled her closer again."Good."

Her heart fluttered.

He planted a quick kiss on her lips, released her, and hopped to his feet.

She felt a bit woozy, and then realized she'd forgotten to breathe. She forced herself to take several deep, slow breaths.

He asked, "What do you say we find ourselves a relic?"

Feeling the wooziness dissipate, she glanced at the map. "There's one problem."

"More than one, I'd say."

"Yes, but this map is the first problem we have to solve." She let out a deep sigh, her shoulders sagging on the exhalation. "The most important section of the map is gone. And I see only one way that we can retrieve the missing information." She looked up at him. "We need to talk to the priests of Amun-Ra."

"Unless you can communicate with the dead, there's precisely zero percent of a chance we can contact them."

She had an idea about that, but she knew he wouldn't like it. In fact, she felt reasonably certain he would flip out at the very suggestion and also mildly concerned that he might lock her in the trunk of his car to prevent her from enacting her idea.

He frowned at her. "Do I want to know what you're thinking?"

"Probably not. But it may be the only chance we have." She took a deep breath, squared her shoulders, and leaped off the metaphorical cliff. "I need to talk to Samuel Wessick. Maybe he can send us back in time to right before the pharaoh and his relic vanished."

Alex's frown condensed into pursed lips. Lines emerged and deepened across his forehead. He said, "Aside from working for the Aten, Samuel Wessick is the one who hired Oded Rassul, the psychopath who tried to kill us both. We have no idea how dangerous Wessick might be."

"Got to at least try." She took hold of his hand, cupping it in both of hers. "It's our only shot."

"I suppose you'll insist on talking to him alone."

"Yes, I think it's best."

He gazed at her for a moment. She could practically see the thoughts bouncing around behind his eyes. No doubt he wanted to order her to stay away from Wessick. The thought of confronting the secretive owner of Revenant House gave her an uneasy feeling in her stomach, but they'd run out of options.

Sighing, Alex pulled his hand away from hers. "All right. But this only happens under one condition."

"What's that?"

"I hear and see everything that goes on during this meeting."

"We just agreed I should speak to him alone."

A sly grin spread across his face. "There are plenty of ways to be alone with someone without being *alone* with them."

"I don't get it."

"You will." He turned and started for the door. At the threshold, he paused to glance over his shoulder at her. "Stay here. I have to get something from the car."

With that, he left.

H ALF AN HOUR LATER, ERIN AND ALEX STOOD IN HER BEDROOM. HE HAD photographed the overlay and transferred the images to the tablet computer for easier analysis. After that, he set about turning her into a human surveillance system. Inside her ear, she wore a little doohickey that contained a microphone. A small brooch attached to her blouse incorporated a tiny video camera. Whatever happened during her meeting with Wessick, Alex would hear and see all of it.

Assuming Wessick didn't jam the signals. Alex laid that caveat on her a few minutes ago. Either way, she intended to see this plan through to its completion.

One thing hindered her plan. Wessick had yet to respond to the message she sent him earlier.

"So," Alex said, "how do you intend to contact our mystery man?"

As yet, Alex knew nothing about her initial attempt to contact Wessick. She said, "Actually, I already tried."

He regarded her with a look of suspicion. "What did you do?"

Erin tried to look innocent, though she doubted it worked. Despite the knots cinching tight in her gut, she related to him the incident with the hand-scrawled note and the hidden camera. Her attempt to contact Wessick seemed downright harmless in comparison with her suggestion they should travel back in time to meet the priests of Amun-Ra.

Alex had a different opinion. She saw it in the flattening of his lips and the tension in his body, and she heard it in his voice.

"You did what?" he said.

She laid her palms on his chest. "Let's not argue about what's already done. The important point is that Wessick has not responded. I have to try something else to get his attention."

"Such as?"

She bit her bottom lip. "I have an idea, but you're not going to like it."

He laid his hand over hers. When he spoke, his voice was calmer and softer. "Tell me anyway."

"It might be best if I show you instead."

They stared at each other for a moment, neither willing to concede defeat by looking away. He wanted to know what she intended before she did it, but she knew that his reaction would be less than supportive. If she told him first, he would try to talk her out of it. And he just might succeed.

Keeping her inner coward at bay took constant vigilance.

Alex might say it was her inner daredevil, not her inner coward whispering in her ear.

Criminy. She was talking herself out of it all on her own.

"Wait here," she said, "and watch me on the hidden camera. After I make my attempt, I'll hang around in the study for awhile to see if he responds."

Retrieving her gun from a drawer in the bedside table, she popped out the clip to make sure it was fully loaded. Alex watched her. She felt his gaze on her even when she turned her back to him to open the drawer. After shoving the clip back into place, she snagged another item from the drawer. It was a folding knife, with a blade four inches long and a curved black handle. Warner gave her the knife a week ago because he said every woman should have both a gun and a knife.

Yeah, he was a little weird. But she liked that about him.

She tucked the gun inside her waistband, flush with her spine. The knife she shoved in her pocket. From the closet she grabbed a sweater jacket and slipped into it. The bulky garment concealed the gun well.

Alex waylaid her as she marched toward the door.

"I'll wait here," he said. "But I reserve the right to storm the study at any time, if I deem it necessary."

"Agreed."

She walked out of the bedroom, heading toward the staircase. Just as she reached the stairs, a flash of light drew her attention down the corridor to the window at the opposite end. Erin halted. The breath froze in her lungs.

A glowing orb floated outside the window. It bobbed a little, side-to-side and up-and-down.

Erin forced herself to inhale, then exhale, and repeat the process that should happen unconsciously. Right now, though, several of her autonomic functions had lost their auto. Her eyes began to burn, so she reminded herself to blink.

The orb watched her.

She felt she ought to do something. Shout at it. Flap her arms to chase it away. Stupid idea. Like flailing her arms could frighten an inanimate object. Maybe if she—

The orb surged toward her, straight through the glass. Before she could react, it closed the distance between itself and her. The orb stopped two feet from her face, level with her eyes. She squinted in its brightness. Its heat radiated onto her face.

Alien thoughts intruded into her mind. The words of the orb's masters, delivered by their servant.

Heed our warning. Find the relic.

The orb zipped around her and sailed down the corridor toward the door to her bedroom.

She ran after it.

The orb disappeared through the bedroom door. Erin skidded to a stop in the doorway a second later. Heart pounding, mind cluttered with a melee of thoughts, she peeked around the doorjamb.

Alex sat on the bed with his bag beside him, its top open. He was messing around with the equipment he needed to listen in on her conversation with Wessick, which included a laptop computer. Focused on his task, he seemed unaware of anything else.

The orb floated behind his head, inches from him.

How could he not feel its heat? Erin opened her mouth, intent on warning him. The words refused to form.

A glittery wave swept across the orb's surface. Words that were not her own popped into her brain.

Next time he dies.

The orb zipped away from Alex. It shot straight out the window and out of sight.

Erin considered saying something to Alex. Knowing about the orb and its threat would accomplish nothing except to amp up his already elevated anxiety. Though neither of them wanted to admit it, they both felt the elements converging around them, transmuting into a new and terrible danger that threatened more than their own lives. It threatened everything. She felt it, and she sensed that Alex did too.

He didn't need to know. She knew, and she would make certain no one hurt him again. Whatever it took. The Aten would hurt no one else.

Alex swiped at the back of his head, as if belatedly aware of the orb's heat. He glanced over his shoulder toward the window. As he swung his head back around, he spotted her in the doorway.

He asked, "Something wrong?"

She hesitated. "Do you think we should check the microphone thingy is working?" Erin pointed at her ear.

Nodding, Alex tapped keys on the laptop. "Walk out in the corridor and say something."

She retreated into the corridor, taking several steps past the doorway. Then she said, in a voice neither too loud nor too soft, "You are not expendable."

Alex's voice sounded in her ear. "Glad to hear it."

"You didn't tell me I'd be able to hear you too."

"Didn't I?" His voice turned soft and deep, tinged with concern. "Be careful down there."

"Yes, sir."

She trotted down the stairs to the study. The door to Wessick's private chamber was shut. She dug the skeleton key out of her pocket, unlocked the door, and thrust it open. The room stood empty, lifeless, silent except for the ticking of a grandfather clock.

Her pulse outpaced the clock's ticking.

Erin sucked in a deep breath, let it out slowly, and strode into the study.

She headed straight for the desk. Once behind it, she knelt in front of the drawers on the left-hand side. A shiver coursed through her. Did someone watch her at this very moment?

I hope so.

Pulling the knife out of her pocket, she flipped it open. The drawers were locked, as she and Alex had determined previously. Using the knife as a crowbar, she struggled to break into the top drawer. It refused to budge. She tried another drawer. Then another. None succumbed to her attempts. The knife simply wasn't enough. She considered whipping out the gun to blast the drawers' locks to bits. Revealing her weapon this early would rob her of the element of surprise when and if she needed the gun to defend herself.

Rising, she surveyed the room. A floor lamp in the corner looked promising. She tromped to it and studied its body. Metal, for sure. Grasping the lamp, she lifted. Her muscles twanged in complaint. The darn thing was heavy.

Good.

She yanked the lamp's plug out of the socket. Taking hold of its long, thin body with both hands, she carried the lamp to the desk. The square base of the lamp offered some nice sharp corners. She raised the lamp, positioned the base so that one corner of it would strike the top drawer, and prepared for the assault.

"That won't be necessary."

Erin froze. She glanced at the doorway. A man stood there observing her, his hands locked behind his back. He wore a charcoal-gray suit, a matching tie, and spiffy leather boots that for some reason reminded her of Sherlock Holmes. His salt-and-pepper hair was cut short, his face clean shaven. He kept his hazel eyes trained on her.

A tinkling sound emanated from behind him. Erin recognized the sound as the jingling bell on the collar of Bastet, the resident feline. A second later, the cat slunk out from behind the man in the doorway. Bastet rubbed her head against his calf.

Erin set the lamp on the floor. Fixated on attacking the drawer, she failed to notice that she was no longer alone. She really hated when that happened.

The stranger crossed the study, halting across the desk from her.

Erin straightened, meeting his gaze. "Mr. Wessick."

He smiled without parting his lips. "Ms. Turner."

"What took you so long?" she asked.

"I didn't receive your message until after our encounter in the woods."

"Our what?" Realization cascaded through her. "You're the groundskeeper. Why the masquerade?"

"My visits to the summerhouse are private."

By summerhouse he must mean the gazebo thingy in the woods. The next time he visited it, he'd find its condition more deteriorated, thanks to Jerry's overzealous attempt to protect her. Right now, his visits to the summerhouse were irrelevant.

"You and I need to talk," she said. "I want candid answers, not cryptic responses and threats of violence. Can you manage that?"

"Yes."

He picked up a chair that sat across from the sofa and relocated it to a spot in front of the desk, facing the executive chair behind it. He patted the top of the chair he'd just moved, a high-backed number upholstered and ornamented in what looked to her like a Victorian style.

"Take a seat," he said, "in whichever chair you prefer."

She dropped into the executive chair.

His lips twitched in something resembling amusement. Seating himself in the froufrou chair, he sat as straight as the back of the chair itself, arms on the chair's arms, attention still focused on her.

She crossed her legs, leaned her head back against her chair, and looked at him.

"You work for the Aten," she said, "don't you?"

The amusement vacated his features, replaced by an expression she could best describe as pleasant yet noncommittal.

"It's far more complicated," he said, "than a simple working arrangement."

"Explain it to me."

"Thirty years ago the Aten conscripted me. I'm tasked with assisting them in the realization of their goals."

The word conscripted implied he had no choice. She let that go for the moment and asked, "And what exactly are their goals?"

"To obtain the relic, naturally. And also to prevent the world at large from discovering the truth of their existence and the extent of their technology."

He lapsed into silence. She waited.

For about five seconds. Then she said, "Please elaborate."

"You know about the artifacts Rassul collected for me." He linked his hands over his lap, keeping his elbows on the chair's arms. "I believe you also realize that those artifacts embody evidence of the Aten's time travel technology. They would prefer not to have the technology revealed."

"Uh-huh. What I really want to know about is the relic. What is it, why is it so damn important to the Aten, and what in the hell gave them the idea I could find it for them."

He moved his shoulders in a barely visible shrug. "I can't offer you answers concerning the relic. I know only what the Aten tell me."

"And what have they told you?"

"That the relic must be found and that you are the one to find it."

"Drop the cryptic villain act and give me some real answers."

"I have no better answers to give."

She glared at him. "Don't you think it's a bad plan to tick off the one person you and your masters expect to find the relic for you?"

He flinched at the word masters. The expression was subtle, but she definitely saw it.

"I'm not being difficult," he said. "I simply have no answers. I don't know what the relic is, and I've come to the conclusion that the Aten don't know either. As for why they chose you, that question I can answer." He paused. "Though you may wish I hadn't."

"I want to know."

"Very well."

Samuel Wessick searched Erin's face for some clue as to how she might react to the news. In her face, he of course saw irritation—and also an unmistakable spark of curiosity. She sought more than answers.

She craved knowledge.

If he believed in portents, he would accept her curiosity as a favorable one. He had hoped to ease her into the truth. That option was no longer available to him.

"Spit it out," Erin said.

He appreciated many of her attributes. Her patience, however, left much to be desired.

Wessick rose, circling around behind the chair. Movement helped him think, and he needed a great deal of help in order to frame the narrative correctly.

"The story begins," he said, "in deep antiquity, before the dawn of civilization in Egypt."

"I wasn't born in deep antiquity. Skip ahead."

He rested his hands atop the chair's back. "You cannot fully understand your own destiny without the proper background."

She scrunched her lips. Then, with a resigned sigh, she said, "Fine. Have it your way."

"Thank you." He strolled toward the bay window. "As I said, the story begins in deep antiquity. In fact, no one is certain how far back in time the trigger event unfolded. But it initiated a chain reaction that continues to this day, culminating with the Aten's search for the relic."

"What trigger event?" Erin asked.

He turned to look at her. "The activation of the time machine."

"When did the Aten turn it on?"

"No one knows, not even the Aten. The time machine was both invented and activated so long ago that no memory of the trigger event persists. Everyone, including the Aten, know *that* it happened but not *when* it happened."

Her lips quirked in a skeptical expression. "If they don't know when it happened, then how can they know for sure it did happen?"

"Because if it hadn't," he said, "they would not have the ability to travel through time."

She stared at him, all expression gone from her face.

This part required the most explanation. Despite decades of working within the rules, full comprehension still eluded him. He could not explain why the rules existed, or how they came to be, yet he knew they did exist. Most people encountered great difficulty in accepting things they could never fully understand. Yet if anyone were capable of accepting such things, it was Erin Turner.

Facing the window, he clasped his hands behind his back. "The machine opened a time portal which may be accessed from anywhere on earth, using specialized devices. We may only travel backward in time, and we may go no farther back than the moment when the machine was activated. We have yet to reach the limit."

"How far back have you traveled?"

"I have traveled no further back than the fourteenth century BC. The Aten have traveled much farther, though I don't know precisely how far."

She made a derisive noise. "I thought you were the Aten's lapdog. Aren't you supposed to know all their secrets?"

Anger spiked through him, hot and sharp. The Aten's lapdog indeed. A lapdog was a pet, not a trusted advisor. Perhaps Erin grasped his situation better than he imagined, better than he had understood it for so many years.

He waited a few seconds for the anger to dissipate. When it had, he strode to the desk, halting several feet from Erin. She rotated her chair toward him, awaiting his next revelation with a composure beyond her years. Did she feign it to hide her true anxiety?

The reason for her composure made little difference.

"You recall the artifacts," he said, "that Rassul collected. Those items betrayed the Aten's greatest secret, their ability to travel through time—if anyone cared to examine the evidence. You see, the Aten have been navigating the seas of time for so long that mistakes inevitably occur. Mistakes such as artifacts dropped in a time or place where they do not belong."

"Right," Erin said, "and that's why you and Rassul snatched all those artifacts."

"Precisely."

"Get to the part about the relic."

"I will." He paused to gather his thoughts. "They once thought the anomalous artifacts were no threat to them, until people like your friend Alex MacKay began to investigate and document the artifacts. In the nineteenth and early twentieth centuries, explorers found some of these anomalies, but their discoveries became forgotten footnotes in history. The Aten felt free to ignore the discoveries, as did history itself. But the situation has changed, and the Aten have adapted their tactics."

Erin observed him without comment.

He continued, "The artifacts are a side note. The relic is the keystone. Whoever finds it will hold the power to destroy the Aten."

"How do they know it can destroy them if they don't even know what it is?"

"They do not know, they believe." He lowered himself into the chair. "Tell me something, Ms. Turner. Do you believe in evil?"

11

"Evil?" Erin asked, furrowing her brow. "Do you mean like the devil?"

"In a manner of speaking. You see, the Aten do believe in evil. Their belief system may not resemble anything we humans would recognize as religion, but they hold as fast to it as any human holds onto religious faith. You might say the relic is their beast, and the one who possesses it is their anti-Christ."

"Beast as in 666?"

He nodded. "The knowledge, or perhaps the legend, of the relic has been passed down through the ages and has become shrouded in mysticism, becoming the centerpiece of their belief system. Unlike human religions, such as Christianity, the Aten's beliefs do not inspire them to seek enlightenment or to toil for the betterment of the world. The legend of the relic inspires nothing but fear and desperation, borne out of the fervent belief that their very existence depends upon controlling the relic."

He felt the urge to stand up, to move around, yet doing so might convey restlessness. In turn, restlessness implied discomfort. He felt nothing of the sort. And yet the urge to rise welled up in him once again.

Quash it, he commanded himself.

With the urge thoroughly quashed, he looked at Erin again. "At any given point in the Aten's history, only one of their kind has known the secrets of the relic. This individual, always a male, was known as the keeper of the Relic. He knew both its location and its function, and what it looks like. Each keeper served for fifty years, then he passed his knowledge on to another and committed ritual suicide. This ensured that only one living Aten knew the relic's secrets.

"Then one day, the system broke down. The ruling elite among the Aten decided they must seize control of the relic and use its power to control the human race. They demanded the keeper hand over the relic at once. The keeper refused. They tortured him, yet still he refused. Finally, they threatened to raze an entire continent unless he complied."

"Raze?" Erin said. "You mean blow it up or something?"

"I mean obliterate every living thing, from animals down to bacteria, and render the land uninhabitable. Its earth would become virtually poisonous."

Though her expression remained unchanged, her silence spoke to her state of mind. He was overwhelming her with bizarre and disturbing information. If he continued, Erin's disquiet would surely grow. He felt an odd sensation in his chest, a tightness unfamiliar to him. It meant nothing.

Whatever her reaction, he had no choice but to continue.

"The keeper gave in," he said. "He promised to lead his fellow Aten to the relic, which he said lay hidden in a cave on the ancient land mass today known as the Sahul subcontinent. But instead he used the voyage to Sahul as an opportunity to escape from their custody. He and the relic disappeared."

"Sahul was Australia, New Guinea, and Tasmania," Erin said. "Sea levels were much lower back then and so those three landmasses became one. But sea levels rose again, and by seven thousand years ago the three landmasses had separated. When did all this happen?"

"Approximately eight thousand years ago."

ERIN STARED AT HIM WITH WHAT MUST'VE LOOKED LIKE A BLANK EXPRESSION. She felt blank. Clueless. Empty— at least mentally. Everything Wessick had told her so far had drained her mind.

"If all this happened eight thousand years ago," she said, "then why do all the clues I've been given point to events in the fourteenth century BC?"

Wessick propped his elbows on the chair's arms and steepled his fingers, resting his chin lightly atop them. He looked amused, which ticked her off. She tried to swallow her annoyance.

No good. The anger stuck with her. For the first time in her life, she wanted to deck someone. *Really* wanted to deck him. Or better yet, shoot him. In the kneecap, naturally, so as not to kill him but so that he suffered.

She made a low noise that embodied her anger.

A voice chuckled directly into her eardrum. She jerked in surprise. Through the device wedged inside her ear canal, Alex said, "It's nice to know I'm not the only one you growl at."

Wessick arched an eyebrow. "Are you all right?"

He couldn't hear the voice in her ear, of course. She lifted a hand to cover her mouth, pretending to scratch the bridge of her nose, and muttered to Alex, "Zip it."

To Wessick, she said, "I'm fine. Don't change the subject."

"For many years," Wessick said, "the Aten searched for the keeper. He seemed to have vanished into thin air, and finally they gave up looking for him. Several thousand years passed. Then, in the year we call 1395 BC, a clue emerged. The keeper's grave was discovered. It seemed he had fled to predynastic Egypt, where he eventually died. The Aten came to believe, or perhaps they merely hoped, that the keeper had passed on his knowledge of the relic to one of the Egyptians, who in turn passed it down to another, reinstituting the tradition of the keepers through the Egyptians.

"This posed a significant problem for the Aten. When they walk among us they...stand out. Their presence in Egypt would likely incite either fear or awe, and in both instances chaos would result. This is when they began to conscript human agents to work in their stead, individuals who could blend in and thus attract no attention to the Aten's quest. These agents scoured the land, in secret, searching for the one person who might have inherited the keeper's knowledge."

"That's how the Brothers of the Aten got started," Erin said.

Wessick nodded. "The brotherhood served as the eyes, ears, and hands of the Aten on earth. After several years of searching, to no avail, the Aten decided more drastic measures were in order. They believed that only by oppressing the Egyptians could they root out the new keeper. And so they began the gradual process of transforming a minor Egyptian deity known as the Aten into the sole god presiding over the land. Through the brotherhood, they managed to convert the pharaoh Amenhotep III to Aten worship, though he retained his belief in the other gods as well. When Amenhotep III died, his son Amenhotep IV became pharaoh. And in Amenhotep IV, the Aten saw their opportunity to seize control of Egypt. They—"

"Hang on," Erin said. "The Aten may have been a minor deity up until then, but it had been a part of Egyptian mythology for a long time before that. How is the deity Aten related to the...beings who call themselves the Aten?"

His lips curved upward a smidgeon in an almost smirk. "An excellent question. The deity must have originated from the traditions passed down by the keeper. It's unclear exactly how it happened, but whatever knowledge the keeper passed on to the Egyptians must have, over time, spurred them to create the deity Aten based on fragmentary and ill-understood information about the real Aten."

Erin asked, "At what point did the Aten replace the pharaoh with a double who looked more like them than like an Egyptian?"

A look of surprise flashed across his face, gone as swiftly as it had come. Once his expression shifted back into neutral, he said, "I assume you derived that information from the scroll you found here inside the manor."

"Yep."

Alex's voice whispered into her ear, "Don't tell him too much about the scroll."

At least this time she didn't jump at the sound of his voice beamed directly at her eardrum. How dumb did he think she was? She intended to tell Wessick nothing more than was necessary to get information out of him. He knew about the map scroll because he'd bugged the entire house, except for her bedroom. She and Alex retreated to her bedroom whenever they worked on deciphering the scroll.

Wessick stood, linking his hands behind his back, and turned partway toward the bay window. "In Amenhotep IV, the Aten saw an opportunity. He was weak and pliant, not a virile warrior like his father. Most importantly, however, he bore a striking resemblance to one of the Aten's own. During the reign of Amenhotep III, when the pharaoh began to revere the Aten deity, his son also came to venerate the Aten. So when Amenhotep IV became pharaoh, the brotherhood had no trouble luring him to a remote location in the desert—alone—ostensibly to commune with his god, the Aten. There, the switch was accomplished."

Erin held up a hand. "Hold on. You said the Aten stand out from humans. So they must look strikingly different from us, but you expect me to believe they switched the pharaoh with one of their own and nobody noticed?"

The map scroll talked about the god Ra escorting the pharaoh through the *akhet* and beyond the *duat* to a place where he was reborn as the son of the Aten. The text also said the pharaoh, upon returning from his otherworldly journey, had been magically transformed so that he resembled "his father the Aten." She knew all this, but she wanted to hear Wessick's explanation.

He lifted his chin off his steepled fingers. "The facial features of Amenhotep IV bore a striking resemblance to the features of one of the Aten. When the imposter took the pharaoh's place, he explained away the differences in his appearance by claiming he'd undergone a spiritual transformation of such magnitude that it altered his outward appearance. The Brothers of the Aten, some of whom had previously manipulated their way into positions of power within the government, came forward to support the pharaoh. And the Aten orchestrated what you might call a mass UFO sighting over Thebes to reinforce matters. No one dared question the pharaoh's story."

"I'm assuming," Erin said, "that's when Amenhotep IV changed his name to Akhenaten and banned all the old gods."

"Yes."

"And the quest for the relic?"

"The Aten, through their imposter pharaoh, seized control of Egypt and oppressed her citizens more than anyone alive today realizes. Despite this, the search for the relic dragged on for years without success. Then one day, everything changed."

Erin knew, from the map scroll, that the pharaoh got hold of something the Aten desperately wanted. From that description alone, she assumed the pharaoh had found the relic—except he didn't give it to his Aten brethren. She was getting the feeling that neither they nor Wessick knew anything more than the author of the scroll did about what the pharaoh found and what he did with it.

Wessick leaned forward, locking his gaze on hers. "The details are murky. What we do know is that the Brothers of the Aten learned the pharaoh had found an object believed to hold great power. They informed the Aten, but it was too late. The pharaoh had absconded with the object."

"The Aten think it was their relic," Erin said.

"Yes. The pharaoh told his closest advisers, one of whom was loyal to the brotherhood, that the item in question was an object from another era that held the power to save or to destroy Egypt. He called it the Shadow of the Aten."

"If Akhenaten found the relic," Erin said, "why didn't he give it to his Aten buddies?"

"Because he was mad."

THE PORTAL TELESCOPED SHUT BEHIND HER. THE WHITE LIGHT THAT ILLUMINATED the seller winked out with it, sinking the room into darkness. Desheret flicked on a pen light.

Rows of wine racks surrounded her. The dank smell, coupled with the darkness and the lack of windows, made her feel as if she'd stepped into a tomb that lay sealed for millennia. Her own tomb. She should have died long ago, after all. No other woman she knew of straddled as many lifetimes as she, the one who called herself Desheret.

No one knew her true name—except Samuel. Until recently, she would have entrusted him with her secrets without reservation. No more. Despite his protestations to the contrary, despite his best efforts to conceal it, beneath his aloof exterior beat a heart infected with warm, sticky human emotions. She smelled it. When he touched her, she felt it on her skin. *Disgusting.*

Desheret marched to the cellar door, flung it open, and stepped out into the sunshine. She stood there for a moment, letting the sun's heat cleanse her of Samuel's infection. The memory of it tainted her tongue with a revolting sweetness. Samuel cared what happened to Erin Turner. He turned his back on the Aten, those who made him the man he was, because he cared for *her.*

And now she—Desheret, not his beloved Erin—must rectify his mistakes.

Retreating into the cellar, she closed the door and wended her way through the racks of wine bottles to another door. This one she unlocked with her key. Then she eased it open a few inches, peeking through the opening. The doorway opened into the downstairs, directly under the second floor landing of the staircase. No one lingered in the passageway beyond.

Desheret slipped through the doorway, shutting it behind her. The lock engaged with a faint click. Voices, faint yet discernible, echoed down the passageway from the direction of Samuel's study. Desheret tiptoed down the passageway. She kept her back to the wall, her footsteps light. Ten feet from the door to the study, she halted. A female voice carried through the open doorway.

Erin. Desheret clenched her jaw.

"What do you mean he was mad?" Erin asked.

"Akhenaten was not of sound mind," Samuel said. "Illness had robbed him of his faculties."

Desheret backed away from the doorway. The conversation was of no interest to her.

Once she retreated out of earshot, she turned and trotted up the staircase to the second floor. Erin might've hidden her secrets in the bedroom she thought of as her own. In reality, Revenant Point and everything on it belonged to the Aten. What their agents acquired in their stead, they owned. The agents themselves belonged to the Aten as well, whether they realized it or not. Samuel behaved as if he were free. Now she must remind him of his true nature.

He served the Aten. He lived at their discretion.

She strode down the passageway toward Erin's bedroom. A rustling sound issued from within.

Desheret froze. She pressed herself to the wall alongside the doorway, bent her neck, and peered through the opening into the room.

A figure sat on the bed. She could see only one leg and a portion of the torso. Yet from that limited information, she knew the person's identity.

Alex MacKay.

No one else would linger in Erin's bedroom. The two of them had spent many hours together, often in the seclusion of the bedroom, the one location where Samuel refused to install surveillance equipment. Another portent of the human feeling eating away at him. She would kill Samuel now, but the Aten commanded that she give him one final chance. As for Alex MacKay, the Aten offered no instructions.

Once, she believed Erin's relationship with Alex MacKay might encourage her to find the relic. The opposite proved true, however, as the little librarian expended too much time and energy fretting over MacKay. Could she trust him, did he like her, would she see him again. Desheret clenched her fists. Erin nattered on and on about a man when she ought to focus her energies on finding the relic.

Desheret *needed* the relic. To be free. To be powerful.

To punish the men who betrayed her.

She reached under her shirt. Grasping the hilt of her knife, she slid it out of its sheath.

Time to free Erin of her distraction.

I DON'T GET IT." ERIN DRUMMED HER FINGERS ON HER THIGHS. "IF THE PHARAOH was sick, why didn't the Aten heal him? One of their orbs healed me."

Wessick arched an eyebrow. "You know about that?"

"It's kind of hard to miss it when you wake up to see a glowing orb hovering inches from your face."

"You were meant to sleep through the encounter." He leaned back in his chair. "The orbs can heal minor injuries such as yours, and they can sometimes heal more serious injuries such as puncture wounds or broken bones. But they cannot heal immunological conditions."

"Immunological?" She squinted at him. "Do you mean like the flu or something?"

"Much worse, I'm afraid. The Aten have, as a rule, avoided any and all contact with our atmosphere and the living things inhabiting the earth. Because the Aten came from another world, they lack any immunity to the pathogens we encounter daily. Since before dinosaurs walked the earth, the Aten have struggled to develop vaccines or genetic modifications to give them the ability to walk among us. All their efforts have failed."

"Then how did they expect Akhenaten to survive?"

He shrugged. "They administered a cocktail of drugs to enhance his immune system, in hopes of staving off illness, at least long enough for him to complete his task. It was the best they could do."

"Did Akhenaten volunteer for the job?"

"No. The Aten conscripted him, and they assured him the drugs would protect him. He was not a scientist or physician, but simply a pious man who believed in the sacred quest for the relic. And so he did as they wished."

"They used him." Erin shook her head. "Real sweethearts, aren't they?"

"They don't think the way we do."

She let out a harsh chuckle. "No kidding. They're evil."

He said nothing, regarding her with an odd expression. He still hadn't explained what any of this had to do with her, and the tether of her patience was about to snap.

With great effort, she kept her voice even as she asked, "If they know when the relic was stolen, why don't they just go back in time to snag it beforehand?"

"They can't. Time won't allow it."

She stared at him. Her mind seemed unable to comprehend his words, and the only syllable she could muster was "huh?"

He smiled in the bland manner of a teacher tutoring a difficult student. She wanted to deck him again, but instead she dug her fingernails into her thighs. Maybe the pain would defuse her annoyance.

No such luck.

"Time travel has rules," he said. "You cannot go forward in time. You may go backward, but not to any point within your own lifetime. And above all, you cannot change the past."

She felt the tether fraying. "What, the Aten are so uptight they can't break their own rules? No wonder they lost the rel—"

"No." Wessick rose from the chair. "You misunderstand. These are not rules the Aten devised. These are the rules set forth by time itself. They are immutable."

She was silent for a moment, as she tried to wrap her metaphorical hands around the concept. Her physical hands she wrapped around the chair's arms.

Finally she said, "You talk about time as if it were a person."

He crossed behind the desk. As he perched on the corner to her left, his expression shifted into neutral again. "Perhaps it is a being, though not of any sort that we might understand. Then again, perhaps it's a force governing the universe. Call it fate or God or whatever you like."

Instinctively, she pushed her chair a few inches further from him. She asked, "Has anyone tried to change the past?"

"Of course. The Aten have tried for thousands of years. Nothing they do has any effect on the outcome of events." He slid closer, still perched on the desk's edge. "That is why they need you."

"I don't get it. Why do they think I can find the relic?"

"Because they made you for the task."

She blinked once, twice, as if clearing her vision might clear her thoughts. Nothing this man said to her made sense. Was he bamboozling her? Trying to brainwash her? Or was he just completely insane?

"Your mother," he said. "She was abducted shortly after learning she was pregnant with you."

Abducted. Once again, the word lodged in her brain. A chill shimmied down her spine.

"How do you know about that?" she asked.

"I know about it," he said, "because the Aten abducted her. They performed an in utero procedure to alter your DNA by inserting elements of ancient genetic material into your genome."

She couldn't speak. Couldn't breathe. Her muscles had turned to stone. His words sounded like a foreign language, though she fully understood their meaning.

It was impossible. He was lying.

Wessick knelt beside her chair. He settled a hand lightly on her arm. Without a hint of emotion, he said, "They made you for this task. Genetically speaking, you are both modern and ancient. You may be the only person in history who could find the relic."

Both modern and ancient. The words reverberated through her mind. *Made for the task. Time travel has rules.*

She swallowed against the lump in her throat. Her heart beat as fast as a hummingbird's. *Modern and ancient.*

The incarnation of another time.

12

HER THOUGHTS SEEMED TO HAVE GROUND TO A HALT. HER PULSE RACED, THE blood thundered behind her eardrums, and the breath froze in her lungs. The world felt like a three-dimensional movie playing out around her. A ringing started in her ears, faint at first, then growing louder. She felt herself swaying, though in the small part of her brain that still functioned she recognized that she sat stone-still.

Erin shut her eyes. She inhaled a breath, slowly, and exhaled at the same pace. As she repeated the process several more times, she willed her muscles to relax. Willed her heart rate to calm. A minute or two, maybe longer, passed before she felt ready to open her eyes. The swirling dizziness dwindled into stillness. The ringing silenced.

The grandfather clock tick-tick-ticked.

She opened her eyes.

Wessick still knelt beside her chair, one hand barely touching her arm. The gesture implied concern, but his expression remained impassive, as detached from his actions as she had felt from her emotions a moment ago.

"Why did they pick me?" she asked.

Pulling away from her, he perched on the desk's edge once more. "They performed the procedure on thirty-two fetuses. Most of the pregnancies ended in miscarriage. Of the ten subjects that survived, seven died in infancy. You are the only one left."

"Your math sucks. Ten minus seven is three. Where are the other two?"

"One was born with severe brain damage, and the other suffers from a variety of mental and physical illnesses. Both are useless to the Aten."

"Their guilt is touching. Why did they wait until now to come after me?" She couldn't believe she was about to say this but jeez, it seemed obvious. She had to know. "Why didn't they just kidnap me when I was a child and brainwash me to be their relic-hunting slave?"

Wessick cocked his head, probably the closest thing to an emotional response she'd get out of the man. He said, "They lost track of you. They chose women at random for the experiment and never bothered to collect personal information about them. The Aten are used to relying on their technology in such matters and, since they inserted tracking devices into each of the mothers, they felt confident in their ability to keep tabs on the subjects. When the babies were born, the Aten intended to insert tracking devices into them as well."

"I sense a 'but' coming."

He folded his hands atop his thigh. "Two weeks after your mother was abducted, her tracking beacon fell silent."

Erin bit the inside of her lip. She lost count of how many times her mother told her the story of the abduction. While driving home from a doctor's appointment, she experienced missing time—the journey took an hour longer than it should have. Erin's father, who had been out of town at the time, dismissed it as hormonal hysteria or some such nonsense. A couple weeks later, a mark on her mother's arm that had looked like a zit developed into an infection. Her mother lanced the wound herself, and removed from it a tiny foreign object. Of course, everyone told her it was nothing. The tiny object went into the trash and life moved on.

A month later, her parents moved out of state.

"It's taken many years," Wessick said, "to find you. And now that we have, it falls to me to set you on the path to your destiny."

"I don't believe in destiny."

"Soon you will." He gazed across the room, out the windows. "You will have no choice but to believe."

"The fact that I'm the only one of their guinea pigs who survived doesn't make me destined for anything. It makes them evil, and me lucky."

"It makes you the *satseshat*, the savior spoken of in texts written thousands of years before you were born. You can find the relic. You must find it."

"Maybe it shouldn't be found."

"If you don't find it—"

"All sorts of badness will ensue. I've heard the spiel." Erin got to her feet. "I have to use the bathroom."

Before Wessick could respond, she tromped out of the room.

Down the hall she raced at a brisk walk, past the staircase to the bathroom beside it. She slammed the door behind her and leaned back against it. Directly in front of her, a mirror reflected her face back at her. Shadows darkened the skin under her eyes. Red veins drew lines across the whites of her eyes. Despite her appearance, she felt strangely alert. The shock had worn off, replaced by a feeling she couldn't quite identify.

Evil aliens made her into the embodiment of time travel. They messed with her DNA, mindless of the consequences to her health. They screwed with her life. Threatened her loved ones. Murdered anyone who got in their way. Covered up the truth. Yet somehow, they expected her to sort out their own mistakes and set things right.

Was it right to find their relic for them? Damned if she knew.

Alex would have a few things to say about it. Maybe together they could figure out the right thing to do.

She pushed away from the door. Alex. Why hadn't he said anything? The doohickey in her ear let him both listen in on her conversation with Wessick and talk to her whenever he liked. He'd been none too shy about expressing his opinion earlier—and scaring the bejesus out of her. Yet during the entire conversation about the Aten's genetic experiments, he said nothing.

Not one word. Not even a grunt or sigh.

Erin bolted out the door.

SHE STUMBLED TO A HALT IN THE BEDROOM DOORWAY. IT TOOK A MOMENT FOR her mind to sort out the scene displayed before her.

Alex's computer lay on the bed. A headset microphone plugged into the computer dangled by its cord over the foot of the bed.

Torso twisted, legs bent and arms askew, Alex lay sprawled on the floor beside the bed.

A woman stood over him, straddling his body. Long black hair cascaded down her back and over her shoulders. In her right hand she grasped a knife.

Bending her knees, the woman leaned closer to Alex. She raised the knife as if preparing to strike.

Erin shouted.

The woman froze for a second. Then she leaped up, spun around, and with a hoarse cry launched herself at Erin. Black hair swirled around the woman's face. She struck Erin with the force of a linebacker, punching the wind out of Erin. The instant Erin's back hit the floor, the woman sprang off her and flipped her onto her stomach. The woman pinned Erin to the floor with one arm across her back. Erin's own torso pinned her arms to the floor. One hand was jammed into her stomach, the other crushed against her rib cage. She couldn't wriggle them free. She could barely breathe, with her face mashed into the floor.

Dark hair spilled around her head as the woman bent close to her ear.

In a voice roughened by rage, the woman whispered, "You live for one reason alone—because they wish it. When their patience runs dry, as it soon will, everyone you love will die one by one as you watch."

The woman drove her elbow into Erin's spine. Pain sliced through her. She winced, gritted her teeth.

"You have one purpose," the woman rasped. "Fulfill it. Or when the Aten have finished with the ones you love, they will wipe this world clean and start anew."

The woman jumped up. She slapped one booted foot on Erin's back to restrain her.

Her voice no longer raspy, but throaty and confident, the woman chuckled. She said, "And now your beloved shall die so that you may understand your place."

Erin tried to shout but the floor muzzled her. She tried to kick her legs but managed only to flail her feet.

The gun. She no longer felt it nestled against her spine under her waistband. It must've fallen out during the struggle.

What struggle? The woman trounced her without breaking a sweat. Samuel Wessick might want to take back his comment about her being a savior.

"Release her."

Erin recognized that voice. Not the woman's. The command issued from Samuel Wessick.

The woman said, "I am only doing what you should have done long ago. I am reminding her of the consequences she incurs by refusing to find the relic."

Footsteps approached from the direction of the stairs. The woman pressed her boot heel deeper into Erin's back, triggering a fresh wave of pain. Erin gasped. Luckily, nobody could hear it.

"Release her," Wessick said. "Now, Desheret."

The menace in his voice seemed to chill the air. After a slight hesitation, the woman withdrew her heel from Erin's spine. The sudden release of pressure shocked Erin almost as much as the initial impact that had knocked the breath out of her.

Footsteps clip-clopped swiftly down the corridor toward the stairs.

Erin pushed onto her side. Wessick crouched beside her, no emotion evident on his face. Not that she expected to find any there. The man's facade never cracked.

He offered her his hands, and she took them. As she struggled to her feet, he steadied and assisted her. Finally, she stood on her feet once more. Out the corner of her eye, she glimpsed a shape on the bedroom floor.

Alex.

She ran to him, dropping to her knees beside him. His eyes were closed. He lay limp, either unconscious or too dazed to react. Grasping his arm, she spoke his name.

Nothing.

She shook his arm and ordered, "Wake up, MacKay."

He groaned. His eyelids fluttered open. He mumbled, "Since when do you call me MacKay?"

Relief flooded through her with such force that she felt dizzy for a second. He was alive and awake.

She took a breath, slow and easy. "I thought it might jar you into consciousness."

He palpated the back of his head. "Please don't call me that anymore. It seems inappropriate coming from you."

Inappropriate?

Alex struggled to sit up, and Erin offered her arms to steady him. He leaned back against the bed's footboard, with his legs drawn up in front of him, one arm resting on each knee. His hair was mussed, his expression foggy.

She brushed her hand across his cheek. "Do you remember what happened?"

"I was attacked by a human tornado."

"Does anything hurt?"

The corner of his mouth twitched, as if he fought back a smirk. "My pride. That was a girl who ground me into the floor, right?"

"Yeah. But are you hurt? She had a knife and—"

He grabbed her hand. "I'm okay. My head's throbbing a little, but I'll live."

"Did you hit your head?"

He cleared his throat. "I may have sideswiped the bed post."

"You should lie down." She hopped up, tugging on his hand to encourage him to stand. He gave her a long-suffering look, sighed, and pushed up onto his feet. She told him, "On the bed. Now."

Alex glanced at Wessick, who lingered in the doorway. Then he returned his attention to Erin. A smile tugged at the corners of his mouth. "In my dreams, I said those words and we didn't have an audience."

Heat rose in her cheeks. Averting her gaze, she muttered, "Just get on the damn bed."

Without a word or a smirk, he complied. Erin gathered his electronic equipment and set it on the floor. As she picked up his laptop, she noticed the video streaming onscreen. It showed the feed from her brooch camera, with a flashing red circle and the letters REC indicating that Alex was recording the video. She snapped the laptop's lid shut.

By the time she set the laptop on the floor and straightened, Alex had settled onto the bed. She adjusted the pillow under his head. He watched her face with a look of mild interest and—she swore—a hint of self-satisfaction. When she'd finished with the pillow, he folded his hands over his belly.

"Thank you," he said. "I should get pummeled by crazed females more often."

She planted a hand on either side of him. Bending down close to him, she stared into his eyes. "I think you've gotten in enough trouble for one day. So just lie here and rest."

"Yes, ma'am."

She glanced over her shoulder at Wessick. He watched them with his usual expressionless expression.

Fixing her gaze on Alex again, she whispered, "Did you get a look at her face?"

"No. I told you she was a tornado."

Erin straightened. She hadn't gotten a look at the woman either. A human tornado, as Alex called her, attacked with such ferocity and cyclonic swiftness that her features blurred into her dark hair, which whipped around her face as she moved. Something about the hair gave Erin the impression it was fake. She couldn't put her finger on exactly what it was. But she felt certain the woman wore a wig.

The woman seemed shorter than Newman, her sole suspect in the mystery woman lineup. Erin couldn't rule out the brittle Brit, however, because her entire encounter with the mystery woman unfolded in chaos. And for most of the incident, Erin lay facedown kissing the wood floor.

Yeah, her pride was bruised too.

She took a step away from Alex. He grabbed her hand. She stopped to look back at him.

"If you leave my sight," he murmured, "I'm coming after you."

Combative words popped into her brain. She balled them up like mental paper and tossed them to the back of her mind. Alex had good reason to worry. First a crazy woman attacked both of them. Now she was preparing to convince Samuel Wessick to send her back in time so she could find a relic that supposedly held great power—a phrase that, as far as she could tell, never indicated anything good. And the folks who wanted this lovely object? They were evil bastards capable of destroying the world if they got tired of waiting for her to find the relic.

No pressure.

She patted Alex's hand. "I won't leave the room."

He let go. She sauntered across the room to Wessick.

The man leaned back against the doorjamb, arms folded across his chest.

"Tell me something," Erin said, "how do the Aten know for sure I'm their *satseshat*?"

Wessick averted his gaze to the window. "Rassul collected a DNA sample from you."

A memory played in Erin's mind. Rassul assaulting her. Slamming into her from behind. Cinching his arm around her neck. Punching her in the gut. Hurling her into a ditch. Later she discovered Rassul had stabbed her with something that left a small red puncture mark on her upper arm.

Through clenched teeth, she hissed, "You sent Rassul to assault me."

"No. He was meant to steal into your bedroom while you slept and extract a DNA sample, a blood sample, without your knowledge. But Rassul changed the plan."

"What did you expect? Rassul was a vicious animal." Erin paused to collect herself. Harping on the Rassul thing got her nowhere, because she already knew her enemies would stoop to any level to get what they wanted. She had to sweep the anger aside and move on to more pressing questions. "Why did the Aten mess with my DNA? What did they hope to gain by giving me ancient genes?"

"They did not give you ancient genes. They inserted ancient genetic material into your genome, not entire genes. In fact, I doubt any modern DNA test could detect the difference. The Aten's technology is so far beyond anything in our world that attempting to understand it is futile. We might as well try to comprehend the thought patterns of a virus."

"Viruses don't think." Erin glared at him. "You didn't answer my question."

"Time is relative to each individual," he said. "This is why we cannot change the past, because even the most ancient event may bear some relation to our own life."

"Right, you might cause a paradox. If you kill your own grandfather then you don't exist even though you do exist. That sort of thing."

"Yes." He exhaled a long breath. "Only someone native to a certain timeline can affect that timeline. The Aten have tried sending agents back in time, but their efforts achieve no results. They've tried recruiting individuals native to the timeline in question, with little success. They hoped that imbuing you with ancient genetic material would grant you the ability to straddle two timelines."

"Sounds like a long shot to me."

"They were desperate." He took a step toward her. Gazing down at her, his dark eyes locked on hers, he said, "You are their penultimate strategy."

"Penultimate, as in next to last?" Despite the sinking sensation in her gut, and despite feeling reasonably certain she knew the answer, she had to ask. "What's their ultimate strategy?"

"Annihilation."

He spoke the word matter-of-factly, yet it struck her with the force of a meteorite impact.

Annihilation.

Obliterate every living thing, from animals down to bacteria.

Wessick's words came back to her now. He used that phrase to describe what the Aten threatened to do if the keeper of the relic refused to disclose the relic's location to them. No wonder the guy took off for parts unknown.

Push the fear aside. Focus on the task at hand. Don't think about what kind of weapon might generate enough power to wipe clean an entire planet.

She started to turn her head.

Don't look at Alex. If she did, she might lose any composure she clung to now.

Focusing on Wessick, she said, "Are you suggesting I should go back in time to look for the relic?"

"Yes."

She intended to keep certain facts to herself, such as the fact that she wanted him to send her back in time so that she could contact the priests of Amun-Ra. At this moment, she wanted something else from Wessick too. And she needed him to believe she was doing him a favor, or else he might never give her the other thing she wanted.

"I'll do it," she said, "on one condition. I want you to fix Alex."

Wessick furrowed his brow. "Fix him?"

"Get one of your orbs to heal him, like it healed me."

"I don't need fixing," Alex said.

Erin kept her gaze locked on Wessick as she said, "Fix him. That's the deal."

Wessick looked at Alex, then at Erin. He said, "I'll need a few moments to arrange it."

"Fine."

With a curt nod, Wessick spun on his heels and exited the bedroom. Erin lingered in the doorway until his footsteps retreated down the stairs, dwindling into silence.

She approached the bed and sat on the edge of the mattress beside Alex.

He raised onto his elbows. "I don't need fixing."

She took his face in her hands and kissed him. "Shut up and rest."

He held still for a moment, eyeing her with a narrowed gaze. Then, letting out a sharp sigh, he flopped back onto the pillow.

THE CEILING WAS PAINTED OFF-WHITE, WITH A SMOOTH FINISH INSTEAD OF the popcorn balls often used on ceilings. Too bad. He would've preferred counting popcorn balls to lying here flat on his back, accomplishing absolutely nothing.

Alex sighed again. He drummed his fingers on his abdomen.

Erin laid her hands on his, forcing him to stop. She said, "Relax."

He grunted. She might as well have asked him to stop his heart from beating. Getting thrashed by a woman, albeit an insane one, left him with a feeling of general uselessness. If he couldn't protect Erin from a girl, what good was he?

He was the sidekick, the one who got beat up every five minutes, the one who needed the hero to save him. Or in this case, the heroine.

He looked at Erin. If no one could change the past, then how had the priests of Amun-Ra known about the *satseshat*? Wessick, or one of his minions, might've time-traveled back to ancient Egypt and inadvertently mentioned the Aten's genetic experiments. If so, wouldn't that constitute altering the past?

His head throbbed. He closed his eyes and tried to will the pain away. Thinking about this time travel nonsense served no purpose other than to worsen his headache. He needed to follow Erin's advice and relax.

Like hell.

He opened his eyes. Erin was staring at him. She squeezed his hands.

In the corridor beyond the doorway, a light flashed.

Alex stiffened. He squinted at the gloom beyond the doorway.

A ball of bluish-white light floated through the doorway.

Erin clamped her hands tighter around his.

The orb floated toward the bed, halting an arm's length away. It bobbed up and down ever so slightly, as if waiting for something.

"I think it wants you to move," Alex said.

Fixated on the orb, she neither moved nor spoke.

He pulled his hands out from under hers and prodded her leg. "Move. You want this thing to fix me, don't you?"

Switching her gaze to him, she nibbled at her upper lip.

He prodded her thigh once again.

She hopped off the bed, backing away a few yards.

The orb floated over the bed. It stopped directly over his chest.

He closed his eyes. He had a feeling he didn't want to see what was about to happen.

Nothing happened.

Cautiously, he opened one eye, then the other. The orb hovered three feet above him. Its mottled interior writhed.

In slow motion it descended. Six inches from his chest, the orb stopped.

White light engulfed him. He squeezed his eyes shut against the brilliance, but it penetrated his eyelids. All of a sudden this seemed like anything but a good idea. The Aten harbored no love for him. What if they took this opportunity to incinerate him?

He tried to sit up. His muscles refused to move. He tried to call out to Erin. No sound, not even a squeak, issued from him.

Heat blanketed him. Like belly-flopping into a hot spring. Not exactly painful, but not exactly benign either. This had been a horrible idea, the worst idea in the history of human thought. If he lived, he'd—

The heat penetrated his flesh, his muscles, his bones. It felt like everything inside him was softening.

The light vanished. The heat dissipated.

He felt…relaxed.

And for some reason that realization made him tense again.

The mattress jiggled. He felt a weight pressed against his hip, then a familiar pair of hands grasped his.

He wheeled his eyes to open, and his eyelids peeled apart. Erin stared at him, eyes wide, face pale.

"I'm fine," he said, and noticed his voice sounded stronger than before. He hadn't realized how pathetic he sounded just a few minutes earlier. "You can stop worrying. I'm fixed."

She looked unconvinced.

He sat up, pushed her off the bed, swung his legs over the edge, and jumped to his feet. Unbuttoning his shirt, he tore off the bandage that had covered his burn. The skin beneath the bandage looked normal.

"See," he told her, pointing at the healed skin. "All better."

She smiled. The expression illuminated her face from within.

His heart skipped. He reached out to pull her into his arms.

Samuel Wessick clomped into the room. He halted in the doorway, one hand in his pants pocket, the other dangling at his side.

Alex dropped his arms to his sides. He truly disliked that man.

Wessick glanced at Alex's partially unbuttoned shirt. Arching an eyebrow, he said, "I see the healing has been accomplished."

Erin faced Wessick. "Thank you."

She thanked him? Alex clenched his teeth. The orb that attacked him in Texas had probably executed orders that came directly from Wessick. The man deserved no thanks. Besides, Wessick healed Alex because he thought he needed to do Erin a favor before he could convince her to do what he wanted. Wessick had no idea Erin would've agreed to the time travel anyway.

Maybe Erin was being polite. She owed Wessick no gratitude.

"It's time," Wessick said.

"I know," Erin replied. "I'm ready."

Alex strode forward. He positioned himself between Erin and Wessick, though he stood off-center of them so that she could still see Wessick. She would need to lean sideways to peek around Alex's shoulder, but technically she could still see Wessick.

Technically was all she'd get.

"Let's go then," Alex said.

"I'm afraid," Wessick said, "you won't be making this journey, Dr. MacKay."

Alex took a step closer to Wessick. "Oh yes I will."

Wessick pulled his hand out of his pocket and swung it toward Alex's left forearm.

Alex felt the prick just as he swung his right arm up to grab Wessick's hand. Too late, he closed his fingers around the other man's wrist.

Darkness swallowed him.

13

ALEX CRUMPLED. WESSICK TOOK HOLD OF ALEX UNDER HIS ARMS AND EASED him onto the floor, laying him flat on his back. Alex's eyes were closed, his lips parted, his entire body slack.

Erin hopped over Alex to seize Wessick's lapels. She shook him hard. "What did you do to Alex?"

"I drugged him."

He lifted his right hand, unfurling his fingers to reveal the object clasped in his fist. It was an autoinjector, like the ones used by people with severe allergies to bee stings. Stab the injector into flesh and a needle sprang out to inject the medicine.

She glanced down at Alex. Her heart skipped with a painful thud. Her throat constricted. Swallowing against the tightness, she glared at Wessick and shook him harder. "If you hurt him, I will kill you myself."

"He won't be harmed. The drug will render him unconscious for several hours."

"I need his help."

Wessick shook his head as that patronizing smile tugged at his lips. "I disagree. Despite your many wonderful talents, you consistently underestimate yourself."

"You don't know me." She let go of him and stepped back a few feet. "Stop acting like you do."

"As you wish." He reached behind his back, under his jacket. When he withdrew his hand, he held in it her Smith & Wesson 9mm. Holding it by the barrel, with the muzzle aimed at the floor, he offered its grip to her. "If you want to kill me, you might need this."

She'd lost the weapon when the mystery woman attacked her. Wessick could've held onto it, leaving her unarmed. Instead he returned it to her, most likely as a gesture intended to foster her trust. Earning her trust would require a lot more effort than that.

Accepting the gun, she muttered, "Thanks."

She popped out the gun's clip. A full complement of bullets filled it. She snapped the clip back into place.

"Your lack of trust dismays me," Wessick said.

"Are you kidding me?" She aimed the gun at his chest. "You drugged Alex. You work for the Aten. You bugged this entire house. Why on earth should I trust you?"

He remained silent, and avoided glancing at the firearm zeroed in on his heart.

Erin tucked the gun under her waistband, flush with her spine. She wished she had a holster for the gun, but when her parents gave it to her they assumed she would carry it in her purse for self-protection. Sometimes, though, carrying her purse proved too cumbersome.

Did the laws of time travel allow for carry-on baggage?

Wessick moved into the doorway. "We must go now."

"What do you mean go?"

"Back to Akhenaten's time." The barest hint of annoyance colored his voice. "We have no time to waste."

"Actually, we have lots of time, don't we?" She folded her arms over her chest. "We are traveling through time after all."

He sighed heavily.

Erin met his gaze head-on. "Besides, I'm exhausted. It's been a long day. I need to get some rest in the present before I tackle the past."

He stomped toward her, halting inches away. As he stared down at her with that eerie look devoid of all feeling, he said, "You can sleep once we reach our destination. But we will go *now*."

A pit of ice congealed in her gut. This man would do whatever it took to achieve his goal, though she suspected his goal might not match the Aten's. What was his agenda? His thought processes seemed as alien to her as those of the Aten.

If she wanted his help getting back to the fourteenth century BC, then she had to do what he wanted.

"Okay," she said.

Wessick turned toward the door.

She slapped his arm. Hard.

He half turned toward her, raising both eyebrows.

"We are not leaving Alex like this," she said, pointing at the unconscious man on the floor. "Help me get him on the bed."

Wessick nodded.

Moving a dead weight, especially a large one, proved harder and more awkward than she expected. Even with Wessick's help, maneuvering Alex onto the bed involved a lot of gasping and grunting, a few sotto voce curses from Erin, and possibly several strained muscles for each of them. After several minutes, however, they completed their task. Alex reclined on the bed again, this time without his consent. His hair was mussed and his shirt had pulled out of his waistband, but otherwise he looked unharmed.

He was okay. She hoped.

Unless Wessick lied about what he gave Alex.

She pressed two fingers into the soft flesh of his neck. His pulse thumped rhythmically against her fingers. Well, he was alive anyway.

Alex's leather bag lay on the floor near her feet, leaning against the bedside table. Kneeling, she opened the bag's main compartment and dug out the tablet computer.

"Now we leave," Wessick said.

Erin rose, the tablet cradled in her hands. She turned to face Wessick. "I'm ready."

He looked at the tablet. "You can't take that with you."

She pursed her lips.

"It's an anachronism," he said. "Leave it here."

"You said no one can change the past. So what difference does it make if I bring along my own little anachronism?"

"If anyone else wanted to bring such a device into the past," he said, "I might be willing to allow it. But you may be the one person in all of history who can rewrite the past."

He snatched the tablet from her hands and tossed it onto the bed. It landed a few inches from Alex's elbow.

Wessick said, "We can't risk it."

"In other words, I'm only allowed to change the past when it suits you and your masters. " She clenched her fists at her sides. "If you guys believe I can change the past, then why did you make me waste all this time searching for the relic in the present? When you could've sent me back to Akhenaten's time weeks ago?"

"We do not take time travel lightly. And we hoped your unique genetic makeup might give you singular insight to help you find the relic. The advantage proved insufficient."

"So you figured threatening my family might help. Great plan, Einstein."

A muscle in his jaw twitched. His voice stayed as smooth as cream, and just as bland. "If you're through testing my patience, the time for our departure has arrived."

"What about your girlfriend?" Erin asked. "Is the homicidal darling joining us?"

"My relationship with her is not what you imply."

"Don't really care what it is. All I want to know is, will she be tagging along?"

"No. Desheret is gone."

Erin narrowed her gaze on him. "Are you sure?"

"I escorted her out of the manor myself when I retired downstairs to make the preparations for our journey."

"You mean when you prepared your little sedative cocktail."

He closed his fingers around her arm, just above the elbow. His grasp was firm, though not painful, and it told her everything she needed to know. She had to go with him. Right this minute. Without the map, without Alex's translation of the text, without…

She glanced at Alex.

Wessick pulled her away from the bed. Like his grip, the pressure he applied to urge her forward was gentle yet resolute. No longer would he give her a choice or wait for her to succumb to his wishes. He would make her submit, make her go with him.

Into the past.

As he ushered her out the door and into the passageway, she stole one last glimpse at Alex. He'd told her she held the power. The Aten needed her to find the relic. But if she believed Wessick, the Aten held more power than any human being could hope to acquire.

And she was about to step into their world.

Alone.

ERRANDO WARNER SHIFTED HIS POSITION ON THE MAKESHIFT BENCH, A HALF-rotted fallen tree that might or might not withstand his weight for an extended period. Unfortunately, he'd sat down squarely on a large knot in the trunk. In the darkness, he hadn't noticed the knot. It felt like sitting on a rock.

His night vision goggles were tucked inside his pack, and his pack was strapped to his shoulders with its bulk hanging down his back. Another strap around his waist further secured the pack. He disliked night vision technology, because it robbed him of his natural night vision. Granted, the artificial version offered greater definition. Yet reliance on technology often proved dangerous, even deadly. He preferred to rely on his own senses. The night vision goggles he saved for emergencies. At the moment, however, he wished he'd thought to take out the goggles before he wound up seated on this tree.

A hairy hominid towered before him, the one Erin called Jerry.

Warner spied other shapes moving among the trees behind Jerry. He couldn't distinguish the shapes, though, which meant he had no idea how many creatures circled him.

A few hours earlier, Alex called Warner to ask him to keep an eye on Revenant House from outside. Although Alex sounded uneasy, Warner refrained from questioning the younger man about his state of mind. Events of late seemed sufficient explanation. But since Alex worried more about Erin's safety than his own, Warner knew Alex's request must have its source in a threat to Erin.

Warner agreed without hesitation. And so, shortly before sunset, he began his vigil in the woods. Only Erin's car occupied the driveway. Two vehicles arrived during the day, one belonging to Anna Newman and the other belonging to Alex. Newman left shortly after arriving, and since then all seemed quiet on the estate.

Until Jerry appeared.

Warner considered himself adept at covert maneuvers, in any conditions. Rarely did anyone get the drop on him. Although some might call his confidence arrogance, he cared little for what others thought. His track record spoke for itself. Yet when it came to the hairy hominids, his skills and experience proved woefully inadequate. The creatures were not merely skilled at stealth. They embodied it.

No one had taught Warner humility, until he met a hairy hominid.

Jerry grunted.

Warner did not move, did not speak. He kept his gaze on the ground. Despite ten minutes of trying, he had yet to puzzle out why Jerry detained him. A hairy hominid had snuck up behind him, seized him by the straps of his backpack, and hurled him onto the ground in front of the fallen tree. The situation improved somewhat thereafter, as the hominid no longer threatened to beat him with a large, jagged rock.

Over the years, Warner gained a rudimentary understanding of the hairy hominid language. Abstract human concepts still confused the creatures, however, and the logic of the hairy hominids equally baffled humans. Erin seemed to have gotten the impression he was fluent in the hominid language. He saw no reason to disabuse her of that notion.

In the staccato language of the hominids, Warner asked, "How have I angered you?"

The hominid stomped his foot. "Daughter of Setesh. Here."

Each time Warner asked for an explanation, Jerry responded with the same phrases.

Since first encountering the culture of the hairy hominids, Warner learned much about ancient Egyptian mythology, because it played a central role in the beliefs of the hairy hominids and their pseudo-gods, the Planners. Nevertheless, Warner realized his knowledge of the ancient culture fell short of the expert level. Setesh, aka Seth, served as the god of chaos and destruction, the personification of the deadly Western Desert. But Warner knew of no daughter of Seth in the Egyptian pantheon.

Alex knew about these things. Warner should consult him.

He doubted Jerry would allow him a phone call.

Perhaps the situation called for a different approach.

In the hominid language, he said, "Daughter of Setesh?"

Jerry made a rumbling noise deep in his throat. "Danger. Aset."

Warner stiffened. Aset must refer to Erin, since the last time he encountered Jerry the hominid had referred to her as Aset, the Egyptian goddess also known as Isis. If Erin was in danger, he needed more information about the threat.

He tried to ask for it, phrasing his request as precisely as he could given his less-than-fluent grasp of the awkward language of the hairy hominids.

"Danger," Jerry repeated. "Aset. Daughter of Setesh. Here."

The hominid stomped his foot, punctuating the movement with a grunt.

Warner groaned softly. Why had it taken him so long to understand? Jerry meant that a dangerous woman had arrived on the estate and that she posed a threat to Erin. The woman, like the god Setesh, represented evil and chaos, at least in Jerry's mind. A woman matching that description had made her presence known once before—when Erin witnessed the woman committing a murder.

Warner told Jerry, "I will help Aset."

The hominid tilted his head down, regarding Warner from beneath a heavy brow.

Warner averted his gaze.

Jerry threw his head back and let out an ear-splitting whoop. Other voices answered from the woods behind Jerry.

The hominid turned and lumbered off into the trees. Within seconds, he merged with the night.

Warner leaped off the fallen tree. He crept, with swift but silent steps, in the direction of the manor. At the edge of the rear lawn, he paused to reconnoiter. A light glowed upstairs, inside Erin's bedroom. On the ground floor, a single light burned within the confines of Samuel Wessick's study. The bay window of the study looked out on the rear lawn. He would make his way around the back of the house to the bay window of the study.

A figure ducked around the far end of the house. The newcomer approached the bay window. Dark clothing masked the newcomer's figure, but the glow from inside frosted the woman's face with pale, golden light. Her long, dark hair spilled down her back as she lifted her chin to peer over the window ledge.

The daughter of Setesh? No one else would undertake such a brazen, and foolish, attempt at spying. The murderess had already demonstrated her lack of both conscience and shame.

Warner dropped onto his belly to slither across the open expanse of lawn between the edge of the woods and the nearest corner of the house. Once there, he rose to a crouch.

The woman lingered at the bay window. Her attention was glued on the scene inside the study.

Sneaking up on her would require little stealth.

He slid his Glock 9mm out of its shoulder holster. Rising to his full height, he kept his back against the house and followed its contours toward the woman's position. The house was U-shaped, with a wing protruding from each end. He followed the shape of the east wing, then jogged south along the wall of the main house until he reached the west wing. There, he angled left again to follow the wall. At the corner, he stopped. He leaned forward just enough to peek around the corner with one eye.

The woman was fifteen feet away. She had risen onto her tiptoes, so intent on watching events inside the study that she ignored all else around her.

Perfect.

He rushed at the woman. She grunted as he slammed his full weight into her, knocking her to the ground. He landed on top of her. Pinned to the ground facedown, she managed to twist her head sideways to glare at him with one eye.

"Release me," she hissed, "or I will scream."

He caressed her cheek with the Glock 's barrel. "No, you won't."

She wriggled under his weight.

"What do you want with Erin?" Warner asked.

In a voice thick with rage, she said, "To hug her and wish her well."

She shut her eyes and exhaled slowly. The anger melted from her features, replaced by an expression of calm certainty.

Certainty of what? The young woman looked far too pleased with herself, given her current predicament.

Warner tapped the Glock's barrel against her cheek. "Open your eyes."

She complied. Her lips curved into a smirk.

"Actions have consequences," she said, her voice as calm as her expression. "And you are about to meet the consequences of yours."

Warner squinted down at her. "Who are you?"

She chuckled, the sound soft and menacing.

To his left, a light flashed. Warner turned his head a few millimeters, enough to glimpse the ball of glowing light that raced across the lawn toward him.

He hooked his free arm around the woman's waist.

The orb sped toward them.

He sprang to his feet, lifting the woman with him. Before she could wriggle free, he shifted his arm to pin her arms at her sides.

She stopped fighting.

As he raised the gun to her temple, he spun them both toward the approaching orb.

"You summoned it," he said. "Tell it to stop."

She chuckled.

The orb halted ten feet from them. It hovered at eye level, its interior shimmering, its bright rim muting into a soft glow.

Warner stared at the orb.

It shot forward, straight at his head.

He ducked. The orb whizzed past his right ear.

The change in position loosened his grip on the woman. She rammed an elbow backward into his gut. Warner gritted his teeth against the pain and struggled to regain his hold on her. She twisted her head around and sank her teeth into his jaw.

Pain seared his face. He slapped his palm hand on her face and shoved.

Free at last, she stumbled backward a few steps. Then she turned and ran.

The orb rocketed out from behind him. It paused for half a second, an arm's length away and level with his eyes. A sensation of static electricity raised the hairs across his torso and head.

He spun around and, for the first time in his life, fled from an enemy.

Erin SQUINTED AT THE DARKNESS BEYOND THE BAY WINDOW. A SECOND AGO, she thought she saw movement outside. It must've been her imagination.

Wessick shut the study door. Erin stood behind the sofa, kitty-corner to the desk. Wessick strode past her to circle behind the desk. She trailed in his wake, stopping alongside him.

A couple feet away from her, he knelt in front of a drawer. It was the same drawer she'd threatened to bash open with the floor lamp.

"Tell me," she said, "does the name Broderick Covington mean anything to you?"

He stiffened, for the space of a heartbeat. "Why should it?"

"How about Ridley Covington?"

The corner of his mouth twitched. He narrowed his eyes, just a hair, enough to tighten the lines that I fanned out from his eyes.

"Ring any bells?" Erin asked.

From his pocket, Wessick produced a key. He unlocked the drawer, sliding it open.

The drawer looked, from the outside, like a file drawer. She expected to see an array of hanging folders inside the space. Instead, she saw wire brackets stacked three levels deep. Each level held six rows of foam-lined metal cradles inside of which nestled drawstring bags fashioned from a metallic fabric. Bulges in the bags' fabric suggested they each contained a small, round object.

Wessick plucked one bag from the drawer. Cupping the bag in his palm, he shut and locked the drawer before turning to Erin.

"The passage will do nicely," he said.

"You mean the hallway? It'll do for what?"

"Patience, my dear."

"I'm not your dear," she said. "And I don't like being kept in the dark."

He smiled. Although his lips remained firmly sealed, the expression altered his entire face. He looked somehow younger, and definitely more attractive.

In one step he reached her, took her hand in his, and said, "You are about to step into the light."

His hand was warm and muscular, his skin slightly rough. Before she could yank her hand away, he tightened his grip and led her out the door and into the passage.

They stopped midway between the study and library doors.

Wessick released her hand. He opened the drawstring bag that he cupped in his other hand. With his thumb and two fingers, he reached into the bag and extracted a small object. He held it between his thumb and forefinger, rotating his hand to give her a better view of the object.

It was an orb. A couple inches in diameter, the orb looked like the tiny twin of the glowing spheres that had both terrorized and healed her—and healed Alex upstairs.

The orb's interior writhed as if liquid flowed inside it. Tendrils of blue and white swirled, merged, and split apart again to repeat a never-ending cycle. Unlike the larger orbs, this one sported no brilliant white rim. The exterior layer of this orb resembled clear crystal, smooth on the surface but faceted underneath. The light from the study refracted into faint rainbows in the orb's outer layer. It was…beautiful.

"Open your hand," he said.

She lifted her hand, flipping it palm up as she flattened out her fingers.

He set the orb in the center of her palm.

The orb felt warm, maybe a few degrees warmer than body temperature. She lifted her other hand and touched her index finger to the orb's surface. It felt oddly soft, and it dimpled under the pressure of her fingertip.

"We call them *akhet* balls," Wessick said.

She glanced up at him. "*Akhet*? As in the Egyptian word for horizon?"

"Precisely." He plucked the orb from her palm, once again grasping it between his thumb and forefinger. "This is how we tap into the wormhole created by the time machine."

She made a face. "That itty-bitty thing will send us back in time?"

"This tiny sphere holds within it more energy than the combined yield of every nuclear weapon ever manufactured."

Erin stared at the *akhet* ball. A shiver coursed through her. Maybe the orb wasn't so beautiful after all.

"How does it work?" she asked.

"Mind over matter."

Wessick dropped the orb into his palm, wrapping his fingers around it. He closed his eyes.

Seconds elapsed. Tick, tick, tick.

Erin said, "Are you—"

He opened his eyes and tossed the orb down the passageway.

It sailed through the air for fifteen feet, arcing upward. Then, at the instant its trajectory angled downward, the orb froze in midair.

Light exploded.

Erin winced, flinging up an arm to shield her eyes.

When she lowered her arm, the breath caught in her throat. Her heart hammered. She gaped at the sight before her, unable to move or speak. She'd seen this phenomenon before, yet this time was different.

In the middle of the passage, suspended maybe a foot off the floor, hung a portal to another time and place. Through the spherical window, she looked out on a desert landscape.

"We must enter outside the city," Wessick said. "It's the only way to be certain no one will see how we arrive."

She forced herself to breathe. And blink. And form thoughts.

When she spoke, her voice sounded depressingly wispy even to her own ears. "What city?"

Wessick grasped her shoulders. He looked into her eyes, waiting until she focused on him in return. When she did, he said, "The city of Akhetaten. Capital of ancient Egypt during the reign of Akhenaten."

"Oh." She found herself tilting a little bit, like a sapling in the wind. Each time she listed to the right, she glimpsed the portal behind Wessick. "I don't know ancient Egyptian. The language, I mean."

"I think you'll find language isn't as much of a barrier as you expect."

Erin took a deep breath and shook off the haze, steadying herself. Alex knew ancient Egyptian, at least the written variety as modern scholars understood it. He stood a better chance of understanding the ancient, spoken language than she did. The pronunciation of the real language might prove different than what modern scholars thought it sounded like, but she didn't even know enough to recognize the difference.

Shrugging off Wessick's hands, she took a step back from him. "You better not be leading me into a trap."

"I hope one day you'll see that I'm not who you think I am."

"I already don't know who you are." She glanced down at her attire. "What about our clothes? We don't look very ancient Egyptian."

In lieu of a response, he turned and stepped through the portal.

He walked several paces beyond the portal, halted, and turned to wait for her.

She gnawed the inside of her cheek. Travel back in time. Meet the priests of Amun-Ra. Find out what they knew about the relic. It sounded easy. But now, standing in front of the actual portal to an actual ancient world, the whole plan felt like bullshit.

Alex lay upstairs, unconscious. Once he woke up, he'd have no way of knowing where she went or how to get there himself. She had no choice.

Oh, she really hated it when that happened.

Erin took another deep breath, and stepped through the portal.

14

Desheret stole into the manor through the cellar door. She peeked around the corner into the east passage at the instant that Samuel entered the portal.

Erin Turner stood near the other end of the passage facing the portal. Desheret knew fate had given her this chance to eliminate her nemesis, in this moment when every one of Erin's protectors had been removed from the equation. Desheret clutched the knife in her fist. Samuel once convinced her they needed Erin to find the relic. Now she realized he simply wanted to protect his precious Erin.

In her mind, Desheret played the possible scenarios for accomplishing her mission. She paused on one scenario in particular. Ah yes, that one would do nicely.

At the end of the passage, Erin stepped into the portal. The window to another world telescoped shut.

Desheret stormed down the passageway. At the door to Samuel's study, she halted. The study was empty. She glanced rightward into the library, which also stood empty.

No. Desheret slammed her boot into the wall. Why had she taken so long to examine the options? Why had she bothered to think about it at all, losing her chance to eliminate Erin Turner?

Why? Because Samuel taught her to think through every situation. He excoriated her for rushing to action. For so long had she listened to his lectures that she found herself obeying his decrees even now.

No more. The next time fate offered her a chance to dispatch one of her enemies, she would seize it. No analysis. No thought. Pure instinct must guide her from this point forward.

She strode into the study, straight to the drawer where Samuel kept the *akhet* balls. The drawer was locked, of course.

An orb sailed through the bay window, crossing the study to her. An arm's length away from her, the orb came to a halt.

She planted her hands on her hips. "Is the stranger dead?"

The answer emerged as an alien thought in her mind. *He is irrelevant. We will not waste energy on destroying him.*

Desheret scowled. "I wished him dead. You owe me this favor."

We owe you nothing. You serve us.

A memory unreeled in her mind. The muscular man clad in camouflage, his head sheathed in a knit cap of the same colors, his face painted black and green to match. He knocked her down, threatened her with his weapon, held her hostage. No one humiliated her in such a manner. No one.

She wished him dead. After her years of service to the Aten, they owed her some compensation for the suffering she endured in their name.

We owe you nothing, they repeated, speaking through their luminous emissary. *Follow them.*

"I cannot." Desheret tugged on the handle of the locked drawer. "I require an *akhet* ball to do so, and Samuel has locked them all away."

The orb shimmered and pulsed. She felt a rush of electricity in the air.

The drawer popped open.

The other has failed in his mission. You must complete it.

Desheret tilted her head to one side, her scowl melting away. "Do you mean—"

By whatever means necessary, force Erin Turner to find the relic. Then kill her.

She stifled a smile. "As you wish."

The orb vanished. In its wake, tiny sparks swirled and dissipated.

Desheret let the smile spread her lips wide. She snatched a bag from the drawer. Oh yes, she would do exactly as they wished.

Kicking the drawer shut with the toe of her boot, she hurried into the passage. It seemed fitting that she should depart from the same location as Samuel and his beloved Erin. Desheret positioned herself in the spot where she estimated Erin had stood moments earlier. She opened the bag, dumped out the *akhet* ball, and initialized it with her thoughts.

She tossed the ball down the passage. The portal opened in a brilliant flash.

Erin Turner crossed into a foreign world where she neither knew the language nor properly understood the culture. The scales of fortune now tipped in Desheret's favor, for the world of the past was not foreign to her. Besides, Samuel would insist that Erin follow his ridiculous rules, and like a good girl, she would oblige. Desheret followed no one's rules. Nothing would stop her now.

Desheret marched into the portal.

THE DINING ROOM LAY AT THE WEST END OF THE HOUSE. THE DINING ROOM window, as it turned out, offered a clear view straight down the main passageway toward the west end of the house.

Warner arrived at the dining room window in time to see the woman exit the study. Lifting a pair of small binoculars to his eyes, he focused in on the woman.

She tossed an object down the passage. A blast of light blinded him. He winced, lowering the binoculars for a second or two. When he raised the binoculars again, the woman was gone. The flash of light must've been connected to her departure. He suspected he knew how.

A portal.

Erin told him about the portal she saw Wessick's man use to escape her. The woman must've used such a portal as well. But where did she go?

And where was Erin?

Given the time of night, perhaps Erin had gone to bed. Given the events of the day, however, he doubted Erin wanted to sleep. Besides, Alex's car was still parked out front.

Warner brought out his cell phone, turned it on, and dialed Alex's number. It rang six times before switching to voicemail. Warner disconnected the call.

Something was wrong. Very wrong.

He tried to open the window. Locked.

Forgoing stealth, Warner tramped around the house to the front door. He twisted the knob. Locked.

Although he'd learned a few things about lock-picking over the years, picking a lock required tools—which he did not have. Oddly, he never considered bringing a lock-picking kit along with him on wilderness surveillance missions.

The other doors and windows would likely be locked as well.

Warner pulled out his Glock and fired a shot at the door lock. It shattered. Kicking the door open, he surged through the doorway into the foyer.

A few minutes later, he finished searching the first floor. No sign of life. He trotted up the stairs, angling left toward Erin's bedroom. The door hung open. A light glowed inside the room. He peered through the doorway.

Alex sprawled on the bed, his eyes shut.

Warner eased through the doorway, glancing left and right. No one else was in the room. He checked the closet and the attached bathroom. No one there either.

Approaching the bed, Warner gazed down at Alex, who appeared to be sleeping. Appearances often deceived, however, a fact Warner always kept in mind.

He grasped Alex's shoulder and shook. No response. Setting the Glock on the bedside table, Warner took hold of both of Alex's shoulders and shook hard. Nothing. Warner checked for a pulse, finding it slow but steady. The evidence suggested one conclusion.

Something had rendered Alex unconscious, most likely a blow to the head or the forced administration of a sedative.

Warner let out a heavy sigh. He could do little else for the moment, save wait for Alex to awaken on his own.

On the other side of the bed, a chair sat near the window. Warner headed for the chair. He might as well make himself comfortable. This could turn into a long night.

Akhetaten, Egypt
Circa 1335 BC

THE SUN BLINDED HER. ERIN RAISED A HAND TO SHIELD HER EYES. IN FRONT OF her, the desert stretched away from her toward the horizon. A breeze tickled her skin and billowed her hair away from her face. A hawk circled overhead, checking out the newcomers.

Wessick was nowhere in sight. He had stepped out of view just as she entered the portal.

She felt nothing when she stepped through, no disorientation or tingling or anything. Walking through a wormhole into the past ought to result in some physical effects, she thought. Yet it felt no different than walking through a doorway into another room.

How odd.

Erin turned slowly in the opposite direction. The portal was gone. Wessick stood a dozen feet past where the portal had been, facing away from her. Beyond him, no more than fifty feet away, a wall of rock filled her view. The steep ridge stretched out to the left and the right, approximately north to south as far as she could determine from the sun's angle. Did the sun move along the same path thousands of years ago?

Not thousands of years ago. Right now. In the present. The past had become her present. Christ, she'd go insane trying to sort out the logic of time travel in her head.

She bent her head back to search for the ridge's summit. More than a hundred feet above her head, the cliff reached its apex.

A flutter of movement drew her attention away from the cliffs, back down to ground level. She spotted Wessick meandering away from her in the direction of the cliffs. After a few paces, he paused to look back at her.

"This way," he said.

Erin scanned the desert around her. In the opposite direction from the cliffs, she spotted what looked like a town, most likely Akhetaten. It looked far away.

With nowhere else to go, and no other guide to follow, she trailed after Wessick.

He led her into a narrow crevasse. When she bent her head back, she glimpsed a sliver of sky high overhead. The crevasse provided just enough breadth that she could, if she wanted to, spread her arms out to the sides and touch the cliff with the tips of each middle finger. Wessick slowed his pace to let her catch up to him and then sped up, forcing her to trot to keep pace with him, though his longer legs carried him onward at a brisk walk.

After what felt like an eternity, but probably amounted to less than a minute, he slowed down again. She leaned sideways to peek around his shoulder. A short distance ahead, the crevasse dead-ended.

Wessick halted so abruptly that she nearly bumped into him. The tip of her nose brushed against his back.

He strode forward three steps, veered left, and disappeared into the crevasse wall.

Erin stood there for a moment, her mind blank.

Wessick reemerged, waved for her to follow him, and vanished again.

Erin scuffled forward. A shadow on the left wall of the crevasse seemed to widen as she neared it. Her mind felt hazy, her thoughts indistinct. Oh lord, she was tired—way too tired for this enigmatic stuff. A little clarity, a bit of straight-forward behavior from Wessick, those things she craved more than food or water at this moment. She stopped alongside the shadow and turned toward it.

The shadow marked an opening. The space measured a little wider than her body, and perhaps six feet high. Wessick must've needed to turn slightly sideways to squeeze through the gap.

Erin walked through the opening, into darkness.

For a moment, she was blind. Then as her eyes began to adjust, she picked out shapes in the darkness as blurry and mysterious as shadow monsters.

Scratch. A tiny flame ignited to her left.

Wessick, crouching a couple yards away, held a match. Its flame danced in the draft from the doorway. He picked up an object from the floor and lowered the match to the object. A larger flame erupted from inside the object, which she recognized as an oil lamp crafted out of clay. The lamp resembled a flat, oblong bowl with a wide lip that overhung the interior. A wick floated in the oil. The flame cast a shimmering twilight throughout the cave.

The chamber looked natural. It extended for perhaps fifteen feet ahead of Erin, a dozen feet to her left, and three or four feet to her right. The ceiling sloped downward toward the back of the cave. A few yards from the cave's entrance, a simple wooden chest hunkered near the left wall. Wessick had opened the chest's lid, propping it against the wall. He set the oil lamp on the floor and set about carefully rummaging through the contents of the chest. He lifted out what looked like several items of clothing, setting them on the chest's lid. As he brought out another mound of folded fabric, he offered the item to Erin.

"I've kept it simple," he said, "so you won't stand out from the crowd."

She unfurled the fabric. The white linen had been cut and sewn into an ankle-length sheath dress, sleeveless, with two wide straps to go over the shoulders.

"The locals prefer to go barefoot," Wessick said. "But your feet aren't conditioned for walking barefoot across the desert. You'll need these."

He handed her a pair of sandals. She took them, tilting them so that the light from the oil lamp illuminated them better. The sandals were intricately woven from plant material, most likely rushes. The toes of the sandals curled upward.

Scooping up the items he'd set on the chest's lid, Wessick tromped toward the cave entrance. At the opening, he paused and said, "I'll change outside."

He left.

For a minute or two, Erin stood there motionless. The lamplight glimmered around her. A draft wafted through the cave entrance. She felt like a coma patient immersed in a vivid dream, aware that she was dreaming but unable to shake off the virtual reality, vaguely cognizant of the real world that moved onward without her, beyond her sight though not beyond her perception.

Snap out of it, she urged herself. Shaking her head, as if to jostle the cobwebs out of her mind, she took a slow breath.

She dropped onto her butt on the ground and started to unlace her boots.

A few minutes later, she had shed her twenty-first-century clothing and donned the sheath dress and sandals Wessick gave her. The dress followed the contours of her body without being skintight, and it gradually loosened over her thighs so that the skirt flounced a bit when she moved. Only a sliver of cleavage showed above the straight neckline. She couldn't remember the last time she wore a dress of any kind.

The sandals felt floppy and awkward. She'd get used to it, she figured.

From outside, Wessick called, "May I come in?"

"Yes."

He ambled through the entrance, took a couple more steps, and halted. His old clothes he carried folded and draped over one arm. His new outfit consisted of a linen kilt secured with a leather belt. Other than a pair of sandals similar to hers, he wore nothing else. The suit and tie he sported before had masked his body, whereas his current apparel left little to the imagination. The kilt covered him from his waist to his knees, but everything else was on full view. She found herself staring at his lean and muscular frame, especially his chest. Though he may have been a villain, she couldn't deny he had a very nice chest.

Arching his eyebrows, he asked, "Is something the matter?"

"Uh, no."

She forced herself to look at his face. With his usual stoic expression, he surveyed her appearance as if analyzing the workmanship of his new BMW.

"I'm afraid I was mistaken," he said, meeting her gaze. "You won't blend in, no matter how plain the garments."

"This dress is quite lovely, I think." She swished the skirt. "And surprisingly comfortable."

"On you, it is lovely. On anyone else, it would look drab."

She blinked. "Did you just pay me a compliment?"

"Of course."

She scrunched her face. "Stop being nice. You're the bad guy, remember?"

He said nothing, skimming his gaze over her one more time. Something flickered across his features, a micro-expression reminiscent of appreciation.

Turning sideways to him, she bent down to gather up her clothes. She didn't trust him but she had trouble despising him, and that fact ignited a spark of unease deep inside her because she knew exactly what Wessick was doing. He wanted her to like him. The second she gave him what he wanted, he would have the advantage.

Alex's face popped into her mind. She felt no qualms about liking him—more than liking him, actually. Anytime she felt herself wavering in her opinion of Wessick, she must think of Alex. The contrast between the two men would snap her back to reality.

Erin gathered her clothes into a loose bundle. Her gun lay on top of the clothes. Cradling the bundle in her arms, she rose.

Wessick waved a hand at the bundle in her arms. "The pistol stays here."

"I'm not going anywhere without it."

"If you can change history," he said, taking a step toward her, "then you must take care not to do anything that might irrevocably alter our world."

"A lot of scientists think that messing with the past would create an alternate reality, essentially leaving our world untouched."

"They are mistaken."

"How do you know? Since you've been unable to change the past."

"It's a risk we cannot afford to take."

He reached for the gun. She clutched the bundle to her chest, burying the weapon between the fabric bundle and her bosom.

"Have it your way." He lowered his hand. "But precisely where do you intend to conceal the pistol?"

Good question. She bit the inside of her lip, staring into space as she contemplated the problem. Wessick moved to the chest and knelt in front of it. He set his old clothes inside the chest, then lifted out a bowl-shaped basket equipped with two handles. The container brimmed with accessories such as bracelets and armbands. Rising, he began to rifle through the basket's contents.

"Place your things in the chest," he told her.

She obeyed, but kept the gun clasped in her right hand, the muzzle pointed at the ground. Under no circumstances would she agree to leave the weapon behind. Walking into an unknown situation in a foreign land and an alien time seemed beyond dangerous, especially with shadowy enemies lurking everywhere around her. One of those enemies stood beside her now. In spite of his strange, stoic charm, she could never trust Samuel Wessick.

The gun went with her.

She glanced down at her dress. Where in tarnation would she hide the gun? A sheath dress, though feminine and elegant, offered no spaces where she might conceal a weapon. Even a knife would be difficult to hide.

Wessick plucked an item out of the basket, handing it to her. The item was a bracelet in the form of a gold ring about an inch wide, inlaid with rectangles of bright-blue stones separated by squares of deep-red stones. Erin recognized the stones as lapis lazuli and carnelian, respectively.

"See if it fits," Wessick said.

She took the bracelet and slid it over her left hand, up to her wrist. "I thought I was supposed to blend in."

"Indeed." He resumed fishing through the basket. "But you are meant to pass for an upper-class woman, not a commoner."

He presented her with a necklace. The single strand of lapis lazuli and carnelian beads, with a gold bead in the center, matched the bracelet. She donned the necklace, then asked, "Don't I need a wig? I thought Egyptians all wore them."

"Wigs are mainly for special occasions. Your hair will suffice."

He bent over the chest again.

Suffice? Guess he was done with the compliments.

Next Wessick produced a makeup kit, which they both used to apply the traditional black eyeliner with green coloring on the lids. Properly adorned at last, Erin felt like an actress about to take the stage as the star of a play that had no script.

She felt a little ridiculous.

"We're ready," Wessick said. He gestured at her gun. "Except for that."

She looked at the basket of jewelry on the floor. Maybe she could use the basket to somehow conceal the gun. Picking up the intricately woven container, she dumped its contents into the chest.

"What are you doing?" Wessick demanded.

She plopped the gun into the basket. "I need something to cover this with."

His lips tightened as he narrowed his eyes. He stared at her for a moment, then turned his gaze to the basket, and finally to the chest.

With a heavy sigh, he bent down to search through the chest. He straightened a few minutes later, clutching several objects in his hands. First, he took a scrap of fabric and draped it over the gun so that the cloth's folds disguised the weapon. Next, he laid a small mirror in the basket along with the containers of eye makeup.

"Satisfied?" he asked.

She nodded.

He snapped the chest's lid shut and started for the entrance. Over his shoulder, he said, "We'll see how you feel about it after carrying that package for the mile-and-a-half journey into town."

Mile and a half? Erin tucked the basket against her hip, holding it in place with her arm. Though the weight was manageable now, she felt certain the basket would seem to grow heavier the longer she carried it.

She stooped beside the chest. Lifting its lid, she surveyed the contents without touching them. A thick bundle of folded linen caught her attention. She set down the basket and picked up the linen bundle. It was a single piece of fabric folded over many times. She unfolded the linen to its full length of about twelve feet and full width of four feet.

Approaching from behind, Wessick loomed over her. He said, "That's meant to be a shawl. You may wear it if you like, but the method of fastening it is rather complicated."

She folded the linen widthwise and laid it out on the floor. Placing the basket in the middle of the fabric, she crouched with her back to the long strip.

Wessick furrowed his brow as he watched her reach backward to take hold of the linen at either side of her hips. She lifted upward, inch by inch, careful to keep the basket in place. Once she'd raised the basket to a position between her shoulder blades, she drew the linen around her shoulders and secured it with a knot over her breastbone. The ends draped down nearly to the floor.

She flung the ends over her shoulders. "Let's go."

Wessick gaped at her, his lips parted in a bemused smile, his forehead crinkled, his eyes no longer squinting but wide open and fixed on the contraption she had attached to herself.

Even his voice lost some of its equanimity as he said, "You are a strange creature."

"I am not a creature." Erin lifted her chin. "I'm a librarian."

She marched out the cave entrance.

THEY SKIRTED THE CLIFFS FOR SOME DISTANCE, ADVANCING ROUGHLY NORTH until they came upon a footpath that headed westward. The sun beat down on Erin's head and shoulders. The heat felt like a physical weight pressing on her, squeezing out beads of sweat that trickled down her temples. She swiped one end of the shawl across her forehead.

At the edge of the footpath, Wessick halted. The path emerged from a wadi in the cliff face. The wadi sloped upward at a moderate grade, rising toward the plateau at the apex of the cliffs. The footpath traced the wadi down from the summit, and then continued across the desert floor in the direction of the town, which appeared in the distance as geometric shapes protruding from the earth.

Wessick lifted the basket from Erin's makeshift sling. He tucked it under his arm and strode off down the footpath, away from the cliffs.

He must've hoped she would ditch the basket, and the anachronistic weapon tucked inside it, after lugging it on her back for awhile. The basket had swiftly begun to feel like a large chunk of granite strapped to her backside. Nevertheless, she would've carried her load as far as necessary.

Probably.

It hardly mattered now. Despite his protestations about the dangers of screwing up the timeline, Wessick apparently held onto enough manly pride that he couldn't let a woman cart a parcel on her back for a mile and a half. Still, though the act was considerate, it failed to earn him bonus points on the Erin Turner Scale of Gentlemanliness. He'd racked up too many debits already. Besides, he let her carry the basket for a good while before he oh-so-generously rendered aid.

Erin untied the shawl. She draped one end over her head, letting it droop low over her brow to shield her face from the sun. With the other end of the shawl, she covered her shoulders and arms. The linen dipped down her back as well, sheltering her upper back.

The footpath seemed to go on forever. The buildings in the distance drew closer but still looked far away, even after countless minutes of slogging across the desert. Her feet ached. Her leg muscles burned. She felt less like an Egyptian princess than like a captive on a forced march toward execution.

She got what she wanted. Wessick brought her back in time. Despite reaching her destination, she knew her problems were far from solved. How could she find the priests of Amun-Ra? Akhenaten outlawed worship of the old gods, a decree that forced devotees of those gods to offer their prayers in secret. The priests of Amun-Ra most likely went into hiding, or at least concealed their loyalty to the forbidden deity. Wessick might know how to find the priests, yet she couldn't ask him because doing so would expose her true motivations for accompanying him on this temporal expedition.

If he knew, then the Aten knew. She could not risk it.

She liked Wessick, sort of, but she absolutely would not trust him. The man kept too many secrets. Every word he said was chosen with precision and deliberate intent, a tactic that to her seemed to indicate he wanted to tell the truth but felt compelled to conceal it. So, prohibited from telling her anything vital, he couched the truth in carefully composed statements. When he told her the Aten "conscripted" him to work for them, his word choice hinted that he did not enter into their service willingly—at least not entirely. Yet Samuel Wessick struck her as the kind of man who forged his own path through the world. Why then would he allow the Aten to conscript him?

Because he had no choice. The Aten knew how to coerce a person into serving them. Erin knew firsthand their talent for engineering duress.

And what about the relic? The Aten expected her to find the thing, though she knew nothing about it. Even the Aten seemed ignorant of not only the relic's location, but also its appearance and its function. Since they referred to it as a relic, or an "object from another time," she wondered if the object originated from a time so deep in the past that all memory of its creation had slipped away.

Erin halted. Wessick told her the time machine was created and activated so long ago that no memory of the event persisted. She searched her memory for a particular phrase from Alex's translation of the altered map scroll. The text declared that when the *satseshat* found the relic, she would destroy the source of the Aten's power and become...

The ruler of time.

Could it be? Erin swept her gaze across the desert landscape around her. Thousands of years before her birth, the priests of Amun-Ra prophesied that the *satseshat* would find the relic and save humanity from the Aten. They seemed to know things about her that she hadn't known until today. They called the relic "the object from another time." They also said whoever controlled the relic controlled time— for what else could the phrase "ruler of time" mean? Maybe the relic was more than an object created in another time. Maybe it was an object *of* another time, linked to the past and the present, a device capable of bridging the distance between eras.

The relic was the time machine.

"Erin."

The sound of her name spoken aloud jarred her out of her reverie. She forced her eyes to focus on the man standing in front of her. Wessick grasped her shoulders lightly, staring at her with an intensity that belied his impassive expression.

"What is it?" he asked.

She shrugged off his hands. Summoning a breezy tone, she said, "Nothing. I suddenly realized I forgot to turn off the lamp in my bedroom."

He stared at her for a few seconds. Then, he spun on his heels and set off down the footpath.

Erin hurried after him. Absorbed in her own thoughts, she must've looked as vacant as an empty turtle shell. No wonder Wessick thought there was something wrong with her. She supposed that his laser-sharp stare qualified as an expression of concern. With any other man, concern might come wrapped in irritation or outright anger. But with Samuel Wessick, nothing scratched his perfectly polished facade.

Not nothing. When she'd jury-rigged a sling to carry the basket, a look of mild surprise broke through his ever-present composure. She felt an odd satisfaction in knowing that she had elicited an emotional response, however tiny, from the unflappable Wessick.

Something else inspired the sense of lightening that rushed through her. The weight pressing down on her had lifted a fraction. For the first time, she knew the identity of the relic. She felt the truth, despite a lack of concrete evidence. She *knew*.

No wonder the Aten wanted the relic so badly. At last she understood why the keeper refused to hand over the relic, enduring torture in order to protect it, and why the priests of Amun-Ra risked everything to hide it from the Aten.

The relic was a time machine. Whoever controlled the relic controlled time.

Erin marched faster, each step infused with an energy she had never felt before. She had a purpose. The reason for her quest. She knew what must be done.

Find the relic and destroy it.

THE FOOTPATH MERGED WITH A ROAD WIDE ENOUGH TO ACCOMMODATE chariots or wagons. Wessick led Erin eastward down the road, toward the distant outlines of the city of Akhetaten.

Sweat sheathed her face and dribbled down her spine. She covered as much of herself as possible with the shawl, yet the sun's heat and the long hike combined to wring every last drop of water from her flesh. Wessick marched onward as if unaffected by…anything. Erin found herself staring at the ground to avoid the painful brightness of the sun. She longed for pair of sunglasses. Unfortunately, they hadn't been invented yet.

The sun dipped lower to the west as the city drew nearer to the east. They approached Akhetaten from the southern end, and the rest of the city stretched northward along the banks of the Nile. The silhouette of the town began to separate into individual buildings. Most of the city's buildings would be constructed of mud brick, blocks of earth and straw dried in the sun. The plaster that covered the mud brick gleamed in the waning sunlight.

They followed the road into the city, passing the one-room hovels occupied by the lower classes. Erin saw men with deeply tanned skin herding livestock into their homes. She remembered reading that the poorest Egyptians housed their animals inside their homes at night, along with their families. Another man was repairing the plaster on his home.

As the sun disappeared below the horizon, Wessick led her deeper into the city. They crossed the main thoroughfare, a road three times as wide as the one that brought them into town. On the other side of the thoroughfare, they continued down the narrower street. The houses got larger and more elaborate, their grounds enclosed by walls. Red-painted gates offered access to the grounds. Most of the larger homes included a second story that rose above the height of the enclosure wall.

Wessick halted in front the gateway to a home of moderate size, compared to the others in the neighborhood. He swung open one half of the gate and motioned for her to enter. Erin tiptoed through the gateway. She felt like a trespasser, though she assumed this home belonged to Wessick. He entered behind her, shutting the gate.

Directly in front of her, the two-story house hunkered at one end of the enclosed grounds. Both floors featured a handful of rectangular windows, set high in the walls. To her right, just visible in the twilight, a garden filled one quarter of the enclosure. Several palm trees, of varying heights, grew in the farthest corner. Behind the garden, adjacent to the house, steps led down into a round hole in the ground. The hole was lined with bricks. A well, she surmised, based on its similarity to pictures she'd seen in books. Those pictures depicted the remains of ancient water wells.

A man armed with a sword patrolled the front portion of the grounds. If she walked around the back of the house, she suspected she'd find another guard there.

Wessick ushered her to the home's doorway. Like the gates, the wooden door was painted red. The doorframe looked like sandstone. The plaster around the doorway lent it the appearance of a temple gateway. A line of hieroglyphs appeared above the doorframe. Though Erin squinted at the glyphs, trying to puzzle out the meaning, her weak grasp on the ancient language hindered her.

"It says this is the house of Meru," Wessick told her.

She cast a sideways glance at him. "Are you Meru?"

He nodded. "Courtier and fourth god's servant in the temple of the Aten."

"Does the pharaoh know who you really are?"

"No." He swung the door inward, glancing back at her. "Do you?"

She didn't answer. She didn't know how to respond. He kept insinuating that everything she knew about him was untrue. She accepted that was possible, since the Aten apparently had the power to erase public records. They made certain no trace of Broderick Covington remained, save for the one piece of paper in T. R. Young's possession, which the Aten had now destroyed.

Wessick led her into the house, shutting the door.

They stood inside a small and dimly lit entryway, similar to but smaller than the vestibule of Revenant House. An oil lamp, carved from alabaster, perched atop a small table alongside the wall. On the right-hand wall, a mural depicted geese taking off from the waters of a marsh. They continued out of the entryway and down a set of steps into a long, rectangular room. Four stone columns stood equidistant from each other in the room's center, forming a line. The column's surfaces were smooth, but their tops were carved to resemble lotus flowers. A table hunkered against one wall, with oil lamps situated atop it. Two low stools squatted near the table. The room held no other furnishings.

Without pausing, Wessick escorted her through a doorway into another, similar room outfitted with lotus columns and similar furnishings. In one corner sat a chest identical to the one in the cave.

"The bathroom is through there," Wessick said, pointing at a doorway to her right.

Straight ahead, through another doorway, she glimpsed what looked like a kitchen, though unlike its twenty-first-century counterpart, this kitchen had no countertops or tables. Utensils lay scattered on the floor. Rather than heading into the kitchen, Wessick turned leftward to stride through another doorway that opened into a stairwell. The steps carried them up to the second floor. There, they entered a wide hallway. Doorways equipped with blue-painted wooden doors opened off the hall, two on each side, all shut.

Wessick opened the first door on the right. They walked into a small, square room furnished with just three items—a chest, a low table that supported an alabaster lamp, and a bed raised on squat legs, the feet of which looked like lion's paws. A thin mattress covered the bed frame.

"You will sleep here," Wessick told her, handing her the basket that concealed her gun.

Erin scuffled into the room, her sandals scratching on the stone floor.

Wessick turned to leave.

She seized his arm. "I have a few questions first."

He shut the door, folded his arms over his chest, and gazed down at her.

A million questions ricocheted inside her brain. Okay, maybe not really a million. A whole heck of a lot of them for sure. She needed to decide not only which question to ask first, but which questions she could safely ask him without revealing her plans and the state of her knowledge about the relic.

He arched an eyebrow at her. "Well?"

"Does the pharaoh know you work for the Aten?"

"No. He would never allow me into the palace if he knew. In fact, he would not let me live if he suspected my true motives."

"How do you intend to explain me?"

"I've already spread the word that I'm expecting a distant relative from Iunu to pay me a visit."

"Iunu?"

"One of the major cities of ancient Egypt, a center of learning and religion. It was known to the Greeks as Heliopolis. The city lies near the modern site of Cairo."

"Oh." She clasped her hands behind her back. "Don't the people here call their country Kemet?"

"Yes. Among other things."

Everyone here would assume she came from Iunu, a city of intellectuals. Better try to sound smart then. She had a master's degree, but she rather doubted that achievement would mean much to the Egyptians—or rather, the Kemetians.

"To find the relic," Wessick said, "you'll need to foster a relationship with the pharaoh."

Cripes. She didn't have time for that. Of course, she had the power of time travel at her disposal. Well, not exactly at *her* disposal. She needed an *akhet* ball in order to sail the waters of time, and Wessick kept those hidden. Since she saw him take only one ball out of his desk drawer, he must have more here. Otherwise, they would have no way of getting home. Maybe he kept them in the chest in the cave, or in the one downstairs.

Spending time getting to know the pharaoh, and convincing him to trust her, sounded like a huge waste of effort. She needed to contact the priests of Amun-Ra. They created the map scroll, and they could tell her what information the missing portion of the map held. In this time, however, worshiping the old gods was forbidden. The priests of Amun-Ra might be in hiding.

Or dead.

Her throat constricted. She swallowed against the tightness. The priests could not be dead. She had not traveled all this way, risking her life and the lives of everyone she cared about, only to smack into a dead-end. She would find the priests of Amun-Ra. She must find them.

But how? She knew nothing about this city. She couldn't even speak the language.

Wessick had clearly lived in this city for quite some time. He was, he'd told her, a courtier and the fourth god's servant in the Temple of the Aten. A god's servant was a priest. She didn't know exactly what a courtier was, but it sounded like someone with access to the palace and, perhaps, the pharaoh himself.

Did she dare ask Wessick about the priests of Amun-Ra?

She bit her lip. If only Alex were here...

He wasn't. The decision rested in her hands alone.

"Is there anything else?" Wessick asked.

She stared past him, not really looking at anything.

He cleared his throat.

She looked at him. "I was wondering—no, that's it. For now."

"Try to rest. I'll take you to the palace in the morning." He waved a hand in the direction of the chest that sat on the floor. "You will find jugs of clean water in the chest. I assumed you wouldn't want to drink beer or wine."

"For once, you assumed right."

He squinted slightly, for no more than a second. She supposed the slight expression indicated annoyance at her persistent lack of trust in him. Let him feel miffed. So far, he'd given her no reason to risk trusting him.

"The jugs hold purified water," he said. "I would advise against drinking water from any other source."

And then he left. Erin stared at the door for a few minutes, suddenly exhausted. Back in Revenant House, she told Wessick she needed sleep because she wanted to wait for Alex to wake up from his drug-induced slumber. Yes, Wessick had been right about that. Despite her exhaustion, however, she no longer wanted to sleep. How could she? In this house. In this city. In this time.

Footsteps shuffled outside the door. It sounded like more than one person. Erin pressed her ear to the door. The wood muffled the voices of two distinct individuals, both male, as far as she could tell. Stepping back, she waited until the footfalls silenced.

With deliberate slowness, she eased the door open six inches and peeked through the gap.

A man stepped in front of her. A sword dangled from his belt. His tanned face bore a hard expression matching the tension in his body. He spoke words she didn't understand, gesticulating with one hand. He wanted her to close the door, she thought.

Another, familiar voice spoke to the man in the same language.

The guard moved out of sight. Wessick stepped into the space the guard had vacated.

"Sleep," Wessick commanded. "Do not try to escape. Akhetaten is a treacherous place."

"Escape?" She scowled at him. "So I'm a prisoner."

"You are in my protective custody."

Seizing the door handle, he yanked it shut.

Trust him? Impossible.

Erin shambled to the bed, settled down onto it, and closed her eyes. Sleep would not come, she knew, but at least she might rest. In the morning, when Wessick took her to the palace, she would find a way to slip free of his custody. And, somehow, she must find the priests of Amun-Ra.

Piece of cake.

DESHERET WAITED UNTIL THE FAINT GLOW FROM THE WINDOW IN SAMUEL'S bedroom extinguished. She slipped through the gates, approaching the guard at the front door. He looked at her with dispassion, his gaze pausing briefly on the bag slung over her shoulder, and then he returned his gaze to the surroundings. She sauntered into the house.

Bathed in the half-light from the oil lamps, Desheret skulked through the house to the stairs and up to the second floor. The guard stood in front of the door to one of the bedrooms. Like the guard outside, this one scrutinized her with a dispassionate gaze.

Desheret reached for the door handle.

The guard clasped her wrist.

She scowled at him.

In a voice barely above a whisper, he said, "By the master's orders, no one enters."

Desheret replied in an equally soft voice, "Meru wishes me to attend to our guest."

"I obey the master."

Of course they served Samuel and not her. No one served her. But soon she would possess the kind of power that would force everyone, including the Aten, to bow down before her.

The knowledge bolstered her. She plastered a sweet smile on her face and gazed up at the guard through her eyelashes. She said, "I understand. I will speak to Meru myself."

The guard offered no response, either in words or in his expression. She sashayed past him. Her arm brushed against his. He stiffened, but kept his focus straight ahead. He didn't notice as she grasped the sword's hilt.

Desheret tore the sword from his belt, spun around, and smacked the dull side of the blade into the guard's head.

The guard crumbled.

Desheret raised the sword vertically in front of her. The lamplight glistened on its blade. She would not need the knife in her bag after all. A sword inflicted far more damage.

And she wished to greatly damage Samuel's precious *satseshat*.

Discarding her bag, she stepped over the guard's limp form to the door. She turned the handle and eased the door inward.

Lamplight illuminated a pale-skinned form reposing on the bed.

Gripping the sword in both hands, Desheret crept into the room. She stopped alongside the bed, parallel with Erin's head.

The tale of the *satseshat* ended here.

Desheret raised the sword and slashed downward.

Present Day
Revenant Point

A LEX WOKE WITH A START. COLD SWEAT SLICKENED HIS FOREHEAD. HIS
pulse pounded as if someone had shoved a bass drum inside his head. He
bolted upright.

Erin.

Something was wrong. He had to find her.

In the chair by the window set a figure mostly concealed by the newspaper
raised in front of the individual.

Alex blinked repeatedly, until the blurriness of sleep cleared. The person
sitting in the chair, with one ankle balanced atop the other knee, was not
Erin. The masculine hands gave it away.

And the sheet in the man's hands was not a newspaper. Even without seeing
the painted front side, Alex recognized the papyrus scroll that contained the
map. Alex specifically remembered placing the scroll inside the plastic tube and
stowing it under the bed. On finding Alex unconscious, the newcomer must've
searched the bedroom, stumbling upon the map scroll.

The man in the chair lowered the scroll.

Warner said, "*Guten Morgen.*"

"Morning," Alex replied. "I'm not sure yet if it's a good one."

At seeing Warner, Alex relaxed—a little. He glanced at the window. Red-tinged
sunlight shining through the glass. Sunrise or sunset? How long had he slept? His

sleep had not been natural. He remembered Wessick jamming a needle into his arm. When he found the bastard, Alex intended to slug him.

Right before shooting him.

Rubbing the back of his neck, he asked, "What time is it?"

Warner checked his watch. "It is five o'clock."

"In the morning? What day is it?"

"You slept through the night."

Alex slid off the bed, straightening to his full height. He stretched, yawned, and stretched some more. The stiffness in his muscles softened a bit, but the tension deep within him lingered. The tension had nothing to do with the knockout drug Wessick gave him, or the fact he'd slumbered all night. He knew precisely what triggered the acid in his stomach, the tightness in his chest, and his overall feeling of unease.

Through clenched teeth, he asked Warner, "Where's Erin?"

Warner rose and laid the map scroll on the bed. "I don't know. She was gone when I arrived."

"Wessick?"

"Also gone." Warner massaged his jaw. "I ran into a vicious female who nearly fed me to an orb. I escaped—as did she. I saw her enter a portal."

A vicious female. Yes, Alex was acquainted with the woman in question.

If the woman had captured Erin...

"I saw no one else with the woman," Warner said. "I believe she left alone."

Warner's assurance did nothing to reassure Alex. If the woman hadn't taken Erin, that left one possibility. Wessick took her.

Into the past.

A portal must've transported them there. But as for how Wessick controlled the portal, Alex had no idea. Without the knowledge, he could not find Erin.

The hidden camera.

How could he have forgotten? He supplied Erin with the brooch that host a tiny video camera. He watched her encounter with Wessick on his laptop, via the wireless feed from the brooch camera.

His laptop was on the floor. Nabbing it, he perched on the edge of the bed and opened the laptop's lid. The screen came to life. The words "signal lost" flashed over a black screen.

Of course he lost the signal. Even the best surveillance equipment couldn't receive a signal emanating from three thousand years in the past. Luckily, he recorded the entire meeting. He queued up the recording, selected the last few minutes before the signal was lost, and hit play.

The image was jerky. The brooch, pinned to Erin's shirt, jostled as she moved. Alex turned up the volume to maximum.

Wessick was saying, "— be certain no one will see how we arrive."

"What city?" Erin asked in a whispery voice.

Alex's heart thudded. She sounded tired, or drugged, or terrified, or simply over-whelmed. He couldn't tell which, and the uncertainty made his jaw tighten.

In the video, Wessick stood directly in front of Erin, so close that only his neck and torso were visible. His body blocked the camera's view, but an eerie glow flickered behind him. Wessick told Erin they would travel to the city of Akhetaten, the capital of Egypt during the reign of the pharaoh Akhenaten. Erin muttered something about not knowing the language. Wessick's response was muffled. Erin listed side to side as if intoxicated.

What had Wessick done to her? If the lying, conniving, drug-administering snake hurt her—

Erin's voice snapped him back to reality. On the screen, she said, "You better not be leading me into a trap."

Her voice sounded strong and clear. Maybe Wessick hadn't drugged her after all.

Alex still wanted to throttle the scumbag.

He'd missed whatever Wessick said in response to Erin. She said something about their clothing.

Wessick turned and stepped away from Erin, revealing the shimmering portal behind him. The bubble-like doorway to another time and place offered a panoramic view of a desert landscape. Wessick strode into the portal.

A moment later, Erin followed him.

The portal telescoped shut.

Alex snapped closed the laptop's lid. He gritted his teeth, forcing himself to breathe. A rage he had never felt before boiled inside him. Wessick took Erin. So what if she went along willingly. He knew she must've felt she had no choice, because their sole hope for finding the relic revolved around decoding the map scroll, a task they could accomplish only with the help of the priests of Amun-Ra. The priests lived thousands of years ago. The only way to reach them was via time travel, and the only one who could take Erin into the past was Samuel Wessick.

Alex sighed, the sound emerging as a hissing growl. He didn't blame Erin for going with Wessick. He blamed the slimy, poisonous serpent of a man for coercing her into going alone.

Dammit. Alex slammed his fist down onto the bed. His hand sank into the cushioning of the quilt and mattress, dulling the impact but not his anger. He must find Erin. To do that, he must know how Wessick opened the portal.

Flipping open the laptop, he reopened the recording and located the spot where it started playback the first time. He backtracked from there, to a point a couple minutes earlier in the recording. He started playback.

Wessick stood in front of Erin, grasping a silvery ball between his thumb and forefinger.

Erin said, " How does it work?"

"Mind over matter," came Wessick's reply.

The snake-man turned and tossed the orb. The portal opened with an explosion of light.

Alex pursed his lips. Okay, he needed one of those orbs.

Selecting an earlier spot in the video timeline, Alex hit the play button.

Erin stood beside Wessick at the desk in the study. Wessick was unlocking a file drawer. As Wessick pulled the drawer open, Alex saw that it contained not hanging folders, but racks of metallic pouches. Wessick removed the pouch, then shut and locked the drawer.

Alex fast forwarded through the video as Wessick led Erin into the passageway and showed her what the pouch contained. It was the orb Wessick used to open the portal. Pressing play again, Alex heard Wessick say, "We call them *akhet* balls."

Alex stopped playback. He shut the laptop.

Warner was observing him from across the bed. The older man squinted his eyes, pressing his lips together. Warner said, "I suspect you're concocting a foolish plan."

"Damn right." Alex jumped to his feet. "I'm going after Erin."

"You don't know where she is."

"Yes, I do. She's in the fourteenth century BC."

Warner's concerned expression morphed into mild amusement. "I doubt even my fastest jet can fly you there."

"I know the way."

Alex spotted his attaché lying on the floor at the foot of the bed. He knelt beside the bag and pulled out the Glock 9mm stashed inside it, along with the shoulder holster that protected it. After strapping on the holster, he threw on his leather jacket. His tablet computer lay at the foot of the bed. He grabbed that and shoved it into the attaché too. Couldn't hurt to have it, for as long as the battery lasted.

To Warner, he said, "Bring me the map. And the tube it was in."

Warner retrieved the tube from the floor near the chair. He brought both the tube and the map scroll to Alex. Carefully rolling the papyrus, Alex slid it into the tube. He screwed on the cap. Plucking his attaché from the floor, he shoved the tube inside and pulled the zipper shut until it bumped against the tube. The top foot and a half of the plastic tube stuck out of the attaché, but he could live with that. The map was essential, and he would not leave it behind.

Hooking the attaché's strap around his neck, he slung it diagonally across his chest. The soft-sided leather bag draped over his hip.

"Now what?" Warner asked.

Alex marched out of the bedroom.

Warner followed him down the stairs, around the corner, and down the passage to the open door of Wessick's study. Alex stomped across the room to the desk, circling around behind it. Locating the file drawer, he tugged on its handle. Locked. He'd expected as much, but it had been worth a shot.

Alex reached for his Glock.

Warner raised a hand to stop him. "Allow me. If one of us is to be deafened, it might as well be me."

Alex shrugged.

Pulling out his own Glock, Warner took aim at the drawer's lock.

Alex plugged his ears with his fingers.

Warner fired. Even with his ears plugged, Alex winced at the detonation.

The lock shattered.

Yanking the drawer open, Alex grabbed four of the metallic pouches. He stuffed three of them into the attaché. The fourth pouch he opened, shaking out the orb within it. The crystalline sphere landed on his palm.

Although Warner said nothing, Alex felt his mentor's gaze boring into his skull. He brandished the orb for Warner to see.

"This," Alex said, "is the way to find Erin."

Lines deepened across Warner's forehead as his brow knit together. "You know how to open a portal?"

Alex stared at the orb in his hand. What had Wessick said to Erin when she asked how the orb worked?

Mind over matter.

The other orbs, the glowing ones that burned flesh, they had the capability of transmitting thoughts into a person's mind. Though he had yet to experience the phenomenon, he knew Erin had. She told him about it. Thought transmission suggested one of two possibilities—telepathy or technology.

Alex studied the writhing interior of the orb. He'd bet his life that the apparent telepathy evidenced by the Aten's orbs stemmed from a technological source. When Wessick said the portal-opening orbs worked by "mind over matter," he must mean that to control the technology a person needed to exert his will via thought control. Think it, and the orb obeyed.

Think about where he wanted the portal to take him, and the orb would enact his desire.

Either he'd wind up exactly where he wanted, with Erin, or he'd get himself killed.

"I know what to do," Alex told Warner.

The older man glanced at the orb. "I pray you do."

"It works by thought control," Alex said. He fingered the orb. "I think."

Alex strode out of the study, turning to face the open expanse of the passage. He tossed the orb, catching it in his palm. With his fingers extended, and the orb balanced in the center of his palm, he closed his eyes and concentrated on one thought.

Take me to Erin.

Then a ghost of doubt slithered through him, and he amended the thought.

Take to me Erin, in the city Akhetaten during the reign of Akhenaten.

A surge of static electricity swept over him, starting in his hand, spreading through his entire body.

He hurled the orb down the passage.

The portal opened in a burst of light. Through the spherical doorway, he spied a dimly lit hallway in a building that looked nothing like Revenant House.

Warner touched Alex's shoulder. "I will go with you."

"No." Alex glanced at Warner. "I need you to guard Erin's parents. I have a feeling the Aten are about to get antsy."

Warner nodded. He reached into a coat pocket and produced three spare clips of ammo. Offering them to Alex, he said, "You may need these."

Alex took the clips and tucked them into his pocket. "Thank you."

"Good luck."

Alex stepped through the portal.

He glanced over his shoulder just as the portal shrank into a pinpoint and winked out, revealing a set of steps that descended into darkness. Soft, yellowish light flickered around him. Turning away from the steps, he took in his surroundings. He stood perpendicular to a blue-painted wooden door that hung open at his right. Other doorways, all shut, led off the hallway.

A man clad in a linen kilt lay unconscious on the floor a feet away.

Judging by the man's attire and the oil lamps affixed to the white-plastered walls, Alex realized he must've reached his intended era—namely, ancient Egypt. But had he reached the exact date and place where he might find Erin?

And why was there an unconscious man on the floor?

Withdrawing his Glock, gripping it firmly in one hand with the muzzle aimed straight down, Alex rotated toward the open doorway. The light of a single oil lamp cast flickering tongues of muted light throughout the room beyond the doorway. A woman in a long, billowy dress stood beside a bed, a sword raised over her head. On the bed, another woman reclined on her side, facing the wall. The light brown locks of the slumbering woman's hair splayed out across the mattress behind her head. Even without seeing her face, he knew the identity of the slumbering woman.

Panic ripped through him.

The murderess stabbed her sword downward at Erin's head.

Alex bolted through the doorway.

E RIN FELT A PRESENCE BEHIND HER. SHE OPENED HER EYES A SLIVER, JUST
enough to see the shadow that draped over her and spilled onto the wall. The
silhouette of a person.

"Erin!"

Alex's voice.

Erin flipped onto her back. Lamplight glinted off a metal blade as it arced
downward at her head.

She flung herself at the shadowed figure beside her. She hit her attacker at knee level,
bowling the woman over and sending them both skidding across the floor. The sword
bounced off the edge of the bed and clattered onto the floor.

Erin rolled sideways away from her attacker.

The woman roared with rage, leaping to her feet.

The sword lay several feet away on the floor. Erin scrambled toward it.

As she spotted the sword too, the woman sprang forward.

Another figure lunged out of the semi-darkness. Erin glimpsed a familiar face
as the figure seized the crazy woman around the torso, locking her in a straitjacket
embrace. Alex lifted the woman off her feet. The madwoman thrashed her legs
as she let out staccato cries of anger and frustration.

Erin crawled to the sword, wrapping her hand around its hilt.

The woman nailed Alex in the shin and he grunted. She threw her head back,
twisted her neck around, and sank her teeth into his collarbone. Alex shouted.

Erin lifted the sword as she jumped to her feet. The blade sagged in her grasp.
Pain lanced through her arms. The blasted sword weighed a ton.

The crazy woman thrashed violently in Alex's arms. He staggered sideways, tripped, and the pair of them tumbled to the floor. Limbs flailed. Arms clashed. The woman's skirts tangled around both their legs. Alex shoved the woman away, disentangling himself from her skirts with a jerk of his feet and explosive grunt.

Erin mustered every bit of strength within her. She raised the sword and swung it at the madwoman.

The lunatic rolled away amid a vortex of twisting and billowing skirts.

The blade smacked into the floor. The concussion reverberated through Erin's bones. She lost her grip on the hilt and the sword popped out of her grasp.

The madwoman fled out the doorway. Her footsteps clapped down the stairway.

Erin stood frozen for a moment, breathing hard, bones still vibrating.

Alex sat on the floor, propped up on one arm. He looked at the sword, then at Erin. A crooked grin flashed across his face.

Erin responded with a wan smile. She said, "The human tornado strikes again."

Alex clambered to his feet, rushing to her. He pulled her into his arms and kissed her. She felt the tension within her melt away as she relaxed against him.

A shadow fell over them.

Alex lifted his head to glance at the doorway. Erin followed his gaze.

Samuel Wessick glared back at them.

She could almost feel the wave of hot anger that rippled through Alex as his entire body tensed.

Wessick fixed his gaze on Alex. "I should have known you would find a way to interfere."

Erin slipped an arm around Alex's waist. She said, "He's not interfering. I want him here."

A muscle in Wessick's jaw twitched.

Out the corner of her eye, Erin saw Alex smirk. He really didn't give a fig what Wessick thought—and, she realized, neither did she. The darkening of Wessick's expression seemed to light a tiny flame of joy inside Alex, the glow of which brightened his expression. Erin suppressed a smile. Maybe she ought to feel bad about the relish Alex took in aggravating Wessick.

Nah.

Alex hooked his arm around Erin's waist, pressing her closer to him.

"I can explain *your* presence," Wessick said, waving a hand dismissively at Erin. His lip curled as he fixed his glare on Alex. "But *his* presence is impossible to explain. He must go back. Immediately."

Erin straightened her spine, lifting her chin. "No."

Wessick ground his teeth. His jaw muscles worked and twitched.

Erin held his gaze without blinking or flinching, maintaining an erect but relaxed posture. She couldn't see Alex's expression without breaking eye contact with Wessick, but she felt pretty sure he was still smirking. His hand rested on her hip in a casual, yet slightly territorial, gesture. She didn't mind a little protectiveness, so long as he didn't take it too far. In fact, she rather liked it.

How bizarre.

Wessick broke eye contact first. He glanced at Alex, then switched his gaze to the gloomy airspace to Alex's left.

After the briefest moment, Wessick spun and stamped out of the room. He veered right, disappearing out of sight down the hallway.

For the second time in less than a day, Samuel Wessick had lost control of his emotions.

And strangely, that knowledge buoyed Erin's spirits.

ALEX STROKED ERIN'S ARM. SHE LOOKED UP AT HIM, HER FACE SEEMING TO glow in the lamplight. The tension that had contracted every muscle in his body, and set his gut to seething, evaporated in the instant she laid her hand on his chest and smiled up at him.

He had thought she needed him to rescue her. How wrong he'd been.

Of course if he hadn't shouted her name, she might've failed to notice the deranged woman about to decapitate her. Maybe she needed him after all, just a little.

Wessick strolled back into the room. His face now wore the customary mask of composure, tinged with slight curiosity. Alex let his smirk settle into a neutral expression of his own. Wessick wasn't the only one capable of hiding his contempt.

Casting a cursory glance at Alex, Wessick told Erin, "He may stay. But we must remain in the house until dawn. Then I will take you to the palace."

Alex coughed.

Wessick added, "Both of you."

Erin shook her head. "Take us to the palace *now.*"

"That is imposs—"

"Right this minute."

Wessick stared at Erin for a second. "As you wish."

"Good," Erin said. "Let's go."

Wessick stomped out the door, pausing in the hallway. He gestured for them to follow.

Alex took Erin's hand and led her into the hallway. Wessick ushered them down the staircase, through one room and into another. Through a doorway, at the end of a short entranceway, Alex noticed a red-painted door. The exit, no doubt. Ancient Egyptians liked to paint their outer doors red.

Wessick halted. He eyed Alex as if appraising a horse before purchasing it. Finally, he said, "His clothing is thoroughly improper."

Alex snorted. "And I should care why?"

"You'll draw attention to us."

"Maybe I like to be the center of attention."

"Do you also enjoy being publicly executed?"

"As long as I get to see you drawn and quartered first."

Erin stepped between the two men, angling sideways to slap one hand on Wessick's chest and the other on Alex's. To Wessick, she said, "Back off."

Alex felt the smirk tugging at his lips again.

Erin swung her head in his direction. "Don't look so pleased with yourself, doctor. He's right. You need to change."

Wessick approached a wooden chest that sat against the far wall. Crouching beside the chest, he flipped up the lid and dug through the contents until he found what he wanted. He lifted an item of folded white linen out of the chest as he rose. He tossed the item to Alex.

"That should fit," Wessick said.

Alex unfolded the item, which turned out to be a kilt similar to the one Wessick wore.

Holding the item with one hand, its length draping down, Alex pursed his lips. He said, "This will look awfully silly with a shoulder holster and my attaché."

Wessick clenched his hands into fists. "You cannot bring along anything from our world. The risk to the timeline—"

"I can't change the past, remember?" Alex couldn't stop the smirk from reemerging. "Erin is the only one who might be able to alter past events. You said so yourself."

Wessick opened his mouth and clamped it shut again. Though his expression stayed impassive, the heat of his glare nearly set the air on fire.

He said to Alex, "How do you know what I told Erin?"

"I read *Audio Surveillance for Dummies* too."

Wessick turned to Erin. "You must convince him. His clothing is simply unacceptable. Everyone will notice him, and in a city as oppressed as Akhetaten, attention is not desirable."

Erin traded glances with Alex. Then she told Wessick, "He does have a point. You said nobody can change the past." She sighed with what sounded like mock resignation. "Besides, Alex is stubborn and he won't listen to me anyway."

Alex tossed the kilt back at Wessick. "Thanks for the fashion tips, but I won't be needing this."

Wessick stood mute and motionless for so long that Alex wondered if he'd suffered a stroke and become paralyzed standing upright.

Abruptly, he marched out of the room into an adjacent chamber. A moment later he returned, bearing two torches that appeared to be made out of reeds lashed together. Wessick lit the torches from the flame of an ornate alabaster lamp. He handed one torch to Alex, keeping the second for himself.

Without a word, Wessick conducted them through the entranceway to the red door. A guard posted outside the door shuffled aside as they filed out of the house into the night. Wessick swung open a pair of gates, waving Alex and Erin through the pillared entrance. The trio set off down a wide road, with Wessick leading the way. Alex and Erin trailed a few paces behind him.

The houses they passed were dark, the occupants likely asleep. Historians explained that the ancient Egyptians, hindered by their lack of real artificial lighting, stuck to the schedule nature laid out for them. They went to bed at dusk, and awakened at dawn. But did everyone followed nature's timetable? So far, the evidence before his eyes suggested they did.

Alex scanned the gloom for shapes. The human tornado was out there somewhere, without her sword but armed with enough deadly rage to take down an army. The woman would find another weapon. She would hunt down Erin.

Ducking his head to whisper in Erin's ear, he asked, "Did you see the woman's face? When she attacked you, I mean."

"No," she answered in an equally soft voice.

"Neither did I." He slid his hand into hers, interlacing her fingers. "But whoever she is, she wants you dead very badly."

Erin sped up, dragging him forward with her. When they pulled up parallel to Wessick, she matched her pace to his. Wessick glanced at her.

"A word of advice," she said. "Keep your psycho girlfriend away from both of us."

Wessick arched an eyebrow. "Desheret acts alone. I have no control over her."

"Then you better get some control," Erin said. "Because I'll make sure that whatever she does to Alex happens to you too."

Erin strode faster, outpacing Wessick.

Alex couldn't help the self-satisfied smirk that once again warped his lips.

Glancing at him sideways, Erin shook her head. "You're awfully chipper for someone who's wanted dead by more enemies than I can count on all my fingers, toes, and hairs on my head."

"We'll survive. Together."

She squeezed his hand.

He nodded over his shoulder, indicating Wessick. "I think he's afraid of you."

"Of course he is. He's learned the most important lesson of all."

Wessick rushed past them to retake the lead position in their procession. As he passed them, the older man cast a furtive glare at Alex. The man really disliked him, Alex mused, which suited him fine.

"Tell me," Alex said, "Precisely what lesson has our host learned?"

Erin aimed a sweet smile at him. "Don't mess with a librarian."

18

THROUGH THE CITY THEY TREKKED, WITH WESSICK IN FRONT WHILE ALEX AND Erin trailed behind him hand in hand. No moon brightened the night. The houses stood dark, silent. The torches shed inconstant light on the buildings they passed, so that the hulking shapes seemed to wriggle as if alive. Erin felt a strange kind of claustrophobia as she traveled down the wide streets, surrounded by mud brick monsters. Whenever the feeling struck her, she first glanced up at the star-speckled sky, then looked at Alex.

He would cast a sidelong glance at her, as if he sensed her gaze on him. His lips would stretch into a partial smile, and the feeling of walls closing in around her would dissipate.

Wessick was right. Alex would stand out. Erin surveyed his appearance one more time. His jeans were a deep blue, the denim still smooth and the creases still crisp despite his tussles with a madwoman. His flannel shirt also evidenced a stunning resistance to wrinkling. A light coating of dust on his leather boots proved the sole side effect of recent events. A leather jacket and his leather bag, the one he called an attaché, completed the ensemble. A faint bulge along the intersection of his left arm and torso hinted at the presence of a shoulder holster under his jacket.

She concluded that he looked nothing like the intrepid archaeologists in the movies. Yet the graceful confidence in his step, the straightness of his posture, and the calmly resolute expression on his face lent him all the heroic appeal he needed.

Ahead, the road dead-ended at a group of smaller buildings. Wessick led them through a narrower alleyway between the corners of two buildings. The alleyway emptied into an open expanse that extended leftward into the darkness. At the far end of the open area, Erin spotted the pale outlines of buildings. Straight ahead loomed a wall at least thirty feet high, its surface covered with white plaster that glowed in the ambient light.

Wessick directed them toward the wall.

At the barrier, they veered left to trace the wall's perimeter. After a minute or two, they found a pair of wooden gates set into the wall. The gates hung ajar. One at a time, they filed through the opening.

Beyond the gateway lay another open expanse, this one enclosed on three sides by the gleaming white wall. Wessick opted to cross the courtyard on a diagonal path, headed toward a dark area that presumably signified a break in the wall. To the right, the fourth side of the rectangular courtyard ended at the front wall of what looked like an immense building. As they neared the structure, Erin realized it was another wall. The central section of the wall consisted of a monumental pylon—a gateway formed by twin wedge-shaped towers that stood at least a hundred feet tall and were presumably built from mud-brick encased in plaster, a common building technique of this era. Nestled between the pylon's halves, a massive stone threshold led into the building. The threshold stood completely open, with no gates or guards to control access.

The torchlight failed to shed its glow on the bulk of the structure, and the ambient light proved barely sufficient. Despite the poor lighting, however, Erin found herself struck with awe at the splendor of the structure. Reliefs painted in brilliant colors unfolded across the walls and spread the height and breadth of the pylons. She noted animals, gods and goddesses, and the pharaoh himself rendered among the depictions of boats and chariots. On the left-hand tower, positioned near the top, the disk of the Aten hovered above everything else. Its rays stretched down toward the pharaoh. Tiny hands, some proffering the crosses known as *ankh*s, extended from the terminus of each ray.

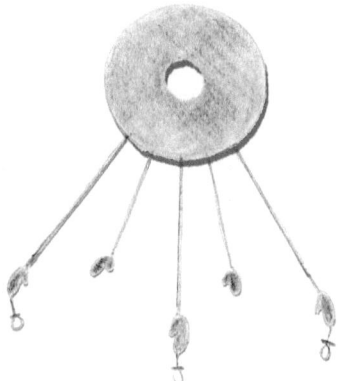

Erin halted, letting her hand fall away from Alex's. She stared up at the tableau. The *ankh* represented life. In essence, the tableau depicted the Aten deity granting life to the pharaoh—and therefore, the imagery also suggested the beings known as the Aten somehow granted life. Maybe it was a wish, rather than a fact. The Egyptians prayed the Aten might grant them life, might let them continue to exist in this life, instead of smiting them.

What had Wessick said about the city of Akhetaten?

In a city as oppressed as Akhetaten, attention is not desirable.

Historical evidence bore out his assessment. Egyptologists usually described Akhenaten's reign as a time of oppression, when worship of the old gods became verboten and any representations of those gods were destroyed. After Akhenaten's death, the nation returned to its old ways. Images of Akhenaten suffered the same vengeance that the heretic king had exacted upon the old gods. Representations of Akhenaten were destroyed, his name erased from official histories.

Perhaps the Aten spearheaded the revisions. If Akhenaten, one of their own, took off with their precious relic, then the Aten might've seen fit to wreak the one sort of vengeance available to them. They could destroy all memory of the pharaoh who betrayed them.

Alex grasped her shoulder. She met his gaze.

Several paces ahead of them, Wessick stopped to glance back in their direction. He waved a hand in an impatient gesture urging them to come. He called to them, "That is the Mansion of the Aten. The palace is this way."

Erin remained immobile, her attention fixated on the Aten disk emblazoned on the pylon's tower.

"What is it?" Alex asked her.

"Nothing," she said. "What is the Mansion of the Aten?"

"The smaller temple." Alex turned in a semicircle, studying the surroundings. He pointed at the walled enclosure kitty-corner to the temple. "That must be the Great Palace. The Great Aten Temple, or the House of the Aten in Akhetaten, must lie beyond the palace."

Erin forced herself to turn away from the pylon. The massive gateway was part of a *smaller* Aten temple? She couldn't envision how gargantuan the Great Temple must be.

Capturing her hand in his, Alex encouraged her to walk forward. They rejoined Wessick, and their host escorted them toward the wall directly ahead, perpendicular to the pylon structure. As they neared the wall, Erin glimpsed the tops of buildings inside the enclosure. The opening in the wall turned out to be a road that separated the pylon structure from the other walled enclosure. The road must've measured a hundred feet wide or more. An alleyway, much narrower than the road, separated the Mansion of the Aten from another walled enclosure that must contain buildings. As in the residential section of the city, everything here stood dark and lifeless.

Down the road they marched, three abreast, a procession of foreigners. Shortly, they came to a bridge that spanned the road to connect the walled enclosure on the right with the fortified domain of the palace. Three impressive piers supported the bridge, at a height of some fifty feet above the roadway. The openings between the piers allowed traffic to pass under the bridge. Brightly colored scenes of the royal couple frolicking in a garden decorated the plaster that encased the piers and the bridge. Shadows played across the upper portion of the bridge, lending an eerie quality to the scenes depicted on its surface.

A shiver coursed through Erin. She bent her head back to scrutinize the sky. Stars twinkled back at her, laid out in constellations she didn't recognize. Of course, the only constellations she knew by sight were Orion and the Big Dipper.

Did the Aten watch from high above?

The shiver raced through her anew.

Wessick headed for the left side of the bridge. As they neared the wall, the torchlight revealed a staircase set into the bridge's pier. They ascended the steps single file, rising high above the roadway until shadows engulfed it. Erin felt as if the bridge floated on a black sea—or in empty space.

The bridge descended over the wall via a long ramp, which they traversed at a brisk pace. On both sides of the ramp hunkered pale silhouettes of buildings situated within the fortification wall, inside the complex known to twenty-first-century archaeologists as the Great Palace. Erin wished she could see it in daylight, with all its glory revealed in the bright sunlight. Instead, she caught glimpses of wall frescoes and ornate columns as they filed down the ramp, through a large doorway, into a courtyard. Torches mounted at intervals along the courtyard walls provided enough light to reveal the more-than-life-size statues of the pharaoh that lined the enclosure. The flickering light drew shadows that advanced and retreated like high-speed tides, sometimes cloaking a statue's face, other times exposing it in golden hues. Deeper shadows lingered behind the statues, making the stone colossi stand out from the courtyard walls.

Elsewhere in the city, life had vanished from view. Houses stood dark, a silence permeated the air as sharply as a sour odor, and the streets lay empty save for the three foreigners traipsing through town by torchlight. A powerful sense of unreality had penetrated Erin to her core during the journey from Wessick's house to the royal district. Now, as they tromped out of the gloom into the courtyard, reality slammed into her with the force of a body blow.

Men sporting swords on their belts, presumably guards, scurried back and forth across the courtyard. Voices, hushed yet infused with ominous intensity, echoed through the space. Erin couldn't make out the words, but the tone of the men's voices conveyed panic. Her stomach flip-flopped. She gripped Alex's hand tighter. Whatever was happening here, she felt certain it bode nothing good.

She glanced at Wessick. Lines of worry creased his forehead as his eyes darted side to side, tracking the flurry of human activity in the courtyard. Wessick led them partway into the courtyard, then halted. She and Alex stopped as well, waiting for Wessick to speak or start moving again.

He held still.

To their left a shallow ramp accessed a doorway through which Erin spied the darkly lit interior of a roofed area. It might've been a building, or simply a roofed patio. In this light, she couldn't tell for sure.

A figure rushed out of the doorway, half running, half skidding down the ramp. In one hand, the man grasped an oil lamp, a clay model similar to the one she saw back in the cave. His head was bald and smooth, wrinkles lined his face, and his belly swelled with a slight paunch. Despite his portly figure, the curves of muscles in his arms and legs hinted that the man was in good shape.

At the base of the ramp, the bald man stumbled to a halt and visually scanned the courtyard. His gaze settled on Erin, Alex, and Wessick. The bald man scrutinized Alex for a long moment. His eyebrows lifted, then knit together as he squinted his eyes.

With a tight shake of his head, the bald man shifted his gaze to Wessick. The two men nodded at each other, as if in recognition. The bald man trotted across the courtyard to them.

Wessick spoke to the man in a language Erin didn't understand—the language of this land, she supposed. Historians of her day called it Ancient Egyptian. Well, she could hardly call it that now. Neither the term ancient nor the name Egypt applied to the place. This time was the present, and this land was not Egypt yet. Kemetian seemed as good a name as any for the language, since Kemet was one of many names given to this land by its inhabitants.

Alex let go of her hand. His attention was focused intently on Wessick and the bald man as the pair engaged in a clipped, fast-paced dialogue.

Leaning close to Alex, raising onto her tiptoes to whisper in his ear, Erin asked, "Do you understand them?"

"No," he muttered, the syllable buried in a heavy sigh.

"But you know the language."

"I can read and write the ancient Egyptian language, in both hieroglyphic and hieratic scripts. But never before in my life have I heard the language spoken by a genuine ancient Egyptian." He frowned, expelling another deep sigh. "The language sounds nothing like I expected. It's incomprehensible."

She patted his arm. "Relax, honey, I don't expect you to know everything."

He shot a sideways glance down at her.

"What?" she asked.

"You called me honey."

Heat rose in her cheeks. She mumbled "sorry" as she pushed away from him, focusing her attention on Wessick and the bald man. Alex said nothing more and, gradually, her blush faded.

Wessick and the bald man stopped talking. Turning slightly toward Erin and Alex, Wessick raised a hand to gesture at the bald man.

"This is Khety," Wessick said, "an adviser to the king. He brings disheartening news."

"Wonderful," Erin said. "What is it?"

Khety took a step toward her. In a voice tinged with only the barest accent, he said in twenty-first-century English, "The king has vanished. I believe he has departed the palace, along with the great royal wife, their children, and a company of soldiers."

Erin gaped at the man—actually *gaped*. Her mouth dropped open. Her eyes bulged. She wondered if her tongue stuck out a little too, though the shock spreading through her like quick-forming ice dulled her senses to the point where she no longer felt in control of her body.

Khety spoke English. Fluently. Beautifully. Better than some residents of the twenty-first-century. But how on earth did Khety learn English?

A phrase Wessick had said to her replayed in her mind. Right before they exited their own time, she had expressed concern about the language barrier they would surely encounter here in the past. Wessick had replied with a typically cryptic statement.

I think you'll find language isn't as much of a barrier as you expect.

The ice of shock melted in a heartbeat. She shot an accusatory look at Wessick.

"Explain to me," she said, "how this man knows English."

In a tone he might use when explaining adult concepts to a child, Wessick said, "For thirty years, I have lived in two timelines, traveling between the two in the manner that some people travel back and forth between a winter and a summer residence. I've had ample opportunity to teach the English language to several residents of this timeline."

Erin crossed her arms over her chest. "Gee, that sounds an awful lot like changing the past. Which you said is impossible."

"Clearly, my actions have not altered our past. No one in our time knows that anyone in this time spoke English."

She harrumphed.

"Besides," he said, "I've instructed my allies to speak English only in the presence of myself or the *satseshat*."

"What if somebody decides to write a little note in English?"

Wessick bent forward, ducking his head close to hers, and murmured, "I haven't taught them to write English."

His position between her and Khety likely prevented the elder man from hearing his statement. Alex, on the other hand, seemed to hear it fine. He slapped a hand on Wessick's shoulder. With a brief but forceful shove, Alex pushed Wessick away from Erin.

Wessick stumbled, caught himself, and steadied. He now stood several feet away from Erin.

She opted not to chastise Alex. After all, she wasn't too happy with Wessick at the moment either.

"Did you ever think," Alex said, "that one of your cohorts might try to write English words using an Egyptian script? They could spell out the words phonetically, either in hieroglyphic or hieratic."

Wessick shrugged at the suggestion. "It would make no difference. No one but the *satseshat* holds the power to change history."

Erin scowled at Wessick. "Stop calling me the *satseshat*. I have a name."

"You're ignoring the salient point," Wessick said. "The pharaoh is gone—which means the relic is gone as well. We are too late."

19

E RIN ROLLED HER EYES AT WESSICK. "THERE'S NO SUCH THING AS TOO LATE. WHY don't we just use one of your fancy little orbs to go back further in time? To a point before the king took off."

"We cannot travel through timelines indiscriminately. One cannot travel back to a moment where one already exists. Time won't allow it. Because I have lived in this timeline for many years, I can't go back to four hours ago or even four days ago in this world."

"So send me back," Erin said. "I didn't exist in this timeline until a few hours ago."

"You would never gain access to the palace complex, much less the pharaoh."

Alex reached into his attaché. "We'll see about that."

Erin shot Alex a questioning glance. He started to smirk, but then froze. His eyes widened as he withdrew his hand from the bag and spun in a circle, searching the ground with his gaze. Torch in hand, he jogged back up the ramp and out of sight. He returned seconds later, a look of contained panic on his face. Before Erin could ask what was wrong, he seized her arm and pulled her toward the ramp doorway. They halted several feet from the opening.

Wessick and Khety observed from their positions several dozen feet away. They would not be able to hear whatever Alex wanted to say to her. She assumed that's why Alex dragged her over here.

"What's going on?" she asked.

Alex grasped her shoulder with his free hand and lowered his head. With their noses no more than an inch apart, he stared into her eyes and said, "I lost the map scroll."

"You brought it with you?" When he nodded, she asked, "How did you lose it?"

"I had it in my attaché, inside the plastic case, but the tube was too large to completely fit in the attaché. Part of it stuck out." He closed his eyes, letting his shoulders sag. "It must've fallen out at some point."

The plastic tube was white and rather large. If it stuck out of his bag, she certainly would've noticed it, particularly back in Wessick's house when she and Alex had their arms around each other.

"I never saw you with it," she said. "Did you have it with you at Wessick's house?"

"Yes." He opened his eyes. "At least I did when I came into the house."

A thought occurred to her, and she asked, "How did you get here anyway?"

"I, uh, watched the recording of you and Wessick departing the twenty-first century. Then I sort of…procured one of his *akhet* balls and used it myself. When I stepped through the portal, I wound up in the hallway outside your room at Wessick's house."

She flashed back to the moment when the madwoman Desheret tried to skewer her with a sword. Though the woman brandished the sword as if it barely outweighed a feather, when Erin grabbed the thing she almost toppled over under its weight.

Brushing aside the memory, she told Alex, "You showed up in the nick of time. That crazy woman is stronger than I am."

"Maybe in body, but not in spirit or mind."

She took his face in her hands and planted a firm kiss on his lips. "Thank you."

"For what?"

"Riding to my rescue, so to speak."

"I told you," he said, lifting his hand to touch her face, "whenever you need me, I will always come for you. And I meant it."

"I know."

A frown distorted his mouth, infecting his entire expression. He offered her the torch, and she accepted it. With both hands, he dug through his bag until he found what he wanted.

"Take this," he said, handing her a drawstring bag made from a metallic fabric she recognized.

It was a pouch containing an *akhet* ball. So he "procured" more than one of the little orbs, no doubt by breaking into Wessick's desk.

"You keep it," she said. "This outfit doesn't have any pockets."

He scrunched his lips, eyes focused on the little pouch. She could practically hear the thoughts bouncing around in his brain as he considered his options. Dropping the pouch into his coat pocket, he pulled the strap of his leather bag over his head and shoved the bag toward her. She shook her head. He grasped each of her hands in turn, forcing her to take hold of the bag. When she opened her mouth to protest, he laid two fingers on her lips to silence her.

"Take it," he said. "There are three more *akhet* balls inside. They work by thought control—think of a time and place and, poof, it'll take you there. If you need to get away quickly, don't hesitate to use them."

She stared at him for several seconds as the underlying meaning of his words and actions sunk into her brain. He kept one *akhet* ball for himself, and gave the others to her. He instructed her to use the orbs to escape, and his wording suggested she would do so alone.

"Where are you going?" she asked.

He cleared his throat, looked at the ground, kicked at the stone tile of the courtyard floor. Then, squaring his shoulders and lifting his head to look at her, he said, "I'm going back to Wessick's house."

"What? Why?"

"I know I had the scroll after I walked through the portal. I must've lost it in the struggle with our feral friend."

She thrust the bag at him. "We'll go together."

"No." He gently pushed the bag away. "It's too dangerous. Who knows where the human tornado went after she attacked you. And if word spreads that the king is missing, the situation will only get worse."

Clutching the bag to her chest, she glared up at him. "What makes you think I'm any safer here?"

"Wessick will protect you." His lip curled slightly when he spoke Wessick's name. "I may dislike him intensely, but I wouldn't leave you here if I didn't believe he'd protect you."

Scuffling erupted behind Alex. He turned to look in that direction. A group of men swarmed down the ramp from the bridge, each bearing some kind of weapon—bows and arrows, swords, battle axes, and spears. Erin and Alex hurried out of the way, ducking to the side. The armed men stormed into the courtyard shouting in Kemetian. Khety approached one of the men, and the pair engaged in an animated conversation that lasted a minute or two.

While Khety conversed with the armed man, Wessick moved closer to Erin and Alex, who huddled near the wall beside the ramp's end. From beyond the palace walls echoed the shouts of both men and women. The pounding of hooves suggested horses, probably pulling chariots, cantered down the road. Word must've spread quickly that the pharaoh had vanished.

The armed men must be soldiers. Were they mobilizing to quell a swiftly rising tide of panic? Only moments earlier, everything seemed quiet within the city of the sun disk. The news of the pharaoh's departure would likely spread first through the palace complex, then radiate outward into the city at large. How long did they have before chaos ruptured the quietude? In an oppressed city, the pharaoh's absence opened a door to power that at least some of the citizens might surge through in order to seize control of not just the city, but the nation itself.

Erin nestled closer to Alex. Politics had never been her strong suit, but the ramifications of the pharaoh's disappearance seemed obvious. The floodgates had begun to open.

Her mission just got a lot more complicated—and immeasurably more dangerous.

Finished with the soldiers, Khety strode toward Erin, Alex, and Wessick. He halted in front of Erin, as if she were the leader of their three-man army. Well, she was the *satseshat*. People kept telling her how important that made her, so maybe she was the leader.

"The secret has been released," Khety said, bowing his head as if in shame. "Our efforts to conceal it have failed. Soon every citizen will know of the king's departure."

Alex slipped an arm around Erin's shoulders. He said, "But it's not just the king who's left."

Khety sighed. "His chief advisors, the royal family, and a number of soldiers have also left."

"Which creates a power vacuum."

Alex's words triggered a furrowing of Khety's brow. The phrase "power vacuum" must not mean much to a man of this era.

"Never mind," Alex said. Then he canted his head, eyeing Khety. "Why didn't you leave with everyone else? You are an adviser to the king."

"I was instructed to await the arrival of the *satseshat*." Khety glanced at Wessick. "My fealty lies with the Brothers of the Aten, not with the king."

Erin felt a scowl pinching her features. Great. Khety was another lackey for the Aten.

"I don't understand," Alex said. "How did word of the king's departure spread so fast?"

Wessick spoke at last. "Even without the Internet, rumors propagate and mutate as swiftly as a virulent disease."

Khety nodded his agreement. "The soldiers who entered the palace a moment ago had been told Hyksos assassins breached the palace and murdered the king."

Footfalls pounded from the direction of the bridge. Within seconds, a stream of soldiers poured down the ramp into the courtyard, fanning out in discrete groups. Most of the soldiers were markedly different in appearance from the Kemetians. Asiatic and dark-skinned complexions dominated the faces that rushed past Erin and Alex. The darkest-skinned men must've been Nubians, natives of the kingdom to the south of Kemet.

Khety grabbed for Erin's arm. She instinctively pulled away. Glancing at the newly arrived soldiers, Khety aimed a pleading look at her.

"You must come," Khety said. "There is a place you may hide. Your safety is paramount."

Alex dropped his arm from her shoulders. He said, "Go with Khety."

Once again, Alex's wording implied that he would not be with her. He intended to trek back to Wessick's house alone. With panic dispersing through the city, and danger nearly palpable in the air, she would not let Alex go anywhere alone.

"You're not coming with me," Alex told her.

"If it's too dangerous for me, then it's also too dangerous for you."

Wessick interrupted. "What is going on?"

Erin waited for Alex to say something. When seconds passed without a peep from him, she told Wessick, "Alex left something back at your house. He insists on going back for it, but I say it's too dangerous for him to go out there alone."

"Whatever you've left behind," Wessick said, "I suggest you forget it."

"It's important," Alex said. "*Very* important."

Wessick shifted his gaze from Erin to Alex, then back to Erin. "I will accompany him."

"Oh no," Alex said, "I positively do not need any help from you."

"Under these circumstances," Wessick said, as he gestured at the troops disseminating through the palace, "navigating the city will be even more difficult. I know the way. You do not."

Alex's jaw worked. He seemed to be quite literally chewing on the dilemma.

"All right," Alex said, his tone resigned. "You can come along. But your brother there had better make certain nothing happens to Erin."

Wessick turned to his "brother" Khety. The bald man simply nodded, his expression solemn.

"I want to hear it," Alex hissed through clenched teeth.

Khety squared his shoulders, straightening his spine. He lifted his chin to meet Alex's gaze head-on and said, "I vow to defend the *satseshat* with my life."

Apparently satisfied, Alex turned to face her. He asked, "Do you have a weapon?"

"Does it look like I have a weapon?"

He looked down at her dress. Though not skintight, the linen left no room for anything larger than a bobby pin.

"I see your point," Alex said. "You should've brought your gun."

"I did, but in all the confusion I forgot it at Wessick's house."

He pulled his Glock 9mm out of its shoulder holster and, flipping it around to grasp it by the muzzle, offered its grip to her. "Take this."

She shook her head. "You need it more than I do."

"I can pick up your gun at Wessick's."

"And between here and there you'll be defenseless."

"Thank you for the vote of confidence." He shoved the Glock at her. "Take this, dammit."

She clutched his bag to her chest but made no move to accept the gun.

Alex stared at her for a moment. Another contingent of armed men streamed down the ramp past them, and Alex tore his attention away from her to squint at the soldiers. His lips curved upward ever so slightly. She knew that look. He had an idea. One she would hate, no doubt.

Facing her again, Alex unzipped the main compartment of his bag with one sweep of his hand. Before she realized what he was doing, he dumped the Glock into the compartment. She nabbed the gun. With its muzzle pointed at the ground, she thrust the Glock at him.

"Take it back," she said.

He smiled, the expression so serene she knew for certain he was about to do something crazy.

She waggled the gun at him.

Spinning on his heels, Alex strode toward the nearest soldier. He reached for the man's sword. The soldier balked, shouting what probably amounted to Kemetian curse words.

Alex punched the soldier in the jaw. The sword slipped from the man's grasp, clattering to the ground. Alex snatched up the sword as the soldier crumpled.

Other soldiers cried out, swarming toward Alex.

Erin kicked Wessick's leg. When he glanced at her, she said, "Help him."

Wessick frowned. Erin kicked him again.

Muttering under his breath, Wessick marched toward Alex. He raised a hand at the advancing soldiers. They hesitated, eyes on Wessick.

In an authoritative tone, Wessick issued what Erin assumed were orders, though she couldn't understand his words. He spoke Kemetian, she assumed. Two of the soldiers stepped forward to help their comrade onto his feet. Wessick issued more orders, and the soldiers exited the courtyard through a doorway opposite the shallow ramp that led into the roofed area. The last soldier to leave handed his sword to Wessick before hurrying after his buddies.

Sword in hand, Alex returned to Erin's side. In a triumphant tone, he said, "I've got the weapon situation covered."

The sword resembled the one Desheret used in her attempt on Erin's life. Alex brandished the sword as if its weight bothered him little. Wessick held his sword in one hand, the tip hanging down toward the ground. Erin felt a twinge of envy. Everyone else seemed adept at handling cumbersome weapons. She felt like a weakling—the damsel in distress, waving a hankie out the window of her prison tower, wailing for a brave knight to save her.

She was not weak. Besides, she had Alex's gun. Pulling the trigger was one task she could manage without falling on her butt.

"I'm coming back," Alex said. He kissed her forehead and added, "Stay in the palace until then."

He took the torch from her and turned to Wessick. The older man motioned for Alex to precede him up the ramp to the bridge. Alex shook his head.

"I want you in front of me," Alex said. "And keep your hands where I can see them. No more hypodermic sneak attacks."

Wessick headed up the ramp. Alex started up the incline, then paused to look back at Erin. She managed a tight smile and a little wave. He strode up the ramp out of sight.

Erin's throat constricted. Her chest felt tight too. Tears stung her eyes, and she blinked them away. No crying. No imagining the worst possible outcome. Alex would return, and they would find the relic together. In the meantime, she needed to get out of sight. Getting herself caught in the melee would only hinder her mission.

As if he knew her thoughts, Khety cupped one hand over her arm. Touching her with the lightest pressure, he urged her to hurry across the courtyard toward the shallow ramp. Outside the palace, galloping hooves thundered down the main road. Men shouted. While Khety led Erin up the smaller ramp, chaos descended over the city of the sun disk. Yet Erin sensed a greater threat looming out of view, high above their heads. Would the Aten wait much longer for her to find the relic? How much time did she have until they enacted their ultimate plan?

She glanced up at the sky. A light flashed, brighter and larger than any star or planet. Maybe the Aten knew her thoughts, or maybe the flash of light was coincidence. Either way, she knew the answer to her own question. They wouldn't wait long. She must find the relic this night, or the Aten would wreak their vengeance on the entire world.

A single word echoed in her mind.

Annihilation.

20

AFTER MEANDERING THROUGH A MAZE OF SMALLER COURTYARDS AND ROOMS, Khety led Erin through a pair of massive wooden doors that hung partway open, allowing enough space for three people to enter side-by-side. They hurried into a spacious chamber decorated in bright, lavish colors.

The floor featured paintings of marshland scenes, complete with geese rising from the grasses and weeds, about to ascend into the sky. Other scenes depicted cattle gamboling beneath airborne geese. On the walls, vivid colors brought to life sunken reliefs of lotuses and cornflowers, geometric borders, and scenes of the royal family. The roof rested atop high columns ornamented with geometric designs and the ever-present geese.

At the other end of the room, facing the doorway, sat a small but magnificent chair lifted above the floor on a stone dais. The chair, clad in gold leaf, served as the only furniture in the room. The legs of the chair terminated in lion paws and lion heads capped the arms, so that anyone seated in the chair would rest his hands atop the feline heads. The chair's back framed a gold panel embossed and painted to depict the pharaoh and his chief wife, Nefertiti, adoring the Aten deity. The sun disk hovered high above their heads, with its hand-tipped rays stretching downward as if to caress the royal couple's faces.

Halfway across the room, Khety halted.

"You will be safe here," he said.

He turned to leave.

Erin stepped in front of him, blocking his path to the door. "Where are you going?"

"I must attend to other matters."

Erin chewed the inside of her lip. She needed to find the priests of Amun-Ra, who most likely lived in hiding—assuming the pharaoh hadn't killed them as part of his efforts to eradicate the old gods. Khety spoke English, which made him the only person she knew of in the city who could understand her. Yet by his own admission, he was loyal to the brothers of the Aten and therefore to the Aten themselves. Her enemies. The evil aliens.

If the priests still lived, Khety was her only shot at finding them. If the priests were dead, then she was out of options altogether.

"My lady," Khety said, drawing her attention to him once more. "Do you require my services?"

"Um…" Trusting Khety was a risk, a potentially deadly one, but she really had no choice. So she said, "You told me you would protect me with your life. Does that include protecting my secrets?"

"I will die before revealing your secrets, just as I will die before letting another harm you."

She expected a hesitation as he considered the ramifications of helping her in a manner that might lead to defying the Aten. If they demanded to know what she told him, after he promised to guard her secrets, then he would be forced to either defy the Aten or betray the *satseshat*. Though his facial expression revealed nothing, in his eyes she sensed spiritual turmoil.

Khety's vow and Alex's unspoken promise seemed, on the surface, quite similar. Khety said he would die to protect her, and Alex promised to always be there when she needed him, no matter what. Alex didn't need to say that he would risk his life for her. She already knew it, because he'd done it before. That was the difference between Khety and Alex. Both men promised to let no harm come to her, but when Alex spoke those words, Erin knew beyond any doubt that he would never succumb to the Aten, no matter what they did to him. Her trust in Khety came tagged with a question mark.

"What about the Aten?" she asked.

"You are the *satseshat*. Where loyalty is concerned, no one ranks higher."

"Okay. Good." She squared her shoulders, lifting her chin. Time to leap off that cliff. "I need to find the priests of Amun-Ra."

Khety didn't blink. He stared at her for several seconds, then glanced around the room as if afraid someone might be eavesdropping.

"Speaking the names of the old gods," he said, "incurs harsh punishment. Worshiping them is punishable by death."

"I didn't ask for a lesson on penal codes." Erin planted her hands on her hips. "I need to find the priests of Amun-Ra. Can you help me or not?"

He looked at the floor and sighed. "I am not certain anyone can help you. The priests at the Temple of Amun-Ra in Waset were among the first to suffer the king's wrath upon his return from the mountains, when he declared the Aten to be the only god. Two escaped the massacre at the temple, but the king dispatched soldiers to hunt and eradicate them. I believe they are dead."

"But you don't know for sure."

"I cannot be certain, as I was not present at their execution."

Erin glanced around at the floor paintings, the golden throne, and the painted reliefs carved into walls hewn from stone rather than mud brick. When it came to building his new capital city, the pharaoh must've poured resources into the project with utter abandon, stealing from his people in order to fund the construction of opulent temples and palaces. Every pharaoh built such edifices, yet Akhenaten did more than squander resources. He beat down his people, forcing them to adopt a new way of life whether they liked it or not.

The Aten encouraged oppression. They wanted to control humanity. Their efforts to find the relic depended on such control. The Aten expected her to find the relic for them, even though their own actions were directly responsible for her current dilemma. The only people who knew where to find the relic were dead. The Aten killed them.

An Aten killed them.

Erin refused to recognize the distinction. One of the Aten's own, whom they conspired to place in a position of power, snuffed out the only chance she had of locating the relic. They should blame no one but themselves. She knew they wouldn't accept culpability though. They would blame her. Exclusively.

"Can you think of anyone," Erin said, "who might know whether any of the priests survived?"

Khety thought for a moment. "There is a man imprisoned in the House of the Aten, the main temple. The priests of the Aten guard him within the *gem-pa-aten*. No one is allowed to see this man."

"What makes you think he can help me?"

"I have heard rumors about this man. They say he speaks a strange language and is a great enemy of the Aten."

He ticked off the Aten? She liked him already. And she had no other leads anyway.

Alex told her to stay in the palace.

She hadn't promised to do it.

"Take me to him," she said.

"Yes, my lady."

Khety moved toward the doors. Halfway there, he froze. As Erin came up alongside him, she saw the look of intense concentration—and worry—on his face.

"Someone comes," he whispered.

Tilting her left ear toward the doorway, Erin listened. A faint clapping sound might indicate the approach of someone. Khety must have superb hearing.

"You must hide," Khety said.

He clapped his hands at her in a gesture that urged her to back away with utmost speed. She stumbled backward. Khety directed her, with frantic gestures, to stand against the wall adjacent to the left-hand door. She complied. Since the doors opened inward, and they stood partially ajar, the colossal hunk of wood concealed her from view. Given the current state of affairs in the capital city, hiding seemed prudent.

In the hallway, the footsteps clapped nearer.

Khety sauntered through the doorway.

Erin sidled closer to the huge wooden door. A gap of perhaps a half inch separated the door from its frame, allowing room for the hinges. She positioned one eye over the gap. Khety stood within her sight line. The newly arrived person, however, lingered somewhere to the left, out of Erin's view. Khety spoke to the newcomer in words Erin didn't understand, undoubtedly Kemetian.

Khety's gestures and facial expression grew animated. He seemed to be arguing with the other person. The voice of the unknown person sounded female.

And familiar.

An icy fist clamped tight around Erin's stomach. She knew the voice because she'd encountered the speaker before. It was the human tornado—Desheret, the sword-wielding madwoman.

Khety shook his head, muttering something.

The woman stepped into view from the left, her body sideways to Erin but her head facing away. Desheret wore a long, tan sheath dress with a matching shawl that covered her arms and shoulders. A large knot situated just below her breastbone secured the shawl in place. Across her collarbone draped a wide necklace composed of multiple strands of red and blue stones interspersed with gold ornaments. Encircling each wrist, gold bracelets, also inlaid with red and blue stones, chinked each time she moved. Long black hair framed her face, cascading down her back and over her shoulders in front. She held her right arm bent across her abdomen, with her hand beneath the shawl.

Desheret turned her head, exposing her face in profile.

Erin choked back a gasp. She knew that face. Even with the elaborate eye makeup and the dark wig, the features matched a face engraved in Erin's memory. She imagined the dark wig replaced with fiery red hair.

The madwoman was Chloe Pelletier.

Erin's friend. The one who encouraged her to take the job at Revenant House. The one who vanished without explanation. The one who told Erin, in a terse text message, to stop calling her.

Suddenly, everything made sense. Chloe showed up in Erin's life a year ago, after taking a job at the library where Erin worked. Despite Erin's distrust of other people, Chloe wormed her way into Erin's life as a friend, keeping in touch even after they both lost their jobs at the library when the institution closed due to municipal budget cuts. Chloe refused to talk about her past, but expressed keen interest in Erin's life. Then, after the Rassul debacle, Chloe vanished altogether—and Desheret roared onto the scene like a rabid lioness.

Chloe had never been Erin's friend. It was all a lie. Chloe-Desheret insinuated herself into Erin's life to keep tabs on her and to encourage to her to do what the Aten wanted. The girl served the Aten, perhaps more fervently than either Rassul or Wessick. Desheret was the most dangerous of them all.

"Stop this charade at once."

The words yanked Erin out of her thoughts. She squinted through the narrow gap at the woman who spoke the syllables, the woman who once played the role of Chloe Pelletier. The dress, the wig, and the makeup made her appear slightly older. Erin might've recognized her sooner, however, if not for the difference in her voice. As Chloe, she'd spoken in a higher and more youthful tone. As Desheret, as herself, she spoke in a more sultry voice.

Was Desheret indeed this woman's true identity?

"I know you speak English, old man," Desheret said. "Stop pretending you don't."

She had spoken the words a few seconds earlier that snapped Erin back to the present. Of course Desheret spoke English. She spoke it as well as, if not better than, native citizens of the twenty-first century. Fluency was required for the girl to succeed in her role as Erin's betrayer.

Not that Erin ever really trusted Chloe. She'd liked the girl, but trust did not come easily.

Except with Alex.

Anger twisted Desheret's features. She jabbed a finger in the air inches from Khety's chest and spat words at him. "Where is Erin Turner?"

Khety feigned ignorance. "What is Air-in-tor-ner?"

Desheret whipped her right hand out from under the shawl. In her long delicate fingers she grasped a 9mm handgun.

Erin's heart thudded. It was her gun.

Well, she did have another one.

Grasping the zipper of Alex's bag between her thumb and forefinger, she pulled it open millimeter by millimeter. The unzipping sound was faint. To Erin, though, it seemed as loud as a jet engine.

Neither Khety nor Desheret behaved as if they heard the noise. Thank heavens.

Suppressing a relieved sigh, Erin stopped unzipping the bag. The gap was wide enough for her to snake a hand inside the bag and close her fingers around the grip of Alex's Glock. She withdrew the gun cautiously. The bag she left unzipped. Nothing important would fall out of the six-inch opening and she didn't care to tempt fate again by re-zipping the bag.

Khety gasped.

Erin glanced through the gap between the door and jamb. Desheret had jammed the gun's muzzle under Khety's chin.

"Tell me now," the woman hissed, "where you have hidden Erin Turner, the *satseshat*. Or I shall use this weapon to blast a hole through your skull from bottom to top? Even you are capable of understanding what I propose."

Perhaps unconsciously, or perhaps believing Desheret wouldn't notice, Khety glanced at the gap through which Erin watched their exchange.

A vicious smile spread across Desheret's face in slow motion.

Oh crap. Erin clenched her hand tighter around the Glock.

Khety's eyes widened until they seemed about to pop loose from their sockets. He shook his head with a vehemence that rattled his jowls.

The madwoman turned her eyes to look at the gap between the door and the frame.

Erin sprang backward. Her heart thumped as she flattened against the wall.

A chuckle echoed through the hallway and into the throne chamber.

"Come out, Erin," Desheret said in the bright voice of her Chloe persona. "Sweetie-pie, we've gotta catch up. It's been way too long."

Erin gulped. The lump refused to dislodge from her throat. She licked her lips, but her tongue felt parched, like the rest of her mouth. Her heart thumped so hard and so fast she feared she might pass out.

Oh for pity's sake. She was not a damsel in distress.

Okay, maybe she was. But she could handle this. She *must* handle this. So what if Chloe had a gun—Erin's gun. The girl was insane, easily overwhelmed by her desperation to kill Erin. Besides, Erin had a gun too. Besting the madwoman should be simple.

Yeah right.

Tucking both arms behind her back, Erin clasped her left hand around her right wrist to hold her gun-toting arm in place, out of sight. The Glock would remain hidden while she assessed the situation. Maybe she wouldn't have to shoot Desheret. But if she saw no other options…

She would do it. She would kill Desheret. It wouldn't be her first kill.

An image of Rassul flashed in her mind. She shoved it back into the recesses of her brain.

Erin sucked in a breath, squared her shoulders, and pushed away from the wall. A flick of her thumb disengaged the Glock's safety. She stepped out from behind the door, striding across the threshold into the hallway.

"Here I am," Erin said.

Desheret's smile turned triumphant. Still in her Chloe voice, she said with mock amazement, "Well, if it ain't the righteous and blessed *satseshat.*"

"Drop the act," Erin said. "Your impersonation of a sane woman won't fly anymore."

"Fine." Desheret's voice shifted into the lower range, which Erin suspected was her normal tone. The madwoman said, "Bring your hands out where I can see them."

Erin stiffened. She had two choices now—reveal the gun and be forced to hand it over to Desheret, or swing the gun out and shoot the woman. The former meant surrender, but the latter felt an awful lot like cold-blooded murder.

The woman was threatening to kill Khety. Did that make homicide justifiable?

"Now," Desheret commanded. "Or this man dies."

Could she raise the gun and pull the trigger before Desheret shot Khety?

Erin felt her shoulders slump as the answer to her own question surfaced in her mind. Though she knew how to use a gun, her skills fell short of the expert-marksman level. She could not risk another person's life based on slim odds.

Dammit.

She swung her arms out from behind her back, holding the gun with its muzzle directed at the floor.

Desheret said, "Drop the weapon and kick it to the side."

Erin complied. The Glock skittered across the stone floor until it bumped into the gargantuan door at Erin's right. She stood a couple feet from the left-hand door. Several yards separated her from the gun.

"Where is the relic?" Desheret asked.

"I wish I knew."

"Do not lie to me. You came here to retrieve it, there's no other explanation for your presence in the City of the Aten."

"I thought I could get here before the pharaoh left." Erin shrugged. "I was wrong."

Khety gulped, his Adam's apple pressing against the gun. Desheret shoved the muzzle deeper into his flesh.

"Why didn't you go with the pharaoh?" Erin asked.

Desheret's upper lip twitched. Her nostrils flared. "He forbade me to go with him. Someone exposed me as a servant of the Aten, and His Incarnation labeled me a traitor, though one so pathetic and ineffectual that I was not worthy of execution. He merely banished me."

Erin arched her eyebrows. "You don't look very banished to me."

"I made my way back to the city. Thanks to you."

"Me?"

Desheret chuckled, the sound soft and menacing. "I was banished to the twenty-first century. The other Aten, the ones Akhenaten betrayed, helped me to return. If you had not won Samuel's heart, and inspired him to disobey the Aten, they would never have deigned to help me."

The old inner chill, so familiar to her now, leeched into Erin's bones once again. She really hoped Desheret was wrong about Wessick's feelings for her. It was too weird to consider. He might grudgingly like her, but oh lord, she prayed it ended there.

Khety smacked his forearm into Desheret's.

For a moment, Erin didn't understand what was happening. She stood frozen as her brain struggled to sort out what it saw.

The gun popped out of Desheret's grasp. It clattered to the floor, skidding away from Desheret and Khety in the opposite direction from Erin. Desheret swung her knee up and slammed it into Khety's groin. A hoarse cry burst from him as he bent forward.

Desheret flung herself toward the gun.

Khety hurled himself on top of her. Hands and arms and legs flailed and interlocked, then yanked free to flail again.

"Go," Khety bellowed. He twisted his head around to glance at Erin. "Quickly."

Erin dove for the Glock. The instant her fingers closed around its grip, she sprang to her feet and spun toward the battling duo.

Their heads were mere feet from Erin, yet Desheret and Khety were so entwined that if she tried to shoot Desheret, the bullet might strike Khety instead. The ongoing struggle between the pair complicated matters further. Limbs flailed and skirts billowed until the entire scene became a blur of flesh and fabric.

"Go!" Khety shouted.

Erin hesitated. She must find the relic. Everyone's lives depended on it. Besides, Khety could surely subdue the smaller and less-muscular Desheret.

No, she would not run like a coward.

A slender yet powerful hand lashed out to grab Erin's ankle. Her foot flipped out from under her. The gun popped out of her grasp. She lost her balance and flung out her arms to steady herself, kicking at the restraining hand as she regained her footing. Desheret yanked Erin's ankle. The motion twisted Erin around just as she lost her footing, and she tumbled to the floor face-first. Though she caught herself with her hands, her hips struck the floor. Something crunched.

Erin did a lightning-fast inventory of her body. Everything felt okay. The crunching must not have originated from shattering bones. Maybe she imagined the sound.

Whump.

That sound she hadn't imagined.

Desheret cried out.

Erin rolled onto her side, looking back at Desheret.

The madwoman's fingers popped open. Erin yanked her foot free and scrambled forward to grab the Glock. With the gun clutched in her hand, she leaped to her feet.

Khety must've struck Desheret, for she looked dazed. He flipped her onto her stomach, pinning her arms behind her. As he struggled to his knees, maintaining his grasp on her wrists, he looked up at Erin.

"Leave," he said. "I will see that she is detained."

"How do I get out of here?" Erin asked.

"Go through the door behind you and continue in that direction. You will cross through two more doors and finally into the courtyard."

"Why didn't we come in that way?"

Desheret wiggled. He rammed a knee into her spine, quelling her struggle. To Erin, he said, "I hoped to deter anyone from following us, and therefore conceal your whereabouts." He glanced at Desheret. "I failed."

"No, you didn't. You saved my life." She managed a smile. "Thank you."

Then she ran out the door.

Through one door. Then another. Up ahead, a wider doorway opened onto the ramp that spilled out into the courtyard. Exactly as Khety had told her.

She raced down the ramp.

Pow!

Erin skidded to a halt as the report echoed through the courtyard. A gunshot.

Khety and Desheret. Erin forgot about the other gun. Who shot whom?

She could not go back to find out. She might walk straight into an ambush. Whatever the outcome, Khety wanted her to leave the Desheret problem in his hands. She must find the temple.

The clamorous noises outside the palace walls grew stronger every minute. Time was running out.

Erin bolted across the courtyard to the doorway that accessed the bridge ramp. Up the incline she ran, her legs aching with the effort. When she reached the staircase that led down to the main road, she glanced out at the view before her and stopped dead.

Soldiers fought soldiers. Unarmed men shielded women and children with their own bodies as soldiers turned on the ordinary citizens once they'd felled their comrades. Other citizens skirted around the soldiers as best they could, keeping close to the walls on either side of the road. A chariot pulled by two black horses and driven by a muscular man in soldier's garb stormed down the road, straight through the crowd. Someone screamed as the horses trampled the throng.

An aura of utter chaos pervaded the scene. It wasn't merely the violence or the noise. A sense of terror and desperation infected everything, even the air. She swore she could smell it, hear it, taste it.

The onrush of death.

Alex was out there. Unarmed. Unaware. Desheret had Erin's gun, which left Alex only the sword for protection. As far as she knew, he wasn't trained in sword combat. Worst of all, however, he had no idea that Desheret was Chloe. If she removed her wig, and slipped back into her goofy girl routine, she might catch Alex off guard.

Erin squeezed her eyes shut. Tears threatened to spill out, and she did not want to cry. Not yet. When this was all over, she'd let the tears flow. Until then, she must get ahold of herself. Alex wasn't stupid. If Chloe approached him, he would recognize the danger.

Please God, let him recognize it.

A few slow breaths brought her heart rate under control. She opened her eyes and allowed herself one last panoramic look at the chaos around her.

The gun felt solid in her hand, its metal warmed by her flesh.

She bounded down the stairs.

A GROUP OF WOMEN AND CHILDREN CONGREGATED ON THE LEFT SIDE OF THE road. On the right side, soldiers argued with civilian men. A team of at least five chariots squeezed through the middle single file, forced to proceed at a walk thanks to the dense crowd around them.

Erin hesitated, considering her options. She must get past the bottleneck. Alex mentioned he thought the Great Temple, aka the House of the Aten, lay beyond the palace. To get past the palace, she must first navigate through the crowd that blocked the road. The group on the right-hand side was embroiled in a heated argument, complete with violent gesticulations. The women and children seemed calm, if wary.

Through the left side then.

Keeping her head down, she charged into the crowd of women and children. She kept her right hand, which held the Glock, tucked inside the unzipped the main compartment of Alex's bag. Some of the women, and a couple of the children, gave her funny looks as they noticed the big leather bag slung around her neck and across her torso. She ignored the attention and pushed onward. Acknowledging the curious looks would only attract more interest to her, and she remembered what Wessick said about attention being dangerous. Though she doubted much of what he said, she accepted his advice on this one point. Drawing attention seemed like a really bad idea.

Traffic on the street thinned out once she made it through the bottleneck. Up ahead, on the right side, a stone wall towered high above the road. Compared to other structures in ancient Egypt, the stone blocks of the wall seemed tiny. Erin knew without examining them that the blocks measured about two feet wide by ten inches high. No pharaoh except Akhenaten used such small blocks. The stones were carved and painted in the vivid colors favored by the artisans of Kemet. The torches from neighboring buildings and passersby flicked tongues of light across the wall's artwork, but the flames seemed lilliputian in comparison with the barrier itself, which must've risen at least a hundred feet in the air. Midway down the enclosure, a pylon twice as high as the wall offered access to the interior. A glow whiter and brighter than a full moon swelled above the wall and spilled out the opening between the pylon's halves.

The sterile glow sent a shiver through Erin. The light was unnaturally pure and bright, indicative of something more than oil lamps or torches. No light source of the pre-electricity era could produce such a glow. Whatever the light's source, whatever lay inside the temple enclosure, she would find out soon enough.

She broke into a trot, and then a full run, racing straight for the pylon.

A stone ramp led up and through the pylon, descending into the interior of the enclosure. Erin skidded to a halt with one foot on the ramp and the other on the ground.

A light almost as bright as sunlight, but far colder, enveloped her and overwhelmed her vision. She swung up an arm to shield her eyes. Even as she stumbled forward another step, her eyes began to adjust to the new conditions. Squinting, she lowered her arm.

And spotted the source of the light.

She swallowed against a tightening in her throat. No history book spoke of this.

At regular intervals along the interior of the enclosure wall hung large globes that radiated a cool yet brilliant light. What powered the globes, she couldn't tell. No power lines or wires were visible. One thing was obvious and undeniable, however. The globes represented a technology far beyond oil lamps or even fluorescent bulbs. They embodied the technology of the Aten.

Naturally, the Aten provided the technology to light only the temple dedicated to their worship. The rest of the city scraped by with inferior technology—oil lamps, hand-dug wells, and no indoor plumbing. The average people slept in the same house with their livestock, for pity's sake. Yet the Aten refused to share their technology with the people they conspired to oppress.

The Aten were evil. She knew that already. Matters of greater urgency needed her full attention.

Standing at the foot of the ramp, she surveyed her surroundings. Behind and to her left stood a flat-roofed rectangular building. Straight ahead, aligned with the enclosure's pylon, hunkered a long and narrow building fashioned from limestone and fronted by a massive pylon of its own. A ramp sloped upward through the pylon. To the building's right, a field of offering tables stretched down the length of the stone structure. The field contained hundreds upon hundreds of offering tables, made of mud brick or stone, lined up in neat rows.

She thought back to everything she'd read about Akhenaten, and the Great Aten Temple in particular. The field of offering tables indicated that the long, narrow building in front of her was the central area of worship. Khety told her the priests of the Aten had imprisoned the mystery man in the House of the Aten, within something called the *gem-pa-aten*. If she remembered correctly, *gem-pa-aten* referred to the building she faced now.

Pulling her hand out of the bag, she held the Glock muzzle-down at her side. Her trigger finger she flattened against the barrel, just above the trigger. No one seemed to be around, but she'd take no chances. She wanted the gun out and ready for use.

Lifting her chin, rolling back her shoulders, she stalked across the open ground between the pylon ramp and the one leading up into the *gem-pa-aten*. This ramp did not descend again on the opposite side of the pylon, but rather deposited her on a flat stone floor higher than the ground outside. She found herself inside a portico populated by gargantuan stone columns laid out in rows of four, two on each side of the pylon. Massive beams connected the tops of the columns. Vivid paints colored in the hieroglyphs and other artwork incised into the stone faces of the columns. Shadows cast by the columns cleaved the brilliant glow from the lights outside, lending an eerie ambience to the portico.

At the near end of each column row, facing the front wall of the structure, stood massive stelae fashioned from sandstone. The stelae, flat slabs mounted to stand upright, featured images of the Aten and the pharaoh adoring the god, above inscriptions that probably offered verbal praise to the Aten.

Erin repressed the urge to fire every round in the Glock at the stelae. Disfiguring the image of the Aten might give her a little pleasure, but would waste ammunition.

In the center of the aisle between the columns, steps accessed an empty platform. It probably served as another place where the pharaoh worshiped the Aten. It seemed strange that Akhenaten worshiped his own race, especially since the other Aten claimed he betrayed them.

Maybe he was keeping up appearances to fool his brethren. After all, the Aten didn't realize Akhenaten had betrayed them until after he absconded with their relic.

So much for their omniscience.

Erin walked down the aisle between the rows of columns, diverting around the platform. The portico ended at another pylon. She walked through a narrower doorway into an open courtyard. At either side of the central path squatted more offering tables identical to those outside the *gem-pa-aten*. At the far end of the courtyard, yet another pylon blocked her view of what lay beyond. She crossed the courtyard at a brisk pace, hurrying through the pylon's threshold into another courtyard virtually identical to the first. Another pylon insulated the second courtyard from the next section of the building. Unlike the previous pylons, this one included a pair of doors fit for a giant. Erin jogged through the courtyard to the doorway.

She raised her hand to knock, but froze.

Goosebumps prickled her skin. Abruptly, she realized what triggered the sensation—the silence within the *gem-pa-aten*, indeed within the entire temple complex. The chaos outside had yet to invade the temple complex, yet the silence seemed deeper than it should've been. The air felt…vacant. Devoid of life. Like a tomb floating in outer space.

Oh sure, that made sense. She was paranoid, nothing more.

Shaking off the paranoia, she rapped on the door. Seconds ticked by with no response. She rapped harder three, four, five times. Several seconds elapsed. She raised her hand to knock again.

On the other side of the door, a mechanism chunked. It sounded like a lock or a latch being disengaged.

Erin dropped her hand.

One half of the door pivoted inward. A face jutted out from behind the slab of wood. The man was bald and smooth skinned, save for faint wrinkles around his eyes. He looked younger than Khety but likely older than she or Alex. Priests kept their heads shaved, she recalled. This man must work as a priest of the Aten, and so probably knew about the mysterious prisoner.

The priest settled one hand on the door's edge, below his chin. He eyed the bag draped across her torso, and the Glock in her hand, before settling his gaze on her face. He spoke to her, his voice a soft tenor. Despite Wessick's assurance the language barrier wouldn't hinder her, she had no idea what the priest said to her. Wessick may have taught his allies to understand English, but the majority of Akhetaten's residents knew nothing of her world.

Wait. This man was a priest of the Aten. Didn't that make him an ally of Wessick?

One way to find out.

She gave the man a pleasant, if restrained, smile. "Do you speak English?"

His brow furrowed.

"*Parlez-vous anglais?*" she asked, immediately realizing how dumb it was to repeat her question in French. She didn't know how to ask in Kemetian. Although her French was basic at best, it still ranked far superior to her ancient Egyptian.

The priest muttered something. He slid his hand off the door, leaning back as if about to shut the portal in her face.

Erin groaned. Tonight she had turned into a bumbling moron—as well as a coward, considering the way she abandoned Khety. The man had wanted her to flee. That knowledge did little to temper her guilt. She left him with a madwoman who probably killed him, judging by the gunshot she heard while fleeing the palace like a lily-livered damsel in distress. Never again.

Use your brain.

"Um," she began, not so auspiciously. "I, uh…"

The priest ducked his head behind the door. The wood slab inched forward.

Erin slapped both hands on the door. "Wait!"

The movement stopped. The priest's head poked out from behind the door.

Erin reestablished her smile. Then she lifted a hand, pointed at herself, and uttered the only Kemetian words she remembered. "*Satseshat. Hem ky rek.*"

She'd just called herself the daughter of Seshat, the incarnation of another time. If this man knew Wessick, then he would know about the *satseshat* too.

She hoped.

The priest's eyes widened. "*Satseshat?*"

Erin nodded. When he gave no reaction, she realized he might not understand the gesture. She pointed at herself and repeated, "*Satseshat.*"

The priest said nothing, his wide eyes unblinking as he stared at her.

How could she prove she was the *satseshat*? Maybe by telling the priest something only the *satseshat* would know. She bit the inside of her lip.

A memory teased her brain. The map scroll referred to the relic as the object from another time. If she could remember how to say it in Kemetian, the priest might believe her. If she remembered. Since *hem ky rek* translated as "incarnation of another time," and she knew *hem* meant incarnation, that told her the phrase *ky rek* must translate as "another time." Now, which word meant object? The answer lingered just beyond her mental grasp.

Erin let her eyes shift out of focus. She thought back to the day when Alex translated the scroll for her. They'd both been leaning over the desk in the library at Revenant House, poring over the scroll. Alex had run his fingers over the hieroglyphs as he translated them aloud. When he spoke the word object, his fingers ran over hieroglyphs that looked like...

A circle with bars across it. Above a semicircle.

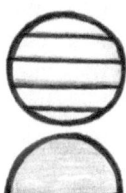

The symbols hovered in front of her mind's eye. By some miracle, she even remembered what sounds they represented.

Erin fixed her gaze on the priest's and said, "*Khet em ky rek.*"

The priest blinked, tilted his head ever so slightly, and stared at her some more. He gripped the door's edge in both hands. Just when she thought he might shut the door, he scuffled backward and swung it wide for her.

She crossed the threshold into an open courtyard. Like the others, this courtyard housed stone offering tables, though unlike the others it measured substantially smaller. The back portion of the courtyard segued into a portico, similar to but smaller than the one inside the main pylon of the *gem-pa-aten*. Beyond the portico, she spied another blasted pylon barred by a door.

Shuffling in a semi-circle, she faced the priest.

He shut the door, dropping a wooden bar into slots on either side of the double doors. With the doorway thus locked, he turned to Erin and gazed at her with a questioning expression.

He expected her to speak. To explain her presence. To say what she wanted.

She bit her lip, searching her brain for Kemetian words. Alex knew more than she did, though she'd tried to bone up on her Kemetian over the last two weeks. Her mind went blank. She'd used up her entire Kemetian vocabulary when she first encountered the priest.

A curse popped up in her mind, but instead she said, "*Satseshat. Khet em ky rek.*"

The priest clasped his hands over his belly, wringing his fingers.

Erin repeated the phrases. She tried to inject a note of authority into her voice.

Dropping his hands, the priest shuffled past her. At the edge of the portico, he paused to glance back at her. He raised one arm and flicked his hand. She decided that meant he wanted her to follow him, and so she did.

They passed between the paired rows of stone columns. At the pylon door, they stopped. The two halves of the door were connected by a wooden bar, which itself appeared to be sealed in place by a rectangular wood box mounted vertically over the bar. The left end of the bar included a slot on its top side.

The priest grasped her shoulders and pressed down lightly, then released her. He said something, but she must've looked as confused as she felt because he emphasized his statement with a hand gesture. Combined with his pressing on her shoulders, she decided he meant for her to stay put.

She smiled, hoping the expression conveyed her compliance.

The priest trotted between the rows of columns in the portico. The shadows engulfed him. A moment later, he emerged from the columns carrying an object in his hand.

Erin watched the man approach the pylon doors. The object in his hand was a long piece of wood, one end of which bent at a shallow angle, lending it the appearance of a spatula. Instead of being slotted, however, the angled end held three metal pegs.

The priest leaned closer to the bar that held the doors closed. He inserted the wooden spatula into the slot in the bar, pegged end first. When the spatula apparently would go no further into the slot, he lifted the handle upward. Inside the vertical wooden box, a mechanism clicked.

Releasing the spatula's handle, the priest slid the bar out of the vertical box. He pushed the left door inward and walked through the opening.

Erin glanced down at the gun in her hand, and then she walked through the doorway.

They walked down a short, narrow hallway, into a small rectangular room. At either side of them, wooden shrines sat atop stone pedestals. The closed doors of the box-like shrines concealed whatever sacred items lay within them. Directly in front of Erin and the priest, a door-size opening led into another chamber. Visible through the opening, a stepped platform supported a golden table piled high with offerings of food.

The priest led her into the chamber. They angled rightward to bypass the offering table on its platform. Erin noted the smaller stone offering tables lined up at either side of the platform, and the dual niches, more like open-topped booths, attached to either wall. Each niche housed a statue of the pharaoh. Since the Aten deity had no face or body, she supposed statues of the pharaoh substituted for the statues of gods like Amun and Horus that had once adorned the temples of Egypt. Akhenaten was, in a real sense, the embodiment of the Aten.

Behind the offering-table platform, another door-size opening accessed a narrow hallway. The rear wall held six niches, three at each side of the hallway entrance. The priest ushered her down the hallway into another little room flanked by an opening into another offering chamber. This anteroom, however, harbored no shrines. Instead, the right-hand side accommodated a bed similar to the one she'd slept on, or attempted to sleep on, in Wessick's house. The left-hand side of the room was empty, save for a gray-haired man who sat in the corner, slumped against the wall with his knees drawn up in front of him.

The priest gestured at the man as if expecting Erin to do or say something. When she didn't, the priest scurried out of the room, back the way they'd come.

Erin looked at the gray-haired man. A gray beard, trimmed short like his hair, covered the lower portion of his face. His green eyes sparkled in the secondhand glow from the globe lights outside the building. He wore a sleeveless, knee-length tunic of linen. Sandals like the ones Erin wore protected the man's feet.

This man must have something to do with the relic, otherwise the priest wouldn't have brought her to him. She took a cautious step toward the man.

His expression brightened as if he recognized her. He got to his feet, walked to her, and clasped her hand in his. "Hello, Erin. It's nice to finally meet you."

"How do you know my name? Who are you?"

"Can't you guess?"

She shook her head.

"The name's M.J. Harriman." He patted her hand. "But you can call me Harry."

THE ROOM IN WESSICK'S HOUSE WHERE ALEX HAD FOUND ERIN EARLIER THAT evening looked exactly as he remembered it. Austere and gloomy. He knew this was the style in ancient Egypt. After years of studying to become an Egyptologist, augmented with field research, he knew how the ancients must've lived. Yet seeing it in person, experiencing the ambience of it, felt completely different.

Of course, this was Wessick's house. Not every Egyptian lived the way Wessick did. Everything the man touched, from this home to Revenant House, felt as cold and unlived-in as a crypt.

Wessick entered the room first. He carried an elaborate oil lamp fashioned from alabaster that featured six wicks. A plurality of flames lit the room in shimmering, dancing light.

Alex spotted the white plastic document tube right away. It lay in the corner directly to the left of the doorway, where it must've landed after the battle. He retrieved the tube, unscrewing the cap to make certain the scroll was still inside. It was. Once he'd replaced the cap, he glanced around the room in search of Erin's gun. He saw nothing. Though he now realized he should've asked Erin where she stowed it, the thought hardly helped him.

Two places might conceal the weapon.

In three wide steps he reached the bed. He patted down the mattress but felt nothing inside it. Bending down, he checked under the bed. Nothing there either. In a crouch he waddled toward the wooden chest tucked into the far corner of the room. Lifting the lid, he squinted down at eight gallon jugs of the plastic variety used to store liquids—in the twenty-first century. The jugs appeared to hold water. All were full, save for one. Someone, presumably Erin, drank perhaps an eighth of the gallon.

The gun was not in the chest.

Which left three possibilities. One, Wessick had spotted the gun and somehow grabbed it without Alex or Erin seeing. Two, one of Wessick's men found the gun after the three of them left the house. Three, the human tornado got ahold of the weapon.

The final possibility was the most disturbing. A murderous lunatic roaming the streets armed with a 9mm handgun, intent on eliminating Erin.

He had to get back to her. Immediately.

"What is that?" Wessick asked, indicating the document tube.

"Nothing you need to worry your pretty little head about."

"Is it the papyrus scroll you found inside Revenant House?"

"Shut up. It's time to go." Alex pushed Wessick through the doorway, into the hall. "You stay in front. That way if we get attacked, they'll lop off your head first."

"Unless they attack from behind."

Alex gritted his teeth. Never before had he truly despised another human being. This man, however, scraped raw every nerve in his body. He'd met ticks and leeches, of the nonhuman variety, that he liked better than Wessick. Of course, as a semi-rational person, Alex understood the ultimate root of his disdain for Samuel Wessick.

Erin liked the man. Sort of. For reasons Alex couldn't comprehend.

He gritted his teeth harder, then exhaled as he forced his jaw to relax. Erin preferred him over Wessick. He knew it. Wessick knew it too.

But Alex still reserved the right to despise the man.

The house was silent as they tromped through the rooms on their way to the front door. Either no one else actually lived here, or the other inhabitants of the house slept like blindfolded deaf-mutes. Maybe they were deaf-mutes. People unable to hear or speak lacked the capacity to betray their master. He hoped the Aten never got that idea, because with their level of technology that just might find a way to make it happen—to everyone on earth.

They must stop the Aten. Tonight.

When they rushed out of the front door, the guard posted there shot a perplexed look at Wessick, though he said nothing to his master. The guards patrolling the grounds managed to suppress their confusion, though they halted in the middle of their rounds to watch Alex and Wessick exit through the wooden gates. In this time and place, no one dared question authority.

So far, the chaos was confined to the royal district. That wouldn't last long. Panic spread faster than gossip.

Alex carried the document tube in his left hand, the sword in his right. Wessick held both a torch and a sword, because Alex suffered a brief moment of generosity and let the man keep his weapon. Soon, they might need these weapons. The street looked peaceful, as before. The distant clamor sounded a little closer, however, and further down the road the golden glow of torches flickered where previously darkness had loomed. People were waking up, learning about the tumult, weighing their options. Alex would've preferred to stick to darker side streets, but avoiding the main thoroughfare meant lengthening their journey back to the palace.

They had no choice. They must head straight for the flickering torchlight.

With each stride, they drew closer to the source of the torchlight. The amorphous glow disunited into individual cones of light, each with a brighter flame at its center. Blurry shapes separated into human figures. Men and women and children milled about in the street. Some argued, some cried, and some hovered at the periphery, their faces pinched by worry and confusion. Two children of perhaps eight or ten dashed into and out of the crowd, weaving back and forth as if navigating an obstacle course. No one except the children seemed to be enjoying themselves. Everyone else looked at best tense and at worst terrified.

Alex and Wessick squeezed through the crowd. Within a few minutes, they passed through the logjam of people and walked swiftly down the road once more. The vacant solitude of the city had been shattered. A smattering of people traveled the roads, and most of them looked bewildered or outright scared. No one paid much attention to Alex and Wessick.

A rumbling, as of thunder, erupted in the distance. Alex saw no lightning. In fact, stars glittered in the heavens. The sound originated somewhere ahead of them, in the direction they traveled.

Wessick slowed his pace. Alex prodded him with the sword. Wessick sped up again.

The rumbling intensified second by second. It seemed to move toward them faster than they moved toward it. Soon the rumbling became a familiar cadence.

Hoofbeats.

Out of the gloom surged four chariots, each pulled by two horses, lined up side-by-side across the width of the road. A pair of soldiers manned each chariot. One man held a whip and controlled the reins while the other brandished a bow and arrow. The company of chariots thundered down the road, driving everyone else out of their way.

Wessick halted.

Alex stopped just behind him. If they didn't move, the chariots might trample them.

Instead of hustling out of the way, Wessick raised his torch. He swung it back and forth in front of his face.

One of the charioteers shouted. The drivers all tugged on their reins and the company slowed to a trot, then a walk. The charioteers approached Wessick, stopping fifteen feet away. The soldier who had shouted orders to the others, obviously the commander of the chariot brigade, hopped down from his chariot. The sword attached to his belt swayed in its scabbard. The commander walked straight up to Wessick and began to speak—in Kemetian.

Alex had long since stopped trying to understand every word the Kemetians said. By letting the words tumble through his mind, he discovered he could understand bits and pieces of their speech. The more he heard the language, the more of it he comprehended. His fluency in reading and writing Kemetian helped, no doubt, but he needed more time before the immersion method would grant him fluency in the spoken language. The experts in his time got more wrong than he'd ever suspected when it came to the spoken version of genuine ancient Egyptian. That's why he no longer thought of it as ancient Egyptian but as Kemetian, the true language of the Two Lands, the empire of Kemet.

And Kemetian tested his linguistic skills.

He understood enough of the current conversation, however, to feel unease creeping into his psyche. The soldier spoke rapidly, nevertheless Alex caught select words and phrases.

Evil. Death. Enemy. The commander seemed obsessed with the darker side of things. Worse yet, each time the man uttered the words he punctuated his statement by jabbing a finger in the air to point at Alex.

Wessick interjected phrases, but the commander cut him off each time. It sounded like Wessick was trying to calm the soldier. The commander was having none of that. The man's face reddened, clearly a sign of anger rather than embarrassment or fear. His posture rigid, he kept one hand resting lightly on his sword's hilt. He squinted at Wessick, casting his glare on Alex each time he spoke of evil, death, or the enemy.

None of this assuaged the unease swelling inside Alex. He wished with every ounce of his mental power that he had a gun, preferably an AK-47. He adjusted his grip on the sword. If the soldiers wanted a fight, he'd give it to them. But frankly, he wasn't at all certain he could win.

The commander pointed straight up at the sky. He spat a machine-gun burst of words at Wessick.

Alex gritted his teeth. He caught one phrase in the outburst—rage of Sekhmet. What the lion-headed goddess of war had to do with him, he couldn't guess.

So he tapped Wessick's shoulder and asked, "What's he saying?"

"He thinks you are the harbinger of death and that your arrival will bring Sekhmet's rage down on the Two Lands."

According to the mythology, Sekhmet held the power to destroy but also to heal. Too bad the commander didn't decide to ascribe the goddess's good traits to Alex. How he became the devil in all this was one mystery he had no interest in solving. He also had no time for this nonsense.

"Tell him I'm nothing of the sort," Alex said, "and let's get moving again."

"I'm afraid if we try to pass, they will stop us." Wessick glanced sideways at Alex. "We are outnumbered."

Alex rolled his eyes. "Fine, you stay and chat. I've had enough."

He whirled around and took two broad steps in the opposite direction.

Something whizzed past his left ear.

Thwack. An arrow struck the ground a feet in front of him.

Alex stopped. He glanced over his shoulder.

Wessick looked at him with a self-satisfied expression. "I believe that was a warning. The next shot will—"

"I know."

Alex glanced around but spotted no place where he might hide, even if he could run faster than the archer could loose his arrows. Muttering a string of curses under his breath, Alex returned to the spot he'd vacated a moment earlier.

"What now?" he asked.

"I don't know," Wessick replied.

The commander leaned closer to Wessick. His features contorting with anger, the soldier uttered words in a near whisper.

The smugness washed out of Wessick's expression, replaced by a pallor.

Alex asked, "What's wrong?"

"They want to prove their obedience to Sekhmet." Wessick swallowed. "They intend to execute us."

"When?"

"Soon."

Four soldiers dismounted their chariots and marched toward Wessick and Alex. Two took up positions on either side of Wessick, forcing him to give up his sword. The other pair surrounded Alex and confiscated his weapon.

The commander drew his sword.

"Very soon," Wessick said.

The soldiers around Wessick seized his shoulders. They shoved him down onto his knees.

The commander raised his sword, aligned it with Wessick's throat, and swung the blade backward. He paused for second as he glanced up at the sky. His gaze zeroed in on Wessick once again.

He slashed the blade down toward Wessick's neck.

W ESSICK SHOUTED IN KEMETIAN. THE COMMANDER FROZE WITH THE BLADE a hair's breadth from Wessick's flesh. Head canted to the side, the soldier listened as his prisoner rattled off more Kemetian words.

Alex strained to hear whatever Wessick was saying. The man's first shout had been a command to stop—in the name of the Aten, if Alex understood the words correctly. Now Wessick spoke quickly and in a hushed tone, a combination that hindered Alex's efforts to translate. He had a hunch Wessick intended it that way.

The commander muttered something in response to Wessick. He prodded Wessick's shoulder with the tip of his sword.

Wessick reached inside the folds of his kilt and slid out an object.

The kilt had a pocket?

Alex dropped the thought as he saw Wessick hand the object to the commander. It looked like a scarab amulet, a piece of stone carved to look like a beetle. The commander took the amulet, flipping it over to read whatever was inscribed on its flat backside.

The commander closed his fist around the amulet. He murmured to the two men who held Wessick and they released their prisoner, retreating to their chariot. The commander offered his sword, hilt first, to Wessick.

As Wessick accepted the sword, the commander dropped to his knees. He bowed his head to Wessick.

What the hell?

Wessick issued orders to the commander. From the tone of the man's voice, Alex knew the intent of the words, even if he didn't understand the exact meaning. The commander rose and conveyed the instructions to his men. The pair manning one chariot dismounted, as did the archer from the commander's chariot. The soldiers hopped into two of the remaining chariots, squeezing in with the men already occupying them. With the manpower thus reallocated, a pair of chariots stood empty.

Wessick tromped to Alex, snatched the document tube from his hand, and spun on his heels to head for one of the empty chariots. Wessick climbed into the contraption. He plucked up the whip lying on the floorboards. Grasping the reins in one hand, he snapped the whip in the air above the horses' flanks. The horses took off at a gallop.

The commander picked up the sword his men had taken from Alex. He twirled it in the air, then strode to Alex. With another flourish, the commander raised the tip of the sword to Alex's neck.

Alex gazed over the commander's shoulder, down the road where Wessick disappeared in the chariot.

The bastard had left him to die.

Erin ripped her hand away from Harry's. Away from the man who called himself Harry Harriman. She really had no clue if he was actually Mallory J. "Harry" Harriman. She'd never met the man, and Alex never showed her a photo of him.

"Where's Alex?" Harry asked. "I figured you kids would stick together."

"He had an errand to run."

Harry's brows knit together. "An errand in the fourteenth century BC?"

She shrugged.

Harry sighed. He gazed at her with a look of paternal dismay.

She scowled at him.

"It's me," he said, as if those two words explained everything.

"Isn't that what an imposter would say?"

"Fair point." His shoulders sagged. He seemed to think for a moment, then he straightened and curved his lips in a slight smile. He said, "Did you get the present I left for you at Revenant Point?"

She almost asked if he meant the map overlay, but caught herself at the last second. Instead she asked, "What present?"

"The cloth that changes the—" He glanced around as if looking for something or someone. "We shouldn't talk about it here."

He knew about the cloth. She assumed that meant either he was Harry Harriman or the Brothers of the Aten already knew about the map overlay. Since the latter option was depressing, she opted to believe the former.

"Fine, you're Harry." She paused. "I mentioned the relic and the priest brought me to you. Why?"

"Dunno."

She made a face at him. "That's the best you've got?"

"Afraid so."

"Why are you just sitting in here like you're bound and gagged?" When he simply shrugged in response, she said, "Let's get the heck out of here."

"We can't just sashay out of here."

"I don't think I've ever sashayed in my life. But why can't we just leave?" Erin glanced at the hallway down which the meek priest had retreated. "You can't be afraid of the mouse who brought me here."

"I take it you haven't met Panehsy."

"Who?"

As if in response, footfalls erupted behind her. Soft at first, the sound intensified into the slapping of sandal-shod feet stomping across the gypsum floor. Erin glanced over her shoulder to see another priest storming down the narrow hallway that led into the next chamber. She hadn't heard any door open or close. Given her current mental state, she might've overlooked a bomb exploding. Then again, maybe the priest had waited in the next chamber, listening to their conversation until he deemed the moment appropriate for his entrance.

She took a breath, then another. Nothing like oxygen to clear the mental cobwebs.

The second priest traipsed right past her without so much as a glance in her direction. He headed down the corridor into the portico beyond. She heard muted voices.

Seconds later, the new priest stormed back into the chamber. He halted beside Erin and Harry. The priest's gaze bored into her, triggering a new wave of goosebumps that swept down her body from head to toe. The priest towered a good six inches over her, and muscles fleshed out his broad frame. His caramel-brown eyes might've looked attractive, if not for the cold glint in them. Hard angles, capped by a square jaw, delineated his facial features. Bronzed skin, bushy black eyebrows, and a hint of stubble hardened his appearance further.

Squinting down at Erin, the priest compressed his lips. Muscles in his upper arms flexed as he twitched his fingers.

Harry cleared his throat. He pointed a thumb toward the priest. "This is—"

"I am Panehsy," the priest said, his deep voice reverberating through the courtyard, "first servant of the Aten in the House of Aten and chief overseer of the Brotherhood of the Aten."

Yes, now she understood why Harry didn't fight his way out of here. Panehsy could crush each of them in one hand without breaking a sweat.

"*Satseshat*," Panehsy said, "you were not to arrive until morning. Where is Meru?"

Erin almost asked who Meru was, but then remembered. It was the name Wessick used in this time. The priest must be an ally of Wessick, or perhaps cohort was a better term. Either way, she couldn't trust him.

"Meru was detained," she said. "I'm sure he'll arrive soon. He sent me ahead."

Panehsy glanced at Harry. "Why do you consort with this man?"

"You better start treating the *satseshat* with a little more respect. Your bosses won't like it if you tick me off and I forget how to find the relic."

His eyes narrowed into slits as his mouth set in a line. She knew this routine well. No matter what timeline she found herself in, men all behaved the same way when they wanted to intimidate a little woman. At least, the obnoxious ones did.

Erin lifted her chin, folding her arms over her chest. The Glock, gripped in her right hand, protruded above her left forearm.

The priest caught sight of the weapon. Raising one eyebrow, he met her gaze.

Erin refused to look away. She bent her head back to study his face. Chief overseer of the brotherhood? This man was no ally to her. He was the enemy.

Panehsy took two steps toward her. They stood a foot or two apart, so close that his bulk cast a shadow over her. Staring down at her face, he said, "You are in my domain. And you shall not leave until you reveal the location of the relic."

She lowered her left arm, still holding the Glock in front of her chest.

"I have seen weapons such as yours before," Panehsy said. His lips twitched in a half-suppressed smirk. "It will not save you this time."

He tilted his head back, shutting his eyes.

Out of the bright glow above the temple, an orb swooped down toward them.

And then another. And another.

Soon, a pack of orbs hovered around them at the periphery of the chamber. A single orb floated in the center of the entrance to the corridor. The one that led into the portico. The only escape route.

Panehsy raised his outstretched arm, swiveling his head to admire the orbs. His smirk transformed into a look of pure satisfaction.

Erin took hold of Harry's arm and backed away from Panehsy several paces, dragging Harry along with her. She dropped her left arm to her side, raising her right hand to aim the Glock at Panehsy.

The priest gazed at her with that look of pure contentment. It gave her the creeps.

"Let us go," Erin said, "or die."

Trouble was, she knew she couldn't keep the promise—and if she knew, then Panehsy knew. An orb had disabled her gun once before, when Rassul confronted her on the road to Revenant House. Her threat acted more as a stalling tactic than anything else. Keep the priest occupied until she thought of a way out.

"You shall find the relic," Panehsy said, "and I will take control of it. I am through serving the Aten. The power of the ages shall be mine and mine alone."

Panehsy smiled. His teeth gleamed white in the glow of the orbs, whiter than the teeth of any ancient person should look. Maybe he wasn't a Kemetian. The Aten brought people from different timelines into this one, in their efforts to track down the relic.

And he said he'd seen guns before.

"There is no escape," Panehsy murmured. "You are mine, *satseshat*."

ALEX COUNTED THE SOLDIERS, JUST TO MAKE SURE. EIGHT AGAINST ONE. HERCULES might win a battle with these odds, but what chance did an archaeologist have?

The commander lowered his sword. He barked orders at his men.

The soldiers at either side of Alex seized his upper arms. They propelled him toward the empty chariot, half carrying and half pushing him. He stumbled. The soldiers held him up until he regained his balance, but to do so each man had to hold one of Alex's arms in both of his own. They hauled him toward the empty chariot, waiting at the far end of the line, separated from the other two chariots by at least thirty feet. The other soldiers loitered by the remaining chariots.

Alex pretended to stumble again. He let both of his knees buckle, forcing the soldiers to support the entire weight of his body. He sagged in their grasp.

The soldier holding his right arm released it.

Alex bit the hand that restrained his left arm.

The soldier cried out as his hand reflexively popped open. Alex rammed his head into the soldier's abdomen. The man tumbled backward, hitting the ground sprawled on his backside. Before the other soldier could react, Alex sprang to his feet and slugged the man in the gut.

Other voices shouted.

Alex snagged the sword from the belt of the man he'd just walloped. Brandishing it in one hand, he leaped onto the chariot, grabbed the reins, and slapped them firmly but lightly on the horse's flanks. The team broke into a canter, and then a full gallop. The chariot bucked and swayed. He dropped the sword onto the floorboards, stamping one foot on the blade to hold it down. With one hand he clutched the chariot for support, and with the other he steered the horses.

The city flashed past in a blur as the chariot slalomed down the streets. It swerved around corners at such speed that one side of the contraption lifted off the ground and he feared it might topple over, spilling him onto the ground. But when he leaned into the airborne side, the wheel smacked back onto the earth with a force that jarred his bones. At least he wasn't crushed under thundering hooves or impaled by a wheel spoke. He thanked heaven for that.

The chariot rounded another corner, lifting the right wheel. He leaned to the right. The wheel smacked down just as the chariot roared out of the city street into the open field in front of the Mansion of the Aten, the smaller-yet-still-mammoth temple.

People. Everywhere. Milling in the field. Fighting. Yelling.

Alex jerked back on the reins. The horses slowed to a trot. He tugged again, and they reduced their pace to a brisk walk. The pedestrians scattered around the chariot, opening a circuitous path across the field. At the other side of the field, Alex urged the horses to a complete stop. The road leading to the palace was choked with human traffic.

And bodies. Blood-stained, lifeless bodies.

Erin.

Alex dropped the reins. Plucking up the sword, he bounded off the chariot and ran straight into the melee.

No one attacked him. The people seemed intent on fleeing, though to where, he didn't know. Soldiers roamed the entire city. Maybe he shouldn't assume the citizens were fleeing the soldiers. A much greater threat loomed somewhere above them, hidden and silent.

For now.

About a hundred feet down the road, Alex passed an abandoned chariot. He had no doubts that Wessick came this way, because he had no doubts the snake intended to find Erin and drag her off to who-knew-where so he could do who-knew-what with her. Wessick had the map, after all. If he got his scaly hands on Erin, he might find the relic.

No. Erin would never help Wessick.

Unless he coerced her.

The bridge emerged from the chaos and shadows up ahead. Alex ran toward it, bounding up the staircase two, and sometimes three, steps at a time. Down the ramp he sprinted, through the entryway into the courtyard.

He stopped with a trip and a slide.

The courtyard was empty, save for a solitary man who lay slumped against the far wall near the shallower ramp that led into the rear of the palace.

Even from this distance, Alex recognized Khety.

He bolted across the courtyard, falling to his knees beside the man. Blood streamed from a small, round wound on his left shoulder. The blood oozed down his arm and the left half of his torso. The injury had a familiar size and shape.

A bullet wound.

The tanned surface of Khety's skin could not veil the pallor rising from beneath it. As the man lifted his gaze to Alex's face, he grimaced.

"Desheret," Khety mumbled.

The madwoman. Alex felt his chest tighten. "Did she attack you? Where's Erin?"

"The *satseshat* escaped before Desheret overwhelmed me. She has gone to the temple—*gem-pa-aten*. You must find her before Desheret..." Khety's words faded away.

"I'll get help for you," Alex said. He glanced around the courtyard, but saw no one. "Where did everyone go?"

"To seek safety." Khety heaved a breath. "My injury appears worse than it is. I will survive. You must leave me and go to find the *satseshat*."

The quaver in Khety's voice belied his assertion that he was okay. Nevertheless, the man struggled to push himself up into a more upright position. Alex reached for the man's arm to help him, but Khety shook off the hand. He propped his back against the wall so that he sat straighter and taller.

"Leave," Khety said. When Alex didn't move, Khety smiled faintly and added, "You are as difficult to rid myself of as she was. Go at once, before her enemies find her."

Alex studied the man for a moment. Rising from his crouch, he turned to leave. As he lifted his foot to take the first step, however, he hesitated.

"Did you tell anyone else where Erin went?" he asked.

Khety shook his head.

"Good," Alex said. "If you see Wess—I mean if you see Meru, don't tell him either."

"She asked me to keep her secrets. I would not betray the *satseshat*."

Alex nodded. He jogged toward the ramp.

The clapping of sandals on the stone floor made him pause to glance backward. Three women of around Khety's age had caught sight of the man slumped against the wall and halted in their flight from the palace. After a brief discussion, accompanied by hand gestures, the women trotted across the courtyard to descend on Khety. They knelt around him. One woman examined his wound while the other two chattered in hushed voices that echoed through the courtyard. Khety might be fine after all. He would certainly receive medical attention.

Alex bolted up the ramp and out of the palace.

23

PANEHSY SAUNTERED DOWN THE HALLWAY INTO THE CHAMBER BEYOND, passing straight through it into the next hallway and the portico. He disappeared into the shadows there. The orbs hovered at intervals along the walls, suspended at chest height.

Erin let her arm drop to her side, with the gun aimed at the floor.

"That's why I haven't blown this joint," Harry said. "I tried a few times, but Panehsy always sics his little glowing minions on me to herd me back into the corral."

Erin tapped her free hand against her thigh. "There must be a way. I haven't come this far just to fail."

"Maybe Alex'll find us."

"I won't cower in here waiting for someone to save me."

Harry shrugged. "I have."

Erin looked at him. Although he met her gaze, the way he compressed his lips and hunched his shoulders suggested discomfort. He looked slightly embarrassed.

She resisted the urge to give him a quick hug. Instead she asked, "How long have you been here?"

"A week."

"Where were you for the three weeks before that?"

"Three weeks? I was shanghaied in the Albuquerque airport nine days ago."

Erin stared at him, probably looking as if she'd spotted a third eyeball on his forehead. She took a second to iron out her expression, and then said, "You disappeared a month ago, Harry. Alex and I found no trace of you." A memory bobbed to the surface, and she told him, "Except for a passage in the unfinished manuscript written by Ridley Covington. He wrote about meeting a man called M.J. Harriman while in Egypt. But Ridley died in 1858."

Harry shook his head, neither in disappointment nor derision but rather in amusement.

"Hasn't anyone filled you in?" he asked. "Time is relative."

"Yes, I've heard. Frankly, the whole topic of time travel gives me a massive headache."

"I know the feeling." He clapped a hand on her shoulder, squeezing lightly. "It's easier if you quit trying to understand and just go with it. Suffice it to say that every *place* has its own timeline and so does every *body*. In my timeline, a week has passed since Rassul abducted me from the Albuquerque airport. In your timeline, it's been a month."

Erin shook her head so forcefully that she swore she felt her brain colliding with her skull. Like a computer asked to solve an impossible equation, her mind seemed stuck in an endless loop.

"That's impossible," she said. "A month can't be a week."

He squeezed her shoulder again. "In the twenty-first century, I've been missing for a month. Here in the old fourteenth century before Christ, I rode into town a week ago." She must've looked horribly confounded, because he lifted his hand from her shoulder to pat her cheek. "Remember, you time-traveled back to this day. You pretty much circumvented the natural progression of time."

Jeez, she'd never wrap her mind around the intricacies of time travel. In the end, it hardly mattered anyway. She was here. Harry was here. And they both needed to escape from this labyrinthine temple so they could find the confounded relic.

The thought reminded her of something. She asked, "Where did you get that gift you hid for me? The one that goes with the—" She glanced at the orbs hovering at the room's periphery. "—with the other thing that I already had."

"I got it from an acquaintance," Harry said.

"Did this acquaintance know anything useful?"

Harry frowned. "This isn't the spot for spilling the beans."

"Right." Erin rested her free hand on her hip. "Let's get out of here then."

"How?"

She waved her gun-holding hand to shush him. They needed a way out. An escape route.

Alex gave her one. In fact, he gave her several.

Unzipping the bag, but still hung diagonally across her body, she dug around inside it. The bag contained some papers, though nothing that looked important, as well as Alex's tablet computer. A silvery powder coated the bottom of the bag. A single *akhet* ball lay wedged into one corner. What happened to the other two? She rummaged through the contents again, but found only the one *akhet* ball.

The crunching sound.

When Desheret had grabbed her ankle and yanked her off her feet, she'd heard a crunch as she belly-flopped onto the bag. The balls must've been crushed then. If she used the ball to get out of the temple, she'd have no method of escaping from this timeline. No way to get home.

She picked up the *akhet* ball. It felt slightly warm in her hand, as she remembered from before. She couldn't use the ball to escape from anything—not this temple or this timeline—unless she knew how to use the technology. Alex said something about that. She rocked the ball in her palm, between her fingers and thumb. Alex told her the *akhet* balls worked by thought control. If she concentrated on the time and place where she wanted to go, a portal would open to take her there. Aha.

Holding the ball in her palm the way she'd seen Wessick do it, she closed her eyes and focused on where she wanted to go.

Take me to the relic.

She opened one eye partway. Nothing had happened. Blinking her eyes open, she grasped the *akhet* ball between her thumb and forefinger and scowled at it.

"Problem?" Harry asked.

"Alex told me these things work by thought control, but I can't get it to work."

"What were you thinking about?"

"The relic. I commanded this stupid thing to take me to it."

Harry sighed. "You asked it to carry out an impossible task. The Aten made the *akhet* balls, and the Aten don't know squat about where the relic is."

She stashed the ball inside the bag. "Worth a shot."

"Got any more of those gizmos?"

"No." She zipped the bag shut. "I don't want to waste the one I've got. I might need it to get home, or to get to the relic."

"Better save it. I bet Alex will show up eventually."

Erin adjusted the bag's strap. She was getting tired of lugging the thing around, especially since it contained nothing that helped her. Except the *akhet* ball. It might come in useful later.

The sentinel orbs glimmered all around them.

The orbs. They looked a lot like the *akhet* balls, except that the orbs glowed. Both technologies might work on similar principles. If the *akhet* balls were activated by thought, then maybe the orbs were too.

Panehsy called in the orbs without saying a word. He held nothing in his hands, and so it seemed unlikely that he commanded the orbs using a remote-control device. The priest had simply raised his arms and shut his eyes.

Thought control.

Using her thoughts to command the orbs might alert the Aten to her escape plans. On the other hand, the orbs didn't seem to be continuously connected to the Aten. Panehsy no longer worked in the Aten's name, yet the orbs obeyed him. The orbs also apparently lingered nearby at all times, invisible to the human eye, ready to wink into sight the instant they received a command. So, using the orbs for her own purposes might not alert the Aten.

Her theory made more sense than most anything else she encountered lately.

Erin closed her eyes one more time. In her mind's eye she pictured the orbs stationed around her, near the walls. As she pushed all other thoughts from her mind, she concentrated on what she wanted the orbs to do.

Leave.

Harry gasped.

She opened her eyes. "What is it?"

"That one pulsed." Harry pointed at the orb positioned in the hallway entrance. "I thought it was getting ready to blow."

It must've heard her thought. Instead of obeying, however, it pulsed in response. Was the orb threatening her, or resisting her control? Time to find out.

She shut her eyes and exhaled, letting the tension roll out of her on the breath as she cleared her mind. She pictured the orb. Then, with every ounce of mental strength she possessed, she shouted her thoughts.

I am the satseshat. Do as I command. Go away!

"They're still here," Harry informed her.

Keeping her eyes closed, she fisted her hands and commanded the orbs once more.

"Go away!"

It took a few seconds for her to realize she'd actually shouted those two words. When she cracked her eyelids apart, the look on Harry's face confirmed it. He watched her with wide eyes, his mouth ajar.

The orbs snuffed out. Tiny sparks showered down from where each orb had hovered.

The central orb still floated in the hallway entrance.

Erin took a step toward it, tilting her head to study it.

The orb shot straight up into the air and vanished.

"Nice work," Harry said. "How'd you scare them off?"

"Thought control."

Either he knew what she meant or he didn't care, because instead of asking for an explanation, he tromped down the hallway. Erin trailed after him. As they crossed through the adjoining chamber, she glanced around but saw no one. The niches along the walls might hide a human being, though. Panehsy had come this way. The priest might lurk out here, inside one of the niches.

No one jumped out at them as they swerved around the offering platform. They hustled down the next hallway single file and broke into a trot as they made a beeline for the wooden doors that barred entrance to the inner sanctum. Erin glanced sideways at the offering tables on either side of them. A smaller man like the mouse who admitted her to this area might hide behind the tables, but a man as large as Panehsy seemed unlikely to find shelter here.

Where was the high priest?

The doors stood closed. On this side, no bolts or handles offered a way to open the doors. Harry pushed on the wood. The doors did not budge. He pushed with his shoulder, leaning all his weight into the effort. Nothing.

Erin came up alongside him. She raised a hand to rap on the door three times.

Silence followed. No pattering of footsteps on the opposite side of the door. No sign anyone heard the knocks. Or at least, no sign anyone cared to let them out.

Erin pounded on the door with the bottom of her fist. The sound echoed through the chamber.

A noise erupted on the opposite side, faint, indistinct. She leaned her ear against the door to listen.

Shuffling. Like footsteps. The shuffling stopped, followed by another sound. She lifted her head. Someone was jiggling the bolt that sealed the doors.

"Erin?"

Despite the muted effect of the thick wooden doors, she recognized Alex's voice. He called her name loud enough that she could hear it, though not so loud as to draw unwanted attention. He stood mere inches from her. It might as well have been miles.

She leaned close to the sliver of space between the two doors. He might hear her better this way without the need to raise her voice.

"I'm here," she said. "With Harry."

The pause that followed indicated, she assumed, a surprised silence as he absorbed the information that Harry was not only alive, but standing beside her. Finally, he said, "The door's locked."

"I know. There's a key."

"Where?"

"Nearby. I don't know exactly where."

Another pause. Alex grunted and said, "If only I had a cannon in my pocket."

"That's not helping."

"I do have a sword."

She glanced down at her hand, spotting the Glock clutched in her fingers. "No, I have a better idea. Stand back."

"Do I want to know?"

"Shut up and get away from the doors."

His response came in the form of renewed shuffling.

She herded Harry away from the doors. Returning to the wooden barrier, she raised the gun in front of her. Harry slapped his hands over his ears. Erin wanted to plug one ear with her free hand, but she lacked the confidence to hold the gun in one hand. Gripping the gun in her right hand, she supported it with her left. Then she aligned the Glock with the space between the doors and slipped her finger over the trigger.

It would be loud. Very loud.

Gritting her teeth, she pulled the trigger.

The detonation bounced off the stone walls, ricocheting like a bullet. She fired again. Wood splintered, but the doors held. The ringing in her ears muted the explosion and she fired two more rounds at the doors. The right-hand door sagged outward a hair.

Harry frantically waved his arms at her. Though his lips moved, she couldn't hear his words.

Erin shook her head, gesturing at her ears. "I can't hear you."

She might've shouted the words. She couldn't tell for sure.

Harry trotted to her. He flapped his hands, which she took to mean he wanted her to lower the gun. She dropped her arm into her side.

The doors jiggled. Harry's lips moved again, though this time he was looking at the doors.

The right-hand door swung outward.

Alex stood outside. He held a sword in one hand, and a portion of the door bolt in one hand. The jagged end of the bolt suggested it had sheared off. Alex tossed the hunk of wood to the side.

Harry pushed her through the doorway. She staggered a few steps past Alex, hopping aside to let Harry enter the portico.

Alex grabbed her, lifting her onto her tiptoes as he hauled her into a suffocating embrace. Thankfully, he released her a second later. She liked that he was glad to see her, but she liked breathing even better.

Harry and Alex spoke to each other. She knew this because their lips moved. Since she could neither read lips nor hear their conversation, she turned her attention to the surroundings. The columns threw shadows across the portico's depths, masking anything that might hide there. Up ahead, past the rows of offering tables in front of the portico, the other pair of wooden doors blocked the path. Those doors locked from the inside, and she noted that a simple bolt sealed the doors, without the added protection of a locking mechanism.

Harry marched past her. Alex clasped her left hand and led her after Harry. They opened the doors without trouble, heading down the central aisle of the larger court-yard beyond. She glanced at the rows of offering tables. They cast minimal shadows, barely enough to conceal a dog. Not that she saw any dogs.

Passing through the entrance to the next courtyard, they upped their pace. Erin surveyed her surroundings as they hurried onward. The rows of offering tables, identical to those in the previous courtyard, concealed nothing so far as she could tell. Unless Panehsy had tucked himself under a pile of meat and bread offerings, the high priest did not lay in wait here. His absence bothered her. Maybe he trusted the orbs to guard her and Harry, assuming they obeyed his commands alone. Then again, maybe he observed them even now. Waiting. Following.

Hoping she would lead him to the relic.

She looked up at Alex. He wore a serious expression, his gaze focused on the path ahead. She needed to talk to him, to warn him about Panehsy. The ringing in her ears, which drowned out everything else, complicated things. For the moment, she must assume Harry told Alex about the threat posed by the high priest.

Acid churned in her stomach. Trusting other people still did not come easy for her. She tightened her grip on Alex's hand. She trusted him, no one else.

Alex glanced down at her. His features crinkled into a questioning expression.

She flashed a closed-mouth smile.

Apparently satisfied, he averted his gaze to the space ahead of them. Another corridor deposited them into the first large courtyard, identical to the previous one. They proceeded past the stelae, through the main entrance to the temple's interior, into the outer portico. Still no Panehsy. Erin kept pace with Alex as they exited the portico, heading down the ramp and onto the ground. Harry slowed down a little to let them catch up and then, side by side, the three of them tromped up the large ramp, through the pylon that bisected the stone wall of the temple complex. Past the pylon, the ramp angled downward to the main road. They turned left, back toward the palace complex.

Erin wanted to ask what in blazes they were doing. Returning to the central part of the city seemed like a bad idea to her. The men strode down the road's shoulder as if they knew precisely where they were going, so she opted to keep silent. The ringing in her ears had lessened somewhat, but she still wouldn't hear much of their responses if she questioned them anyway.

Just past the wall of the temple complex, they veered left to dash between two long, narrow buildings far shorter than the wall next door. How far they traveled into the dark alley between the buildings, she couldn't say. Eventually, they ducked through a doorway into the leftmost building. The room within looked like a storage room littered with cooking utensils and pottery vessels she thought might be bread molds. Most vitally, the room had no windows but did feature a wooden door to shut them out from the world outside. It was a perfect hiding place.

Well, almost perfect. Its proximity to the temple and the palace awoke slithering creatures in her gut. She wanted to get far, far away from this place.

Alex found an oil lamp hidden among the bread molds. He carried it to Erin. Without a word, he unzipped an outer compartment of the bag strapped across her torso, his bag. He brought out a lighter. After several flicks of the lighter's ignition switch, he elicited a tiny flame that he used to ignite the oil lamp.

Harry shut the door.

The lamp lit the room in murky shades of yellow and orange.

Alex cleared his throat. And she heard the sound. The ringing in her ears had abated enough that she heard softer noises, including Alex's throat clearing and, she abruptly realized, the flicking of the lighter seconds earlier.

When Alex spoke, he raised the volume on his voice and emphasized every syllable with exaggerated lip movements. "Harry and I thought we should discuss—"

"I can hear you," Erin said, at a normal volume.

He let out a relieved sigh. "Good. We need to discuss our strategy. But first Harry has something to tell you."

She directed her gaze at the older man.

"The priests of Amun-Ra," Harry said. "I'm afraid they're all six feet under. I met the last surviving priest a week ago, not long after I was shanghaied. The priest was being held in that same room inside the temple where you found me. Either the Aten figured neither of us could break out of the temple, so it didn't matter if we shared information, or Panehsy ignored their orders. Anyhoo, the priest and I got to talking and he told me about the relic and the *satseshat*."

If the priests were dead, then her plan was torpedoed. Unless…

"You said the priest made you memorize the prophecy," she said. "But you didn't recite it to me verbatim. Do you remember every word?"

"Sure do. Didn't recite it verbatim because the full text is sort of long-winded. I gave you the highlights."

"Okay." Time to find out how much he really knew. "Since you distributed the map and the overlay, you must've seen them. Did you get a good enough look at the overlay to remember what it looked like?"

He matched her whisper. "Reckon I could. But why does that matter?"

"Because the overlay was damaged. Part of it's missing." She stepped in front of him to look him in the eye as she asked. "If I showed you the overlay, could you tell me what's missing?"

"Sure." She must've looked less than convinced, because he added, "My memory's not photographic, but it's pretty darn good. Show me the overlay and I'm sure I can rustle up the information you need."

"Good." She had a few more questions before they delved into the map-overlay issue. As she thought back to his previous statements about the priest of Amun-Ra, her first question surfaced. "What exactly did the priest say about the relic and the *satseshat*?"

"You want verbatim or paraphrased?"

His tone was mocking. She rolled her eyes and said, "However you like it."

"Thanks bunches." Harry took a breath, then said, "The priest told me he was the last priest of Amun-Ra and that he'd been charged with a sacred duty, passed down through the generations. He was to protect the most important, and most dangerous, treasure ever conceived. He was the keeper of the relic."

"Did he tell you where it was?"

"Nope. He would only reveal that information to the new keeper, the one who was supposed to take his place when he kicked the bucket." Harry scratched his beard as if the action might enhance his memory. "The Aten had already tortured him in hopes of squeezing the knowledge out of him, and he knew the torture wasn't done. They'd keep at it until either he told them what they wanted to know or he died. So he cooked up the map as a means of passing on the information to the new keeper."

"I'm confused," Erin said. "How did he expect to get the map to the new keeper?"

"He didn't. He hid the map here, in this timeline, to protect it. When the time came for a new keeper to take over, he planned on spilling the beans about the map. The overlay he intended to keep. The Aten were hot on his trail, though, so he gave me the overlay." Harry scrunched his face, rubbing the back of his neck. "I was supposed to take the overlay back to the twenty-first century to give it to you. Priest gave me a couple of those nifty little *akhet* balls. His instructions about how to use them were, uh, kinda vague. Or maybe my thought control just isn't that controlled."

Erin sighed. "What happened?"

"I meant to go back to the twenty-first century in the Upper Peninsula. Instead, somehow I wound up still in Egypt but in the nineteenth century. I hung around for a few days trying to figure out what I did wrong, and working up the courage to try my last *akhet* ball. That's when I met Ridley Covington. I'm sure he never knew it, but his passion for truth inspired me to give it another go." Harry rubbed his neck again, this time rolling his eyes up to gaze into the heavens. "I screwed it up again. Found myself where I wanted, but not when I wanted. Then she showed up."

"Who?" Erin asked.

"The woman who calls herself Desheret. I managed to get away from her long enough to hide the overlay, with a little help from a new friend. Luckily, I squirreled it away before Desheret caught up with me and, well, caught me."

Alex asked, "Who was this new friend?"

"He was…a Sasquatch."

She blinked once, twice, three times. Bigfoot helped him? She had no time to ponder the issue, so she forced herself to concentrate on what mattered at this moment. "How did the priest get his hands on *akhet* balls when you were both imprisoned in the temple?"

"He helped me escape. For a pious man, he was surprisingly sneaky. After we snuck out, he gave me the overlay along with my instructions and the *akhet* balls, which he got from a secret cache. By then Panehsy's stooges were nipping at our heels. The priest distracted them so I could get away. " Harry frowned at the floor. "He died in the process."

The bag's strap was digging into her ribs. She shifted her weight mostly onto one hip, hoping to relieve the pressure, but to no avail.

Alex reached for the strap. He flicked his fingers in a visual request to hand over the bag. Erin lifted the strap up and over her head, freeing the bag from her torso. Alex took it and slung the strap over one shoulder. She glanced at him with a look she hoped expressed gratitude.

Then she asked Harry, "What did you do with the map?"

"Exactly what the keeper asked, I divvied up the parts. The overlay I hid in Michigan, for you to find, and the scroll I gave to Ridley Covington."

"In Egypt. In the 1800s. How did you get there?"

"I had a couple of those nifty little *akhet* balls that the priest gave me. Used one to find Ridley and give him the scroll.

"You changed the past?"

"No." He scrunched his face, giving his head a little shake. "At least I don't reckon so. The map meant diddly-squat to Ridley. He couldn't crack the map's code. Actually, he never realized it was a map. So giving him the scroll did not change my past."

"But the map text told him about the *satseshat* and the relic."

"Oh, he already knew about that. The Aten told him, when they drafted him into their cabal."

Erin stared at him, unable to think of what to ask him next. The information he imparted so far left her brain in a muddle.

"There is a crucial part you should know," Harry said. He met her gaze, taking two steps closer to her. "The priest of Amun-Ra also knew about the *satseshat*."

"So what?"

"The Aten didn't clue him in." Harry paused, apparently considering his next words. "The keeper knew about the *satseshat* because the man who kept the secret of the relic's whereabouts also kept the secret about a prophecy more ancient than Egypt itself. The keepers believed the prophecy had its origins in the same era as the relic itself, a time so remote that no one knows the date. The prophecy talked about a lady who would foil the Aten's scheme to gain control of the relic. It talked about the *satseshat*."

Alex said, "The Aten altered Erin's DNA to create a *satseshat*. It's hardly a surprise that they knew one would arise."

"You don't get it. The prophecy predates the Aten. They started their whimsical little genetic experiments because they wanted to control the prophecy, to control the *satseshat*. Because the *satseshat* is the new keeper of the relic."

"But I—" Alex shook his head. "This makes no sense."

"The prophecy was specific in describing the *satseshat*. Only one person fits the bill." Harry took hold of Erin's shoulders. "It's you."

She tried to form words but only managed to grunt "huh?"

Harry locked his gaze on hers. "The prophecy describes you, Erin."

24

E RIN BLINKED ONCE, TWICE, THREE TIMES. HER EYELIDS LOWERED AND raised as if in slow motion. Harry's words seemed to bounce off her eardrums, unable to penetrate her mind.

"Are you saying the priest was psychic?" she asked.

"No," he replied, drawing out the word as if it tasted funny. "I'm saying someone long, long ago jotted down a prophecy that named you as the one person capable of both finding the relic and stopping the Aten."

"Where is this prophecy written?"

"Oh, the written version was destroyed long ago so the Aten would never get their grubby hands on it. Each new keeper memorizes the text of the prophecy." Harry hunched his shoulders, reaching out to a nearby table to run his finger along the top edge of a bread mold. "The previous keeper couldn't pass on that knowledge to his successor. There was no time. He asked me to memorize it instead, and pass on the information to the new keeper."

"Which you claim is me," Erin said.

He nodded.

Erin took a few seconds to sort out the questions tumbling through her mind. Then she said, "You said the prophecy describes the *satseshat* so accurately that it could only refer to me. What exactly do you mean by that?"

Dropping his hand from the bread mold, Harry flattened his palm on the tabletop to lean against it. He said, "The prophecy describes your eyes, your hair, your figure, your skin…" He looked straight into her eyes. "And then there's your name. The prophecy calls you the peaceful one."

"That's not my name."

"Actually, it is. The name Erin means peace."

She stared at Harry. This was nonsense. Utterly, indisputably nonsense.

Alex cleared his throat. She felt him watching her as he said, "The map text called you the peaceful one too. I didn't make the connection."

"It took me awhile," Harry admitted. "But when I remembered that Erin means peace, I couldn't brush off the prophecy anymore."

"It's ridiculous," Erin said. "It must be some kind of hoax."

"Maybe not," Alex said.

She whipped her head to the left, staring up at him. Alex rested a hand on the small of her back. He gave her a slight smile, the kind designed to soothe her. It didn't work.

"Think about it," Alex said. "If the relic is a time machine, then whoever made it had the ability to travel forward in time and see you. See who you are and what you mean to the quest for the relic. Based on that knowledge, they wrote the prophecy."

She shook her head. "That doesn't add up. Harry said the Aten messed with my DNA in order to fulfill the prophecy, which means the prophecy must have existed first."

"Not necessarily," Harry said. "It's possible the Aten's rejiggering of your DNA had no effect on the outcome of events. You might've already been the *satseshat*."

"Okay," Erin said, "but tell me this. How did the guy who wrote the prophecy know about me?"

"You assume it was a gentleman and not a lady."

"I have to choose a pronoun." She virtually spat the words of him. "And apparently all the keepers have been men." She planted her hands on her hips. "You're ignoring my question. How could the prophet know about me?"

"Isn't it obvious?" Alex asked. When she simply twisted her mouth into an irritated expression, he explained, "Whoever wrote the prophecy had the technology for time travel. The prophet might not have been a prophet in the true sense but rather in the sense that he saw the future. He saw it because he visited it."

"But then the prophecy would've changed the past," she said.

"Not the *prophet's* past."

Erin swayed a little. Thoughts twirled and collided in her mind until the violence of it shifted her slightly off balance and left her numb. The room seemed to grow darker around her.

Alex slid his arm around her waist. He pulled her tight against him. The contact grounded her, in body and in mind, despite the confusion still roiling within her. She took a long, deep breath and let it out slowly. The room brightened, no longer immersed in the oily shadows of her distress.

Resting a hand on Alex's chest, she said, "I'm okay."

He kissed the top of her head.

Harry watched them with a half-suppressed smirk tugging at his lips.

She scrunched her lips. "Why do you look so pleased with yourself, Professor Harriman?"

"Because it worked." The smirk broke through, widening into a grin. "My first stab at matchmaking worked."

"What are you talking about?" Erin asked.

Alex groaned. "That's why you sent me to find Erin. Not because you realized how important she was, but because you're a meddlesome codger with too much time on his hands."

"Oh, I had an inkling of her importance," Harry answered. "When I realized someone was tailing me, I decided to mail my book to Erin. Then I reckoned she might need a hand, so I sent her another present. I sent her you."

"That's—" Alex pointed an accusing finger at Harry. He sputtered, trying to finish his sentence. Finally, he exhaled a loud sigh and threw up his hands in resignation.

Erin shook her head at Harry. "I had no idea you were so devious."

"Was I wrong?" Harry asked.

She tapped the Glock against her thigh. The fact that he'd been right irritated her, and under no circumstances would she give him the satisfaction of hearing her admit it aloud. He knew it anyway.

"None of this matters now," she said. "We have a job to do."

Harry smirked, bouncing on his toes.

Erin glanced at Alex, noting his distinct lack of luggage—aside from the bag he took from her and the sword he held in his right hand. She asked, "Where's the scroll?"

He looked at the floor and raked a hand through his hair. "Um...Wessick took it."

"What? Why on earth did you give it to him?"

"I didn't give it to him." He jammed the sword's tip into the dirt floor, jerking his head up to look at her. "Soldiers captured us. Wessick somehow convinced them to let him go and he took the scroll. Leaving me there to die, I might add."

Her heart skipped a beat. "They tried to kill you?"

"Well, I doubt they were hauling me off to a birthday party."

"If Wessick took the scroll, where did he go with it?"

"I assumed he'd find you and coerce you into taking him to the relic. He's wanted to ditch me from the beginning."

Erin chewed the inside of her lip. Where did Wessick go?

"Without the scroll," Alex said, "we're lost in the woods without a compass."

A thought popped into her head, bright as the proverbial lightbulb. She spun toward him, fumbling for the zipper on his bag. Although he watched her with intense interest, he said nothing as she unzipped the bag's main compartment and plunged her hand inside. Her fingers grazed the smooth surface of the tablet computer. She grabbed it and hoisted it out of the bag.

Holding up the tablet, she said, "Photos of the map and overlay are on here."

Flicking the power switch, she waited for the tablet to boot up. The screen remained dark.

Alex took the tablet from her. He flipped the power switch off and on several times. The screen stayed dark, he pushed other buttons. Nothing happened. He slapped the back of the tablet, as if that might wake it up.

He muttered noises that sounded like slurred curses. "It's dead."

"I guess time travel was too much for it," Erin said.

"Dammit." Alex shoved the tablet back into his bag with such force the bag's strap popped off his shoulder. The bag plopped onto the floor. Snatching it up again, he said, "We have to find Wessick. And when we do, I'm going to strangle that slimy, scaly snake of a—"

"Calm down," Erin said. "We'll find him and we'll get back the map and the overlay. Somehow."

Click.

In unison, the three of them turned their gazes to the source of the sound—the door. The click had signaled the latch disengaging.

The door swung inward with a triplet of soft, staccato creaks.

Alex leaped in front of Erin, planting himself squarely between her and the door. She peeked around his shoulder at the silhouette that blocked the doorway.

The figure took a step into the room. The light from Harry's lamp revealed the newcomer's features.

"There you are," Wessick said.

In his right hand, he held a sword. In his left, he grasped the document tube.

Alex's voice deepened into a near growl. "How did you find us?"

Wessick jerked the sword to point toward Erin's wrist with the blade's tip. He said, "Her bracelet. I equipped it with a tracking device."

"Of course you did," Alex hissed.

Lowering the sword, Wessick twirled the document tube.

Alex glowered at him. Erin rested a hand on Alex's upper arm.

"Now," Wessick said, jiggling the tube. "Tell me about this."

Shadow Bay, Michigan
June 8
Present Day

Warner stood at the window in Erin's bedroom, a mug of hot tea in his left hand. The overhead light was turned off, as were the two lamps in the room. He'd left the bedroom door open, so that the bluish glow from an LED night-light in the hallway provided minimal illumination. Enough that he didn't stumble into furniture. Yet not so much that it ruined his night vision.

Erin's parents had gone to bed an hour ago. Since Erin and Alex time-traveled to ancient Egypt, he thought perhaps they might return quickly. After all, they needn't wait three days to return simply because their task in the past took three days. Then again, perhaps the rules of time travel made as little sense as the U.S. tax code.

A voice whimpered behind him.

He glanced over his shoulder at the dog, Freya. With her chin flat on the floor, she gazed up at him and thumped her tail on the carpet.

"Don't worry," he said. "She will return soon."

He leaned against the window frame, focusing on the view outside once again. His shoulder holster rubbed against his arm uncomfortably. He shifted his position just enough to relieve the pressure. The holster kept his Glock 9mm handgun at the ready, in case he needed it. He would sleep wearing a shoulder holster— if he slept. A feeling of unease niggled at him from deep inside. He could neither identify nor dismiss the source of his unease. Each time he looked out the window, the feeling intensified.

Closing his eyes, he sipped the tea.

His cell phone warbled. He plucked it from its belt holster and answered the call.

A woman's voice said, "I thought you should know, you've got a big problem."

The voice belonged to Katy Bergren, head of the Human Origins Project, the organization that both he and Alex worked for, though "work" seemed a misnomer for their activities. For Katy to call him, the problem she mentioned must indeed be serious.

"What is it?" he asked.

"Our contact at the FAA called a few minutes ago. Radar just picked up an unidentified target moving across Lake Superior from west-northwest of Isle Royale, heading southeast. Straight for you."

"What altitude?" he asked.

"They couldn't tell for sure. Radar tracked it across Lake Superior until it got almost to the Keweenaw Peninsula. Then the target vanished."

"You don't believe it's gone."

"Not for good. I'd bet anything that they wanted to get picked up by radar briefly, so you'd know they're coming."

"How large was the object?"

"The radar can't distinguish size. But a park ranger on Isle Royale called our toll-free number to report seeing a globe-shaped object as big as his fist held at arm's length. The object was glowing faintly, like a light bulb. He couldn't gauge its altitude, so the exact size is hard to guess. From the tone of the guy's voice—" She paused. "I think it's big, Warner. *Really* big."

A light flashed outside the window.

Warner glanced up, holding perfectly still.

Though fading fast, the last vestiges of daylight allowed him to discern the trees at the edge of the woods, perhaps a hundred feet away. A light bobbed inside the woods.

"Hang on," Katy said. He heard voices, muffled as if Katy held her hand over the phone, and then she came back on the line. "We just got another report. From a family camping in McLain State Park, about fifteen miles from where you are." Papers rustled. Katy continued, "They saw a round object, dark like a silhouette. No lights on it. Bigger than a football field, they estimate. And it was heading in your direction."

"No longer glowing?"

"Apparently not." Katy paused. "What on earth are they up to?"

"Psychological warfare." He watched the light still bobbing in the woods. "Thank you for the report. I must go."

He disconnected the call without waiting for a response. Tucking the phone into its belt holster, he set the mug of tea on the bedside table.

The light in the woods surged out of the trees. It sped across the rear lawn straight toward the house—straight for the window of Erin's bedroom.

Warner did not move. He rested his hand on the Glock's grip.

The orb halted a dozen feet from the window. Warner stared back at it without flinching, without so much as moving a finger or blinking an eye.

The orb glittered. A wave of brighter light swept across its surface.

Static electricity tingled over Warner's skin. Yesterday, he fled from an enemy for the first time in his life. He fled from an orb like this one. Now, he felt the urge to flee rising within him once again. This time, however, he refused to heed that urge.

Tonight, he would stand and fight.

Lights flashed in the woods. Orbs raced out of the trees, splitting off to surround the house.

A much larger, globe-shaped object was headed in this direction. The smaller orbs, he knew, served the Aten. Did the larger object house the Aten themselves? He would find out soon enough.

He grabbed his cell phone. The screen was dark. He punched buttons. No response.

Tossing the phone onto the bed, he stared out the window. The first stars glimmered in the heavens. The sun had long since dipped below the horizon, but the last grayish remnants of its glow allowed him to distinguish the outlines of trees and bushes. He also saw a four-legged animal, most likely a deer, grazing at the far end of the lawn.

The orb positioned a dozen feet from the window pulsed iridescent blue.

A shadow fell over the house. The darkness crept across the landscape as a dark, round shape floated across the sky, blotting out the stars. Soon the shadow encompassed the house, the yard, and much of the woods surrounding the property.

The room sank into pitch-darkness. He glanced over his shoulder. The night-light in the hallway was out. With sunlight gone, and even the stars extinguished, the evening seemed blacker than the darkest moonless night.

He returned his attention to the window, tilting his head up.

The object hovered stationary in the sky. Precisely how far above his head, he couldn't judge. They wanted it that way, he presumed.

In the exact center of the craft, a blue-white light pulsed.

He felt no shame in the shiver that coursed through him.

The battle was about to begin.

Akhetaten, Egypt
Circa 1335 BC

E RIN RIPPED THE BRACELET FROM HER WRIST. SHE HURLED IT TO THE FLOOR at Wessick's feet.

"What else am I wearing," she said, "that you've bugged?"

He gazed at her without expression. "Nothing."

She squinted at him.

With a faint shrug, he said, "Why would I lie when I've already admitted to placing a tracking device in your bracelet?"

Alex answered the query. "You lie habitually."

"No," Wessick said as he glanced at Alex. Then he fixed his gaze on Erin again. "I've told you the truth far more often than I've lied to you."

A hiccup of derisive laughter burst out of Erin. Stifling it, she said, "How comforting."

Alex snatched the gun from Erin's hand and, with one stride, closed the distance between himself and Wessick. He reached for the document tube.

Wessick ducked his arm behind his back, concealing the tube behind his body.

Alex raised the gun at Wessick. "Hand it over."

"Shoot me if you like," Wessick said. "But you'll never escape from Akhetaten without my help."

"He's not going to kill you," Erin said.

Alex didn't look at her. "Maybe I will."

"Oh for crying out loud." Erin stomped forward, positioning herself between Alex and Wessick. "Put the gun down."

Since only a few feet separated the two men, she found herself uncomfortably close to both Wessick and the gun's muzzle. Alex uncurled his finger from around the trigger and rested it on the barrel. A deep scowl darkened his expression as he lowered the gun to his side.

He wouldn't have shot Wessick.

Would he?

She spun around to face Wessick. Her eyes came to the level of his nose. Separated from him by no more than six inches, she tilted her head back to meet his gaze. He arched an eyebrow.

"Give me the tube," she said, extending a hand palm up. "Please."

His jaw worked for a couple seconds. Then, without so much as an annoyed sigh, he whipped his arm out from behind his back and set the document tube atop her palm.

She closed her fingers around the tube. "Thank you."

"The scroll must be important," Wessick said, "for you to bring it with you. But the hieroglyphic text reveals nothing about the relic's location."

Erin shuffled backward a few steps to stand alongside Alex. He exuded tension. The fingers of his right hand, which clutched the gun's grip, twitched at erratic intervals. With each movement, the tendons across the back of his hand stuck out like cables on a suspension bridge. His jaw looked tight enough to grind granite. His eyes, narrowed to slits, stayed focused on Wessick.

They had the map and overlay. Harry said he remembered what the missing part of the overlay looked like. They also had one *akhet* ball, enough to get them home. Strategizing how to find the relic could wait until they got safely out of Akhetaten and back to their own timeline. Finding the relic no longer required the cooperation of the Aten or their minions.

Wessick was irrelevant now.

She laid a hand on Alex's arm. "You're right. We don't need his help anymore."

He relaxed, a little.

"Let's get out of here," she said.

Alex nodded.

Wessick shook his head. "The Aten have lost their patience."

Either not listening to Wessick or not caring what the man said, Alex headed for the door. Wessick tried to block his path, but Alex shoved to the older man out of the way. The oil lamp in his hand, Harry trailed Alex toward the door. Erin hesitated, her gaze intent on Wessick.

"What do you mean?" she asked.

"They've grown weary of your antics," he said. "Their patience is all that has held them back—and kept you alive and unharmed. Tonight, the tether has snapped."

Erin stepped closer to him, until her breath must've whispered across his face as she glared up at him. In a rough whisper, she said, "Inform your bosses that if they harm me or any of my friends or family, I will make certain they never see their relic again."

She didn't mention that she'd make sure of that anyway.

Without waiting for a response, she marched to the doorway. At the threshold, she paused to glance back at him.

"About what I just said," she told him. "Chloe is exempt from it. Oh pardon me, you call her Desheret, don't you?" Erin swallowed the anger rising inside her. "She's not my friend."

"You will never escape the city without my—"

"Shut up."

And then she stalked out the door.

Alex and Harry waited for her a few yards away. When she got within whispering distance of them, she said, "What now?"

"We need a private place," Alex said. "I mean a *more* private place where we can show Harry the you-know-what."

The moon glowed high in the sky. Stars twinkled all around, more stars than she'd ever seen in her life, more even than in the skies over the Keweenaw Peninsula. Here, not a smidgen of light pollution obscured the heavens.

A chill slid down the back of her neck. The moon. It looked...strange. The orb glowed with an iridescence that lent it the shimmering quality of water.

Plus, the moon was getting bigger. And she was pretty sure the moon was not supposed to get bigger.

Yet it did. The orb swelled little by little.

She slapped Alex's arm with the back of her hand. When he gave her a curious look, she pointed up at the moon. He traced his gaze up her arm, past her fingertip, to the brilliant object above their heads. Though it held the same position in the sky, the orb had begun to swell faster. It appeared as large as a basketball—and it was still growing.

No. She stared at the orb as it enlarged. The object was not growing in size. It was coming closer.

She, Alex, and Harry watched the craft without speaking. For it was a craft, a vehicle powered by some sort of energy and controlled by intelligent beings. The craft descended on them in complete silence. As it drew nearer and nearer, its apparent size increased exponentially. Its light grew brighter. Squinting, Erin raised a hand to shield her eyes.

The glow extinguished in a split second, as if someone flipped a switch.

The flame in Harry's oil lamp snuffed out.

The darkness blinded her. Still, she sensed the craft descending. Felt it coming closer. A spreading blackness engulfed the stars. Within another minute, she saw no stars at all.

A hand fumbled for hers, clasping it firmly. She wrapped her fingers around Alex's.

Scritch. Scritch.

Erin's heart skipped at the sound. It came from close by. She gripped Alex's hand tighter.

A light flashed no more than a yard from her. Then again. The light was a spark, though from what she had no clue. She heard the scritching sound. The spark erupted into a tiny yellow flame. Alex held his lighter. Harry proffered the oil lamp to Alex, who lit its wick.

She'd wondered why Alex carried a lighter, since he didn't smoke. Tonight, she discovered the answer. And she was extremely grateful he did carry the thing.

At the outer edges of the lamp's glow, she spotted Wessick standing just outside the doorway to the storage room. The soft illumination highlighted the whites of his eyes. He looked like a dark specter straight out of Hell. Unlike an evil specter, however, Wessick failed to ignite fear within her. He was a man, nothing more. He held no power unless the Aten granted it to him.

A light winked on overhead.

All heads turned to gaze upward. A single white light, tiny in relation to the craft's size, burned in the exact center of the object. At least she thought it was the exact center. Hard to tell in the dark.

Lights popped on at either side of the central light. Then, in pairs of one on either side, lights winked on in a straight line across the craft's bottom. The lineup extended out of sight in either direction.

"They've come for your companions," Wessick said.

Erin jerked her head left to look at him. "What?"

Wessick strode to her, entering the heart of the lamplight. He halted a few feet from her. Alex shifted his weight, as if about to pounce on Wessick. Erin squeezed his hand. He stayed where he was, though she felt the tension rippling through him. Wessick ignored Alex, focusing instead on Erin.

"They've come for your..." Wessick nodded toward Alex without taking his gaze off he Erin. His upper lip twitched as he finished his sentence. "For your *friends*. To take them as hostages."

Dread crystallized ice around her heart.

Wessick continued. "I told you, they've lost their patience. We don't have much time. It will take them a short while to locate us, but then they will take hostages." He leaned a hair closer. "Smaller ships have taken up positions over both Revenant House and your parents' home."

"In the future? " she asked. "How is that a threat? All we have to do is go back to before the ships arrived and get my parents out of there."

Wessick shook his head. "They will find you wherever you go. This isn't an action borne out of desperation. This tactic has been a part of their plan from the beginning. Your only option is to do as they wish and find the relic."

She expected Alex to disagree, or at least tell off Wessick. Both he and Harry remained silent.

Overhead, the enormous craft hovered in silence.

She didn't have a blasted clue what to say either.

"I can help you escape," Wessick said. "I know where to find an *akhet* ball."

It took all of Erin's willpower not to glance at Alex's bag. Wessick had no way of knowing the bag contained an *akhet* ball. He must mean that he knew of a stash somewhere in the city.

"Come with me," Wessick said, starting down the alleyway between the buildings.

Alex murmured, "We don't need him."

"Maybe we do." She paused, thinking back on what Wessick had said. "If there are ships waiting to swarm over us as soon as we get back to our own time, then we need someone who knows where we can hide."

"We'll do what you said, go back to before the ships arrived."

She couldn't suppress the exasperation that tinged her voice. "We have one *akhet* ball. The only stash we know of is in Wessick's study. Obviously, the Aten are keeping tabs on Revenant House. We might get there and, whoosh, here comes a big nasty mother ship. Before we can get our hands on another *akhet* ball, they've zapped you and Harry and my parents into their laboratory of horrors."

"What do you suggest we do?" Alex asked. "Follow Wessick around like good little sheep?"

"Let him get us out of here. He won't hurt me—and he knows better than to hurt you."

Harry cleared his throat.

"Sorry," she said. "I meant both of you."

"No offense taken." Harry gestured over his shoulder. "If we're following your comrade, then I reckon we should catch up to him."

Wessick either hadn't noticed their hesitation, or he didn't care. He was indeed continuing down the alleyway at a brisk walk.

Alex said to Harry, "You agree with her?"

The older man shrugged. "I'll defer to the lady on this one. Her instincts seem a tad more reliable than mine. I got myself snatched by the bad guys after all."

Alex looked at Erin. She gave him a tiny smile, not of happiness but of resignation. He let out the longest sigh she'd ever heard.

Then he took off down the alleyway after Wessick, dragging Erin along with him. They caught up with Wessick a few seconds later and trailed him down the alleyway past the end of the long, narrow buildings into an open area. Onward they traveled, half marching, half running. Erin refused to let herself look up at the gigantic ship hovering overhead. Still she sensed it up there, its weight seeming to press down on her. Never before had she imagined a person could feel claustrophobic while outdoors.

They passed a squat building that smelled of cow manure. Beyond that, another open expanse stretched ahead of them. To their left, the great wall of the Aten temple towered like an apparition, darker than the night around it, no longer lit by the stunning brilliance of the globe lights inside the temple complex. The only light came from Harry's oil lamp—and the lights on the underside of the mother ship, which cast the faintest glow on the landscape.

A dark outline up ahead suggested another building or a walled enclosure. Wessick made a beeline for the structure. Erin, Alex, and Harry hustled after him as he upped his pace. As they neared the structure, Erin realized it was a walled enclosure similar to the one around Wessick's house. A similar gateway accessed the enclosed area. The wooden gates stood closed. Wessick approached the gates, halting directly in front of them. A locking mechanism identical to the one in the temple barred anyone from opening the gates.

"Do you have a key?" Erin asked.

Wessick stepped back several feet. He raised his sword over his head and slammed it down on the lock. The wood cracked. Wessick attacked the lock with several more blows. The mechanism splintered. With a bit of effort, Wessick maneuvered the bolt out of the lock. He dropped the slab of wood onto the ground. Kicking the gates open, he strode inside.

As elsewhere in the city, no torches or oil lamps burned here. They must've snuffed out like Harry's lamp. They crossed a small courtyard that fronted a house. A red wooden door marked the front entrance of the building. Unlike at Wessick's house, here no guards protected the house from intruders. The homeowner must've felt the lock on the gate provided enough of a deterrent. Maybe he couldn't afford guards, the size of the house and its grounds suggested otherwise.

Wessick shoved the door open. He stepped across the threshold into a long entranceway. As he led them deeper into the house, Erin glimpsed wall paintings of the Aten and the royal family, as well as geese and other wildlife. Wessick ushered them through one room and into another. Here, he stopped. By the light of Harry's lamp, Erin saw the room's decor was even sparser than at Wessick's house. A single long table, overburdened with unlit oil lamps and pottery vessels, nestled against the far wall. A chest stood tucked into one corner. The wall paintings depicted architectural elements—lotus-topped columns, pylons, doorways—all of which created a false environment around them. Erin felt as if she'd stepped through another portal into a different time and place.

Without a word, Wessick stomped toward the chest in the corner, crouching before it. He lifted the lid and began rifling through the contents. Erin, Alex, and Harry lingered near the doorway.

Erin shuffled closer to Harry so that she might whisper in his ear. She said, "Did the priest tell you anything more?"

"No." He glanced at Wessick. "Shouldn't talk here anyway."

"You won't talk in front of Wessick. You didn't want to talk in the temple. But you and the priest had long conversations about the relic's location while you were prisoners."

He shook his head. "He held back the details until after we'd escaped from the temple. We were hiding out in the workers' village, way out in the desert."

"And you're sure you remember what the map looked like?"

"Yep." He hesitated. "Pretty sure."

Acid churned in Erin's stomach. They were risking their lives based on "pretty sure."

She looked at Alex. He was staring at Wessick, though she got the impression he was also listening to her conversation with Harry.

"Whose house is this?" Alex asked, loud enough for Wessick to hear.

Wessick paused in his search. Without looking away from the chest, he replied, "This is the home of the high priest Panehsy."

A chill rushed through Erin. Wessick brought them to the enemy's stronghold. Since he conspired with the enemy, he probably brought them exactly because this house belonged to Panehsy.

The walls seemed to close in on all sides as the ceiling crushed down on them. Not literally, of course. But she still felt suffocated. Trapped. Powerless.

Baloney. She held the power. If only she knew how to use it.

Wessick slammed the chest's lid shut. He rose, turned toward them, and said, "The *akhet* balls are gone. Panehsy seems to have moved them."

"You must have your own stash," Erin said, "somewhere else in the city."

"The only other cache I know of is in the house I own."

Erin let her shoulders sag. "The house that's clear on the other side of town. Past the gangs of armed soldiers and the rampaging mobs who blame us for their predicament."

He nodded.

Erin felt the remnants of her energy drain out on her breath. Rampaging mobs. Gangs of soldiers.

"We would never make it," Wessick said. "Even if we survive the mobs, the longer we're out in the open, the more chance there is that the Aten will locate us and take us hostage."

Alex snorted. "Nobody cares if you're a hostage."

Erin poked him in the side. He muttered something that she couldn't quite make out.

Arguments and macho posturing helped them not one bit. Erin wished Alex and Wessick would both get over whatever it was that made them so testy. Every so often she got the impression that she was the source of their dislike for each other. But that couldn't be. No one would get this upset over her.

Or would they?

Shaking off the thought, she asked, "What now?"

Wessick said nothing. Alex said nothing. Harry said nothing.

She reached for Alex's bag. He yanked it away.

Erin blew out a breath. "Give it to me. *Please.*"

They both knew she was referring to the *akhet* ball in his bag. The only *akhet* ball within reach. The one chance they had to escape this cursed city.

Through clenched teeth, he said, "What if we need it later?"

"You mean when you're a hostage being tortured by the Aten. Or worse."

"What could be worse?"

Fear gripped her heart like a steel-plated fist. She could imagine much worse things. Actually, she imagined just one worst-case scenario.

"Don't be so dense," Harry said. "She means if you croak."

"Oh." Alex unclenched his teeth, softening his expression as he gazed down at Erin. His voice dropped to a near whisper as he said, "Don't worry about me."

"If you don't want me to worry," she said, "then give me what I want."

Erin reached for the bag again. Instead of handing it to her, he unzipped the main compartment, reached inside, and fished out the *akhet* ball. He gave the object to her.

She kissed his cheek. "Thank you."

He grumbled.

Cradling the *akhet* ball in her palm, she faced Wessick. "Problem solved. We can go home."

"I'm afraid not." Wessick took two steps toward her, still a dozen feet away. "If we return to the twenty-first century, the Aten will find us no matter where on the planet we land. And they will be angry."

"Can the Aten track these balls? Where we ask them to take us, I mean."

"No, the balls are connected to neither each other nor a central system."

"Okay then." She tossed the ball a few inches into the air and caught it again. "We'll figure out where the relic is and use this *akhet* ball to take us there."

She unscrewed the cap of the document tube.

Alex spun toward her. "You're showing him the you-know-what?"

"He's already seen it." She popped the cap off the tube. "And maybe he can help."

Wessick said, "We have no time for this."

"We have no choice," she said. "You just told us we can't go home yet. And we can't waste our one and only *akhet* ball on going someplace else. We'll have no way to get home or to get to the relic."

Alex raised a hand, like schoolboy waiting to be called on by the teacher. But he didn't wait for someone to recognize him before he said, "Why don't we use the *akhet* ball to get back to Wessick's house? Then we can use the *akhet* balls from his stash to go wherever else we need to go."

So his brain did still work, in spite of the testosterone overload.

"Good idea," she said, smiling up at him.

"Yes," Wessick said, as if speaking the word hurt him. "It might work."

Alex met her gaze, and a look of self-satisfaction came over his face. It wasn't arrogance but rather an expression of accomplishment, she thought. He liked to feel useful.

Especially if it ticked off Wessick.

Wessick waved at the room's doorway. "We should go out there. Opening a portal requires a larger space than this room. The entrance corridor will do."

Harry led the group as they exited the smaller chamber into the larger one beyond. The entranceway stood directly ahead of them.

Pow!

Erin yelped as the front door burst inward. Alex flung an arm out to shield her, raising the gun with his other hand.

The door bounced off the wall. It teetered briefly before coming to rest three-quarters open. A figure filled the doorway.

Erin had a sick feeling she knew who the newcomer was.

Crossing the threshold, the man clomped down the hallway toward the room where they stood. He halted just inside the entrance to the room. The glow from Harry's lamp flickered across the man's features.

The man twisted his mouth into a vile grin.

"Who is this?" Alex murmured.

Erin gulped against the lump in her throat. "It's the high priest Panehsy."

In his left hand, the priest clutched a mace. The weapon's wood handle supported a stone ball large enough and hard enough to crack a skull wide open.

"I told you, *satseshat*," Panehsy growled. "You are mine."

26

THE HIGH PRIEST PANEHSY THUMPED THE MACE'S HANDLE ON HIS PALM. HE sneered at Erin. The old lump congealed in her throat again and she swallowed. Hard.

Alex waggled the gun just enough to draw Panehsy's attention to the weapon. Once he had the priest's attention, Alex said, "You mentioned being familiar with these weapons. So when I tell you to drop the mace, you understand the consequences of not doing what I say."

Panehsy glanced past Alex's shoulder. "You might succeed in killing me, but my wife is another matter."

Erin turned her head to track Panehsy's gaze behind them, to a doorway at the back of the room. There in the doorway stood Desheret. In her right hand she grasped a 9mm handgun. Erin's gun.

Desheret held the gun in front of her, aimed squarely at Erin.

Alex muttered a curse.

Wessick turned sideways to glance first at Desheret, then at Panehsy, and finally back to Desheret. The madwoman kept her gaze locked on Erin's face.

His gaze narrowed on Desheret, Wessick said, "Why would you aid your husband? You begged me to release you from your marriage bond."

Desheret cocked her head to the side. "And you refused, Samuel. You spoke of my duty and promised that soon I would no longer be required to feign devotion to the loathsome man whom you and the Aten forced me to wed."

Panehsy slammed the mace's head onto his palm with a smacking sound that echoed off the walls.

"Silence, wife," the priest barked.

Harry and Alex looked at Panehsy. Erin and Wessick kept their eyes on Desheret.

"I will not be silenced," Desheret hissed. Though she glared at Erin, her words were clearly aimed at the priest. "They chained me to you so that I would have access to the palace and the pharaoh, and to the temple. I will be chained no longer."

She pulled the trigger. The gunshot exploded inside the room.

Erin heard the bullet whiz past her head. She ducked down, then realized she felt no pain. Exploring her head with her fingertips, she found no wounds. Her ears rang, but she knew from recent experience the phenomenon would pass in a few minutes. Unless exposure to two deafening gunshots in a short period had permanently damaged her hearing.

Alex shoved an arm under hers. He hauled her up, tilting her toward him. His eyes were wide, his mouth open, his forehead creased with worry lines.

Since his ears must be ringing too, she expressed her okay-ness by shaking off his arm and standing on her own. Relief ironed out the lines across his forehead.

Erin looked at Desheret. An expression of wild triumph spread across the madwoman's face.

Triumph? What had the woman accomplished?

Alex nudged her shoulder. He was pointing in the opposite direction. Erin swung her head to the right, toward the front entrance.

Panehsy lay flat on his back, eyes open but unseeing. Blood seeped from a single gunshot wound on his chest.

Erin jerked her head to look at Desheret.

The woman killed her own husband. Of course, according to Desheret, the Aten and Wessick forced her into a marriage of convenience—their convenience. And Erin learned firsthand that Panehsy was no meek, pious servant of the Aten. The man had been intimidating, to say the least. She couldn't imagine living with the man as his wife.

Erin felt a twinge of sympathy for the woman. She balled it up and tossed it to the corner of her mind. Desheret was no wilting flower. The woman was a murderer. She killed Greg Vertanen.

A question bobbed to the surface of her mind. The ringing in her ears had lessened enough that she could probably hold a conversation.

Facing Desheret, Erin asked, "Why did you kill Greg?"

The woman's triumphant expression disintegrated. The hard line of her mouth suggested, however, that anger simmered beneath the surface of her now-calm expression.

"Greg was nothing," Desheret said. "A whimpering fool. A simpleton. When he discovered my involvement with Samuel, Greg became a problem. I solved it."

"By throwing him off a cliff?" Erin shook her head, unable to comprehend the logic that Desheret clearly saw in her solution to the Greg problem.

"Men deserve no better," Desheret said. She trained the gun on Erin's head. "And neither do you."

Erin eyed the gun in Desheret's hand. "Greg said you bought a gun for self-defense, but I've never seen you carrying one."

"I never owned a gun. It took all my money to pay the rent, since Greg was a useless fool."

"Then how did you learn to shoot? You didn't accidentally hit your husband square in the chest."

Desheret smiled, though the expression conveyed no joy. "I went to a gun club. It wasn't hard to convince men to let me borrow their guns."

So her lies about going to the shooting range weren't always lies. Nevertheless, Greg's suspicions had proved correct. She was involved with someone else, though perhaps not in the way Greg had envisioned.

Out the corner of her eye, Erin saw Alex lift his arm to raise his gun.

"Uh-uh-uh," Desheret said, wagging a finger at him. "If anyone moves, Erin gets a bullet between the eyes. And you know I can make the shot."

Alex stopped moving. A muscle in his jaw twitched.

"Drop the gun," Desheret ordered, "and kick it to me."

Alex hurled the gun at Desheret. The weapon smacked into her thigh and plopped onto the ground at her feet. She didn't even wince. Without looking down, she used the back of her heel to kick the gun behind her.

The madwoman looked at Wessick and then at Alex. "Drop your swords. Both of you."

Both men tossed their swords onto the ground.

Desheret locked her gaze on Erin once more. "Toss me the *akhet* ball. Gently."

Alex muttered syllables that sounded like *don't do it*. Erin saw no other options, though, and chucked the ball toward their captor. Desheret caught the ball in her free hand. Bobbing her hand as if measuring the ball's weight, she said, "Thank you, *satseshat*. You've saved me the trouble of retrieving my *akhet* ball."

"So glad I could help," Erin muttered.

With the same hand, she gestured at the document tube. "You were about to show something to Samuel. I want to see it."

Erin clutched the document tube to her chest.

"Now," Desheret said. "Or your next conversation will be in the afterlife."

Alex looked at Erin. He rolled his eyes in Desheret's direction, indicating that Erin should hand over the map to the madwoman. No way. The vital part of the map was damaged beyond recognition, yet who knew how long Desheret had been eavesdropping on their discussions. Did she follow Erin or Alex into the temple? Did she catch up to them at the storage room? In either case, she might've overheard Harry admitting that he both saw the map before it was damaged and felt certain he could fill in the missing portion. Because of all these concerns, handing over the map seemed like a really bad idea.

When Erin didn't relinquish the map, Alex snatched the document tube from her. He unscrewed the cap and slid out the papyrus and the fabric overlay, which were rolled up together. Unfurling the paired sheets, he held them together by their upper corners with their front sides facing Desheret.

"It's a map," he told her. "The overlay changes the map's appearance. But as you can see, a part of the map is damaged."

What on earth was he thinking, spilling their secrets to this woman? His mind must've snapped from the stress of recent events. He looked fine, though, not at all like a raving lunatic. And she couldn't believe he would break, no matter how intense the pressure. All of this brought her back to her original question. What was he thinking?

His expression gave no clue.

Desheret leaned forward to squint at the items Alex held. The map was, naturally, too far away for her to see much, since she kept a safe distance between herself and her captives. She was crazy, not stupid.

Alex took a half step toward Desheret.

"Stop," she said. "Or you know what will happen to Erin."

Alex stopped. He stretched his arms out as far as possible and said, "Why don't you take the map?"

Desheret studied him with half-closed eyes, her lips pursed slightly. A few seconds ticked by on Erin's mental clock. Finally, Desheret shook her head. One corner of her mouth angled upward in a half smirk.

"Nice try," she said. "But I've dealt with far more devious men than you. You won't trick me into coming closer so that you might wrestle the gun away from me."

Oh, so that was his plan. Erin glanced at him sideways. Worth a shot, she supposed, but the shot had ricocheted. Desheret was, as Erin had already determined, crazy but unfortunately not stupid.

"No more tricks," Desheret warned. "Give Erin the map and back away slowly with your hands in the air." She nodded at Wessick. "You do the same—*darling*."

Wessick shuffled backward toward the entryway where Panehsy's body lay crumpled.

Desheret stomped her foot and screeched, "Do it!"

Erin grasped the corners of the map and overlay, gently freeing them from Alex's grip. He lowered his arms and turned toward her. The tension in his jaw tightened all his features. Even the blue of his eyes seemed sharper than before.

She mouthed, "Go."

A long breath hissed out his nostrils. Fisting his hands at his sides, he faced Desheret and backed toward the entryway.

To Erin's left, a silhouette shifted.

Her heart thudded. She glanced left to see Harry baby-stepping backward. A pang of guilt stabbed at her. Jeez, she'd all but forgotten about Harry.

"No," Desheret said, jerking the gun toward Harry. "Stay, professor. I heard you say you've seen the map in its entirety. I want you and Erin to work out what the missing part shows."

Harry scuffled forward again, coming up alongside Erin.

Desheret aimed the gun at Erin's head once more, though she kept her gaze on Harry. The madwoman told him, "Get on with it."

Rotating toward Harry, Erin held the map with its top edge just below her chin. Harry took hold of the bottom-right corner, grasping it between his thumb and forefinger. He ducked his head and lifted the corner to scrutinize the damaged portion of the map more closely.

Without lifting his head, he asked, "Anybody got a pen?"

"You want to draw on the map?" Alex said. "You can't deface it, it's an ancient…"

"Relic?" Erin finished.

"Yes. But I suppose this is one relic we have to deface." He cleared his throat, reaching for a side zipper on his bag. "I have a fine-point marker. A pen, essentially."

"That'll do," Harry said.

Alex unzipped the small compartment on the front of his bag.

Desheret stamped her foot, letting out an animalistic cry.

Everyone froze and looked at her.

"No tricks," she growled. "Or Erin dies. There will be no more warnings."

At a pace that would put a snail to shame, Alex withdrew the marker pen from the pocket of his bag. He tossed it to Harry, who caught it in his right hand. Thus equipped, Harry slid his left hand under the bottom-right corner of the map to support it and the overlay. He used his teeth to pluck the cap off the pen. As he spit out the cap, discarding it on the floor, Harry raised the pen to the overlay. He touched the pen's tip to the fabric. Brow furrowed, lips mashed together, he drew lines on the fabric inch by inch. He took such care, in fact, that Erin's arms began to ache from holding up the map for him.

No one spoke. No one moved. Even the sounds of turmoil from outside had faded into silence.

Harry lifted the pen from the fabric. He nabbed the cap from the floor and snapped it back onto the pen. Straightening, he said, "Done."

"Let me see it," Erin said.

Taking the map from her, he flipped it around so that she could see its front side. The corner of the overlay now sported a series of curving and jagged lines. The last time she and Alex examined the map with its overlay in place, neither of them could make any sense of it. She felt the same confusion squeezing her brain cells now.

The hieroglyphic text spoke of a river that ran straight through the *duat*, finding its end at what the text called "the excellent lake." The lake also served as the burial place of a pharaoh, or so the text claimed. Mainstream historians said Amenhotep IV underwent a religious conversion and changed his name to Akhenaten in honor of his new god. The map text, however, told a different story. From Alex's translation of the hieroglyphic text, she knew the Aten abducted Amenhotep IV, the human pharaoh. According to Wessick, they lured the pharaoh into the mountains, where the supposed transfiguration took place. In reality, they replaced the human pharaoh with one of their own—who became Akhenaten, the earthbound servant of his brethren.

On first learning of the Aten's clever swap, she'd wondered whether the pharaoh buried near the excellent lake might be Amenhotep IV—the original, human king replaced by the Aten—but she dismissed the idea. The Aten despised humans. They would've discarded the pharaoh's body like so much waste.

Since learning of Akhenaten's betrayal of his fellow Aten, Erin wondered if he might be the pharaoh buried near the excellent lake. To find out, she must first find the lake in question. A line that looked like a river did indeed wind its way across the map. The river appeared to end in the damaged portion of the map, at the edge of the area Harry had just redrawn. Maybe the late pharaoh, whether Amenhotep IV or Akhenaten or someone else altogether, rested for eternity alongside the relic.

Except Akhenaten wasn't dead—yet. The map text explained that the pharaoh absconded with the relic. But the map itself provided the location of the relic.

Hmm.

Erin peered over the top of the map at Harry. "Are you fluent in Kemetian? I mean ancient Egyptian."

"No." He let out a dry chuckle. "The priest said a Babylonian infant could speak Kemetian better than me."

"Then how did you communicate with the priest?"

"He spoke English. Like a pro, I might add."

"How?"

Harry lowered the map a little, rolling his shoulders back. "The priest told me a man called Meru taught him English. Apparently Meru was a big kahuna in the palace. He swore the priest to secrecy about the English lessons."

"Meru?" Erin slowly turned her head to look at Wessick, who regarded her with an impassive expression. She said, "You taught a priest of Amun-Ra to speak English? Why?"

"I thought he might prove useful to you."

"Was this before or after the Aten ordered the deaths of all the priests of Amun-Ra?"

"Before." He shrugged one shoulder. "I helped the priest escape execution."

Erin couldn't think of a blessed thing to say. Wessick worked for the Aten, yet he helped a priest of Amun-Ra escape their wrath. Every time she thought she understood the man, he threw up another screen to obscure her view of his true self.

I hope one day you'll see that I'm not who you think I am.

Wessick spoke those words to her just yesterday. She assumed he him save file was being cryptic, as usual, but maybe he meant the words literally. Here in Akhetaten, he answered to the name Meru. She already suspected that Samuel N. Wessick was not his real name either. The initials SNW, when coupled with ATN—the initials of Wessick's assistant, Anna T. Newman—formed the Kemetian words SNW ATN.

The phrase *senu aten* meant Brothers of the Aten. So the name Samuel Wessick seemed like a pseudonym as well. Who was he really?

The answer would have to wait.

Returning her attention to Harry, she asked, "The priest made the map, right?"

Harry nodded.

"The text on the map says the pharaoh ran off with the relic," she said. "But the map must've been created well before Akhenaten took off. But how could he take off with the relic anyway, since only the keepers know where it's hidden?"

"Your translation of the map is a little…off." Harry glanced at Alex. "No offense."

"Forget it," Alex said. "What's the correct translation?"

"The pharaoh took with him the knowledge of the relic's location, not the relic itself. Akhenaten got his hands on the first draft of the map and took off with it."

"How accurate was the first draft?" Alex asked.

"Almost as good as this one."

Erin dropped the corner of the map. She flung up her hands in a gesture meant to silence the conversation. It worked. Alex and Harry both turned their attention on her.

"I have a question," she said. "You explained the part about the pharaoh and the relic. But who's the pharaoh buried near the excellent lake? It can't be Akhenaten. He's not dead yet."

Harry gave her a patient smile. "Most of the information in the map text, including the bit about the pharaoh, came straight out of the *satseshat* prophecy. The priest of Amun-Ra didn't make it up. He repeated it." Harry sighed. "All I can tell you is that the pharaoh mentioned in the text seems to be Akhenaten. After all, he's the one who skedaddled with the first draft of the map."

Erin felt the room tilt around her. None of this made sense. She listed to the left, coming to rest against Alex's chest. For the moment, she couldn't worry about some ridiculous prophecy. She had to focus on the task at hand.

As the world steadied again, she pushed away from Alex and waved her hands, gesturing for Harry to raise the map higher. He complied, and she focused on the newly restored section. At the end of the snaking river, a small grouping of hieroglyphs, once smudged beyond recognition, now appeared sharp and clear. The other lines Harry had drawn, the curving and jagged ones, reminded her of something. She cleared all thoughts from her mind and let her vision drift out of focus. The markings on the fabric became a fuzzy outline.

Recognition tickled her brain. She couldn't quite latch onto it.

Straightening, she looked at Desheret. "I need Alex's help."

"No." Desheret gripped the gun so tightly that her arm wobbled. "No one but the old man helps you."

"If you want the relic, then let Alex help me. He's unarmed."

Desheret scowled at Erin for a moment, then let out a sharp sigh. She spat, "Fine."

Alex tiptoed toward Erin, keeping his body facing the madwoman. Once alongside Erin, he murmured, "What can I do?"

"These hieroglyphs." She indicated the grouping on the map. "What do they mean?"

He leaned forward, careful not to touch her or the map, probably because he thought Desheret might interpret such contact as a threat. Erin lifted the corner of the map to help him see it better. He squinted at the symbols. With the index finger of his right hand, he traced the series of hieroglyphs that marked the end of the river flowing through the map's center.

After a few seconds, he said, "It translates as the excellent lake of the big waters."

The hieroglyphs in question appeared next to a blue blob that protruded from the river, which itself was rendered in the same shades of blue. The adjacent blob must represent a lake. A short, slender bit of blue connected the river to the lake. The strange symbol she'd noticed before, an *ankh* inside a cartouche, split the main river from the connecting tributary. The shape that ring a familiar tone in her mind represented a landmass situated between the river and the main body of the lake.

Between the river.

What had the hieroglyphic text said? *First buried in the land between the river, in the pyramid mountain at the doorway to the duat, he now rests for eternity in the land at the river's end.* "He" referred to the unnamed pharaoh, possibly Akhenaten.

"You can do this," Alex whispered.

As she scrutinized the outline of the landmass, she noticed a tiny red dot that seemed to mark a spot on the landmass. She couldn't tell for sure whether the dot was intentional or nothing but a dribble of paint or a speck of red dust. Ignoring the dot for now, she focused on the blobby lake that surrounded the landmass. The excellent lake. Big waters. The shape of the landmass. She let her vision slide out of focus once more. The shapes and colors on the map coalesced into one big rainbow blur. Words bounced around in her mind. Excellent, waters, big, lake.

Her body jerked as her vision snapped back into focus.

Alex settled a hand atop her shoulder. "Are you all right?"

"Uh-huh." She pointed at the landmass on the map. "Doesn't this shape remind you of something?"

"I don't know, maybe a shrimp."

She scrunched her lips. "No, not a shrimp." She traced the outline with her fingertip. "It's the Upper Peninsula of Michigan."

27

ALEX GAZED DOWN AT THE MAP AND TILTED HIS HEAD LEFT, THEN right. "I suppose it could be the Upper Peninsula. But it's so vague, it could be almost anything."

"The text refers to the excellent lake of the big waters." Erin crossed her arms over her chest. "Another word for excellent is superior, as in Lake Superior. And the Ojibwa called Lake Superior by another name, Gitchigumi, which means Big Water. Considering the shape of the landmass—" She tapped the image. "—the text must be referring to Lake Superior."

His eyes widened just a smidge. He blinked, glanced at the map, then looked at her. "That means…"

"The relic we've been searching for may have been right in our backyard the whole time." She gazed down at the map. A strange sensation swept over her, a feeling akin to awe mixed with giddiness. Even those words failed to describe the sensation. She'd never felt anything like it before. She felt herself speaking, and heard the hushed tone of her voice as the words escaped her lips unbidden. "Holy mackerel."

Alex slipped an arm around her waist. "I believe, under the circumstances, the more appropriate term is holy shit."

His words broke through her trancelike state. She glanced at him sideways as a grin threatened to part her lips. She couldn't remember hearing him swear before, and she certainly never heard him use the S word. He liked long words that forced her to consult a dictionary to make sure she understood him correctly.

"Back away from her," Desheret barked. "Slowly."

Erin's jubilation fizzled out. Alex withdrew his arm from her waist and shuffled backward. Caught up in her moment of discovery, Erin forgot about the lunatic aiming a gun at her head. She probably shouldn't have revealed every detail of her revelation in front of Desheret. It didn't really matter, she supposed, since the woman would've simply shot Alex or Harry in order to convince Erin to reveal the relic's location. Besides, the U.P. was a big place. Desheret might never find the relic by herself.

The lunatic tightened her finger over the gun's trigger. Glaring at Erin with the intensity of a rabid lioness, she said, "You know the precise location of the relic."

"The map doesn't say exactly where the relic is hidden," Erin replied. She glanced down at the map, to the spot on it marked with the tiny dot, and she knew she'd just lied to a madwoman who had a hair-trigger temper. Pressing on anyway, she said, "Plus, this map is over three thousand years old. The shoreline of Lake Superior has changed repeatedly during that time, as the water level rose and fell. What we're looking for might be submerged."

"Then we will travel to a time when it was accessible."

"I don't know when that would be. And besides, I can't pinpoint the location based on this map."

Desheret raised the *akhet* ball, supporting it with her fingertips. "This will get us close enough."

"And if we pop out the other side into the bottom of Lake Superior?"

"We'll take our chances."

"Great plan, Chloe."

Desheret's eyes widened at the use of her pseudonym. A split second later, she narrowed her eyes again. Her upper lip twitched.

"I'm so sorry," Erin said with feigned contrition. "You like to call yourself Desheret, which even I know refers to the red deserts of Egypt. I assume you picked the name because of your red hair. But what is your real name?"

"None of your concern."

Desheret set the *akhet* ball on the floor, freeing her left hand. Seemingly from within the folds of her skirt, but most likely from a pocket hidden there, she produced a coil of thin rope that she tossed to Harry. He caught the rope and eyed it with curiosity.

"Bind her hands in front of her," she told Harry as she retrieved the *akhet* ball, "and then roll up the map and place it in her hands."

Harry stared at the coil of rope in his hand.

Erin lifted her hands, holding them out for him to bind. She said, "It's all right."

As Harry gave her a pained look, Alex's voice shattered the silence.

"Like hell it's all right," he said, his tone gruff with emotion. "There is no way I'm letting this psychopath take you—"

"It's my choice," Erin said.

She nodded to Harry, and he strapped the rope around her wrists. He tied a knot that was secure and snug, but not uncomfortable. Next, he rolled the map scroll and overlay as one. She clasped her fingers around the roll as he slid it between them.

Desheret told Erin, "Bring the map to me. Make no sudden moves and do not try to trick me, or I will shoot him."

As she spoke the word "him," Desheret swung the gun leftward to level it at Alex's head.

Erin turned toward Desheret. She swore she could hear Alex's teeth gnashing from several yards away behind her. When she reached Desheret, the woman motioned for her to stand to the side. Erin made a three-quarters turn so that she faced both Desheret and the men, except for Harry. Only by turning her head to the right could she see him. Alex and Wessick stood near the far wall, adjacent to the entryway and Panehsy's body. Erin's gaze fell across the corpse. A cold lump solidified in her gut and she averted her gaze. Having killed once tonight already, Desheret would hardly flinch at the prospect of murdering another man.

Wessick stood still, though relaxed, his face devoid of expression. Alongside him, Alex stood stiff and straight while wearing a tight expression that fanned lines out across his forehead and away from his eyes. He caught her gaze just as she looked into his eyes. Somehow she knew exactly what he was thinking—and she knew it would get him killed.

She gave a little shake of her head, just enough to warn him. She hoped.

Either he didn't understand or he ignored her, because he took one large step forward.

"Stop," Erin said.

Alex hesitated.

"Let me go," she said. "Please, it's the only way. You know what has to be done."

He studied her for a moment, and then the anger evaporated from his features as he grasped her meaning. She knew he understood. He remembered as well as she did what the map text said about the relic. It told of the *satseshat* using the relic to destroy the source of the Aten's power. She knew, without a logical reason or conclusive evidence, that destroying the source of their power would end the Aten's reign of terror. She must find the relic. She must destroy the Aten.

And apparently, she must do it alone.

As the realization struck both of them, she felt certain the color was leaching from her face as rapidly as she saw it draining from his.

Desheret held the *akhet* ball to Erin. "Take this."

Erin looked from Desheret to the ball and back again. This felt like a trap, the kind outfitted with sharp metal teeth that sprayed acid. And she was the unlucky mouse.

"You will initialize the ball," Desheret said, "to open a portal to the correct time and place."

The crazy chick plucked the rolled-up map from Erin's hands and tucked it under one arm. She accomplished the feat so swiftly that no one had a chance to take advantage of the moment during which she lowered the gun to grab the scroll. Erin finally understood why the Aten chose Desheret as their hand-maiden. She was smart, quick, agile, and fierce.

Desheret thrust the *akhet* ball closer to Erin. Her voice turned as hard and cold as stone when she said, "Take it."

Still feeling like a mouse reaching for the cheese, Erin took hold of the *akhet* ball. She cradled it in both hands, since she couldn't separate her hands, thanks to the bindings.

"You know how the balls work?" Desheret asked.

"Yes," Erin answered, as she contemplated whether she might get away with requesting the wrong geographic location. Of course, she might end up at the wrong place anyhow.

"You should know," Desheret said, "that I've hidden an explosive device in this house. Once we go through the portal, it will shut behind us. I must disable the bomb before that happens. If you take us to the wrong location, if you attempt to trick me in any way, I won't disable the bomb. Your friends will have no chance of escaping. The bomb will destroy the entire temple district."

Erin snapped her head left to stare at Desheret.

Wessick spoke before Erin could muster her thoughts. He asked, "Where did you acquire a bomb, Desheret?"

"The Aten of course. They approved of my plan."

Either satisfied with her response or rendered speechless by it, Wessick said nothing more.

Erin cleared her throat to regain Desheret's attention, and then she asked, "How do I know you're telling the truth?"

The woman chuckled. "You don't. But are you willing to take the risk?"

No, Erin realized, she wasn't. Gambling with her own life was one thing. Playing Russian roulette with the lives of others proved more than she could stand.

Erin started to close her eyes.

Desheret seized Erin's arm, squeezing it painfully. When Erin directed her gaze at the woman, Desheret said, "Make certain you request passage for two people, no more."

Okay, that was a new one. Alex never mentioned needing to spell out how many passengers would ride the Time Travel Express. Stating the number of people must be optional.

"No stowaways," Desheret said, glancing at the men.

Erin cupped her hands around the *akhet* ball. She needed to go to the location on the map where the tiny red dot appeared. Everything depended on her identification of that dot as a marker, rather than smudge or a speck of dust. Closing her eyes, she summoned her knowledge of the Keweenaw Peninsula to triangulate the dot's location, using Shadow Bay as one of the triangle's corners. Christ, the relic had been practically under feet all this time, so close yet so unreachable. Her request seemed awfully wordy, but she wanted to take no chances on this little adventure. It was too important.

Focusing her mind like a laser, she issued the command in the form of a thought.

The ball vibrated in her hand.

Her eyelids flew open instinctively. She glanced down at the ball. Its innards swirled and glowed, shimmered and churned.

"Throw it into the room behind us," Desheret ordered.

Erin turned and tossed the ball into darkened room behind them.

A blinding light exploded.

When the light dimmed a bit, Erin cracked her eyelids open to peek into the other room.

A portal hovered in the air, about a foot off the floor. Although a faint glow emanated from the portal's skin, the region beyond the portal was pitch dark.

A shiver rattled Erin's bones as her pulse accelerated. All confidence in her plan washed away on a tide of panic. The location she chose might be underwater, or she might've chosen the wrong time and the location lay under a mile of ice.

"We go through together," Desheret said. Then she shoved Erin through the doorway into the other room. Once across the threshold, she waved a hand and said, "Retrieve a lamp from that table."

Erin rotated her head to see a long, narrow table placed against the wall. Atop the table hunkered two ornate oil lamps fashioned from alabaster. One featured several stems, each topped by an oil reservoir with a wick floating inside it. The other lamp consisted of a large oil reservoir with an open-topped globe seated on it and handles protruding from either side of the base. Erin selected the globe lamp. It seemed like it would provide the most light.

Grasping the lamp's handles in her bound hands, she returned to the doorway and glanced backward into the room she'd just left.

Alex had crossed half the distance to her. She shook her head, and he halted.

"You'll have no way to get home," he said.

"Don't worry about me. I'm a librarian."

He looked puzzled but said nothing.

Desheret clutched Erin's upper arm in her steel-plated grip. The madwoman shoved her forward, step by scuffling step, toward the portal.

"Erin."

The sound of Alex's voice made her glance back at him. His mouth hung open, as if he wanted to say something more but couldn't form the words.

She wanted to say something too. Now wasn't the time, though. If she ever saw him again, they'd have a nice long conversation.

Desheret dragged Erin to the portal. In the instant their feet crossed the threshold, a single ridiculous thought popped into Erin's mind.

How cold is it under a continental ice sheet?

Then they were through the portal. In the dark.

Erin wrenched free of Desheret's grasp and said, "Disable the bomb. *Right now.*"

A grin spread across the woman's face. The expression conveyed not cheer, but rather a searing hatred that bit into Erin's soul.

"I'm afraid," Desheret said, "I have tricked *you* this time. There is no way to disable the bomb."

Erin's heart thudded. She spun to face the portal.

Alex stood just on the other side of the threshold. He reached a hand out to her in the instant the portal telescoped shut.

In the darkness, Desheret's voice echoed through the space around them, sending a new shiver coursing through Erin.

"They are already dead, *satseshat*. And the relic is mine."

A LEX STARED AT THE SPOT WHERE ERIN HAD STOOD A SPLIT SECOND earlier. She was gone. The portal was gone too, but evidence of its presence remained. On the wall directly behind where the portal had opened, a circle of blackened mud brick marked its location. He noted glassy particles interspersed throughout the charred area. The shiny black specks reminded him of fulgurites, the columns of vitrified rock sometimes left behind in the soil by lightning bolts. Aside from the charring effect, the wall appeared dented, as if a wrecking ball had slammed into it.

This explained why Wessick said opening a portal required a larger space. It must create a shockwave when it opened.

A memory flashed in Alex's mind. The portal. Erin poised at its edge. Glancing back at him. Desheret shoving her through the portal.

He'd lost sight of Erin in the blackness on the other side. An instant later, the portal snapped shut.

His chest tightened, as if he lay on the floor with a cement block pressing down on his ribs. For a moment, he forgot to breathe—until a ringing erupted in his ears and darkness licked at the corners of his vision. Sucking in a breath, and then another, he turned away from the scorched room.

In the back of his mind, a silent clock counted down the seconds until detonation.

"We have to get out of here," Alex said.

"It will do no good," Wessick said. "Desheret would've ensured we have no time to escape."

"Then let's find the damn bomb and disable it." Alex stepped away from the doorway. "What might this bomb look like?"

Wessick paused, as if considering the question. "If the Aten provided the device, which seems likely, then it would most likely be in the form of a small black orb."

"Does this house have an upstairs?"

"Yes. But—"

"Okay." Alex motioned to Harry. "You and Wessick start upstairs, and I'll start down here. Finding the bomb is our top priority, but keep an eye out for *akhet* balls too."

Harry nodded, then turned to Wessick and asked, "Where are the stairs?"

Despite the frown creasing his features, Wessick led Harry through a doorway and out of sight. Alex commenced searching the downstairs, probing every dark corner, searching every chest, overturning every table to check its underside, even peering into the oil reservoirs of lamps. He found nothing. Desheret might've hidden the bomb outside the house, he decided, and so he marched past the body of Panehsy and out the front door. There, he hesitated. Desheret must've arrived at the house before he and Erin and the others. She couldn't have had much time to hide the bomb. In fact, she couldn't have known they would come to this house. The Aten probably gave her the bomb earlier, after she shot Khety in the palace. She kept the bomb until an opportune moment arose.

That moment came when Wessick hacked apart the lock on the front gates of Panehsy's house, announcing their arrival to anyone inside.

If Desheret were inside the house at that moment, however, it seemed unlikely she would've ducked outside to plant the bomb. If she were outside at the time, he suppose she might've planted it on the grounds near the house, though it still seemed unlikely.

He decided to search the perimeter of the house anyway. Better than doing nothing. Except waiting to get blown to bits.

Overhead, the Aten ship hovered. He sensed it up there, though he refused to look at it. More pressing matters demanded his attention, and besides, he didn't need to look to know it was still there. The Aten wouldn't leave without getting what they wanted.

Finding nothing along the front of the house, he veered around the corner to search another side of the structure. Up ahead, he spotted a pale shape lumped on the earth. He halted at the object in question. It looked like a pile of folded linen. Kneeling, he reached out to poke the fabric. It concealed a firm lump in its center. Cautiously, he picked up the bundle and unrolled the fabric to reveal a single *akhet* ball nestled inside it.

Alex glanced up at the wall of the house. On the second floor, a window overlooked this exact spot.

Desheret said Erin had saved her the trouble of retrieving her own *akhet* ball. The madwoman must've found the *akhet* ball inside the house and tossed it out the window. He thought of two reasons for the behavior. Either she intended to hide the *akhet* ball so that no one else got their hands on it, or she popped the last circuit breaker in her brain and lost the capacity for rational thought.

He preferred the first option. The second meant he'd let Erin go off with a deranged woman.

Gritting his teeth, he picked up the *akhet* ball and hurried back into the house. He hopped over Panehsy's body to get into the room beyond the entryway. Harry and Wessick already waited for him there. When he saw them, Alex froze.

Harry stood to the side of Wessick, partially facing him, gaping at the object in Wessick's hands. In one palm, Wessick cradled a small black orb.

Alex swallowed against the lump in his throat.

Harry aimed his wide eyes at Alex. His voice quavered ever so slightly as he said, "We found the bomb."

Alex took three steps toward the man, closing the gap between them. Now a mere three feet away from Wessick and the bomb in his hand, Alex couldn't take his gaze off the black orb. It resembled the glowing orbs he was familiar with, except for the color of its interior. While the glowing orbs churned with white and blue colors, this little sphere contained a roiling mass of black and dark purple, like a swirling bruise locked within the prismatic glass that formed the orb's surface.

"Does it have a timer?" Alex asked.

"Yes, but it's thought activated. Only the individual who started the countdown has the ability to stop it."

"Can you tell how long we have?"

"Perhaps." Wessick closed his eyes. "Give me a moment."

Harry snorted. "I hope we've got a moment."

Alex shot a silencing glare at Harry, who clamped his mouth shut.

After a couple seconds, Wessick eyelids popped open. He said, in a bland tone, "We have less than three minutes."

No one spoke for several seconds.

Harry broke the silence saying, as he jabbed a finger in the air to point at Alex's hand, "Hey, you found one."

Alex glanced down at the *akhet* ball in his hand.

An idea burst out in his mind. It seemed ridiculous, but then again, what other choice did they have? He refused to stand here waiting for a creepy black orb to incinerate him.

"If we can't diffuse the bomb," Alex said, "let's get rid of it."

"Ya lost me there," Harry said.

"We use this *akhet* ball to send the bomb someplace where it can't hurt anyone."

"Why not stick with your original plan," Harry said, "and use the ball to zip ourselves over to Wessick's house. We can use one of his *akhet* balls to get rid of the bomb."

Wessick shook his head. "I believe Desheret underestimated the bomb's potential. It may well destroy the entire city."

"Wonderful," Alex grumbled. Squaring his shoulders, he raised the *akhet* ball to chest height. "Back to plan A. Where should we send the bomb?"

Neither Harry nor Wessick answered. Although Harry shrugged, Wessick just stood there as if he cupped an oil lamp in his palm rather than an explosive device. The man only showed emotion when Erin was around.

Suddenly, Harry piped up. "Couldn't we send it into outer space?"

"No," Wessick said. "*Akhet* balls are not powerful enough to reach beyond Earth's atmosphere."

Alex looked at the ball in his hand, and then at Wessick. "How high in the atmosphere can they reach?"

"Perhaps fifty thousand feet."

"Well, in this timeline, at least we don't have to worry about air traffic getting in the way."

Harry edged a little closer to Wessick, eyeing the bomb sideways. In a half whisper, he asked, "How much time do you reckon we've got?"

Wessick kept his gaze trained on Alex as he said, "Less than one minute."

Alex spun around to face the entryway.

"There is one problem," Wessick said. "*Akhet* balls are designed for personal travel. It will expect at least one human to cross the portal."

Alex twisted his head around to glare at Wessick over her shoulder. "Thank you for leaving the vital information until the end."

"Um," Harry said, "does the portal care if the human is dead or alive?"

Wessick arched an eyebrow. "I don't know."

"Maybe we could chuck Panehsy in there. Might work, eh?"

Holding silent, Wessick knit both eyebrows.

"Get ready," Alex said, facing the entryway again, "we're about to learn the answer to that question."

He squeezed his eyes shut, commanded the ball to send one person 50,000 feet up in the air, opened his eyes, and pitched the ball down the entryway past Panehsy's corpse.

The portal burst open in a stunning flash.

On the other side, stars shimmered in a dark sky.

Alex whirled, snatched the bomb from Wessick's hand, and hurled it through the portal. Panic knifed through him. What if he'd gotten the timeline wrong? Too late to worry about that now.

"Help me," Alex said as he rushed forward to grab Panehsy's body under the arms.

Harry scooped up the feet while Wessick helped Alex lift the torso. With Alex on one side and Wessick on the other, and Harry holding the feet, they tossed the body through the portal.

Alex's arms ached from the effort. Holy heaven, the priest weighed as much as a life-size granite statue.

The portal shrank to a pinpoint and winked out.

Panting, Harry asked, "Think it worked?"

A boom detonated overhead.

"I'll take that as a yes," Harry said.

Thanks to the muting effect of the enormous ship positioned over the city, the boom sounded distant. That they heard it at all corroborated Wessick's claim about the bomb's strength. The explosion must've been huge.

Alex let out the breath he'd held. Part of him wanted to cheer because they didn't die in a fiery explosion, but most of him couldn't stop thinking about Erin. She was gone. Alone. With a madwoman. In an unknown place and an unknown time.

A glimmer of light drew his attention back to the entryway.

At the end of the hall, just inside the closed front door, an orb hovered.

"They've found us," Wessick said.

Other orbs surged out of the walls to surround them.

A beam of light shot down through the ceiling. The air within the transparent column seemed to glow, with no apparent source for the illumination. The beam terminated in a bright white circle on the floor between Alex and Wessick.

His tone a little breathless, Harry asked, "Are we about to be sucked up into the spaceship?"

"Yes," Wessick said.

The edges of the following column inched outward. Alex stumbled backward.

"Don't bother," Wessick told him. "There is no escape. They've come for their hostages."

29

Keweenaw Peninsula
Date unknown

DARKNESS NEVER FELT SO COMPLETE, SO COLD, OR SO LIFELESS AS IT DID now. Erin opened her eyes wider in a vain attempt to collect more ambient light. No such luck. This space, whatever it was, held no light whatsoever. She had no idea into what place or time the portal brought them, but she prayed the *akhet* ball followed her instructions to the letter. After hearing the tale of Harry's botched attempts at time travel, she couldn't help worrying.

Alex managed it fine. He found her despite the colossal gap between their time zones.

Scritch.

A flame erupted in the darkness. Erin glanced to her left. Desheret held a lighter in one hand, its tiny flame throwing off a flickering glow barely strong enough to illuminate the two of them. Desheret still clasped the gun in her other hand, with its muzzle pointed at Erin.

The woman stretched her lighter-holding hand out to the oil lamp Erin had brought along. Desheret dipped the flame inside the lamp's globe-shaped top, igniting the wick. A brighter glow spread outward to reveal the chamber in which they stood.

It measured about twenty feet across. Shadows veiled the chamber's length where it extended beyond the reach of the lamplight. The walls were stone, rough hewn from the earth itself. Sconces spaced at regular intervals along the walls

228

held what looked like oil lamps. Directly behind them, a section of the wall had been sanded smooth to accommodate pictures and symbols. Erin couldn't identify the carvings from this distance and in this light. The largest carving depicted a human being, or at least a bipedal humanoid being, though the distance and lighting blurred its features.

Water dripped, though from where she couldn't say. Drip, drip. Drip.

Erin shuffled in a semicircle to face the engraved wall. To her right, just outside the range of the lamplight, she thought she saw a shape darker than the shadows. An object hid in the gloom over there.

An urge, stronger than her desire to expose the mystery object, drew her toward the engraved wall. She walked toward it, slowly at first, then faster and faster until she broke into a trot. A few feet from the wall, she stopped.

Footsteps clapped behind her. Desheret halted kitty-corner to her, the gun conspicuously aimed at her head.

"Where is the relic?" Desheret said, her voice thick with rage.

"I don't know."

Erin gazed up at the humanoid figure carved into the stone wall. It was a human being after all. Not just any human being either. Her mouth went dry as a chill shot through her, raising goosebumps all over her body. She recognized the face of the woman depicted in the carving. How could she not?

It was her own face.

A draft wafted over her, intensifying the chill. Erin rubbed her arms, but the goosebumps refused to settle down. Seeing her own face carved on a wall inside a chamber that no one had entered in thousands of years, perhaps longer, it should've done more than give her a chill. It should've sent her spiraling into a mental abyss. Yet somehow, the sight of the carving didn't really bother her. The chill stemmed not from fear, but rather from a sense of rightness. The time traveler who built the relic, and who jumped forward in time to see the outcome of the Aten's totalitarianism, trusted her to end the Aten's reign. Though a part of her recognized the absurdity of it all, in this moment another part of her accepted the challenge.

Standing on tiptoes to get a better look, she squinted at the hieroglyphs inscribed below the image of her. The symbols—at least the ones she recognized— identified the woman in the carving as the *satseshat*, the peaceful, she whose identity is hidden, the incarnation of another time. She knew all this. If only she were fluent in Kemetian, she might glean more useful information from the inscription.

The hieroglyphs lined up in neat vertical registers. The carving of the *satseshat* filled nearly all of one register, with the identifying glyphs beneath it. To the right of the registers, separated from the main inscription, a series of curving lines engraved in the rock caught her eye. She sidled past Desheret, avoiding looking at the gun, until she came up in front of the isolated carving.

It was the Eye of Horus, a sacred symbol in ancient Egypt. The symbol consisted of an eye with an eyebrow above it and two curving lines extending down from it.

A red jewel took the place of the eye's pupil and iris. The jewel stuck out from the wall, almost like a button.

Erin scrunched her lips. It couldn't be. Could it?

What the heck.

She placed two fingers on the jewel and pressed down. Nothing. She pressed harder. Dirt encrusted around the jewel crumbled away, dribbling onto the ground at her feet. She kept pushing, as hard as she could.

With a deep thunk, the jewel sank into the wall.

A pop and buzz followed as one of the sconce lights clicked on, showering pure white light into the chamber. In quick succession, the remaining lights popped to life. White light bathed the entire chamber. She saw the room stretched about fifty feet to her left and to her right. At the leftmost end, a sconce light revealed an opening, perhaps to another chamber. At the rightmost end of the chamber squatted the mystery object, now fully illuminated by a sconce light positioned above it.

The breath froze in Erin's chest. Her heart pounded.

The relic.

There it stood, waiting for her. Its shape mimicked the strange hieroglyph she'd seen on the map, the symbol that looked like an *ankh*, the Kemetian version of a cross, suspended inside a round cartouche. On the actual device, the loop-like cartouche was a ring of metal with two wide feet attached to its bottom. The *ankh* shape seated inside the ring seemed to float there. The entire device towered about nine feet tall and seemed to be made of an odd kind of metal. The color was almost indescribable. The object glistened a dark gray streaked with prismatic rainbows that glimmered in the light.

"I thank you, *satseshat*," Desheret said, suddenly right behind Erin. "You have indeed brought me to the relic."

Erin tore her gaze from the relic, half turning toward Desheret. A wicked smirk warped her lips. She held the gun high, her finger tight over the trigger. The slightest movement of her finger would discharge the weapon.

"You have served your purpose," Desheret said.

Erin dove at the woman in the instant the gunshot exploded. She slammed into Desheret's thighs, tumbling them both to the ground.

A ping resonated through the cavern.

Erin bit Desheret's hand. Despite the deafening effect of the gunshot, Erin heard the woman howl as the tang of blood seeped into her mouth. Desheret's finger loosened. The gun slipped from her grasp, clattering to the rock floor.

A hand seized Erin's hair, yanking her head backward. Pain lanced through her neck into her shoulder. Desheret sliced her fingernails across Erin's cheek. Another wave of hot pain coursed through her, but Erin bit back the cry welling inside her. Desheret rolled them both over, pinning Erin on her back with one arm jammed underneath her at an angle. Pain seared her arm. Shadows licked at the edges of her vision.

Desheret straddled Erin's hips. Still clutching Erin's hair with her right hand, she pulled back her left arm in preparation for a blow.

No. She refused to die like this.

Summoning every iota of strength in her, Erin twisted her head to sink her teeth into Desheret's right forearm.

The madwoman bellowed. Her grip on Erin's hair slackened just enough that Erin managed to free her head. Springing up into a half-sitting position, freeing her other arm.

Desheret swung her left fist down toward Erin's face.

Erin scuttled backward like an upside-down crab.

Desheret's fist grazed Erin's knees and smacked into the rock floor. The woman let out a cry that sounded like a cross between a growl and scream.

Spotting the gun, Erin lunged for it. Her fingers closed around the grip.

Peripherally, she saw Desheret whirl on her knees toward Erin. The madwoman jammed a hand under the folds of her skirt, whipping out a dagger.

Erin snatched up the gun. She rolled onto her back and jerked the gun up.

Desheret raised the knife and lunged.

Erin pulled the trigger.

The ringing in her ears muffled the gunshot, though she felt the weapon jerk in her hand. Desheret seemed to freeze in mid lunge, as if her body hung suspended from wires attached to the ceiling.

Then the madwoman collapsed to the ground.

The knife skittered across the rock floor.

Sweat dribbled into Erin's eyes. She swiped at her brow with the back of her hand.

Desheret's head had landed inches from Erin's left foot. She nudged the woman with the toe of her sandal. Desheret's head lolled.

Erin pushed onto her knees. She scrambled closer to the madwoman's body. Desheret's eyes were open, yet lifeless. Erin pressed two fingers to the woman's throat. No pulse.

Relief surged through Erin. She let her shoulders sag. The pains throughout her body coalesced into a dull aching that infected her every muscle. Even her skin ached. Christ, the pain seeped into every cell of her body from her fingernails to her hair.

With some effort, and a few groans, she managed to stand.

The relic sat unmoving and silent, straight ahead of her.

She shuffled toward it. With each step, some of the stiffness and pain eased. Her shoulder still throbbed, and the scratches on her face burned, but otherwise she felt relatively undamaged. At least, she didn't think she'd broken any bones—or dislocated her shoulder. A selection of bruises might form at various locations across her body. She was alive, though, which counted for a lot.

A half dozen feet from the relic, she halted. One task remained. She must figure out how to destroy the relic. Okay, make that two tasks. Destroy the relic and...

Find a way out of here.

30

Akhetaten
Circa 1335 BC

T HE BEAM EXPANDED MILLIMETER BY MILLIMETER, AS IF TESTING THE AREA or, more likely, trying to frighten them into submission. The Aten enjoyed flaunting their power. They also exhibited an impressive degree of patience, searching for the relic for thousands of years while waiting for the *satseshat* to arrive. They could certainly take their time tormenting their three potential hostages.

Alex kept pace with the beam is he backed away from it. Since they'd penned in their quarry with the orbs, the Aten clearly felt confident their hostages could not escape. Alex would be damned if he'd just stand here waiting to get, as Harry phrased it, sucked up into a spaceship.

He glared at Wessick through the beam. "We have to get out of here."

"If we try to escape," Wessick said, "the orbs will attack us. I believe you're familiar with their capabilities."

"I can stand getting burned if it gets us out of here."

"The burn you suffered was minor. At full power, the orbs can cause much greater damage."

Harry raised a hand. "I vote for not getting burnt to ashes."

Alex felt his jaw clench. He thought about forcing it to relax, but then realized anger might save his life in this situation. So instead, he zeroed his gaze in on

Wessick and through clenched teeth said, "You work for the Aten. You're experienced with their technology. Command the orbs to let us go."

"I can't."

"Can't or won't?"

"I have never been able to command the orbs."

The sensation of static electricity tingled over Alex's backside. During the entire conversation, three of them had kept inching backward at the same pace that the beam inched outward. He must be getting close to the orb behind him. He refused to look back. Doing so served no useful purpose—until they could escape.

"Hang on," Harry said to Wessick. "How come you can't control the orbs? Erin did it."

Wessick's eyes widened as he slowly rotated his head to look at Harry. He stopped moving.

The beam kept advancing. It clipped the toe of Wessick's sandal.

He jerked as if shocked by an electrical current. This time he kept an eye on the beam while he began to back away from it again.

"I did not know," Wessick said, "that Erin had the power to control the orbs. Her powers of concentration must be far greater than mine."

Alex almost smiled. Erin could focus on a task, any task, to the point of shutting out everything else. If a task grabbed her attention, she might forget he was there even when he sat right next to her. Yes, she had incredible powers of concentration.

And Wessick didn't. *That* was the thought that almost made him smile.

"Maybe you can do it," Harry said.

Alex grimaced. "I appreciate the vote of confidence. But I'm not sure—"

"What have we got to lose?"

Harry had a point. Alex glanced at the orbs encircling them. They had a lot to lose by getting captured. They had absolutely nothing to lose by trying to escape.

The beam stopped advancing.

Alex halted. He looked at Wessick, who shook his head in confusion.

The beam vanished.

Above their heads, a faint whirring sound started up. It seemed to emanate from above the house. The noise seemed mechanical, though unlike any machine on Earth, and it intensified with each passing second. Alex recognized the sound. He'd heard it before, in the Grand Canyon, when he and Erin got trapped in a labyrinth of forgotten tunnels. The sound had accompanied a vicious lightning storm of unearthly origin.

A storm brewed up by the Aten.

The air felt charged with electricity. This wasn't an effect of the orbs, he knew, but the precursor to something far worse.

"It seems they've changed their minds," Wessick said. "They no longer want hostages. They want martyrs."

"They're not getting any," Alex said.

He shut his eyes and focused every scrap of his mental energy on one task.

The orbs.

Go away, go away, go away.

Erin's face flashed in his mind. Rather than distracting him, the thought of her strengthened his resolve.

Go away, go away, go the hell away.

Alex felt a sense of release, like a guitar string snapping. He opened his eyes.

The orbs were gone.

"You actually did it," Harry said, a note of surprise in his voice.

Satisfaction rippled through Alex, but only for a second or two. No time for gloating.

"Let's get out of here," he said.

They ran out of the house.

Just as they cleared the gates, the house exploded.

Without pausing, without looking back, they fled past the cattle sheds in the long, narrow building where they'd hidden earlier. Structures exploded behind them, raining debris that pricked and burned their skin. Grit blew into Alex's eyes and he squinted against the discomfort. His eyes watered, forcing him to blink faster to keep his vision clear.

As they veered onto the main road, Alex chanced a look back.

Flames engulfed the Great Aten temple. Smoke billowed out of the temple, blanketing the entire walled complex. The long, narrow building beside the temple complex had been reduced to rubble.

No, it wasn't smoke billowing out of the temple. The cloud consisted of dirt and debris.

No beam of light glanced downward from the ship. He couldn't discern a source for the destruction. Buildings exploded and walls tumbled down as if they simply lost their ability to stand upright, as if every atom within them lost cohesion.

They raced down the main road past the smaller Aten temple and across the open field that separated the royal-temple district from the rest of the city. They passed a smattering of people fleeing from the destruction, but most of the city's residents must've fled already. Alex's legs burned. His chest ached from the effort of each heaving breath. Still he ran, unwilling to slow down or even glance backward again. The booming and roaring behind them told him everything he needed to know.

The Aten were wiping the city out of existence.

Sooner than he expected, they dashed through the front gates to Wessick's house. The door hung open, and the guards were gone. The rumbling of the city's destruction sounded farther away now. Somehow they'd managed to outpace annihilation.

For the moment.

Alex and Harry waited in the entryway while Wessick hurried upstairs to raid his stash of *akhet* balls. Neither of them spoke. They simply stood there listening to the rumbling and roaring. Every twenty or thirty seconds, a deep boom punctuated the rumbling and sent tremors echoing through the earth. Alex felt the vibrations in his bones—and in his soul. Never could he have guessed that in his lifetime he would bear witness to the kind of destruction only the dinosaurs knew.

At least it answered one question for him. The city of Akhetaten was not merely abandoned when the pharaoh died. It was demolished.

Footsteps pounded down the stairs and, seconds later, Wessick emerged from the other room to rejoin Alex and Harry in the entryway. He held a single *akhet* ball in one hand.

"That's all you've got?" Alex asked.

"I'm afraid so." Wessick rolled the ball side to side in his palm. "I thought I had more, but apparently I lost count."

"You're really losing it lately, aren't you?"

Wessick looked pale. Even his lips had lost most of their color. Alex almost felt sorry for the man.

Almost.

Wessick handed the ball to Alex. "You should return to the twenty-first century and wait there for Erin. I'm certain she will find her way home. She is far cleverer and much stronger than anyone gave her credit for."

"I gave her credit for it." Alex curled his fingers around the *akhet* ball. "You're the one who underestimates everyone but yourself."

"I admit I've been guilty of arrogance. And I've paid dearly for it, more dearly than you can know."

The rumbling grew louder, and closer, with each tick of the virtual clock in his head. The booms intensified as well, now rattling the house along with the ground.

"This might be a dumb question," Harry said, "but why aren't they incinerating the city? I thought that was their M.O."

"No," Wessick said. "The orbs and artificial lightning they use as small-scale weapons do inflict heat damage. Their ultimate goal, however, is not to destroy the planet but to wipe it clean of all life-forms so that they may begin again, reshaping the world to their liking."

"Oh."

Harry's tone infused the lone syllable with greater melancholy than a hundred words could conjure.

Alex stared down at the *akhet* ball in his hand. "We're not going back to the twenty-first century. We're going to find Erin."

"You have no idea where she is," Wessick said. "You must know where to ask the *akhet* ball to take you."

"I'll tell this goddamn ball to take me to wherever Erin is with the relic."

Wessick shook his head. "The *akhet* ball you're holding is not connected to the one that transported Erin and Desheret. It does not know where to send you. Commanding it to take you to Erin, without a specific destination in mind, will not work."

"It worked before." Alex looked up at Wessick. "That's how I got here. I asked one of these balls to take me to Erin and, poof, it did."

Wessick stared at him, unblinking, the pallor in his face deepening. Just when Alex decided the man must've suffered a stroke and could no longer speak, Wessick said, "That should never have worked. Time must favor you and Erin more than I realized."

"What do you mean?" Alex asked. "Time doesn't favor anyone. It's not alive, it…just is."

"You are mistaken. Time governs itself in the same manner that a living thing protects its own existence."

The man had cracked. There was no other explanation. Samuel N. Wessick had finally, and completely, lost his grip on sanity.

It didn't matter. Only one thing mattered to Alex now.

He marched outside. Harry and Wessick trailed after him. He halted ten feet from the house, in the empty area between the walled enclosure and the house. This looked like a big enough spot for opening a portal.

Alex closed his eyes and concentrated on the single command he wanted the ball to carry out for him.

He felt energy surge through the ball.

Opening his eyes, he lobbed the ball into the air.

The burst of white light made him fling up a hand to shield his eyes. When he lowered his hand, a portal floated before him, fifteen feet away. The scene on the other side looked like a cave of some sort. Whether the cave was natural or artificial, he couldn't determine.

He didn't see Erin. She was there, though, off to the side out of view. She must be.

"Go on," Alex said as he pushed Harry toward the portal.

Harry glanced at Alex, but then tromped through the portal. Once through, he stepped to the side out of sight.

Alex waved a hand toward the portal and said to Wessick, "Villains first."

"I must stay," Wessick said. "Too many innocents have suffered or died because of my actions. I failed those closest to me. I'll remain here to face the destruction I brought down on us all. I'm sure you'll agree I deserve no better."

Boom. The earth shook beneath their feet.

"Nobody deserves this," Alex said. He took a step toward the portal. "Besides, I told this contraption to expect three passengers. Will the portal close if only two of us go through?"

"Yes. It will sense the change in your plans when you step through."

Alex felt lines of confusion tightening across his forehead. "The portal's telepathic?"

"Of the technological variety, like the orbs and the *akhet* balls. No mysticism is involved."

"Fascinating," Alex said. He jabbed a finger toward the portal. "Let's get moving."

Wessick neither replied nor moved toward the portal. He shook his head once.

Frowning, Alex said, "You have to come with me. Erin will never understand why you think you need to stay behind. She'll be upset."

"She will recover." Wessick balled his hands into loose fists. "And she'll understand soon enough."

Alex glowered at the man, but Wessick still did not move.

Boom!

Across the street, a house exploded. The earth trembled so violently Alex struggled to stay on his feet.

"We don't have time for this," Alex said.

"For once, you're correct," Wessick said. "You must go. If they haven't already, the Aten soon will send a message to the twenty-first century informing them Erin found the relic. They'll begin the cleansing."

"Cleansing?" Alex repeated. "You mean of the planet?"

"Yes, it is their ultimate strategy." Wessick paused as another explosion rocked the city. "This is merely a sampling of what they can do. They'll save their worst for the twenty-first century. In the end, the planet will become so toxic no earthly creature can survive on it."

"I thought they would only do that if Erin failed to locate the relic."

"With each hour that's passed, their frustration with us has grown exponentially. We are no longer amusing pets. Besides, the idea of annihilating the human race has always appealed to them far more than the reality of controlling us."

"They're fed up," Alex said.

"You understand at last," Wessick said. He swept a hand toward the portal. "Now leave, before they annihilate us both."

"If you want to die, it might still happen if you come with us. We have no way to get home."

"Nothing is as certain as you think." Wessick backed away a step. "Go."

Alex took a step toward the portal, then paused to glance back at Wessick. The man nodded, as if they'd reached an agreement of some sort. They had, Alex supposed. He knew that, short of beating the man senseless and dragging his limp body through the portal, he would never convince Wessick to accompany him.

"Take care of her," Wessick said. "And thank her for me. She helped me to redeem my soul."

"Erin doesn't need anybody to take care of her. But I'll pass along your regards."

Alex strode through the portal. His feet clomped down on solid rock. A white glow akin to daylight lit the interior of the rock chamber inside of which he now found himself standing.

The portal telescoped shut behind him.

Wessick was gone, trapped in the ancient past. Why would a man volunteer to stay in a city on the brink of annihilation? He had no hope of saving Akhetaten or its residents. To stay behind was an act of suicide, not bravery.

Alex's train of thought derailed as he caught sight of Erin.

She stood a couple yards away from him. His heart felt as if it sank into his gut when he took in her appearance. Scratches etched dark red lines across her cheek. One strap of her dress drooped off her shoulder. Smears of dirt discolored the white linen. The semitranslucent hues of newly forming bruises speckled the skin of her arms with shades of purple, blue, and yellow.

Before he could speak, she rushed at him and flung her arms around his neck to plant a kiss on his lips. He hooked his arms around her waist, lifting her onto her tiptoes, and kissed her back.

When he finally set her down, she smiled up at him.

The scratches on her cheek elicited a frown from him. He loosened his grip on her waist, worried he might be putting pressure on additional bruises hidden under her dress. He lifted a hand to touch her cheek, careful to avoid the scratches.

"I'm fine," she said. "Got in a little tussle with a crazy chick, but I won."

"I never doubted you would."

Glancing past her, he spotted the body of Desheret some thirty feet away. Harry was maybe twenty feet from the body, scrutinizing a section of the chamber's wall.

Alex returned his attention to Erin. Though he tried to keep his expression neutral, he clearly failed.

"What happened?" she asked.

"Wessick stayed behind." He recounted his conversation with Wessick and then asked, "Do you know what he meant about redeeming his soul?"

"Not a clue. If he said I'd understand soon, I'll take his word for it and be patient."

Erin pushed away from him. Clasping his hand in hers, she tugged as she half turned to walk in the opposite direction.

"Come on," she said. "I need your help with something."

Tugging harder, she tried to drag him after her. He gave in and followed her.

"What do you need my help with?" he asked.

She glanced at him sideways. "Figuring out how to destroy the relic."

31

AFTER SHOWING ALEX THE RELIC, ERIN TOOK HIM OVER TO THE WALL WHERE Harry stood. Alex linked his hand with hers is they gazed at the inscription on the wall.

The relic itself offered no clues. Its metallic surface felt smooth and slightly warmer than the cool air inside the cavern. They found no buttons, no levers, no switches. Nothing on the relic or in its immediate vicinity gave any clue about its workings. They needed an instruction manual. At first Erin dismissed the thought as ridiculous, until she realized the wall inscription might indeed provide the ancient equivalent of an instruction manual. At the very least, it might provide clues.

Alex aimed a blank look at her. "When are we?"

"Huh?" she said, thinking a marble or two must've slipped out his ear during his split-second journey through time.

"I know where we are," he said. "We're under the Keweenaw Peninsula. But *when* are we? What year is it? What geological period?"

"Uh... it's the Holocene epoch, assuming I used the ball thingy correctly. And it should be the year we left, sometime shortly after we left it." She bit her lower lip. "I took Wessick's word that we can't travel to a moment in which we already exist, but I couldn't remember what time it was when I left with Wessick. So I asked to be brought here at a time immediately after I left."

"But we have no way of knowing exactly what time it is."

"No."

"And we don't know if the Aten ship is already positioned over your parents' house."

She shook her head. "We may not have much time."

"Then I'd better get to work."

Alex concentrated his attention on the wall inscription. Erin looked at it too, but with no hope of comprehending the text.

The symbols engraved in the rock lined up in five columns, or registers, with an equal number of lines in each register—except for the first register, which included the image of the *satseshat*. The registers stretched from two feet above Erin's head to within inches of the floor. Before Alex and Harry arrived, she'd gotten a good enough look at the inscription to realize that it actually contained two separate languages. Kemetian hieroglyphs filled the first three registers. Another language, written in a script that resembled wavy lines and chicken scratches, filled the remainder of the registers.

She bumped her shoulder into Alex's arm and asked, "Do you recognize this other language?"

"No."

Leaning forward to glance in Harry's direction, she said, "What about you, professor?"

"Sorry," Harry said. "Looks like gibberish to me."

Alex released her hand and stepped forward to run his finger along the lines of hieroglyphs. His eyes darted back and forth in time with his finger movements.

"What's it say?" she asked.

He shushed her without looking away from the inscription or interrupting his perusal of it.

She supposed he needed time to translate the text. While she waited, she thought back on what Alex had told her about his last conversation with Wessick. It didn't mesh with what she knew about the man. Why would he stay behind knowing he would die? His death served no purpose. The number one thing she'd learned about Samuel Wessick was that he always had a purpose in mind—and he rarely betrayed any emotion. Other than his dislike of Alex and his occasional frustration with her, she had never seen him lose control of himself. If he harbored suicidal tendencies, surely a trace of those emotions would've slipped out once or twice.

And what on earth had he meant about failing those closest to him? How did she help him redeem his soul? None of it made sense. Wessick said she would understand eventually, so until then she must stick to her earlier statement and be patient.

Something else about Wessick's final actions bothered her too, though she couldn't quite pick out the detail that niggled at her.

Crouching in front of the third register of hieroglyphs, Alex reached the end of the Kemetian inscription. He settled a hand on each knee.

"Well?" she asked.

"Most of the text spells out the prophecy of the *satseshat*. The information here corroborates both the map text and what Harry told us."

"That's good to know," Erin said, "but what else does it say?"

He rose, taking a step back from the inscription. "The text also talks about the relic and what it can do. It's more than just a vehicle for traveling through time and across distances." He folded his arms over his chest, frowning at the inscription. "Do you remember how the map text talked about the *satseshat* using the relic to destroy the source of the Aten's power?"

"Yeah, " she said.

"I assumed it was a metaphor. You know, they would lose their power over humanity if they lost the godlike ability to travel through time."

"But it's not a metaphor."

"No." He took in a deep breath and let it out through pursed lips. "The text says, quite explicitly, that the relic collects energy from the atmosphere and transmits it to receivers capable of disseminating the energy to basically any device connected to the receiver. Whoever controls the receivers controls the power supply." He looked down at her. "The Aten have the receivers."

"Of course." She thought for a second and then asked, "What about the orbs and the *akhet* balls? They're not connected to any receivers, yet they clearly siphon power from somewhere."

"From what I can tell," he said, "the orbs and *akhet* balls are receivers in and of themselves. But the relic is the source."

She glanced over her shoulder at the relic. "It doesn't look like it's doing anything. How does it draw energy from the atmosphere when it's underground?"

"I don't know. The text was less clear about that aspect of the relic's operation. It does say that the relic was stored down here both to hide it from the Aten and so that, in the event of a fatal malfunction, the surrounding rock would absorb the blast."

"The blast?"

"If the relic exploded. That's what a fatal malfunction is."

"Oh." Images of an explosion rocking the cavern, caving the roof in on their heads, flashed through her mind. She shoved them aside. "How do we destroy the relic?"

Averting his gaze to the floor, he snaked a hand up to rub the back of his neck. "Um, that's another area where the text was less than explicit. It said the *satseshat* must choose her destiny. She can either seize control of the relic and become the ruler of time, or she can extract the life-force from it and destroy the source of the power."

"How am I supposed to do either of those things?"

He shrugged.

Harry raised a hand, like a schoolboy asking permission to speak. He didn't wait for permission, though, but said, "Anybody want an old fart's opinion?"

"Please," Erin said. "We seem to be out of ideas."

Harry lowered his hand and stepped forward, locking his gaze on Erin's. "Whoever wrote this inscription must've thought the answer would be plain as day—to you."

"Well, it's not."

He gave her a look of parental dismay. "Go over and look at the doggone thing before you give up altogether. And dump the flat-earth mentality. Try to look at the wider picture around you, not just what's straight out in front of you."

"He's right," Alex said.

She planted her hands on her hips. "Now you two are ganging up on me?"

"No," Alex said, laying a hand on her shoulder. "We know you can do it, that's all."

She felt lines tightening across her forehead and muscles tensing down her neck and into her shoulders. Her fingers ached from squeezing them into fists. The first pangs of a headache sprouted behind her eyes. She wasn't angry with Alex or Harry. She was ticked off at the author of the inscription, at the keepers of the relic, and the priests of Amun-Ra. Why couldn't they just come out and say what she needed to do? Why veil everything in cryptic phrasing?

"Time is a scarcity right now," Alex said.

"Rushing me does not help." She exhaled, willing herself to relax. It didn't work. "Besides, we should have a little time before they figure out I'm not handing over the relic."

Alex scratched the back of his neck as he avoided looking at her. "Actually, Wessick said the Aten are so fed up with us that they don't want to wait anymore. They might start their campaign to eradicate humanity at any second." He raised his eyes to lock onto her gaze. "We have to destroy the relic right now and pray losing the power source cripples their weapon of mass destruction."

Erin opened her mouth but couldn't speak. Her fist fell open as her shoulders sagged.

"It's our one and only chance," Alex said as he grasped both her shoulders. "And you're the only one in this cave who can pull it off."

"Gee, thanks. Put all the pressure squarely on me."

Alex squeezed her shoulders gently. "You can handle it."

She whirled away from him and marched straight to the relic. The cursed thing just sat there, silent and unmoving. She moved around behind it. How was she supposed to destroy the relic? With her back to the rock wall, she stared at the thing and tried to squeeze even one drop of comprehension from her brain. Another thought occurred to her instead.

Alex had strolled up to the opposite side of the relic. Separated by about eight feet, they gazed at each other through the space between the outer ring and the vertical bar of the *ankh*-shaped central part of the device.

Erin asked, "How will the Aten know I've found the relic?"

"I don't know," he said. "Wessick only told me they would know, and they'd send a message to our time letting their brethren know about it."

"But how will they find it? After they wipe out humanity, I mean."

He shrugged.

The Aten couldn't track her in the ancient city of Akhetaten. Tracking down her, Alex, and Harry had taken time. Wessick found them quicker because he put a tracking device in Erin's bracelet, but apparently the Aten knew nothing about that. Yet they must have a plan in place for locating and taking control of the relic once Erin uncovered its resting place. Otherwise, what was the point of forcing her to find it? Wiping out humanity rid them of one problem. Unless they controlled the relic, however, they essentially forfeited the game.

Erin surveyed the room visually. Her gaze landed on the body of Desheret, the late handmaiden of the Aten.

Desheret said the Aten approved of her plan to coerce Erin into taking her to the relic, which meant they'd known about it ahead of time. Maybe they had no way of tracking Erin, but what about Desheret? The Aten might've implanted a tracking device inside her body in the same way they placed such beacons in the women they abducted during their attempts to create a *satseshat*. Although Desheret arrived at Panehsy's house before Erin and the men got there, the Aten couldn't have known their handmaiden found Erin. And by that time, Desheret had decided she wanted the relic for herself. What in tarnation the girl thought she might do with it, Erin had no clue. Desheret wanted the device, though, and so would not have alerted the Aten that she captured Erin.

They must've realized it by now. Soon they would zero in on the tracking beacon inside Desheret's body.

Erin stared at the relic. Initially, she thought the *ankh*-shaped part was attached to the outer ring. As she tiptoed closer, however, the strangeness of the mechanism became clear. The ankh hung suspended within the ring, not touching it. A gap of perhaps a quarter inch separated the *ankh* from the ring. Erin stretched out a hand to slide her pinky finger into the gap. No wire. No glass. Nothing connected the two segments of the device.

What had the inscription said? The *satseshat* must take the life-force from the relic.

Life-force. Life. She felt the answer rising inside her about to pop—

"Where's Harry?" Alex asked.

The question ripped Erin out of her thoughts, sending the answer spiraling down into the depths of her mind once again.

"What?" she said.

"Harry's gone." Alex had his head twisted around to look over his shoulder. "He must've found another chamber. Maybe I should go look for him."

"Shut up and let me think."

A hurt look flashed across his face, then he shrugged and trotted off in the opposite direction, presumably to look for Harry.

Erin returned her attention to the relic. She tried to get back to the level of focus she'd experienced a moment earlier. Achieving it seemed to take longer this time, but finally she got there.

Life-force. Life. *Ankh*. The Kemetian symbol for life.

Extract the life-force.

Could it be that simple?

She reached out with both hands, hovering them above either side of the horizontal bar of the *ankh*. A sliver of panic lodged in her chest. She sucked in a breath and closed her hands around the bar.

Nothing happened. She'd half expected an electric shock or a burst of poisonous gas. Instead, she felt absolutely nothing—except the smooth metal against her skin.

"I can't find him anywhere."

Alex's voice echoed across the cavern to her. He was striding out of a shadow-veiled doorway at the opposite end of the chamber. She dropped her hands from the relic. He broke into a brisk jog to cross the distance between them, hurrying around the relic to halt alongside her.

Between heavy breaths, he said, "I found another chamber, a dead-end. But no Harry. It's like he vanished into thin air."

"I think I know how to destroy the relic," she said.

He squinted at her. "What's the catch?"

"Isn't it obvious?" When he just stared at her, she explained, "If I trigger a fatal malfunction—"

"Boom."

"Exactly. We're toast."

A chill raced through her, penetrating every cell. Maybe the icy feeling stemmed from the chilly air in the cavern, but she doubted it. The cold within originated with a realization, and a decision, that she knew Alex shared.

They must destroy the relic. And to do that, they had to die.

"Do it," Alex said.

Erin took the bar in both hands again and pulled. The *ankh* held.

"Let me help," Alex said.

He took hold of the vertical bar of the *ankh*. In the instant his fingers closed around the metal, a sizzling sound erupted. His body jerked and then he flew backward, hitting the wall with a soft thud. Eyes open, he crumpled to the ground.

Erin rushed to kneel beside him. "Alex?"

Though dazed, he rolled his eyes to look at her. "I'm okay. I guess it wants you and only you."

She felt around the back of his head for a wound but found none. No blood trickled from anywhere. Despite looking stunned, he seemed uninjured.

He grabbed her hand to yank it away from his head. "Worrying about me is a little silly when we're both about to die." He let go of her hand. "You know what has to be done."

Chewing on her lips, she watched him for a moment. Then she got up and faced the relic once more.

On the other side of the device floated a glowing orb.

A second orb swooped down out of the ceiling. A third surged upward out of the floor.

"Hurry," Alex said.

Closing her hands around the horizontal bar, she pulled. The *ankh* moved the barest amount, the movement so subtle she almost missed it. But it had moved. She pulled harder, and harder, until her arms ached and her breath came in gasps.

The *ankh* popped free.

Erin stumbled backward. The *ankh* slipped out of her grasp. It clattered onto the floor in front of her. Regaining her balance, she stared down at the *ankh*.

"Did it work?" Alex asked, clambering to his feet.

"I don't know."

A humming noise started up, faint at first but growing louder. It came from the relic, she realized. The outer ring was vibrating. The trembling escalated into shuddering. The humming intensified into whirring.

The vibrations bled into the floor, setting off tremors that pulsed outward in waves. Each wave was stronger than the one before. The pulses came faster and faster too, until the rock floor throbbed from the energy coursing through it.

Erin's heart hammered. Cold sweat dribbled down her temples. This was it. The fatal malfunction. The end of the relic.

The orbs vaporized in a flurry of sparks.

Alex pulled her into his arms. She buried her face against his chest as she clinched her arms tight around him. The relic's thrumming had grown so loud she could barely hear her own pulse thundering in her head. Alex said something, but the clamor around them swallowed his words.

It was over.

They were over.

32

S UDDENLY, ALEX STEPPED AWAY FROM HER. HE LEANED SIDEWAYS TO PEER around the relic.

Erin looked through the metal ring in the direction Alex was staring. She let her jaw drop open as her eyes widened.

At the far end of the cavern, just inside the shadowed doorway, Harry stood there waving his arms frantically. He lips moved as if he were shouting at them. The roar of the relic drowned out his words.

Alex seized her hand and hauled her around the relic, across the cavern toward Harry. She stumbled over a pothole. Alex hooked an arm around her waist to steady her. Joined at the hip, almost literally, they half walked, half ran to the man still flapping his arms at them.

Harry dropped his arms when they halted in front of him.

He leaned forward to shout, "I found an escape hatch."

Without waiting for a response, he spun on his heels and darted through the opening. Alex and Erin ran after him. They passed through a dark antechamber, aiming for a pale light at the other end. The light shined through a five-foot-tall, three-foot-wide opening. Alex pushed her through the opening and then squeezed through behind her.

They wound up inside another small chamber. The wan light emanated from a scaled-down version of the sconce lights in the main chamber. Erin stopped in the chamber's center. Alex came up behind her, stopping as well. The room offered no exits.

Erin glanced at the ceiling but saw no openings there either.

The rock walls between them and the relic did little to dampen the rumbling from its imminent meltdown. The tremors in the floor and walls had strengthened just in the time it took them to get into this chamber. Erin teetered, falling backward against Alex. He steadied her a bit, but the shaking was keeping him slightly off balance too.

Harry waited to their left, one hand resting flat on the wall. He shouted, "Over here."

Alex grasped Erin's shoulders and urged her toward Harry.

The older man pressed his hand against the wall.

A section of rock eased out from the wall, creating a two-foot gap. The slab that had separated from the wall measured as tall as Alex and as wide as his shoulders.

Harry withdrew his hand from the wall. Erin noticed now that he'd pressed his hand into an oval depression in the wall.

Alex shoved her through the gap in the wall.

The space beyond was murky. Yellowish light flickered from inside an oil lamp that sat on the floor a dozen feet away. It was the alabaster lamp she'd picked up in Panehsy's house. Harry must've snagged it from where she'd set it down in the main chamber.

The men squeezed through the gap behind her, and she moved further away from it to make room for them. They were in a tunnel hewn out of the bedrock.

The slab door rolled shut.

Harry nabbed the oil lamp, gesturing for them to follow him.

Single file they ran down the tunnel, with Harry in front and Alex bringing up the rear. Erin struggled to stay on her feet and keep up the pace. The tremors rattling through the rock afflicted her with a sense of instability and of disorientation. She had no idea where they were going, but she fervently hoped Harry did. He acted like he did.

In her mind she heard an imaginary clock ticking down the seconds to detonation. The wall inscription gave no hints about the length of time until the malfunction reached its fatal dénouement. She preferred not to be underground when that happened. Visions of getting buried alive haunted her as they traversed the tunnels. She kept her eyes locked on Harry's back.

They swerved around the corner into another tunnel that angled upward sharply. Her legs pumped harder, battling to keep her upright and to ferry her up the slope. Her thighs ached and burned simultaneously. Her breaths came hard and fast. Her heart pounded against her ribs.

Another turn. And another.

Tick, tick, tick went the countdown clock in her head.

The grade lessened. Still her legs burned. She tripped, and Alex caught her. He lifted her back onto her feet. Harry led them on and on down what felt like an endless tunnel through the underworld, a labyrinth designed to drive cursed souls insane. She prayed for daylight. Ached for it. Hungered for it as if its light alone could sustain her.

These tunnels reminded her of the ones she and Alex discovered in the Grand Canyon, inside the mountain known as Cheops Pyramid. She prayed this little adventure ended better than that one.

No, actually, she didn't. They had survived that adventure. The Aten tried to kill them, but they prevailed. She prayed for just that ending this time around.

The slope leveled out. They ran a little further, until they reached a dead-end.

Harry thrust the lamp at Erin. "Hold this."

She took the lamp, grasping it in both her trembling hands.

Tick, tick, tick went the countdown clock.

Harry motioned for Alex to approach him. "I need your help."

"With what?" Alex asked, coming up alongside Harry.

The older man pointed at the ceiling three feet above Alex's head and said, "Opening that."

Alex squinted at the ceiling, furrowing his brow. "I don't see anything."

Harry drew a square high in the air, as if outlining a shape on the ceiling.

Erin followed the path of his finger. It traced the lines of cracks in the ceiling. At first glance she took them for cracks anyway. Then she realized the lines were straight and formed a perfect square in the ceiling. A protrusion that looked like an imperfection in the rock might, she now realized, actually represent a handle.

"It's a hatch," Harry said. "I need your help getting up there to pull it open."

A deep, muffled explosion rumbled through the tunnels.

A wave of intense shaking rippled through the rocks around them.

Erin stumbled, lost her balance, and crumpled to her knees on the floor. She managed to hold onto the lamp, though some of the oil sloshed out, dampening the floor and her dress.

A cacophony of rumbling echoed down the tunnel toward them. The racket sounded much closer than the explosion.

Harry and Alex both went pale.

"Cave-in," Alex said. "We have to get out of here."

The visions of being buried alive leaped back into the forefront of Erin's mind. A violent shudder racked her body.

Alex linked his hands to form a stirrup. Harry settled one foot onto Alex's hands and pushed himself up as Alex lifted. Harry swung his other knee up to plant it on Alex's shoulder, then Alex pushed Harry's other leg higher until the older man could swing his knee up onto Alex's other shoulder. Alex grasped Harry's calves to hold him in place.

The tremors stopped.

"Maybe it's over," Erin said.

Boom!

Another cacophony of rumbling eruption, this time far too close. The ground shook with such violence that Erin threw out a hand to brace herself against the wall. Harry grasped the handle in the ceiling hatch to keep from tumbling off Alex's shoulders, an action that also helped steady Alex.

Bits of rock rained down from the ceiling.

Erin looked up. And she swore her heart stopped beating.

A crack bisected the tunnel ceiling lengthwise, extending from somewhere deep inside the labyrinth and ending inches from the hatch that Harry grasped.

"Oh shit," Alex said.

Harry yanked on the handle. It didn't move. He jostled it side to side, tugging harder and harder.

The two-foot-wide hatch popped out of its slot and smacked into Harry's shoulder as he struggled to cast it aside. The hatch tumbled to the floor, hitting it with a thunk. Luckily for Harry, the stone part of the hatch was less than an inch thick, with the bulk of it composed of earth and grass. The whole contraption measured no more than four inches thick. Getting hit with it must've hurt, but it probably wouldn't cause serious damage.

Pale sunlight shined down through the hole left by the hatch.

Harry thrust his arms through the opening. Alex pushed up as Harry pulled himself through the hole into the sunlight. His legs disappeared through the opening.

"Who's next?" Harry's voice called down through the hole.

Alex clutched Erin's left arm. "Your turn."

With her right arm, she set the oil lamp on the floor. Alex didn't wait for her to move on her own, but dragged her to him, turning her to face him. She tilted her back to gaze up into the sunlight that bathed them in a muted yellow glow. The boughs of trees formed a canopy high above the hatch. The sunlight filtered down through the foliage.

Alex seized her ankles and launched her entire body up through the hole. She hit the ground on her stomach with her legs dangling through the hole. Harry grabbed her arms and helped her crawl away from the opening.

A new wave of tremors shook the ground.

Alex leaped up through the hole. He grabbed hold of the rim but the rest of him fell back through the opening. Erin clasped his wrists while Harry seized the collar of his shirt. Together they pulled as Alex pushed. He flopped onto the ground seconds later.

A cloud of dust burst out of the hole.

"We better scram," Harry said. "I think the tunnel's about to go."

They scrambled to their feet and took off through the woods. Harry led the way, directing them to what looked like a game trail. How he knew it was there, Erin couldn't imagine. As far as she knew, he'd never visited the Keweenaw before and none of them knew precisely where they ended up.

A whump and a rumbling behind them made all three skid to a halt and glance back. A massive cloud of debris had exploded from the vicinity of the hatch.

The tunnel was gone. She didn't need to see it to know.

The tremors subsided. They stood transfixed as the debris cloud settled down as well and the forest lapsed into silence.

Panting, Erin asked, "Where are we?"

She meant it as a rhetorical question, since none of them could know the precise answer.

But Harry did reply.

"Revenant Point," he said matter-of-factly.

Erin spun toward him. "How can you possibly know that?"

"I've been here before. When I buried the map scroll under the future location of the summerhouse. I told you I'd made a little booboo with my time travel. Instead of coming back to our time, I sent myself to prehistoric days. A couple friendly Bigfoot helped me out. After I buried the scroll for you to find, I was escorted out this hatch." He waved in the direction of the now-collapsed tunnel. "I thought I'd escaped from the wacko Desheret, but she and her cohorts caught up with me in these woods. That's how I found myself back in Akhetaten."

Erin didn't know what to say. *Thank heavens you got kidnapped* seemed uncouth. But if Harry hadn't wound up a prisoner in the Aten temple, for a second time, they might never have found their way out of the tunnels. They would've died in the explosion or the tunnel collapse.

She glanced past Harry. The sky was dark in that direction, unnaturally dark. Black actually.

The hairs on the back of her neck stiffened.

Wessick had said Aten ships were hovering over both her parents' home and Revenant House. The black sky was not sky. It was a ship.

Tilting her head, she listened.

A faint but distinct whirring sound emanated from the direction of the ship.

She ran toward the sound.

"Wrong way," Alex shouted, but she ignored him.

The pounding of footfalls behind her signaled that the men were following. She needed to see the ship, to know if destroying the relic had damaged it in any way, to find out if their efforts yielded any result. She *must* know. To know meant to approach the ship.

After that, she didn't know what she'd do. An instinct told her that seeing the ship would answer her questions. She hoped her instinct proved right.

Turning down other game trails, she wended her way toward the ship. Soon she recognized the woods and the trail she'd just veered down, and she knew the summerhouse lay ahead.

Running, running.

The ramshackle structure loomed out of the woods directly ahead. She raced past it, down the trail she knew headed straight to Revenant House. Not long after, she spied the hulking silhouette of the manor and then she broke out of the woods onto the rear lawn.

And she stumbled to a halt.

Alex nearly slammed into her but swung left at the last instant.

Overhead, the ship hovered. Huge and black and terrifying.

The whirring remained soft, though definitely coming from the ship.

Harry staggered out of the woods. He stopped beside Erin, lifting his head to stare at the ship.

The whirring abruptly ended.

Erin glanced around. No orbs. No human minions. She looked at the ship again.

The ship surged upward.

The circle of darkness it created shrank as the vessel rose higher and higher, straight up into the sky. Within a minute, the ship was gone.

Sunlight beamed down on them, warming Erin's face. She averted her gaze from the brightness.

The Aten had left.

She bolted for the house. Sprinting around to the front, across the driveway and up the steps to the main door, she flung the door open and headed straight for the library. At the desk, she snatched up the telephone receiver and dialed her parents' number.

Warner answered. "It's gone."

Between pants, she said, "The Aten ship?"

"Yes. It left seconds ago. We are unharmed." Warner hesitated, then asked, "And you?"

"I'm fine, we're all fine. Alex and Harry are here too. Tell my parents everything's okay."

She hung up the phone.

Her knees buckled. She staggered around the desk to the chair and sank into it.

Alex and Harry dashed into the library a second later.

"Whew," Harry said, "you run fast. Should've been an Olympic athlete."

Erin laughed. Not at what he'd said, though it was ridiculous. She was no athlete. Pure adrenaline fueled her flight. But no, she laughed because the Aten had fled and she had destroyed the relic.

And they all lived through it.

Alex kneeled beside her chair. He touched her cheek, concern wrinkling his forehead.

"I'm okay," she said. "Exhausted, that's all."

Harry blew out an overdramatic sigh. "Amen to that."

Alex dropped his hand but kept his gaze on her face.

"Cripes," Harry said, "I'm starved. Where's the kitchen?"

Alex rolled his eyes. "Straight the other way and turn right."

Patting his belly, Harry strolled out the door and down the hallway.

Erin turned her head to look at Alex. She smiled.

He arched an eyebrow.

Her smile segued into a grin. "We did it."

He cradled her face in his hands and kissed her.

EPILOGUE

Three weeks later

THROUGH THE BAY WINDOW, ERIN WATCHED A PAIR OF SEAGULLS SWOOP LOW over the rear lawn of Revenant House. They soared upward again, flying out of sight. The world had returned to normal.

Not that the world had any inkling about what almost happened.

Erin sat at the desk in Wessick's study, in the chair Wessick sat in many times before. It was her chair now, and her study—her house, in fact. As Newman informed her less than twenty-four hours after their return from the past, Wessick signed the house and all of Revenant Point over to her before he departed for Akhetaten. His corporation would continue to pay her salary, with a hefty raise tacked on, for her to oversee the cataloging and care of his book collection, which he granted to her on indefinite loan. All of these actions suggested to her that he knew, or at least suspected, he might never return from their mission to the past.

No, she corrected herself, not never. Nobody knew for certain he died during the destruction of the ancient city. The history books still said the city was abandoned, rather than destroyed. The type of destruction the Aten wrought on the city left no clear indications that a calamity struck. Buildings fell. Some people must've died, but most fled before the cleansing began. When archaeologists unearthed a skeleton, they had no way of knowing why a wall collapsed on that person.

The secret remained intact. The world at large knew nothing of the Aten.

Or of what a librarian and a disgraced archaeologist did to save it.

She pulled open a drawer and picked up the envelope that lay inside it. Just as Wessick promised, she finally understood, mostly, why he behaved as he did. Flipping up the envelope's flap, she slid out the two items protected inside the envelope. Newman brought the little packet with her when she arrived to hand over ownership of the manor and its property. Erin had examined the envelope's contents a half dozen times in the past three weeks. Nevertheless, she laid the two items on the desktop to study them once more.

The first item was a daguerreotype, a kind of photograph popular in the nineteenth century. The photo captured two men standing in front of the summerhouse here at Revenant Point. One man held his arm around the other's shoulders in a brotherly gesture of affection. Both men smiled at the camera.

She flipped over the daguerreotype. Handwritten text provided a caption for the image.

```
Ridley Covington
Broderick Covington
at the summerhouse, July 1858
```

Ridley died in the Grand Canyon in August of 1858. She knew the man only as a mummified corpse, and so would not have recognized him in the flesh. The other man, however, she did recognize. He was younger in the photo, certainly, but his features still matched the man she'd known.

Samuel Wessick.

His real name was Broderick Covington. He was Ridley's older brother.

She set down the daguerreotype and picked up the other item, a folded sheet of paper. Opening the sheet, she skimmed the handwritten letter one more time. The handwriting matched that on the back of the daguerreotype. It was Broderick Covington's handwriting. He signed the letter with his given name, perhaps as a way of reclaiming his true identity before marching into the arms of Death. The first line of the letter explained that, although he was born Broderick Covington, throughout his life he lived under various names given to him by the Aten. His last pseudonym was Samuel Wessick.

When explaining the Aten to her shortly before they left for the past, he'd mentioned that thirty years ago the Aten conscripted him to serve them. At the time, she thought his word choice seemed odd. Now she understood. The letter spelled it out for her.

With words penned in a careful and elegant script, Broderick/Wessick explained that the Covingtons hailed from England. Following his parents' deaths in an accident, Broderick became obsessed with the occult and spiritualism in particular. When he learned of rich copper deposits found in America's northernmost territory, the Upper Peninsula of Michigan, Broderick relocated to the Keweenaw. He believed copper deposits held a mystical property that would aid him in his efforts to contact his late parents. Once in Michigan, Broderick purchased a large parcel of land and built a house on it. His younger brother Ridley, along with Ridley's wife and their children, soon joined Broderick in America.

Revenant House, and its surrounding land, inherited its name from Broderick's obsession with the occult.

After the move to America, Ridley became fascinated with ancient history, eventually setting out on expeditions that took him away from his family for months at a time. Along the way, he found out-of-place artifacts that stimulated his curiosity—and attracted the attention of the Aten. They, through their human minions, coerced Ridley into serving them by threatening his family. From that point on, Ridley's expeditions turned from exploration to covering up the Aten's time-travel errors. It was the same job Rassul would later perform for them.

Near the end, Ridley wanted out. But the Aten let no one go. They sent Desheret to ensure Ridley completed his new mission—to locate the relic. Ridley's final and longest expedition took him to the Grand Canyon. He never returned.

Desheret was, as Wessick said in his letter, a mystery no man could solve. She took the knowledge of her origins to her grave.

Shortly before Ridley's death, when the Aten realized his forced loyalty was waning, they sought a replacement. Broderick Covington must've seemed the natural choice. They tempted him with promises of great power that would allow him to contact the dead, and he nearly succumbed. Suspicions about their true motives held him back.

Until the Aten threatened his family.

Or, more accurately, Ridley's family.

To protect Ridley and his wife and children, Broderick entered the service of the Aten. Unlike Ridley, Broderick was initiated into the Brothers of the Aten as a full-fledged servant of the race who deemed themselves superior to humanity. His sacrifice failed to save Ridley, but his brother's wife and children lived on, ignorant of the true reasons for Ridley's death.

After Ridley met his end, the Aten decided on a new tactic. They sent Broderick forward in time to insinuate himself into a new world where they hoped for a new beginning in their hunt for the *satseshat*. They initiated their genetic experiments in the hopes of fashioning the *satseshat* to their own liking. Meanwhile, Broderick worked to preserve the secrecy of their existence and their master plan while both he and the Aten waited for the *satseshat* to emerge. Once they found her, Broderick—now known as Samuel Wessick—was tasked with bringing her into the fold by whatever means necessary. Instead, in his own enigmatic way, he betrayed the Aten to help her find and destroy the relic. He didn't portray himself as a hero, however, but rather as a misguided soul whose mistakes cost him everything.

He was no saint. He did the Aten's bidding for thirty years, employing scum like Rassul to accomplish the dirty work. Despite Wessick's attempts to rein in Rassul, the man attacked and killed anyone who got in his way. Erin knew his brutality firsthand. Whenever she thought about how Rassul attacked her, she could still feel the blows from his fists.

Still, in the end Wessick played a vital role in helping to find and destroy the relic. She must give him credit for that much.

She tucked the daguerreotype and the letter back inside the envelope and stashed it back inside the drawer.

Approaching footsteps drew her attention to the doorway.

Alex sauntered through the open door, halting behind the sofa, in front and to the right of the desk. One hand he stuffed in his jeans pocket, while the other dangled at his side.

"Katy called," he said. "The Planners confirmed that the Aten have left the planet. Where they went, nobody knows. They still have the capability for interstellar travel, since that didn't rely on the energy supplied by the relic."

"I'm just glad they're gone." Rising, she asked, "How goes the search?"

"No pharaoh's tomb yet, but we're not giving up. Searching all of Revenant Point will take a long time. Even ground-penetrating radar can't speed up the process."

She strolled around the desk to lean on the corner nearest him. "You'll find it."

"If it exists."

"The map scroll was right about everything else," she reminded him. "It said the king was laid to rest near the relic, which means an alien pharaoh must be buried somewhere around here."

"Well," he said, crossing the distance between them in two steps, "at least it gives me an excuse to stay close to you."

She stood up and grabbed a handful of his shirt to pull him closer. "You don't need an excuse for that."

"You don't mind having a strange man sleeping in the bedroom across the hall from yours?"

"No." She smiled. "Besides, you may be strange but you're not a stranger."

He bent his head to kiss her, but stopped as a bell jingled in the hallway.

They both turned their heads to look at the doorway.

Bastet, the manor's feline inhabitant, trotted into the room. She ignored Erin, heading straight for Alex. As she purred loudly, the cat rubbed against his calf in a gesture of feline adoration.

Erin made a face. "Bastet still won't let me touch her. How did you win her over?"

"I guess I'm just lovable."

She rolled her eyes.

He snaked a hand into his back pocket and brought out a small foil packet of cat treats.

Bastet meowed.

Erin slapped a hand on Alex's chest and a halfhearted reprimand. "Cheater."

He offered the cat a tiny treat, which she gobbled up while still purring. He tossed the packet onto the desk.

And then he finished what he'd started just before the cat appeared.

By the time the kiss ended, she'd completely forgotten what they were talking about a minute ago.

Alex glanced behind her. A crooked frown warped his lips as he said, "How long do you plan on keeping that thing up there?"

Twisting her head to the left, she looked at the object in question. It was a portrait, an oil painting she found in one of the locked rooms upstairs. When she first came to Revenant House, she wondered why no portraits graced the walls. She understood as soon as she read Wessick's letter. If he'd left the portraits up, she might've figured out his true identity. The portrait hanging on the wall behind the desk showed Broderick Covington, clad in nineteenth-century finery, an expression of serene satisfaction on his face. He looked every bit the English aristocrat, a true lord of the manor.

The other day she'd finally realized what bothered her about Wessick's final actions and how he explained them to Alex. Wessick claimed he forgot that he had only one *akhet* ball left in his personal stash. In the time she'd know the man, however, she came to understand a few things about him. Number one on the list: Samuel Wessick never ever miscalculated his assets, especially a vital asset like the *akhet* balls. So she couldn't help wondering if he kept one *akhet* ball for himself.

Of course, that would mean he sent them off to find and destroy the relic with no way of escaping the blast. Then she decided he probably guessed that initiating the fatal malfunction would sever the power supply for the *akhet* balls. The glowing orbs fizzled out right before her eyes. An *akhet* ball might not have helped them anyway.

Another thought had occurred to her as well. Given Wessick's behavior, and what he said to Alex, the man must've been convinced they would find a way out of the relic chamber. The keeper who hid the relic was an Aten, after all, and the Aten always had a backup up plan.

Like annihilating every living thing on the planet if Erin failed to hand over the relic.

She turned her gaze away from the painting and back to Alex.

"I like the painting," she said. "Think you can get used to it?"

He feigned resignation. "Every relationship involves compromise."

"So I've heard."

Lapsing into silence, he stared at her for several seconds. She was about to question him when he asked, "What did you mean when you said I shouldn't worry about you because you're a librarian?"

"After three weeks, you finally ask me that?"

He shrugged. "I forgot about it for awhile. Now tell me what you meant."

"I don't know." She gave her own little shrug. "It just sounded good."

Shaking his head, he took a step back. Though he tried to frown, the expression faltered and slid into a half-suppressed smile.

Then he strode toward the door, pausing on the threshold.

"Come on," he said, holding out a hand to her. "Let's go find the tomb of an alien pharaoh."

She couldn't think of anything better to do, or anyone else she'd rather do anything with at this moment—or any other.

He wiggled fingers, a silent encouragement. They had solved a handful of mysteries, but countless more awaited them.

She took his hand and followed him out the door.

Continue the adventure!

with more books in
THE HUMAN ORIGINS SERIES
by
LISA A. SHIEL

BOOK 1

THE HUNT FOR BIGFOOT

Katy and Rick tumble into a double-edged mystery—a hidden Bigfoot society protected by an ancient race and a mysterious billionaire willing to kill to preserve the legend. Can they unravel an enigma half a billion years in the weaving?

BOOK 2

LORD OF THE DEAD

Continues Katy and Rick's quest for the truth about human origins and explores the debate between Egyptologists and New Age enthusiasts over the enigmatic Book of Thoth. This time, the fate of the human race itself is at stake.

BOOK 3

RELIC OF THE ANCIENT ONES

Around the world, someone is stealing seemingly un-related ancient artifacts. Drawn into the mystery, Erin and Alex plummet headlong into shocking revelations about humanity's history, and its future, as they chase the evidence to the Grand Canyon and beyond.

BACKSTORIES

TRACES OF BIGFOOT (E-BOOK)

What would you sacrifice to prove Bigfoot exists? In short stories set before *The Hunt for Bigfoot* begins, explore the psychological impact the quest for Bigfoot exerts on Katy, Rick, and Charlie.

available from
your local bookstore, Amazon.com, BarnesAndNoble.com
or
www.JacobsvilleBooks.com

About the Author

L ISA A. SHIEL RESEARCHES AND WRITES ABOUT EVERYTHING STRANGE, FROM Bigfoot and UFOs to alternative history and science. She has a master's degree in library science and previously served as president of the Upper Peninsula Publishers & Authors Association. As a fiction writer, Lisa blends her paranormal interests with sci-fi and romance elements to create her own brand of adventure stories. Her fiction works include short story collections as well as the other novels in the Human Origins Series—including *The Hunt for Bigfoot, Lord of the Dead,* and *Relic of the Ancient Ones.* Lisa's nonfiction books explore topics as diverse as Bigfoot, evolution, and Michigan's quirky history.

www.LisaShiel.com